ADVANCE PRAISE

"If debut author Barry Maher set out to write a book consumed with mayhem, peopled with [characters] in desperate circumstances...and make it a story so compulsively readable that you'll carry it to the kitchen in the middle of the night while you're waiting for your tea kettle to boil, he did, and this is it. *The Great Dick* is pretty great fiction."

– **Jacquelyn Mitchard**, Number 1 *New York Times* bestselling author of *The Good Son* and *The Deep End of the Ocean*.

"What a page turner! Witty, literate, scary, sexy, and powerfully evocative of Southern California trying to leave the Sixties behind. I can't wait to read his next novel. Barry Maher is a brilliant new talent."

– **Gayle Lynds**, *New York Times* bestselling author of *The Assassins* and *Masquerade*.

"Powerful sexual tension...wry self-knowing humor...and a pitch-perfect evocation of an era—[the] classic you always wanted to read, a witches' brew of sexual tension, metaphysical speculation, lurid crime, tabloid scandal, and black magic, all served up with sly wit and some unexpected grace notes. And yes, it's called *The Great Dick*, so it's got that going for it, too.

– **Michael Prescott**, *New York Times* bestselling author of *The Shadow Hunter*.

"I love the writing! Incredibly readable—the pages just fly by—and hands-down the most unique tale I've read in years."

– **Lisa Black**, *New York Times* bestselling author of *Every Kind of Wicked*

"Barry Maher is a highly original and completely delightful new voice... I loved it!"

– **Deon Meyer**, international bestselling author of *The Last Hunt.*

"Novels about catastrophic failures are often the best kind of novels, and Barry Maher's *The Great Dick's* unforgettable Steve Witowski proves himself an indelible part of that canon. Echoes of Denis Johnson, Carl Hiaasen, even Thomas Pynchon—those hilarious laureates of American calamity—abound, but Maher has a deadpan command that's entirely his own. *The Great Dick* is an absolute blast. This book is an utter delight and exceptionally well-realized. Reading it was a total joy."

– **Matthew Specktor**, author of the *American Dream Machine,* and editor of the *Los Angeles Review of Books.*

"With a voice that jumps off the page, Barry Maher delivers a smart debut novel with a wink and a smirk that is part thriller, part supernatural horror. *The Great Dick* is like the product of a lusty, literary one night stand between Anne Rice and Lee Child. Here's hoping Maher progresses his lead character into a follow-up story."

– **Pamela Fagan Hutchins**, *USA Today* bestselling author of the Patrick Flint novels.

"Time and again, I found myself stopping and admiring the way [Barry Maher] has put together a sentence, the words he used. A man on the run, a beautiful woman, and a spooky old church combine with crackling writing, laser humor, and a little bit of magic to create a book that will keep readers turning the pages. Add a touch of the paranormal, a dash of intrigue, and a missing body, and *The Great Dick* is a great read!"

– **Casey Daniels**, bestselling author of *Don of the Dead*.

"Barry Maher has got a wicked voice and a razor-sharp tongue to match. He's found a countercultural cad for the ages with his anti-hero Steve Witowski...a great book."

– **Clay McLeod Chapman**, author of *The Remaking* and *Whisper Down the Lane*.

"WOW! What a fascinating read. Barry Maher has created the ultimate antihero in Steve Witowski. *The Great Dick* is a powerful supernatural thriller that scares the crap out of you. Just when you think you know what's going on, you discover you don't. A well-written, haunting debut that grabs hold and refuses to let you go. This is a book I'm not going to forget. Different and impossible to put down."

– **Chris Goff**, bestselling author of *Dark Waters* and *Red Sky*.

"A rollicking, off-kilter joy ride in the vein of Bret Easton Ellis and Jack Kerouac, *The Great Dick* hits all the laser-sharp high notes of a modern-day hero on the run, as told by one of the more accessible voices I've read in ages. Compelling, twisting, irreverent, and entertaining, The *Great Dick* blends creative fiction and literary thriller in an unstoppable story for current times."

> – **Claire Fullerton**, award-winning author of *Little Tea* and M*ourning Dove*.

"Brilliant! Witty, fast, and fun. Maher's novel makes your own relationship issues pale compared to the protagonist, Stephen Witowski. A failed small-time drug dealer on the lam, his problems are just beginning when he stumbles across a stunningly beautiful woman under assault by a crazed assailant mumbling in Latin. A taste of *Fatal Attraction* with a rewrite by Stephen King [and] twists and turns you cannot predict. Best manuscript tossed my way, ever."

> – **Kevin Tinto**, author of the Indie Mega-bestselling *Ice Trilogy*.

"An enormous amount of fun. Wholly fresh and original. Wickedly funny. Within a couple of chapters you'll think you know where this is going... a few chapters more and you'll realize you were very wrong. *The Great Dick* is a hot, sweaty, magic- and murder-infused rollercoaster of a story that takes you in every direction except the one you're expecting. I laughed. I gagged. I loved it."

> – **David Moody,** author of *Hater* and *Autumn*.

"I loved it...imaginative, told in an exciting voice, and altogether fascinating—reminded me of Graham Greene."

   – **John C. Sheldon**, co-author with Gayle Lynds of *A Triumph of Logic.*

"Barry Maher's *The Great Dick* is a romp equal parts Indiana Jones and Elmore Leonard, with a smidge of Ira Levin for good measure!"

   – **John F.D. Taff**, multiple Bram Stoker Award-nominated author of *The End in All Beginnings* and *The Fearing.*

THE GREAT DICK

AND THE DYSFUNCTIONAL DEMON

BARRY MAHER

Crystal Lake Publishing
Where Stories Come Alive!

www.crystallakepub.com

WELCOME
TO ANOTHER

CRYSTAL LAKE PUBLISHING
CREATION

Join today at www.crystallakepub.com & www.patreon.com/CLP

To Rosie

Who makes everything more worthwhile.

BACK IN THE '60s...

On Wednesday October 13, 1968, a faculty panel recommended the dismissal of Professor John Harris—in absentia, as no one at Harvard had seen or heard from him in weeks. Harris later bragged about delivering his final lecture on "one shitload and a half of LSD." According to the recording made available to the faculty panel, this was the sum total of that lecture:

"Good afternoon. Wow. American Literature, hunh? Let's see. *Moby Dick* today. Right?"

"*Moby Dick*?" asked a confused voice. "No. What happened to *The Scarlet Letter*?"

"Right. *Moby Dick,*" Harris continued. "Great book. None of you have read it. None of you are going to read it. Nobody ever does. What you need to understand is that as far as I'm concerned—and I'm the fucking professor—*Moby Dick* is the same story as *The Great Gatsby*, which some of you may read. I call it, 'the half-assed struggle of the individual to put their world to rights in the face of a failure that threatens to define their life.' I think that's from my thesis. Though maybe it's not pretentious enough."

Harris laughed. "Hey! How about this? *Great Gatsby/Moby Dick*: same story, different era, right? So, if someone someday tries to write that story for this generation, they should call it *The Great Dick*. That'd be perfect, wouldn't it? *The Great Dick*. Alright, that's got to be almost fifty minutes. See you next...whenever. Wow."

TWO WOMEN AND ONE CORPSE

"Any fool can tell the truth, but it requires a man of some sense to lie well." – *Samuel Johnson*

CHAPTER 1

Okay, let me start out by admitting that I was an asshole. I know that. The ludicrous amount of fame and acclaim and money I've had dumped on me since that time only makes it more glaring. The fact that we lived in a different world back in 1982 is no excuse. It was the same world. It just wasn't the world we thought it was.

I remember it was a Sunday night. Sundays always feel different. Looking back now and Googling a 1982 calendar, I'd guess it was Sunday, March 21. I remember waking up and within minutes making the decision to leave. Quickly, before I could change my mind, I eased myself out of the rickety hide-a-bed.

Immediately, Maria rolled over into the spot I'd just vacated, breathing loudly through her nose and mouth, not quite snoring. I hate to say it, but she looked every minute of her thirty years. Her thick dark hair clung damply to her face; her heavy arms stretched outward. The cast on her left wrist looked like a giant manacle.

The grandfather clock beside the cigar store Indian read 1:37, though a few minutes before, it had chimed four times. That made as much sense as anything else in my life. I was thirty-five years old, a Harvard grad who'd spent the previous two years faking his way through a $13,500 a year job as a territory rep for the Richmond Tobacco company. That $13,500 was the most money I'd ever made. You're probably thinking that when you adjust for inflation and translate that $13,500 into today's dollars, it's a lot more impressive.

No, it's not.

I slipped on my jersey and my jeans and gathered the rest of my things in my old gym bag. Fortunately, enough moonlight crept in around the edges of the tattered drapes to give the room a dim glow. I wondered if it would be safe to hitchhike out of there, or if Indiana had already notified the California Highway Patrol that I was wanted.

My situation was bad. But not bad enough to, say, crawl into a grave with a rotting corpse.

That would come later.

Carefully, I wove my way through the assorted clutter and opened the front door to let in more light. The scents of honeysuckle and the sea mingled with the room's stale air. For some weird reason, with my life in shambles, the old, abandoned church across the way suddenly reminded me that briefly, as a child, I'd wanted to be a priest—though not as much as I wanted to be Zorro. I'd read the fourth-grade version of *The Lives of the Saints*, and I thought if I became a missionary I could have a shot at sainthood, maybe even martyrdom. Which was as good as you could get saint-wise. Another realistic goal I hadn't quite achieved. But at least that one was when I was nine.

It took a while, but I finally found a pen on a table back over by the hide-a-bed. Maria had kicked off the covers. I pulled them back up around her. Something clattered to the floor. A diaphragm case, recognizable even in the faint light, probably beige, maybe pink. We hadn't had sex that night, though I'd realized she'd wanted to. If I stayed with her I wouldn't be in the mood more often than not. Maria's body was the earth-mother type I once found so plushly erotic. But in bed and in the back seat of the car that afternoon, all I could see were stretch-marked breasts and puckered thighs.

Okay, I already admitted I was an asshole. And no saint. It's going to get worse.

I tore a piece off a Kentucky Fried Chicken bag and tried to work out a good-bye lie. Something that might leave Maria with a soft memory instead of an acid stomach. She wasn't falling in love with me, and I wasn't breaking her heart, but I had mentioned that once we got to California I might settle down in this area. I'd meant it when I'd said it; going as long as I had without sex can lead to an overactive imagination and the emotional equivalent of premature ejaculation.

But that imagination deserted me now on the note. I finally started it with the truth, explaining that I was running from a drug bust.

"I was no big-time dealer," I wrote. "A friend and I just tried for one good score and messed up. But in Indiana the minimum sentence would be seventeen years, and I couldn't handle jail again. Not anymore. Not for seventeen days."

So much so true. Then I did get creative. "Now I've discovered that I'm not safe even out here."

Since I couldn't figure out when or how I could have made this discovery, I kept it vague. Fortunately, a note wouldn't have to answer questions.

"So, I've got to go. To stay out of jail, and to keep you from getting involved in my crime. Thanks again for the ride and everything. You helped a stranger when he needed it most. I wish we had more time. You're a wonderful lady, and I'm very, very attracted to you. Be sure to thank your uncle for putting me up tonight, and for being so nice. And best of luck with your new life."

I signed it, "Love, Steve."

I stopped short of telling her she was too good for me—a blatant brush-off—though of course she was. The "very, very attracted," was probably overkill. I was making amends for not getting it up in the motel that morning. Fortunately, our second attempt, in the car, had been better. Although it still took me awhile and she must have known I didn't cum. I hadn't had much practice faking orgasms.

Her jacket hung over a nearby chair, and I stuck the tab of the zipper through the note, so she couldn't miss it. My own jacket wasn't around. When we'd arrived, the evening was so balmy I must have left it in Maria's car with my sleeping bag. No problem, I was sure the car was unlocked. Almost sure.

In spite of the dim light and the junk all over the room, I managed to get outside without knocking anything over. I crossed the concrete slab to the car, stepping between two ancient gas pumps, humming a sophomoric lament under my breath. Once more my subconscious had dug out an appropriate soundtrack, a song I'd written years before. I decided to take a moment to roll a joint to bring with me and smoke before I hit the road.

The car was an old Checker cab with a back seat that smelled like a urinal. Three and a half days ago, I'd talked my way inside—in a rest stop a few miles outside of Hamilton, Illinois. I was rumpled and maybe even a touch wild-eyed—if not particularly threatening. At first Maria told me she was only going as far as Iowa, which was just across the river. Within fifteen miles, with a relieved and embarrassed grin, she admitted the truth, and fifty miles later I was sharing the driving. I was never particularly conscious of that smell until the previous afternoon, parked out on that deserted back road near the Arizona-California border, tangled up with Maria in the back seat. With the stench of piss in my nostrils and the corner of one of her paintings digging into my bare hip, it wasn't exactly a romance novel.

Now I climbed into the shotgun seat and cracked a window, letting in the cool night breeze along with the throb of the nearby surf and then the rumble of a semi down on the highway. My jacket wasn't anywhere in the car. *Shit!* The plan—to the extent there was a plan—was to head down to Estero Beach just south of Ensenada. My sleeping bag had fallen apart back in Jerome, Arizona; I'd need that jacket. What had I done with it?

And then I remembered.

The damn jacket was locked in the trunk. The only way in was with the key.

Brilliant.

Oh well, maybe a face-to-face goodbye was what was called for anyway. Though it would be messier for me and possibly more painful for Maria. The note had been fairly believable. Face to face, I'd probably screw it up. I started to get out of the car, then decided I might as well roll that joint first.

I thought I heard a small cry. I paused, listening. Probably an owl.

"Nowhere to go, nowhere to stay," I sang softly. "Wandering down the dark highway."

Christ, I'd really had a way with a cliché even then. In 1966, we'd all been vagabonds. Supposedly. I wrote the song in an expensive dorm my freshman year at Harvard. Fortunately, originality hadn't been an admissions requirement.

How had I ever allowed myself to believe for all those years that I could become a songwriter? Though during my "musical" years, I *had* made it to vagabond. My fellow alumni might have said, "bum."

Through the open window came a snatch of what sounded like a distant conversation. It could have been a TV, except there were only two buildings in sight—and one was dark and the other apparently abandoned. But who would be chatting out here in the middle of nowhere at 1:45 in the morning?

I found the pot right away, but I had to rummage through everything else in my gym bag to find the papers. Not that I had all that much to rummage through. Just what I always carried with me in the trunk of the Richmond Tobacco company car—shampoo, deodorant, toothbrush, toothpaste, a change of underwear—plus a few extra shirts and things

I bought at a Salvation Army store in Chicago before ditching the car in front of Richmond's regional headquarters.

A can of hair spray fell out and landed on my lap. I never used it except at big sales meetings or when the upper brass was riding with me. No need for that anymore, but I shoved it back into the bag.

Now I definitely heard human voices. I couldn't make out the words, but the anger was unmistakable.

I had one cigarette paper left.

Another semi roared by, trailed by several cars. Their headlights winked along the line of trees and bushes bordering the road. The squat cinder block house Maria's uncle lived in was once a store on the old Pacific Coast Highway. Now the new road curved around the house a hundred yards to the south and west, isolating the house and the old church in an empty field.

The new road was still only one lane north, one lane south. Serious traffic took Highway 101, twenty miles inland.

One of the voices was definitely a woman, the other clearly a man. Maybe they'd broken down over on the highway. I envisioned a couple arguing while changing a tire.

A small stick in the pot poked a hole in the cigarette paper. The marijuana was cheap and as usual I hadn't bothered to clean it properly. I almost never smoked dope anymore; I just kept it around from force of habit. I'd brought it with me by accident, forgetting it had been in the bag in the car. That was stupid, and it would be idiotic to hitchhike any farther with it. People were still doing serious jail time for tiny amounts—even in California. And of course, once I was fingerprinted, things would quickly get a whole lot worse.

The shriek was tortured—shrill and sexless—singeing with a hot-ice chill. Once again, I envisioned a man and a woman down by the highway. But now one of them was impaling the other with the tire iron.

CHAPTER 2

The shriek's residue seemed to hang in the air. Suddenly, I felt alone and exposed. Maria's uncle, Jonathan O'Ryan was old and half-senile; his closest neighbor might be all the way back in Santa Lucia, ten miles away. The joint lay shattered in my lap. The pot was sprinkled across my jeans. I held my breath, listening, mentally rerunning the cry. It had been mindless, hadn't it? An animal, run over and dying by the roadside. It'd come from that direction.

Of course, the voices had come from that direction as well.

The second shriek felt electric—as if I was feeling it as well as hearing it. Was there actually a prickling in my fingers and among the hairs of the beard that traced my jawline? Quieter, yet overfilled with terror and pain—or could it have been fury?—it wasn't any animal.

It wasn't any animal.

For a heartbeat, I sat there. I noticed the plain-faced Chesterfield girl painted on the wall of the old store had lost her nose. The small copse of trees behind the building—though nowhere near the screaming—now seemed alive and menacing.

I climbed out of the car, slamming the door loudly behind me, whether to scare off villains or—like a biker revving his engine—to show my potency, I wasn't sure. I told myself that things that go bump in the night almost always turn out to be nothing. Two cats getting romantic in the moonlight. *It wasn't any animal.* Maybe a couple of teenagers with a couple of six packs. Maybe a lovers' quarrel. Him coaxing her back into the car, and her doling out some piercingly loud psychic punishment before coming around. Odds were good Jack the Ripper and the Manson Family hadn't joined forces someplace in the darkness ahead.

Still, heading for the highway, I skulked through the undergrowth like it was a mine field. As I got closer, the grass gave way to ice plant riddled with bottles and cans and paper. I was still hanging on to my gym bag. I thought about going back for the lead pipe Maria and I had found under the old cab's front seat the day before. But I really wasn't a lead pipe kind of guy.

A sheltered clearing held the remains of several campfires. The junction of State Road 64 from Bakersfield was a half mile to the north, making this a perfect campground for transients.

I stumbled upon a narrow path and followed it between two large bushes. In front of me, a small embankment led down to the road. A cursory examination and I'd be out of there. Through a lull in the traffic, the ocean's soothing backbeat sounded close, somewhere just on the other side of the road.

I almost stepped on them.

"Damn you, you frigid bitch," the man sputtered at the woman struggling beneath him. He let out a small, pained cry and muttered something incomprehensible that almost sounded like Latin.

He was tall and thin but wiry—a praying mantis overwhelming a butterfly. She held off his right arm with both hands. He flailed at her with his left.

I froze. For an eternal half-instant. I was aware, without actually focusing, of their labored breathing and soft grunts, of the scent of pinecones, of water running under the highway through a flood control ditch, of a vehicle approaching.

A sliver of reflected light flashed in the man's right hand—a knife, oddly shaped and the color of the moonlight. The lead pipe was back in the cab. A car rounded the corner, lighting the scene. I was staring into the frightened, pleading eyes of the woman—watching her watch me as I did nothing. Finally, I started forward. Then the hand clutching the knife was free. It swooped downward. She gasped. He leaped off her, spun around, and smashed into my chest. Clinging together we toppled over, rolling and sliding down the ice plant covered embankment toward the road.

An elbow caught me in the Adam's apple. My head slammed into the asphalt. I grabbed a handful of his hair, and he flipped over on top of me, rolling us farther out into the street. A horn sounded. The tires of another car hummed by my head—the wind in their wake a warm breath against my skin. He flung dirt or something in my face. It missed my eyes, but my mouth was open; the grit had a sour, metallic taste and smelled like decaying garbage.

I smashed my knee up into him, trying for his groin and hitting his leg. He must have lost the knife because he was crushing my throat with both hands, lifting me off the ground, forcing me out ahead of him into the road. Clutching his jacket, I tried to pull myself down his body, back toward safety. Loose pebbles ground into my skin. I couldn't breathe.

The gaunt face inches from my own reeked of alcohol. Wizened, with a stubbly beard and hair that grew in unhealthy clumps around his head, he was at least fifty, possibly older. Christ, I thought, I was being murdered by the strongest wino in California. My right hand stumbled into his coat pocket, seized on a heavy metal key ring and yanked it out.

Darkness constricted the edges of my vision. The night was pounding rhythmically. Still, I caught the animal terror in the bulging eyes staring down at me.

I lashed out, the keys clenched in my fist like a roll of nickels, but I got no real force behind the blow. Under the pressure of his hands, my throat was collapsing inward. My lungs were on fire. I tried to slash the keys into his face, but they slipped from my hand. Instead, I gouged with my fingers, rending the flesh, groping for an eye. Fabric tore somewhere, and another horn blasted. I was going limp, melting into the night, giving up. Tires squealed. Close. I jerked my head around.

"Introibo ad altare dei," he repeated, clearer this time. It *was* Latin.

"Ad deum qui laetificat juventutem meam," I croaked out in response.

CHAPTER 3

He gave a small, startled grunt. The hands around my neck loosened just a fraction. The pick-up careened around the corner into my vision, hugging the shoulder, bearing down on us. Lit by a southbound car. Shiny. Gigantic. The weight on top of me eased as my assailant tried to back off. Brakes wailed—and locked. The earth rumbled. I could practically feel the impending collision: the truck's bumper smashing into my skull, the front wheel crushing, then dragging me down the road amidst the smoke of tortured tires and the smell of brakes. I forced myself away desperately, with all my strength, grabbing the form crouched above me for leverage. I must have yanked him toward the truck.

The slightest *thunk*. Small. Hollow. Overshadowed by the pick-up's violent roar. And a faint moan like a woman makes when you enter her.

My hands were suddenly empty. My assailant was gone.

A tug tickled my scalp as the truck's rear end skidded over my hair. For an instant, large silver and black snowflakes fell around my face. One bit into my cheek. My throat was free.

I was still awaiting impact as I heard the driver mangling gears, speeding off around the corner as quickly as he had appeared.

It was all I could do to heave myself off the road. Lying on my side on the embankment, sobbing for breath, the right side of my face cooled by the moist ice plant, I forced myself to turn over. *Where was he?*

"Bastard!"

For a moment, I thought she was talking to me. I raised my head, braced to undergo another attack.

He was still there. He'd been knocked five feet away and now he was face up, draped over a low concrete railing at the side of the road. Out cold. The woman had a hold on his jacket, keeping him from overbalancing and plunging over the side into what was probably a drainage ditch. With her other hand she searched his neck for a pulse. A patch of darkness oozed down the side of his face.

Shaking with fear and anger, spitting the sour, powdery taste out of my mouth, I roused myself to my hands and knees. I felt like killing the son of a bitch—for what he'd done, for what I'd done, and for still being here and forcing me to deal with him. I needed to be ready if he returned to consciousness, so I looked around until, in the light from another passing car, I found his knife. It was buried up to the hilt in the hard ground where they'd been struggling—stuck into the earth then yanked diagonally another six inches. It looked like he'd been trying to disembowel her but in the confusion, he'd stabbed the ground rather than the woman.

The handle of the dagger was shaped into what I first thought was a penis. Then I realized it was supposed to be the head of a snake: fangs, sinister eyes and all, though the face was as much human as it was reptile. In any case, the blade was functional, curving to a deadly point. It would do.

The woman made a noise that was someplace between a sigh and a moan.

"You okay, Miss?" My voice was raw and constricted.

At first, I wasn't sure she'd heard me. Then, expressionless, she glanced over for an instant before returning her attention to the man on the railing—holding him now with both hands. She was petite. The smudge of dirt on her forehead and the leaves in her hair and entangled in her fur vest reminded me of a small girl who'd been rolling on the ground in her new coat.

I trudged toward them, keeping the knife ready, smoothing my hair back over the thin spot with automatic vanity. I might have wobbled light-headedly. My neck was bruised, my back scraped. My left shoulder ached. Pieces of mirror glinted on the roadbed. The truck's side mirror must have been what hit him.

Before I reached her side, she turned toward me again. A small crucifix on an excessively long chain dangled almost to her waist.

"He's dead," she said. "The bastard's dead."

The sinking sensation in my stomach was like a blow. Had I killed him? It was hardly deliberate. *It wasn't, was it*? I'd been fighting for my life. Behind the shock was both relief at being safe and a touch of shame. Nobody would be calling me a hero this time.

"Bastard!" she repeated.

In the moonlight, she was like a lady of silver, as delicate as the thin bracelets around her wrists, yet brittle with tension. She was also extraordinarily beautiful. As vulnerable as a young girl perhaps, but nothing less than a full grown, stunning woman. Sometimes my imagination can idealize a woman seen in a dim light (like in a dark bedroom). But I would have expected my ideal to be more sensual—maybe even a little sweaty—and less the high-end woman's magazine cover girl.

The gleam of tears made her appear wronged as well as fragile, but physically she seemed unhurt.

She turned back to the body, slowly, deliberately, then gave it a single violent shove that sent it toppling off the railing. It splashed loudly into the water below.

By the time I reached her side, the corpse had already been carried off by the current. Beneath us, the stream coursed in its concrete pit, swirling over and around rocks and debris, shining in the now erratic moonlight, like a river of ink. Or blood. Only a few feet deep, it was still fast and powerful. I remembered such canals from my songwriting years in L.A. In a few months, there wouldn't be enough water there to break the fall of a sparrow. Even now it was a drop I'd hate to try alive. But then, a corpse doesn't need much of a cushion.

I leaned against the railing stunned. Maybe I was shocked at such harsh wrath from such a delicate person, or maybe it was the irrationality of what she'd done that bothered me, even though moments before I'd felt a similar rage. No matter—he *was* a bastard and she'd done him no harm. He was beyond that.

Never taking her eyes from the water, apparently deep in thought, she fingered the crucifix hanging from her neck. Suddenly, convulsively, she ripped it off and hurled it against the far wall of the canal. It plunged into the stream. The current erased the ripples instantly.

I kept my eyes on the water even after I felt her studying me. After a moment, she gently took my arm, pressing her face against it, as if, I thought, to ask forgiveness—for the corpse, or the crucifix, or perhaps both. And I felt I understood.

I could hardly have been more wrong.

With the breeze dying down, it was warm enough that the sweat was already drying from my body. I didn't feel cold, yet I started to shiver, minimizing it by holding on tight to the concrete rail. I wanted to comfort her, maybe simply put my arm around her, but I was afraid the gesture would be misinterpreted. Or maybe I was afraid it would be properly interpreted.

"I want to thank you," she said softly. Her voice was as rich and as soothing as hot chocolate. "He would have raped me. Probably murdered me. I can't thank you enough."

I started to shake off her thanks, taking my cue from a thousand movies: the battle-weary warrior, saddened by another victory. I ended up just shaking my head in shock. A man was dead—really, actually physically dead. Stephen Witowski dead. And I'd killed him.

"It was him or you...or *us*," she said, touching my hand. "Just thank God you won."

Nodding, I shut my eyes tight. I'd won. And now I wondered if I was more profoundly disturbed by the overwhelming fact of death or by the taint on my "victory"—the image of myself frozen as the knife descended toward her helpless body. I'd gotten into the fight by accident, and I'd come out on top only because of my desperation and panic.

A car roared up. It slowed down as it spotted us, then sped on by, turning the silver woman at my side into a woman with soft golden skin, and stylishly casual golden hair, sensuously disheveled. Her beauty had a familiarity about it, as if I'd seen her recently on TV—or perhaps she reminded me of someone I'd seen.

"My name is Victoria," she said. "Victoria Fairchild."

"Steve Witowski." Either those blue eyes were especially penetrating, or I was still uncomfortable using Stephen's name. Though I'd had the driver's license "proving" I was him for the last several years, I'd been such a solid citizen recently, I'd never needed the alias until now.

"What in God's name were you doing out here this time of night?" I asked.

"I couldn't sleep," she replied. "I guess I was lonely. So, I went down to the beach for a walk in the moonlight. I was on my way back home when that... that man came out of nowhere."

She began brushing herself off and for lack of anything better to do, I started knocking the dirt and leaves off my shirt. When she offered me her back, I just brushed her vest, ignoring all the dirt on her white pants. No telling how a woman like that would react if I tried swatting her below the waist. When she brushed me off, she was more thorough, unselfconsciously wiping the dirt from the seat of my pants and the backs of my legs. With her that close, I was aware I probably smelled like yesterday's jock strap. Her own scent must have come from the rotting leaves. The side of her blouse had been cut, and a small part of the cut was blood-stained. But when she untucked the blouse and pulled it up, the wound underneath was so slight the blood had already coagulated. The knife had merely nicked her on its way into the ground.

"I can't believe I was that lucky," she said.

"It certainly could have been a lot worse," I agreed, without looking her in the eye.

She went to look for her purse on the embankment. I picked up the dagger from where I'd left it on the concrete railing and thoroughly wiped off any part I may have touched. I felt rather than saw that something was scratched deeply into the handle. Then another truck swept by and the light revealed the scratches as carefully, but amateurishly inscribed:

3

Jehovah

Ahura Mazda

Huitzilopochtl

Asmodeus

It took the light from two more cars before I was sure that I'd read the inscription correctly. Then I tossed the knife into the canal. The splash was barely audible. When I turned back, Victoria was watching me, her purse over her shoulder.

"Walk me home," she said simply, yet somehow managing to imply that many men had been refused the privilege.

"Sure. Just let me get my stuff."

I gathered up my gym bag which had spilled open. Once again, the hair spray had fallen all the way out like a guilty secret, as if I really wanted my hair to look like a TV evangelist's, but this thin reddish, permanently tousled effect was all I could manage. As I bent down, I caught a dim flash of reflected moonlight in the ice plant. The dead man's keys. The key that caught the light was thicker than the others and clearly old fashioned. Yet it was shiny enough to be brand new.

Not wanting to make a show of wiping each individual key of fingerprints, I nonchalantly slipped them into my pocket. No point in leaving any potential evidence. I could deal with them later. I knew that this was a good time to make some feeble excuse and get the hell out of there. Instead, I let her take my hand and lead me back up the embankment.

And that, as the poet said, made all the difference.

CHAPTER 4

"Let's just sit for a moment," Victoria said. Still shaken, she plopped down on a low, table-like burial vault. I'm not sure she realized she was sitting on a grave. It was off by itself, not part of a graveyard, beside the old church that was across from Maria's uncle's place. The inscription on the stone was virtually invisible in the moonlight, except for the name which seemed to be Cavendish.

We sat there quietly for a moment, our legs touching, Victoria staring off into the distance. I noticed that oddly enough the church had a back porch. And a double row of windows like those in a regular house—some still with curtains. Judging by the gables in the roof, there were three floors inside.

Several slates fallen from that roof had embedded themselves in the ground. The cheerful thought crossed my mind that it looked as if the earth was being seeded with small tombstones.

"Whew!" Victoria sighed, shaking her head. She massaged the back of her neck, then rolled her head around on her shoulders. "Did you notice he switched out his lights after he passed us?"

"Who?"

"The driver of the pick-up. He didn't want us to read the license plates. He knew he hit something. Someone."

That was a conversation killer. One thing I was sure of, the driver of the pick-up hadn't been at fault.

"I hope you're not beating yourself up about killing that man," she said. "It was clearly justifiable murder."

Not murder, I thought. *It wasn't murder. Homicide maybe.* Trying to pull myself away from the oncoming pick-up. Using his body for leverage. Forcing myself away. And him back? Toward the truck? That horrible small hollow *THUNK*. The sparking flakes from the mirror.

"Are you up for a drink?" I asked, remembering the unopened bottle of J&B in my bag. I bought the pint for hitchhiking out there. For warmth—you could almost see through the second-hand sleeping bag I'd picked up in Chicago. And for comfort—it had been years since I'd slept on roadsides and in fields, and I wasn't into lying awake for hours, jumping at every sound, visions of homicidal maniacs dancing in my head.

She raised her eyebrows and surprised me with a small, teasing smile. "Are you asking me out?"

That took me off guard. I felt like I should say something clever, but I was fresh out. Instead, I simply dug out the bottle, held it up and said "scotch." Then I twisted off the cap and passed her the bottle.

She inspected the label, took a lady-like pull and handed it back. She didn't grimace. My first swig jarred. The second was smoother.

My right forearm felt weird—stiff and itchy. I scratched at it through my shirt; it was sore to the touch. Of course, so were my neck and my throat and my shoulder and the back of my head and several other places.

Small dark clouds slid across the moon. The church's steeple rose in front of us at a slightly tainted angle. The old TV antenna precariously attached to it was even more crooked. Maybe it was her remark about me asking her out, but I was becoming self-conscious and had already moved my leg away from hers. Way back in high school, I was one of those guys who got tongue-tied around the prettiest and most popular girls, the cheerleaders and prom queens and that ilk. Not when asking them out, in those days asking them out was the stuff of fantasy. I got tongue-tied simply talking to them. You would have thought I'd have been around enough in the seventeen or eighteen years since then to have gotten over that. But then, the last few years hadn't been exactly confidence building.

Still, Victoria had said she was lonely. And it was her idea to sit there and prolong the trip back to her house.

I took another drink, trying to forget that *THUNK!*

"San Francisco...D.C., New York, Paris..." she said. It took me a moment to realize I must have asked her where she was from—the basic California question. "All over, really." She gave a little self-deprecating laugh that included me, as if I, of course, understood how it was, though obviously the "all over" wasn't meant to include the likes of South Bend, Indiana.

My right forearm was really starting to ache.

"I moved down here about three weeks ago," Victoria continued. "Looking for a new start. My husband died a while back—Dr. Raymond Fairchild?"

I was apparently expected to recognize the name; it may have been slightly familiar.

"Sorry to hear that," I managed.

She shrugged a dismissal. "It was six months ago," she said in a tone that made it sound like six years. "Have you been through RAM?"

"RAM?"

"Reactional Analytical Motivation. That's Raymond's movement. It's all based on his books and courses. He was an extremely impressive guy—most people thought so anyway. They treated him like a god."

"Interesting," I said, that being the most non-committal word in the English language.

THUNK! Sometimes it's the song you hate the most that you just can't get out of your head.

She was going into a bit more detail about her husband and RAM. I wasn't particularly up on the latest trends of the eighties but I recognized the general concept. It wasn't unique. Cram as many yuppies as possible into a hotel ballroom, charge them enough to make the experience seem worthwhile, and assail them with new age platitudes for hours without letting them pee. Enlightenment through bladder control.

I got the impression that—not surprisingly—Fairchild had been loaded, and that originally Victoria had money too. But apparently everything was tied in with the RAM organization, and it might take a little while before the estate was probated and she got what was coming to her.

"Fortunately," she explained, "I've got an iron-clad will and world-class attorneys. Because those RAM guys are sharks. Reactional Analytical Moneygrubbers. It's like a for-profit religion."

"Ungodly wealth," I tried.

She nodded, no more impressed by the phrase than the music business had been years before by my song *Ungodly Wealth,* satirizing televangelists. Maybe the phrase wasn't as clever as I'd thought.

She touched my knee with a single finger, "It's amazing what people can believe. But tell me about you? Where's Steve Witowksi from?"

"Indiana, originally," I said. "But I've lived in a lot of different places myself since I graduated from Harvard."

She didn't react, but mentioning Harvard was a sign that I felt outclassed, her being not only beautiful, but the widow of a famous person, even if I'd never heard of him. For years, I'd seldom mentioned where I went to college. At first, it sounded like bragging. Later, when I was an aging, failing songwriter, it often seemed to transform me into a tragic or even pathetic figure. Recently, however, I found myself bringing it up more and more.

The ache in my right forearm had become a burning, and suddenly now it felt like it was on fire. I cried out involuntarily and grabbed the arm which made the pain worse.

"What the hell?" I said, pulling up the sleeve of my jersey.

In the moonlight, we watched the face forming on my forearm, at first so faint it was hard to be sure it was even there, then darkening, in gray scale, the size of a medallion, swelling a bit in places for a slight 3-D effect.

And clearly recognizable as the man I had just killed.

We watched in stunned silence as the various shades of bruising and the slight swelling that formed the features faded almost as quickly as they had arrived.

"What was that?" I whispered eventually, astonished.

"It was like a small tattoo of a face."

It was more like an incredibly accurate drawing.

"Did you recognize the guy?" I asked.

"No. Why would I?" She sounded confused and looked away. I wasn't entirely sure she was telling the truth. She looked back at me and added, "How did you do that?"

"Are you kidding? How could I do that? It just happened." I looked down again at my arm. But the face had finished fading away, leaving a lightly bruised, slightly discolored soreness. "And you didn't recognize the face?"

"No, did you?"

When I was looking at it, I'd been sure it was the man from the road. I wasn't quite as sure now. It had been a tough night. Imaginations can play tricks. "It was definitely a face," I said. "Definitely somebody's face. Like a portrait."

She nodded. "It definitely *looked like* a face."

———

I don't know how long we sat there in silence after that, occasionally sipping from the bottle, and when we started talking again it was about nothing. Certainly, it wasn't about the attack, or the dead man or the face that had appeared on my arm.

"And what is it that makes Steve Witowski Steve Witowski?" she asked at one point. I guess she liked the name. Maybe it was a question from a RAM session. Still, she had a way of turning the conversation back to me that was flattering and a welcome distraction. It compounded my natural tendency to babble in the presence of a beautiful woman. I no longer had the good sense I had at fifteen to simply turn red and shut up.

"So, you're an entrepreneur and a promoter," she decided, a few minutes later, extrapolating from a story or two I'd told. That sounded much better than cigarette salesman. And besides the coke deal, Dell and I *had* staged two small concerts and an evening of classic movies. We'd only lost $2,600 each.

Victoria took a sip of whiskey and handed the bottle back to me. She moistened her lips with her tongue, distractedly yet still somehow sensually.

I told another story that gave me a flavor of hip independence.

A single tale from my more distant past implied I'd been the lover of many women.

It was only a matter of time before I maneuvered my songwriting into the conversation.

Almost nothing I'd said was a lie, yet almost nothing was true. It was a performance I'd probably be ashamed of in the light of morning, especially if I realized she'd seen through it, which she probably had. Part of it was the booze coming hard after the strain of the fight and whatever had happened to my arm. Part of it was the knowledge of how far I could get with her with unadorned honesty. Most of it was that look in her eyes as I stood above her, watching, just watching, while that derelict attacked her.

Victoria's glance shifted to my battered old gym bag. She'd seen me rummaging through it to find the J&B and knew that this was my luggage.

"I had some massive business reverses in the last few days," I explained. To me, the $4,500 I'd lost on the coke was massive. "The other night I just decided to chuck the whole thing and took off without a word to anyone. When my car died, I just said the hell with it and started hitchhiking."

A lark, right? A victim of the vagaries of the economic system. True enough. Undercover agents offer the best drug prices, but if I ever buy drugs in bulk again, I'll shop elsewhere.

"The bastard!" She spit it out quietly, slumping forward like an old woman, kneading the bridge of her nose with her fingertips.

"Are you okay?"

She sighed and straightened up, taking my hand.

"I'm glad you ended up here," she said warmly. "Very glad. After... after what just happened tonight, I couldn't face this old place alone. Come on. The wind is starting to come up."

She stood up from the tomb and tugged my hand to join her. By "this old place," she meant the church. Which as we got closer, began to moan. Not the best of all possible omens.

"It's a weird effect, isn't it," Victoria said. "I don't know if it's the wind in the eaves or what. But the windier it is, the louder and the more high-pitched the noise."

Closer up, I could see many of the glass panes in the windows had stickers on them as if they'd been recently replaced, though some of the panes in the attic were still broken.

I stumbled over a wooden shingle. The ground was littered with them, as well as the slates from the roof. The place was going bald. I could relate.

"I've never remodeled a house before," she said.

"It's a big job," I replied informatively. The deep insight I bring to even the most commonplace situations was one of my chief assets as a songwriter. And helps explain my success.

"I got the place for next to nothing from a cult called The Ashram. Speaking of for-profit religion. You'd never know it, but they made a lot of improvements. Just haphazardly. A few here, a few there. They didn't finish any one thing before they gave it up."

Someone had slapped a couple of gallons of white paint on one corner of the porch, perhaps quitting when the thirst of the ancient shingles outlasted either the supply of paint or the stamina of the painter.

"It's more romantic from a distance, isn't it?" I commented.

"Romantic?"

"Mysterious." Even in this shadowy moon glow, a church with a back porch was too mundane, too middle class, to be spiritual; even in decay it wasn't sinister.

"No. Not mysterious. Just dusty and dilapidated. A big job."

"What's a church doing way out here anyway?" I asked.

"According to the realtor who sold me the place, it's all that's left of a small settlement that was here sometime in the mid-eighteen hundreds. The building only survived because around 1880 it fell into the hands of a local character, a pimp named Zandie, who fancied himself an amateur sorcerer, and thought it'd be funny to turn the place into an—as they say—house of ill fame. I guess, occasionally, for laughs, he'd even carry on mock religious services, with himself as high priest, dispensing his own kinds of sacraments and penances."

"That must have gone over big with the locals."

"I'll bet. Though by the time he took it over, I think this was way out of town. And they did have a need in those days for a business like that. Cozy rooms upstairs with the cleaner girls, for the young men and the husbands on a night out. Cribs down in the basement for the farm hands and the migrants who came in for the harvest. Still eventually old Zandie must have gone too far. I understand he ended up getting lynched."

The flashing lights of a police car down on the highway grabbed our attention—racing down on the road then jerking to a stop. Right beside the flood control canal Victoria had dropped the body into.

CHAPTER 5

"Your back door is open," I said. Victoria was still looking at the flashing lights, though with the bushes and the distance, there was no way to tell what might be happening down there.

"What?" She turned toward me.

"The back door of your house—the old church—it's wide open."

"No, I locked it."

"Look," I said, pointing as we approached the back porch. Both the screen door and the door leading into the house were clearly wide open. "Do you think it could be connected with..." I gestured over toward the highway.

She stopped with one hand on the railing of the porch steps, pensively working her bottom lip with her teeth. After a moment, she said, "No. I'd forgotten. I didn't lock it. I thought a friend might be coming by, and there's not really anything inside to steal. Sometimes if you don't close it securely the wind blows it open."

"Are you sure?" There had been a breeze, but a light one. And though the porch wasn't enclosed, it was covered. The door was at least somewhat sheltered.

"Positive. Come on." She bounced up the stairs quickly. "It's fine."

The back entranceway to the old church was the size of an elevator. Half of it was filled by an ancient built-in Kelvinator ice box—not a refrigerator, an ice box—with nine doors, stacked in threes, each maybe fifteen inches square.

"Did you ever see anything like this thing?" Victoria asked, opening one of the doors. "There's another one down in the basement."

"Looks like a morgue for the Seven Dwarfs," I offered. "Ample space for all seven and room left over for the undertaker's family groceries."

"Aren't you the morbid one." Victoria smiled, with surprising innocence, almost flirtatiously, as if we hadn't just watched a man die—killed him really.

"It's been that kind of night," I said. But I thought better of pointing out that the ice box even had a door that could be opened from the porch outside. So, if Grumpy died after business hours you could still get the little mother on ice before he started stinking up the place.

The kitchen was old, huge, and recently repainted a lime green. Victoria switched on a wall lamp. The light was soft and flattering—to her, at least.

I must have expected the place to have a musty, disused odor because now I was surprised that it didn't. It did have a distinctive smell—dark and rich, but not unpleasant. It made me think of lace doilies, and thick, flowered drapes.

She sat me down at the linen covered table and went over to the huge cast iron stove that dominated the room. Quickly and expertly, she laid a fire, lighting it with a long stick match. From a dispenser in the door of a brand-new stainless-steel refrigerator-freezer, she poured herself a glass of water, drank it down in one gulp, then poured another and put on some water for coffee. Neither one of us had yet said anything about the police car outside or, more important, what we should do about the dead man floating down the drainage ditch.

I pulled up the sleeve of my shirt to see what my forearm looked like in this light. It was only faintly bruised though still sensitive to the touch.

Victoria came over to check it out. "It looks fine to me," she offered. "Do you think it was a subconscious response to the shock of what happened tonight? Or maybe it was some kind of weird allergic reaction, some kind of a rash. We saw it in the dim moonlight and maybe after all that stress, our minds just interpreted what we saw as a face. Like seeing the image of Jesus in a tamale."

"A tortilla. I think Jesus tends to favor appearing in tortillas. Appearing in a tamale would be beneath the dignity of the creator of the universe."

"Do you have allergies?" she asked, once again ignoring my babbling.

"Not really, not as an adult. I was allergic to chocolate for a short while as a kid. That guy tonight did throw some kind of weird smelling powder at me. I got a mouthful."

"Maybe that's it."

"Didn't you see a perfectly detailed face?" I wasn't sure what kind of allergic reaction made you break out in faces.

"I saw a face. It certainly could have been a face. But I was almost raped and murdered tonight. And I'll bet that was the first man you've killed? Is it surprising your mind would react strangely?"

Before the coffee was ready, my teeth suddenly began to chatter. I had no idea how my subconscious was reacting, but my body had apparently taken until now to realize how cold it was. I suppose the adrenalin and the alcohol had something to do with that.

"We've got to get you out of that damp shirt," Victoria said, though by this point my jersey was mostly dry. She disappeared up the stairs. A few moments later, I heard water running noisily through the old pipes.

I got up, quickly switched off the lights to kill the glare, and strode over to a gap in the window blinds. *Damn.* Now there were two police cars down there on the side of the highway with their lights flashing, and they probably weren't there for donuts.

So, what were they doing there? Had they somehow found the body? With all the debris in that canal, it wouldn't be hard to believe the body had gotten hung up somewhere. Maybe under the bridge; maybe not far downstream.

And what did it mean if they had found it?

Hearing footsteps coming down the stairs, I flipped the lights on and sat back down at the table.

Victoria returned combed and perfectly made up. She was carrying a green sweatshirt.

"What a mess I am," she apologized with a smile that—if I were standing—would have weakened my knees. Though far more poised, she was obviously several years younger than I was. In this light, her blue eyes were lustrous and almost gray. She said, "Raise your arms."

"Hunh?"

"Raise your arms."

I did and she stepped behind me and reached down to peel my jersey off. As it came up, the shirt stuck to the scrapes on my back. I must have winced. She brushed her fingers over the torn skin sympathetically. I could smell the whisky on her breath, the musk of her perfume. And still the dried leaves. Ordering my arms up again, she helped me on with the sweatshirt. Her fur jacket brushed the back of my neck. She squeezed both my shoulders affectionately before returning to her chair. I was excited and strangely honored by the familiarity. Obviously, she was the type of woman that men delighted in being seen with. The type that the real Stephen Witowski, with that studied disdain of his, called, "Mercedes ladies"—women who were, in and of themselves, status symbols.

"What do you drive?" I asked, thinking out loud.

"What do I drive? Why do you ask?"

"Just curious. And this is America. Don't the cars we select say something about us?"

"Not me. I couldn't care less about cars. It's just a car—some kind of Mercedes. What do you drive?"

"Oh. Well, nothing now, I guess. Like I said, it broke down and I just left it." Which of course made absolutely no sense. At least not unless the car was a complete junker. "So," I said quickly, indicating the large white letters on the front of the sweatshirt, "'Bald and Fat Is Where It's At.' What's that about?" The sweatshirt was extra-large and hung over my hands.

"I got it for my friend Humpert when he was helping me move in," she explained. "But he hasn't been back since then, and I doubt if he ever wore it. Cute, isn't it. He's about thirty pounds overweight, so it's a little more appropriate for him."

I smiled, a closet baldy who wasn't showing yet. Not much at least—in this light.

The water came to a noisy boil.

"What liqueur goes best with freeze-dried Maxwell House?" Victoria laughed. "RAM's holding on to my beautiful La San Marco coffee machine, and I haven't got around to replacing it."

I watched her as she bustled around serving the coffee. According to Stephen back in the sixties, a "Mercedes Lady" was supposed to be beautiful, but not sexy. Times had changed. The last year or so, I *had* been finding my thoughts turning more and more to women I'd met, who—though not exactly of Victoria's type—would have liked to be. And Victoria's firm butt looked amazing as she bent down to get the brandy off a lower shelf.

The combination of coffee and Courvoisier tasted like toothpaste.

What did it mean if the police had found the body?

"I suppose we should call the authorities," she finally said, uncertainly.

I'd been waiting for that. I was surprised it had taken so long.

"I suppose," I said.

"The closest police station's in San Cristobal." That was another fifteen miles past Santa Louisa. "I wonder if the driver of the pick-up already called them?"

I shrugged. The driver hadn't switched off his lights and sped off like that because he was in a rush to call the police. Still, somebody must have called them.

A pure white cat leaped up on the table. It rubbed up against Victoria's arm. When she tossed if off the table, the cat scratched her.

"God, I hate this animal," she said, sounding serious.

We drank our coffee silently.

"The police thing will be a hassle," I said after a bit.

She just looked at me. But sympathetically.

"It's not like they could do anything," I said. "The man is dead now. Just another dead transient." And only a miracle could link him to us—I hoped.

"Still..."

"I know. But God, I don't feel up for it tonight, do you?"

"Well... Not really."

The fire crackled. The new refrigerator made some noisy ice cubes.

"If you want, we could just forget the police," I offered, as if my prime concern was sparing her the discomfort. "We didn't commit any crime. We were simply defending ourselves."

"I guess there's nothing much we could do, is there? The body's long gone by now. I never even got a good look at him, did you?"

I shook my head. Twenty, thirty years, I might be able to close my eyes without seeing the bulging eyes, the acne pits, every detail of those dried up features. But then he was only the second person who ever tried to kill me. The first couple are probably always special.

And that's when the police car pulled up—a sheriff actually. Victoria hurried over to the window, once again worrying her bottom lip between her teeth. Shielding her eyes from the interior light with her hands, she gazed through the blinds for a moment, then suddenly smiled and let out a derisive little laugh.

"I doubt they're in search of desperate criminals," she said. "Instead of the swat team, they sent out a meter maid."

A moment later, a knock sounded on the back door. *Could a passing driver have provided a description of me or of Victoria? Or both of us? This couldn't possibly be about the drug case in Indiana—could it?*

Victoria remained standing. "Yes?" she called. The tone of that one word said it all. She may have been concerned a moment ago, but now she was back in her world, and in that world the police existed to serve her and those like her—and that should be as clear to them as it was to her.

"San Cristobal County Sheriffs. Deputy Galloria."

Victoria stepped over and opened the door. "What can I do for you?"

"I was hoping you could help us out." My guess is she was looking past Victoria and taking in the room, including me. But I'd turned my back to the door. Holding my coffee cup so it was clearly visible, I was making my way to a place where I certainly could have been going to pour myself another cup of coffee—if there had been any there, which there wasn't—but where the open door would definitely block me from Deputy Galloria's view.

"Officer... Gallery, is it?" Victoria asked.

"Galloria. Deputy Galloria."

"Deputy Galloria. You understand that it's the middle of the night. Past the middle actually."

"Yes, ma'am. I'm sorry. I saw your light so I figured it would be okay. It's just that we had a report of a body floating down the flood control channel. I was wondering if you'd seen anything untoward this evening, anything at all that could relate to that."

"Let me assure you, Officer Gall..." Victoria gave a little laugh and a dismissive wave. Her voice was a polite scold, "let me assure you that if I knew *anything* about something like that I would have already been in touch with the proper authorities. So, thank you for stopping by, but it's very late and I've had a long day, and I was just on my way to bed."

"Can I ask your name and what you've been doing tonight?"

Now safely out of sight from the door, I turned. I could see Victoria's stare was a surprised rebuke, as if it were astonishing, even slightly amusing, that the woman would have the nerve to ask her those questions. She said, "Can I ask you if your superiors know what time of night you're out banging on doors, bothering people?"

I have no idea what kind of reaction that generated. But almost immediately, Victoria shook her head and raised both palms in a gesture of surrender.

"I'm sorry, officer. This is a difficult time for me. I'm Victoria Fairchild. I've recently lost my husband. Dr. Raymond Fairchild, the writer? I bought this place to get a fresh start and tonight I imposed on a friend to help me get settled. I can assure you we've seen nothing that could possibly have any bearing on what you're investigating. Forgive me if I haven't been as hospitable as I should be, but it's very late, I'm exhausted and... well, this is not a great time in my life."

Without thinking, I'd been rubbing my right forearm. I realized now that it was starting to burn once again.

CHAPTER 6

And the sheriff left—actually apologized and left. I could remember once speaking to a cop the way Victoria had spoken to Deputy Galloria. After growing up in a solid, white-bread middle class family, in 1967 I'd been dumb enough to let my indignation out the first time I'd been hassled by a cop for walking down the street with long hair.

I remembered it because it was also the first time I ever spent a night in jail. Initially I was charged with resisting arrest. Having an unwieldy mouth and not having learned my lesson, I was dumb enough to point out that there didn't seem to be an actual crime I was being arrested for when I'd supposedly done my resisting. The officer thanked me for reminding him and added a charge of "aiding and abetting a loiterer." Being a particularly slow learner, I pointed out that I'd been alone at the time—apparently somehow thinking that this was an argument I could win. Obviously, the cop explained, my aiding and abetting allowed the evil loiterer to escape. But if I didn't appreciate the fact that I was getting the white man's discount, and I thought resisting arrest required a more serious underlying charge—perhaps a nice felony—there was always the chance I'd also assaulted an officer.

Lesson learned. Even if you're white, the rules are different when you're not a solid citizen.

I sat back down at the table. The stinging in my arm had stopped. The bruise had deepened and was roughly the shape of a face, but no features had yet formed.

Victoria turned from the door and let out a long sigh. "I almost told her what had happened tonight. If it had been a real cop, I probably would have. I'm sure Officer Galloopa there can write a great parking ticket, but who knows what a mess she might have made out of this."

Without asking, she came over and poured another stream of brandy into my coffee cup. She said, "I do want to thank you again though, for what you did tonight." To my discomfort, she added, "You were certainly brave."

I gave a little shrug of my eyebrows with a modesty I only wished was false. It was generous of her to pretend, but I knew she'd seen what really happened. And having a witness to my cowardice made it more concrete, more a part of who I was, and less a one-time accident that could have been the result of being caught off guard. Still, she was being extremely nice to me. Maybe with things moving so quickly, her impressions of the attack were jumbled and incoherent. And as she'd said, it was amazing what people could believe. And what they believed was often what they chose to believe.

"I really didn't have a choice," I said ambiguously.

She smiled again. A genuine smile, I thought, with flawless Miss America teeth. A muscle beside her left eye twitched slightly. When she gave my hand a squeeze, her fingers were cold, and her rings were even colder.

"Introibo ad altare dei," I said.

"What?"

"*Introibo ad altare dei.* He said it twice tonight."

"He was muttering a lot—while he was attacking me at least. It was gibberish."

"*Introibo ad altere dei.* That's what Catholic priests used to say to open the old Latin mass. It means 'I will go to the altar of God.' Why would a rapist say that?"

"I have no idea. If that's actually what he was saying."

"I'm fairly sure it was. Especial because when I gave the altar boy's response—'ad deum qui laetificat juventutem meam, to God who gives joy to my youth'—he definitely reacted with surprise and eased off enough for me to catch a breath. Then that truck came by."

"Maybe that is what he said. Who knows why crazy people say what they say? Or maybe what he said just sounded like that."

"Are you sure he was trying to rape you?"

Her eyebrows shot up. "Am I sure he was trying to rape me? What kind of a question is that?"

"Sorry. Obviously, he was attacking you. But are you sure it was sexual?"

"He grabbed me. He threw me down on the ground. He was all over me. Of course it was sexual. What else could it have been? He grabbed me, not my purse."

"There does seem to be some kind of religious element here. He'd painstakingly scratched four names into the handle of that dagger he stabbed you with: Jehovah, Ahura Mazda, Huitzilopochtli and Asmodeus."

"Jehovah means God, right?"

"The God of the Bible. Ahura Mazda is the Zoroastrian religion's one true god. Huitzilopochtli was a god of the Aztecs."

She waved a hand dismissively. "I'm not religious." Her assumption seemed to be that anyone who was religious would certainly be familiar with Ahura Mazda and Huitzilopochtli. So, I got no points for knowing them. In actuality, I only knew of Ahura Mazda—the Zoroastrian bringer of light and darkness—because of my favorite ninth-grade textbook, *Morey's Ancient Peoples*, and because he's the god the old Mazda light bulbs and the Mazda car were named after. Huitzilopochtli—pronounced Huit-zi-lo-pocht-li, just like you thought—I knew about because Dr. Rogers, my freshman philosophy professor, used the name in his favorite, and most frequently repeated, saying. A saying that was also the opening sentence of the textbook he'd written and of course assigned for the class. I had no clue who or what Asmodeus was.

I wasn't entirely sure, but I thought Dr. Rogers had described Huitzilopochtli as the Aztec god in charge of human sacrifice.

"You are going to spend the night, aren't you?" Victoria asked abruptly. I'd been telling her how nobody even knew I was in the state, forgetting for the moment about Maria and her uncle.

I nodded, trying to stare into those beautiful blue eyes—not sure if that was a proposition or not, but starting to get excited anyway.

"Maybe tomorrow," I said, my voice reasonably even, "we can replace a few more of those broken windows."

"Really?" She brightened.

"Why not? I'm in no rush to get anywhere."

"Listen, maybe you'd like to stay here for a couple of weeks. You could help me fix the place up. It would be great to have someone to work with. Money's tight right now—until Raymond's will is probated—but I've got enough for food and wine and perhaps an occasional low budget night on the town. Then the moment the estate is settled, I'll pay you for everything you've done." Then she quoted a figure that was twice what

I'd been getting from the cigarette company. She reached across the table and squeezed my arm. "What do you say? It could be fun."

"Well," I began, trying to sound indecisive-yet-leaning-to-the-positive, "I was originally planning to end up in Santa Cruz for the summer..."

"Listen, that's months away. Stay for three weeks. Then maybe I'll even drive you up there. I'll have at least some of my money long before then, and we can make it a vacation. Take a few days and drive up the coast."

The implications!

"Please," she said, her eyes lighting up. She sounded like a little girl, as if having me stay was what she wanted for Christmas. "We'll have a ball. I guarantee it."

I never had any intention of turning down a chance to spend three weeks living alone with her in that big house. "Sounds good," I said. "It might be fun. Besides what else do I have to do right now?"

"Fabulous!" She sprang up and gave me a quick hug as I sat there passively, pulse thumping. "You can sleep in my bed tonight. Nothing else is made up and the couch won't be delivered until tomorrow or the day after."

I suppose I could put up with that. Close up, I noticed a scar by one corner of her mouth like the nail mark of a small finger, only doubled, like an "m." Such a tiny imperfection, little more than a dimple, it almost seemed to add to her beauty. It was a blemish only because of the extra make-up she'd used trying to cover it up. But suddenly I regretted all the bullshit I'd handed her earlier. And it wasn't even the morning after yet.

I finished off the last slug of my coffee. I never much liked coffee, and it was cold to boot—but alcoholic enough to help me relax. Then I got my bag, and she led me up a dark enclosed stairway, holding my sweaty hand. For safety?

"This'll be your room when I can get it made up," she said at the first door we passed in the second-floor hallway.

I nodded and kept moving. I had no interest in "my" room.

Gigantic pink roses competed with water stains for control of the hallway walls. The ancient red carpet was more hole than carpet.

"This is the bath," she said, opening the next door down and flicking on the light. "Plenty of towels. There's an extra toothbrush on the bottom shelf of the medicine cabinet if you need it. You'll have to take a bath—no shower yet. Don't worry, there's plenty of hot water. When you're finished my room's through here."

With that she withdrew through a door between the shiny new tub and sink. The door started swinging open after she shut it. I pulled it shut again. It didn't catch, but didn't open much further so I left it that way, unwilling to disturb our budding intimacy by making a big deal out of shutting it airtight.

The bright blue bathroom had already been remodeled. I let the tub fill while I brushed my teeth. Then I combed the leaves out of my hair—gingerly where my head had banged against the road—and took inventory. The bruises on my neck were as dark as they were sore. I had a scrape on my temple and part of my right ear looked and felt raw. The bruise on my forearm was barely visible.

Across from the tub, next to a hamper that matched the blue walls, another door led back into the room we'd passed coming down the hallway; in theory anyway, my room. I opened the door to take a quick peek and discovered Victoria, a pile of old clothes under her arm, gathering up empty beer cans from a night table. I'd startled her. The bed was neatly made.

"Humpert's stuff is all over." Her words held a trace of irritation. "I thought I might get it picked up for you tonight, but it's too much of a mess."

A few pieces of clothing lay scattered around. Magazines, jars of various vitamins and several bottles of cologne cluttered the bureau top as well as the night table. But it wasn't five minutes work to clean up.

"The sheets must be rank," she continued. "He's two hundred and forty pounds of fat. He was supposed to strip them before he left."

I nodded understandingly and ducked back out before I ended up sleeping in there anyway. Had she lied about her bed being the only one made up as an excuse for us to sleep together? Briefly, I wondered who this Humpert was, but two hundred and forty pounds of fat in a separate bedroom seemed little competition.

My beard only outlined my face: the rest of it still needed shaving, at least it did if I was going to be kissing anyone. Then I remembered that Maria had borrowed my razor that evening. Was she psychic, or had I made some comment about hairy legs? No, of course I hadn't. There were limits even to my stupidity.

Among an enormous assortment of lotions and make-ups and tweezers and pluckers in the medicine cabinet, I finally found one of those round female armpit razors. Pink of course. I cut myself twice.

Though only three inches of water had accumulated in the tub, I eased in, bathing quickly. Victoria was waiting. I didn't wash my hair; it looked thinner when wet. The water stung the scrapes on my legs and back.

I could hear Victoria's footsteps back in her room, then silence. Would she want the next bath, or would she already be in bed when I came out? I was beginning to savor the excitement of those first few weeks with someone. Especially someone like this. I was simmering gently, feeling desired. Not too nervous; chances were good we wouldn't actually make love the first night. Not after all that had happened, not when we had all this time together coming up.

Still, it was only natural that sometime before morning we'd begin to kiss and explore each other. It would be better to ease into it gently, anyway. Especially for me. I never really had a problem getting it up—I only hinted that to Maria because I was too embarrassed to tell her what had really happened today—but it *had* been a long time since I'd been with someone I wanted nearly so much as I wanted Victoria.

Remembering the crucifix around her neck and the expression on her face when I caught her in "my" room just now, it occurred to me that, in spite of her beauty and sophistication, Victoria might not have been with all that many different lovers. She could be relatively new at this sort of thing.

I climbed out of the tub and dried myself off. The extra ten pounds of puffy flesh around my waist quivered under the toweling. Like the hair on my head, my pubic hair—once nearly orange—had faded to reddish brown.

The clothes I'd been wearing were filthy. And the stuff I'd crammed into the gym bag looked—not surprisingly—as if it had been crammed into a gym bag. The idea of entering Victoria's room in just my underwear made me realize I'd be entering with my underwear *and* an erection. Maybe if I could focus my mind on something else and then wrapped a towel around my waist, I...

"Listen, Steve," Victoria called, "Make yourself at home. I'll see you later."

Poof! The erection was no longer a problem.

The waterbed was warm and yielding, the smell of Victoria's perfume a suggestive ghost beside me. The quilt was comfortably heavy even against my bruises. In spasms, the late rain rattled the windows, undoubtedly raising the level of water in the drainage ditch, easing the passage of its flotsam to the sea. But this part of the old church was dry and under the covers I was warm. And sooner or later Victoria would return. All in all, I felt good. For an instant my thoughts touched my cowardice, like a cold spot in the bed. They managed to roll away again, back to drowsy images of Victoria.

A low moan broke the silence, reverberating like a dull ache, startling me fully awake. Muted and diffuse at first, it focused and consolidated itself, rising in pitch and volume to a piercing whistle. A moment of ululation, then a hum dissipating into silence.

As a lapsed atheist, as well as a lapsed Catholic, I didn't believe in ghosts or spirits. Obviously, as Victoria had explained, this was nothing more sinister than the wind rushing through the eaves of the old house.

Still when the second moan began, the thought flickered melodramatically through my mind that it was like a lament for the dead. Even though I was fairly sure neither the house nor the cosmos gave a shit.

Two Women, Two Cops, No Corpse

"There are only about 20 murders a year in London and not all are serious—some are just husbands killing their wives."
– *G.H. Hatherill*, Commander, New Scotland Yard

CHAPTER 7

When I opened my eyes, the blinds were drawn. The room was still dim, and as stuffy as a mine shaft. The clock on the nightstand read 7:05. My head matched the room: a dull headache; an embryonic, unfocused remorse, the kind that often accompanies a hangover on mornings after you've probably made a fool of yourself but aren't sure. With all the stiffness, the soreness and the scrapes and bruises, the quilt draped across my chest felt like lead. Most of the previous week, I'd awakened in rest areas expecting to be in my own bed, expecting to get ready and go out to work. Today, I knew where I was.

I wasn't sure what time I'd finally fallen asleep the night before, but it had obviously been late. And what sleep I'd gotten had been fitful, some of it peopled by creatures with silver faces and moaning, whistling knives. I knew if they caught me, I'd betray everything. Other dreams were erotic. Several times I found myself deliberately breathing the dark, musky scent of Victoria on the sheets and pillowcase. Now, without looking, I knew she wasn't beside me in the waterbed. I looked anyway.

Before I'd fallen asleep the night before, Victoria had returned as I'd expected. Picking out something from her closet and some underwear from her bureau, she'd slipped into the bathroom, never noticing I was still awake. On the far side of the closed door, shoes clunked off, grass-stained white pants slid to the floor, the belt buckled clinking as it hit. Her blouse swished off over her head. Every sound was a picture of incredible provocation, so vivid that remembering it later, it almost seemed like I'd actually watched her. I "saw" her bra coming off—though the sound must have been slight—with a snap and a whoosh, panties sliding off, followed by hands slowly rubbing flesh, massaging panty lines from her sleek stomach, from the soft insides of her thighs. A sigh painted a feline stretch for me—the pleasure of sensual tension and release.

I thought I'd left the tub clean, but she swished it out twice before running her bath.

By this time, I was convinced she'd be coming to bed when she was finished. But after the water had all run down the drain, I heard her back in "my" room, cleaning up. I was aroused enough to consider just bursting in and coming on to her, though I knew that would be stupid. A few moments later, she headed downstairs. A door opened and shut, and outside a car started up.

Probably going to her boyfriend's, I thought.

The car drove off, and I felt foolish for letting my imagination run on like that. To me, there'd been a delightful, promising sexuality between us. But what did I expect? A woman like that. And me? I seldom even had sex anymore; I *never* seemed able to get anything going with anyone who could really mean anything to me. Though I was only thirty-five, my once thriving—perhaps even excessive—love life already seemed exclusively past tense. Maybe more than just my love life; I was amazed by how quickly everything had moved from tomorrow to yesterday.

Now in the drizzly light of morning when the chance Victoria might return and spend the night beside me had fully dissipated, I told myself it didn't matter. At least I had a relatively safe place to stay, and I could earn some badly needed money. Besides, even if she had a boyfriend, people break up with their boyfriends all the time.

That crazy derelict with the knife had been all over her, blocking my view of what was happening. Plus, it was dark. And had I really hesitated for all that long? Maybe she figured I was waiting for a good opening.

Sloshing over on my back on the waterbed, I found myself staring up at my reflection in the mirror mounted on the inside of the canopy. It obviously came with the bed. Still, Sister Mary Joseph would have bought the model without the mirror. A second mirror—a long one—was set lengthwise on the wall beside the bed. Another interesting placement. Stuck in one corner of it was a professional eight-by-ten of Victoria, her hair in the Farrah Fawcett style of a few years back.

I'm no great fan of mirrors—I know what I look like, and I looked particularly out of place there. The bedding, the wallpaper, and the curtains were all color coordinated in beiges and pinks. All the wood—bed, bureau, two nightstands—was oak. The total effect—minus the mirrors—reminded me of my cousin Denise's room, which was always a temple of female mysteries to me when I was growing up. Denise was eight years older, and everyone said she used too much make-up and her skirts were too tight. But I loved those black nylons she wore and those gaudy scents. At fourteen, my only ambition had been to someday be one of those people who had sex with a woman. Any woman. Even just once, and I would die happy.

———

The rain had yielded to a heavy mist, but the damp grass on the way back to Maria's uncle's place still soaked my tennis shoes. That of course was not the problem.

The problem was I'd left Maria a note, explaining that I was wanted by the police in Indiana and that I absolutely had to run. And then I'd run a good hundred and fifty yards straight to Victoria. No good could come of that note.

A fading White Rock Sparkling Water thermometer mounted beside the door of the former store read sixty-five degrees. The mailbox beside the thermometer was stuffed full of junk mail. Above the front door, in lettering so faint and faded it could barely be read, were the words, "Penelope Agnes Delgado, Prop."

I knocked softly. I was hoping I'd gotten back before Maria woke up, but it was her voice that called for me to come in.

Maria was at the sink across the room. Though she'd already filled a yellow dish drainer with cups and plates, dirty dishes still swamped the sideboard. Balanced among them were soup and vegetable cans, many with forks and spoons sticking out. The window over the sink had a lovely view of an ancient Esso gas truck abandoned in front of the small copse of trees. By the open hide-a-bed, the jacket I'd pinned the note on had slid into a heap on the seat of the chair, possibly by itself. The note wasn't visible.

I wove my way past easy chairs, eight or nine lamps, stacks of magazines, countless pieces of bric-a-brac including life-size plaster of Paris busts of Rutherford B. Hayes and Warren G. Harding and two dead plants. The room—a combination living room and kitchen—was like a small, badly overcrowded second-hand store. An old bottling machine, a single wooden-shafted golf club, tools and more dishes shared space with a wide selection of soft drink cans and Big Mac wrappers.

I also passed two more White Rock signs, each with a slightly different version of the White Rock girl. According to Maria's uncle, she'd gotten consistently skinnier and taller over the century she'd been hustling soda water, all the while gazing at her own reflection in a stream. The company had originally selected the image as a symbol of purity. Back then, she'd been topless, the way she was in almost all the signs in O'Ryan's collection—if you could call ten or twelve signs scattered randomly throughout the rubble a collection. Apparently though, bare breasted was no longer pure enough. In the most recent version, the company had decided to cover her up.

I remember Stephen—the real Stephen Witowski—once asking, "What kind of creatures find their own procreation—and their own body parts—obscene?"

Maria finished rinsing off a pan and turned to greet me.

"So, Hercules," I said. "How's every little thing around the stables?"

"Aha! Just when I thought I was running out of horseshit, here he is in the nick of time. And what did you do to your forehead? And your ear?"

I was wearing a turtle neck jersey so she couldn't see the bruises on my neck. "Would you believe I cut myself shaving?"

"Looks like you did that too."

Maria searched around for something to wipe her hands on, without success, made as if to wipe them on me, then shook them off in the air and finished the job on her baggy jeans. She stepped close, almost as if to kiss me good morning, but then didn't. The blue flannel shirt she was wearing emphasized the weight problem she'd been fighting her whole life. And though she was more pudgy than fat now, she still had the large breasts of a heavier woman.

"Did you think I'd left?" I asked, meaning: Did you read the note?

"It crossed my mind." She sounded unconcerned.

"How could I leave all this?" I asked, gesturing around the cluttered room.

"And all this." Leering at me archly, she shook her breasts, quickly and theatrically. Obviously she hadn't put a bra on yet. Then she glanced away immediately, as if uncomfortable even pretending to be sexy.

"Careful. You could wrap those babies around your neck and strangle yourself, like Isadora Duncan."

By now, we were grinning at each other. If she was no great beauty—if she was too plain by 1982 White Rock girl standards, or too plump, if her features were a hair too broad, her skin a grade too coarse—her grin broke through all that. And let's not forget I myself had never been mistaken for Burt Reynolds, Richard Gere or even Warren Gamaliel Harding, who famously was initially considered for the presidency because "He looked like a president." I looked like... Well, let's just say I'd always been thankful that women weren't as superficial as men on the subject of looks.

"Isadora?" Maria said, "That's weird. Al once said the exact same thing—even mentioning her. I guess it's true that men are all alike."

"We all spend a lot of time thinking about boobs. Al might have spent more time than most."

Her grin held firm, but her eyes were suddenly shielded, and she glanced away. Still, she'd invoked Al—the husband—with neither masochism, nor self-pity. In the time I'd known her, only rarely did I see the kind of tense shadows on her face that I attributed to what she called "the Al situation."

I said, "I thought you were supposed to keep that cast dry."

The fingers sticking out of the end of her cast were still clearly wet.

"Mostly I used the other hand for the dishes." She smiled. "Maybe not quite mostly enough."

She wiped the fingers on her jeans again; this time hard enough to make her wince. She and Al had been married for the last four years, while he'd been working for his Ph.D. in chemistry at Michigan State. Maria supported them, first by waitressing, then by the sale of her paintings. They also managed one of Al's mother's apartment buildings in return for a rent reduction, though that gradually became just Maria's job. Coming to California was the only promise she ever held him to.

I'd passed a dishtowel or maybe a piece of an old curtain wrapped around a porcelain urn on the way in. I went back, grabbed it, shook the dust out and brought it over to her. Al had slapped at her during an argument someplace in Iowa on the first day of their trip to California. She was driving and tried to block the blow with her right hand—"it was so unlike him" she said—but something snapped in her wrist. He never noticed, but when he demanded to be taken back to Michigan a few minutes later, she did it, getting back on the road again as soon as she'd stopped by the emergency room to have the break attended to. By the next morning when I approached her and asked if she needed help with the driving, the angry adrenalin had worn off, and she was exhausted.

She looked at the towel suspiciously, shook it out again, started to put it aside on the counter, then shrugged and wiped her hands with it.

I stepped up beside her at the sink. "Move over," I said, giving her an intimate little shove with my hip, "I'll do the dishes. You keep your cast dry."

Instead of answering, she suddenly moved to get a better angle looking out the window. Then abruptly she turned back and met my gaze.

"I wonder what the police are doing here," she said with concern. "Sheriffs, actually."

I stepped away from the sink and the kitchen window.

"You didn't rob any banks this morning, did you, Steve?" Maria asked. There was no humor in her voice.

Outside, two car doors slammed. I moved a foot or two closer to the wall, to a spot where I'd be out of sight from either the front door or the window beside it. The knock on the door a moment later was loud and aggressive.

"I'll take care of it," Maria said firmly, walking toward the door. She opened it—just enough to fill the opening with her body. "Good morning, officers. What's up?"

"Can I ask your name, ma'am?"

"Of course, I'm Maria Delgado. And you are?"

"Sorry. I'm Deputy Richard Hartfield. This is Deputy Robert Ramirez. So that's Maria D-E-L-G-A-D-O."

"Right."

A second voice, older, obviously Ramirez, asked, "Can we come in for a minute?" as cops usually do.

I wondered if I could make it into the bathroom without them hearing me. But I knew the drill. One deputy would ask questions while the other wandered around the room. It wouldn't be long before he tried the bathroom door and either opened it or asked why it was locked.

"Unfortunately, I don't have a minute," Maria said amiably. "I'm due in San Cristobal for an appointment. What's this about?"

"We're investigating an alleged body that may have occurred around here," said Hartfield's voice. "Trying to figure out what may have ensued. Have you seen anyone or anything out of the ordinary the last couple of days?"

"I just got here last night—from Michigan. This is my uncle's place. He's out fishing right now. So someone died?"

"A citizen reported seeing a body being swept down a flood control channel," Ramirez said. "The only channel that fits the bill is the one that runs past here."

"We get a lot of transients in this area," Hartfield explained. "Something may have happened to one of them. We don't have a lot of specifics on the situation yet."

"And you don't know when the 'alleged' body may have occurred?" Maria said with a smile in her voice. *Oh good*, I thought, *piss off the cops. What is with these women?*

But Hartfield chuckled. "Okay, I was hoping you wouldn't notice that. You try doing this job after a lifetime of watching TV and movie police. See what you sound like."

"I think it's cute," Maria said.

This time it was Ramirez who laughed. "We all think he's cute, ma'am. That's why we send him out whenever an alleged body occurs."

"And why do you guys always say 'ma'am'?" *Don't push it, Maria.*

Once again the burning in my forearm snuck up on me while I was focusing on something else, and this time it keyed a quick flash of panic.

"We try to keep it impersonal," Hartfield said, "Particularly when we're talking to someone we might be tempted to want to get personal with."

I pushed up my sleeve. The face was coming back, the slight swelling and various shades of bruising already forming a clear portrait of the man who became the alleged body.

"Is that so, Deputy?" Maria was saying, just a bit flirtatiously.

I pulled my sleeve back down. *Keep them away from me, Maria.* I started rubbing the spot intensely, hoping to change the pattern of swelling and bruising.

"I think," Hartfield said, "that this is the spot where I'm supposed to say, 'We ask the questions here, ma'am.' Anyway, in my defense, this particular body *was* just alleged. All we have is an anonymous call. And we checked the entire wash. There's no body anywhere."

"Maybe it was swept out to sea," Maria suggested.

Let's hope, I thought. But in any case, the cops had no idea what this guy looked like. I took a deep breath. I could have his face tattooed on my forehead and it wouldn't mean anything to them.

"That wash hasn't been properly cleared in who knows how long," Hartfield said. "With all the debris, a goldfish couldn't slip through to the sea much less a human body."

"We've pretty much decided it was a prank call," Ramirez added, "Probably high school kids."

"Happens all the time," Hartfield said. "If they're not anonymous, they're Ben Dover or Al Coholic or Mike Hunt."

He paused, probably realizing what he'd just said and trying to figure out what to do about it. He ended up just plunging on. "Anyway, we're just touching all the bases, talking to anyone near the wash that might have seen anything."

"I'll mention it to my uncle. But unfortunately, he's elderly and probably the least reliable witness in the state."

"What about across the way?" Ramirez asked. "Anyone living over there now?"

"The whorehouse?" Hartfield interjected, "Puss... Deputy Galore, she talked to the people over there last night."

"Officer Galore?" Maria asked innocently. "Would that be *Pussy* Galore?"

"Ah...well... it's just a nickname," he mumbled, "Like the James Bond character."

"A nickname? And here I thought her mother named her that. She was at the whorehouse last night? Did Mike Hunt show up?"

"Well..." A long pause. "Sorry."

"You going to keep talking, Rick?" Ramirez asked. "See if you can make it worse? Our apologies, *ma'am*. But that old church across the way is actually known around here as Zandie's Whorehouse or just the Whorehouse. For reasons you can probably imagine."

"I'm sure I can. If not, I'll bet Deputy Hartfield here can fill me in, probably in graphic detail."

"Let's hope not. Anyway, Zandie's long gone, but the name's stuck. So, is there anyone else around who...?"

Maria raised her hands in an "I have no idea" gesture. "I'm sorry, guys, but I've really got to get going."

"We understand," Ramirez said. "Just a few more quick questions if you don't mind."

"I certainly don't mind, but I can't speak for my uterus."

"Excuse me?"

"Since you brought up the subject of Mike Hunt, deputies," Maria said pleasantly, "this appointment I mentioned is with my gynecologist. I can't miss it, and if I'm too late they'll cancel me. I've been bleeding for five solid weeks now and today the flow is heavier than ever. Right now, I'm working on my very last tampon. So much as I might want to stay and…"

"Go," said Ramirez.

"Absolutely," Hartfield added. "There's no body anyway. It was probably just a prank call and we're all just wasting our time here. You get to your appointment."

"I do have a hygiene issue to take care of first, so if you'll excuse me."

"Of course. We're done," Ramirez said. "You have a great day. And excuse my partner, ma'am. He shouldn't actually be allowed to talk to young women. Or older women. Or men for that matter. He *is* outstanding though with rodents and small barnyard animals."

***

"Wow," I offered with a laugh that I hoped sounded unconcerned, "'I am woman, hear me roar.' Bleeding for five solid weeks?"

"Menstruation is the surest way to end any conversation with a man," Maria said. "The more graphic you make it, the quicker it ends. I should have thought of that sooner. Also, I expect points for self-control. I kept wanting to tell Robert that he doesn't look like a Bob, and Richard that he certainly does look like a Dick."

"Probably better to keep that to yourself. And was there a reason you didn't mention me?" I was hoping she hadn't read the note, but just how much did she suspect?

She met my gaze for a long moment. Then she said, "There was no reason *to* mention you."

I nodded. "So what happened to the body?" I mused aloud.

Now she really looked at me strangely. "That's kind of the whole point, Steve. No body. Prank call. Is something wrong with your arm?"

"No, of course not."

"Then why are you massaging it like that?"

"Oh. Just a little muscle pull." I considered showing her the face, to see what she'd make of it. But then I thought better about offering a potential witness evidence that would connect me—even in the weirdest possible way—to the dead man.

"So," she asked, her tone neutral, "what are your plans?"

"I'm staying right around here. At least for a while." I pretended to be interested in the framed snapshots on a nearby table. They were all of the same boy, taking him from toddler to about twenty. "I've got a job already."

"Really? Doing what? And how on earth did you already find a job?"

It made me feel good to hear how pleased she sounded. "The old church next door is being remodeled," I said. In one of the pictures, the boy, about fifteen, was pushing a chunky young girl on a swing—Maria. "The lady who owns it offered me a few weeks work, helping out. Room and board included."

"The lady" might have sounded gray-haired and stately, but hey, I could have called her, "the widow."

"That's great, Steve. I'm going to be living right here."

"You are? Here? I thought you were going to try to rent one of your uncle's places in San Cristobal?"

"Uncle Jonathan's holdings are...no longer as extensive as they once may have been." She smiled and indicated that we were standing in the sum total.

Oh.

"It'll actually be cozy," she went on. "I'll be able to keep an eye on him. He really shouldn't be living alone. And there's an entirely separate apartment in the back of the house. He'd already started fixing it up when he thought my brother might move in. I want to pay rent, of course, but I won't have to mess with a first and last and a damage deposit. And since I have no income..."

She'd left half of what little money she had with her husband. And added to the normal expenses of the trip out there, she spent over two hundred dollars when the timing chain of the old Checker cab died on the cliffs leading up to Jerome, Arizona. I'd helped her out a little, and I'd surreptitiously taken her uncle's address hoping to be able to send her more. Even though she never asked. Especially because she never asked.

"I should go, Steve," Maria said, leaning over and peering out the window. "Since I'm supposedly running late for my imaginary appointment about my spooky female problems. You, on the other hand, have to stay. My new pals, Dick and Bob are still parked out there, talking on their radio. I wonder what they're talking about."

CHAPTER 8

Once Maria was out the door heading for her car, I immediately pushed up my right sleeve. No face, no swelling, not even that much bruising. To quote the real Steve Witowski again, "In every life there are a number of *What the Fuck* moments; some just more *What the Fuck* than others."

This was about as What the Fuck *as it gets*, I thought. Which shows you how little I knew about just how *What the Fuck* things could get.

I hurried over to the chair holding Maria's crumpled jacket. I couldn't see the note until I picked the jacket up. And there it was, still attached to the tab on the zipper tab. I pulled it off and shoved it into my pocket.

I was making good headway on the remaining dishes when the two sheriffs finally pulled out. Maria must have been parked someplace where she could watch them leave because she returned about five minutes later.

"They won't come back," she said. "But if they do, I'll just explain that they made me so late I had to reschedule. Then I'll talk some more about how badly I'm bleeding."

I turned back to the dishes just as the front door slammed open and her uncle burst in, carrying a dripping bucket. He blinked myopically—as if he'd expected to find something but had forgotten what it was. Jonathan O'Ryan was actually Maria's great uncle, the widowed husband of her grandfather's sister. He looked to be somewhere around eighty. He'd met both Maria and I for the first time the night before, and though he'd been anticipating only Maria—and didn't even seem all that sure about that—he'd been charming and gracious if not always focused.

I'd liked him immediately, but I had to admit that the man was world-class ugly. Short and slight, with hairy ears, a bulbous nose, dim, rheumy eyes, yellow uneven teeth and—for some weird reason—badly-dyed thin black hair. Under a skin like cracked leather, facial muscles sagged, as if the power that once assembled and directed his features had ebbed out with the years. He was very neat though; today in a dated blue sport coat and black dress pants.

Now he looked at me, looked at Maria, then back at me again.

"Welcome," he said warmly, coming over to me and extending his hand. "I'm Jonathan O'Ryan. Thanks for coming."

We'd spent the entire evening together the night before, and I had no chance to dry my wet hand but, what the hell, I shook his hand.

"And you are?" he asked.

"Steve... Steve Witowski. We met last night?"

"Of course we did. It's a pleasure to meet you, Steve. But you're no Polack."

"He's not *Polish*, Uncle," Maria corrected, looking concerned. "And actually, I think he is."

"Not with that red hair, he's not."

"My mother was Irish," I tried. "My father Polish."

"Nope. Recessive gene. Both parents have to carry it, even if they don't both have red hair."

So much for my clever fake identity. I laughed, "I always was suspicious of that couple that claimed to be my parents."

"No!" he exclaimed suddenly. "I'm wrong. Malwina Koserowski! A beauty. Came over from Warsaw. Red hair—so thick on her lady parts she didn't need bloomers. Said she once bedded General George Armstrong Custer. Before he died of course."

"That would have been the time to do it."

"Have you had breakfast yet, Uncle?" Maria asked.

O'Ryan focused on her now, clearly confused. He held up the bucket, which was dripping leisurely on the rug and smelled of fish. "I caught breakfast."

"Perfect," said Maria. "That's great. Maybe next time you go fishing, I'll go with you."

"Why is the TV off?" O'Ryan asked with real concern. The TV was a relic of the fifties, with a fully extended set of rabbit ears. "Is it broken?"

"It's fine, Uncle. We were just talking." She gestured toward me. "Turns out Steve's going to be working next door, helping to fix up that old church."

O'Ryan shook his head. "It's a desecration."

"Actually," I said, "it's been a long time since it was a church. I understand for quite a while it was even a...a house of ill fame."

"You mean it was a fucking whorehouse," O'Ryan said cheerfully.

"I guess there's no arguing with the adjective," Maria said.

"That's what they call it nowadays," O'Ryan said. "But what do they know? I'd call it a church of pleasure."

"And did you ever partake, Uncle? Back in the day?"

"Do I look like a guy who has to pay for it?" As we all considered that, he chuckled. "Maybe. But in my day I'd have taken the measure of that diamond-collared she-bitch that's over there now. That... Venus?"

"Victoria," I corrected.

"Man-trap? Venus man-trap? I think somebody said that. I don't know who. She probably eats her young."

"She doesn't eat them alive or anything," I said. "And she hardly ever leaves any large bones lying about on the furniture."

Maria turned toward me. "This Victoria is staying there too, while the place is being fixed up?"

"Sort of. I get the impression she has a gentleman friend she spends most of her nights with."

"She's the motherfucking Whore of Babylon," O'Ryan insisted happily. "But minor league."

"I didn't even know they *had* a league," Maria said.

"You should see the playoffs," O'Ryan deadpanned, surprising me. But then his face clouded over.

Though I was ready to leave, O'Ryan insisted that I stay long enough for him to make us all breakfast. Since I could see that Victoria's car hadn't returned across the way, I figured why not. Astonishingly, it was delicious. He was a first-rate cook, and having clean dishes probably didn't hurt.

After breakfast, I finished washing the rest of the dishes, including more than a few extra that turned up in the living room. Then I went over to where Maria was sitting with her uncle as he watched some loud game show on the TV.

O'Ryan looked up. "You're not Todd," he said matter-of-factly.

"Nope, still not Todd," I responded. Todd was Maria's older brother. The boy in all the pictures. Though O'Ryan was only related to Maria's family by marriage, over the years he'd apparently emotionally adopted the child without ever actually meeting him. I'd heard about Todd at length the night before, when the old man had been convinced his beloved nephew had preceded Maria out there by a couple of weeks, visited for a while, and then run off or something.

"Todd's much better looking," O'Ryan said.

"Most people are," I agreed. "So why is she the Whore of Babylon?" I asked.

"Who?"

"The woman next door."

"I don't know. But I know things."

"Uncle Jonathan," Maria said soothingly, "I'm sure she's very nice."

"I know what I know." His gaze settled again on the wavy people on the TV screen and the multi-colored auras that hung in the air behind them when they moved.

"What do you know, Uncle?"

"I know…" he began then stopped. He looked around, then grinned his somehow charming jagged-tooth grin. He laughed. "I have no idea. I guess I don't know what I know. But I'm sure I know something. Or maybe there's something about her I'm supposed to know. And I'll bet it's good."

"I wouldn't be surprised," I said.

"Did you know there's a place where…where, say you want some connubial splendor…"

"Connubial splendor?"

"Sex."

"Got it."

"First, the young lovely runs off and hides from you…"

"Unfortunately, there are a lot of places like that."

"No, this is an island. So what you do is pick up two hot, burning coals. If you can find her before you drop the coals, she's yours."

"That," said Maria, "sounds like an excellent system. It's really going to be great living here next to you, Unk." The "Unk" came out awkwardly. Not only hadn't they met previously, "Unk" hadn't even recognized her name until she identified herself as Todd's sister.

"Didn't you write me that you were coming out here with your brother?" he asked again now.

"I said I was coming out here with my husband, Al. It didn't happen."

"I must have known that," he said with a small laugh. He shook his head and made a face as if he thought something might be loose. "But the guy who was here before...young and handsome and strong and straight. He could have been Todd—innocent, you know, kind of defenseless."

"Nobody ever described Todd as either innocent or defenseless."

The old man smiled proudly. "I'll bet. He's a big success, right? Head of a giant milk company." We'd been through all this the night before.

"No, Uncle. I said, we were told he was on a milk run. That means an easy flight. It just didn't turn out that way."

"Probably has the ladies hanging all over him." O'Ryan got up slowly and picked up one of his pictures of Todd. "A giant milk company. I'll bet he gets a lot of free cheese." I wasn't sure if he was making another joke. It was difficult to tell with him.

Maria's eyes were moist, but I guess she'd decided there was no point in explaining once again that Captain Todd Delgado had been shot down seven years before. He'd been ferrying a plane load of bubble wrap and other moving and packing supplies into Saigon, right before the fall of South Viet Nam.

***

While Maria and O'Ryan discussed fixing up both of their apartments, I got my jacket out of the trunk of the old Checker cab and my razor out of the bathroom. I wondered if Maria realized my gym bag was already gone. Then I helped her put away the sheets and blankets from the hide-a-bed and fold the rickety thing up. I pretended not to notice when she picked up her diaphragm and a tube of contraceptive jelly.

When I finally left, besides the jacket, I was loaded down with a number of shirts and pants O'Ryan had given me, clothes that "Todd"—who was either entirely imaginary or a case of mistaken identity—hadn't wanted during his visit. The load was a bit of an excuse in the awkward moment when Maria and I had to decide whether or not to kiss each other on my way out. We didn't.

I crossed back to the old church deep in thought. Where was the body and when would it turn up? And why wasn't I even thinking about getting the hell out of there?

CHAPTER 9

Since I had no key for the old church, I'd left the pantry window unlocked. It had occurred to me that I could climb in through the outer and inner doors of the old Kelvinator ice box, but I'd decided a window would be easier. Cleverly, I'd picked one over a sink. I got it open now without too much problem and tossed in the clothes I was carrying. But, halfway in, my belt hung up on a faucet. Freeing myself, I knocked a cup off the counter. It shattered on the floor—one of an expensive-looking matched set, the kind that never holds as much coffee as the good solid cheap cups that are virtually indestructible. Unable to find a broom, I swept it up using one hand and a piece of an empty Special K cereal box. I buried the pieces deep in the trash, and brushed the fine powder I couldn't get under the radiator.

The perfect houseguest.

In my room, Victoria had put clean sheets on the old iron bed. All Humpert's stuff had been removed. The floor could have used a sweeping, but I already knew I couldn't find a broom, so I let that go. I'd been in a lot dirtier.

No reason why I shouldn't just start in working. There was certainly no shortage of things to be done. And it would be nice to be busy when Victoria returned. I hung up the donated clothes in the closet, and brushed my teeth in the bathroom sink.

When I was finished, I knocked on the connecting door to Victoria's room, then eased it open. The room was still dark, cave-like. She'd been there though. A window had been opened.

The bed linen had been changed—now it was maroon; I'd forgotten what color it had been before. A used towel covered much of the throw rug, and the clothes she'd picked out last night were tossed on the foot of the bed. In front of the open closet, a pair of lacy blue panties lay on the floor, shining like a flash of thigh. A matching bra dangled from the doorknob. Quietly, I took a step into the room.

"STEVE! Are you home!?!"

Victoria's voice startled me guilty. Suddenly I remembered Lee Hill and I in junior high sneaking into the girls' locker room during cheerleader try-outs. Thirteen and hornier than we were bright, we'd had no plans, we simply wanted to look at some female underwear. Underwear is a big deal in puberty. Not that we saw any—the girls were all still wearing it under their gym suits. So I simply took a quick look around, and Lee moved a couple of blouses and skirts around from one locker to another for no particular reason except that maybe that was the only way a thirteen year old boy with braces and pimples seemed to be able to have any effect on the girls at that school.

We left the locker room just as Debbie Stamatopolis and Pamela something-or-other were returning from the try-outs. If they'd been less preoccupied with the injustices of their own failure, they might even have noticed the door swing shut behind us. A second or two slower and we would have been caught inside, and I would have gone in an instant from honor student and altar boy to horny little disgrace in need of discipline, psychiatric counseling or worse. It would have messed up my poor mother with the Legion of Mary at St. Anne's, but good.

Today, I was lucky again; Victoria was still downstairs. I made my retreat, flushing the toilet again on my way through the bathroom to explain why I hadn't responded. I was in my room, feeling foolish yet relieved when she knocked on my door. I called for her to come in.

"I was just changing into my work clothes," I said.

"Fabulous." She was sucking on a mint or a piece of hard candy, rattling it around in her mouth. "I really appreciate it, but I could certainly understand if you wanted to take the day off… After last night."

"Well, if *you're* too tired…" I said.

She did appear tired, as well she might. Tired, but still first class. Her tailored shorts were tight, but not unfashionably tight (at least from what I knew of fashion—which was of course nothing). Her loose, pleated blouse suggested rather than concealed. I was suddenly aware of how dirty my hair must be.

"I've got an appointment in L.A.," she said. "And I've got to get the Mercedes serviced while I'm down there, so I've got to run. But come on and I'll be glad to show you where you can start. Better wear something old. It could get grungy."

"I'm ready for grungy," I said, grabbing a shirt and a pair of pants from O'Ryan's donations. "Just give me a second." I stepped back into the bathroom to change. "Did you hear that whistling last night?" I called through the door. "It seemed way out of proportion with the amount of wind."

"I know. It's annoying, isn't it. I had one…visitor who thought it was ghosts. But he was an idiot. Maybe it's bad plumbing—I have no idea. If you can make it go away, I'll love you forever."

A couple of minutes later I came out, twirling around to display a green shirt covered with tiny golfers and a pair of red double-knit pants that had to be belted securely and rolled up at the cuffs.

"Stunning?" I asked. "The very latest from the House of O'Ryan."

"O'Ryan?"

"The old guy next door? He gave them to me."

"How did you meet *him*?" she asked. "Was he over here looking for his 'nephew' again? God! They deserve each other."

I smiled sympathetically, expecting more. When it didn't come, I said, "The sheriffs were over there this morning. They'd gotten a report of a body washing down the flood control channel. But they couldn't find anything and thought it was just a hoax."

"They didn't find anything?"

"Nothing. Maybe it just washed out to sea, though they didn't seem to think that was likely."

She thought for a moment then said, "One way or another, it has nothing to do with us. Some old derelict dies—I'm sure it happens all the time."

And yes, this would have been a good time to slip in something harmless about Maria and the trip out there. I didn't want Victoria thinking I'd lied my way into her bed last night. But I had something more concerning to discuss—that's one excuse.

"One other thing," I said. "While the sheriffs were there, that face reappeared on my arm."

"That face thing again?" She sounded skeptical. "Really?"

"Really."

"Okay. So obviously it *is* a nervous reaction or an allergy of some kind." She smiled. "Maybe you're allergic to the police."

What did that mean? "It was an amazingly accurate likeness of that guy's face."

"Amazingly accurate? But as we decided it's kind of like seeing Jesus in a taco, isn't it. Or is it a tamale? I don't eat Mexican food."

"So, to you it wasn't even a face?" I asked, surprised. She'd certainly seemed more definite about it being a face the night before. And if she hadn't seen what I'd seen—and what I'd thought she'd seen—what did that mean?

"You know, I've been thinking about this play that Fairchild dragged me to last year. He liked to think he was an intellectual. I'm sure he didn't understand half of what they were saying. In any case, the hero of the play was weak and stupid and ended up getting what weak and stupid deserves. But what really made a lot of sense if you think about it was that after he kills a guy—stabs him to death, very traumatic—he freaks out and starts seeing things that aren't there. Ghosts and bloody daggers floating in the air and who knows what-all."

"Macbeth?"

"Some Shakespeare thing. You've been through a traumatic experience, Steve. It's bound to have an effect on you."

I just shook my head and gave a little non-committal shrug. I knew what I'd seen. But how do you make a case for something that can't be explained? Out of necessity, it was a skill I eventually developed—to some extent anyway—somewhat later in my life. But prior to my arm becoming a show-and-tell for murder victims, how often had I quoted Dr. Rogers, my freshman philosophy professor:

"If you can believe in the resurrection of Christ without putting your hands in the wounds, why can't you just as easily believe in Zeus, Shiva, Huitzilopochtli or Skippy, the Squirrel God?"

Or Banquo's ghost, for that matter.

Was there a chance I was still hallucinating this morning, under the stress of the killing and having the sheriffs at the door asking about it?

Obviously not particularly concerned about the issue one way or the other, Victoria started going on about all these old books that were stored away in the attic. Apparently Zandie surrounded himself with books, though of course most of those remaining weren't his. Instead of really listening, I was thinking not about Macbeth but about an article I'd read months before about a woman who'd been kidnapped, tortured and raped by a serial killer. Eventually, he took her out to the desert to finish her off and dispose of the body. By a fluke, she'd managed to escape. But when she told people what happened, no one believed her. Not the police, not her friends, not even her own mother. This must have been the most vivid, most memorable—unfortunately the most real—experience of her entire life. But by the time the serial killer was caught, and he confessed twenty years later, she herself had come to doubt that it really happened.

I knew what I'd seen—twice.

Still, it did occur to me that since I couldn't have seen what I'd seen, maybe I *should* be starting to doubt it.

But I didn't. Not for a minute.

CHAPTER 10

Walking down the hallway in the attic, Victoria and I passed dark rooms that were in even worse shape than the rest of the house. Glass was missing from windows. The floors were littered with hunks of crumbling plaster. Yellow and brown water stains made the walls look like an old whorehouse's sheets. From up there, the place looked unsalvageable—at least, to my ignorant eyes.

She led me into a windowless storage space. Musty books in boxes and in stacks covered large sections of the floor.

"The living room walls are covered with built-in bookcases," she explained. "But The Ashram was into controlling what their people read, so they collected most of the books left in the house over the years and brought them up here."

"Why didn't they just toss them?"

"Somebody had the idea some of them might be worth money—as antiques, maybe even first editions. When I bought the place, they decided they should sell them to me separately, figuring at the very least I'd want them so I could fill up all the downstairs bookcases. I'm sure that's why so many of the books seem to have been kept through a number of different owners."

"You paid extra for these?"

"Humpert, who's also my attorney, explained that they needed to read the purchase agreement they'd signed. I was buying the house *and* contents. That not only meant their washer and dryer—which by the way it turns out don't even work—but everything but their personal possessions. They griped—until he pointed out that if they weren't selling the contents, they'd have to clear *all* the junk out of the place, including from the attic and the basement."

"And you wanted the junk? Wouldn't it have been easier to just have The Ashram take care of it?"

"Oh, I don't know." A flash of irritation flickered across her face. "Some of it might be worth a little something I suppose. And I do have all those bookcases to fill."

The idea of lugging all those tomes down all those stairs must have made its way to my face.

"Don't worry, Love." Victoria smiled. "They can stay—at least for now. But that real estate lady I told you about...? The world's foremost authority on Zandie, the panderer who used to own this place...? Well, she dropped by several times right after I moved in. She's a dowdy thing, forty-plus and trying to look nineteen but well-healed. She's opening a specialty store in a new mall in San Cristobal—designer jeans and dresses and tops and accessories. Wants to call it Zandie's Storehouse, and she said she might be interested in buying any of his things we might come across—especially old books—to give the place atmosphere."

"Zandie's Storehouse? For women's clothing?"

Victoria laughed. "Because this place was known as Zandie's Whorehouse."

"Uh huh, I got that."

"Cute, don't you think?"

No.

"Humpert and I already glanced over the books in here, but we didn't really check each one. So just take a quick look. Separate the ones that were printed before, say, 1924 or '25."

I nodded.

"Better make it anything before 1930, to be safe. And anything undated or in any other language that might be that old. And certainly, anything at all that sounds like it might be weird or supernatural or sexy or something the good ladies of the Junior League would hate for the cleaning lady to find on their nightstand. Just put whatever you find down in the kitchen. I'll take them over to the realtor's office tomorrow morning. All right?"

"Sure."

"Oh, and especially anything handwritten. What she called a holi...holigrat?"

I didn't correct her. "No problem."

"All right. Fabulous. There's beer in the refrigerator and plenty of food if you get hungry. Help yourself and don't worry about it. Remember how much I owe you for last night."

She blew me a kiss and disappeared. I entertained a brief fantasy about my friend Dell and Paula, his old lady, rushing out of their house as I pulled up in a Mercedes sports car, Victoria at my side. The thought of what Dell must have been going through at that very moment, and the small likelihood of my being able to return to South Bend at all, deflated the daydream immediately.

Leaving the door of the stuffy room open so I could breathe—and because small, enclosed spaces remind me of prison—I went at it for the next several hours. Unfortunately, some place along the line Victoria's parting words echoed back into my mind, and the work didn't occupy me enough to drive out thoughts of just how much Victoria did or didn't owe me for my behavior the night before.

Even if she hadn't seen me as a coward, I was one. People had called me a hero years before but it's much easier to be brave as part of a cause, a crusade. Where even if no one would ever know of your bravery, you realized that—if they had known—they would have cheered. Easier to be brave, if you believed the world really could be saved, that even a desperate gesture could make a difference. The night before, I'd hesitated, frozen. It was a miracle he hadn't killed or severely wounded her with that weird knife.

But what should I have done? Wasn't it only natural to spend a moment assessing the situation? I could have jumped him blindly, only to discover he was armed and crazy and four times my size. I could have been turning an apparent rape into a double murder.

He *was* bigger, he *was* armed, and he was probably crazy.

Did that allow me to stand by with my mouth open and watch while he raped her or cut her to shreds? Did that absolve me from helping out?

I'd opened the last four or five books and glanced at the copyright date without registering anything, so I went through them again. Sure enough, the third book back was dated 1901. *Missy Matlor's Happy Birthday.* Obviously, a black magic classic. I set it aside for Victoria and went back to the pile.

If I hadn't been forced into the fight, would I have helped out? What would I have done?

Copyright 1898. *A Lady's Book of Christian Dress.* I stuck it on top of Missy Matlor, but I didn't reach for another book. How close had I come to just abandoning Victoria? How close? Even *I* couldn't have justified that to myself. At least I would hope not.

The real Stephen Witowski would have known what was right and acted instantly. Fifteen pounds lighter, and two inches short of my five-foot-ten, he would have leaped right in, his Jesus cheering him on. The real Stephen was brave. At least when I knew him.

That was before he put that rifle into his mouth: one shot through the back of the throat without touching the teeth or the tongue. A communion with death. With nothingness? *This is MY body. This is MY blood.*

Over the next couple of hours, I gave myself a headache and found three more books. First, *The Collected Sermons of Cotton Mather,* copyright 1904, and something called, *The Fruit$ of Victory: Rumanian $ucce$$ $torie$*, dated 1920. Either of those might easily have been the hit of the whorehouse library.

I also found a copy of Pliny the Elder's *Natural History Volume V*, translated back in 1853 by "the late John Bostock, M.D., F.R.S" and the apparently less learned, but at least at the time still breathing, H.T. Riley, Esq. B.A. Inside the front cover, a bookplate identified this particular copy as a 1891 bequest from Jeremiah Frances Reynolds to the Library of the University of Illinois.

I took a break and sat down on the dusty floor to page through it a bit. I'd heard of the book, but I'd never actually read any of it. The Translator's Preface identified Pliny simply as "a Roman physician and naturalist." It explained the original work was a thirty-seven-volume encyclopedia, and that "for centuries after its creation in 77 CE., Pliny's *Naturalis Historia* was the western world's primary source of scientific information." Volume V of the translation actually encompassed a number of the medical volumes of the original encyclopedia. Old Pliny had a natural cure for everything anyone could imagine and a few things most people probably couldn't.

His cure for inflamed tumors immediately caught my attention. According to Pliny, panace herb should be sprinkled with wine, wrapped in a leaf warmed with ashes and applied hot by a naked, fasting maiden. She should then touch the sufferer with the back of her hand and repeat three times, "Apollo forbids a disease should increase which a naked virgin restrains."

You can understand how this could help. Though I saw no need for the woman to be fasting. Or a virgin. I later discovered that Pliny believed that panace herb cured every ailment—thus the word panacea. The reason he had to fill volume upon volume with other cures—even though $panace cured everything—was that panace was in somewhat short supply since it was entirely mythical.

Other cures in the book were more practical. To quell excessive sexual desire, simply drink "a man's urine in which a lizard has been drowned." The urine of a eunuch would also work, as would a nice glass of pigeon shit and olive oil. And it is hard to imagine anyone wanting sex after that.

On the other hand, "The right section of a vulture's lung worn as an amulet in a crane's skin is a powerful aphrodisiac, as is consuming the yolks of five dove eggs mixed with pig fat and honey."

Bull urine and a pinch of sulfur were recommended for hair loss, dandruff and the dreaded affliction of "scanty eyebrows."

For hiccups or sneezing, simply kiss the nose of a mule.

A mixture of vinegar and boiled frogs was just the thing for toothaches.

Since I did actually have a headache, I looked that up. Pliny offered any number of options. I could rub crushed snails on my forehead. I could swallow boiled owl brains. The next few cures involved either ingredients I'd never heard of or urine from various creatures gathered under differing—and usually unpleasant—circumstances. I stopped reading when he suggested I could get rid of my headache by wrapping a rope from a suicide around my temples—which of course got me thinking of Stephen again. I didn't bother to see if Pliny had a cure for unfocused regret. For all I know it might be suicide, since the nature's cure for every ailment wasn't really panace, it was death.

It was thirsty work. I'd scattered around a lot of dust, breathing in what I didn't swallow. By five o'clock I wanted a beer, but as I left the storeroom, I saw the stairs leading up at the far end of the hall. The church steeple. I couldn't resist.

The brief winding stairway was as dim and dusty as the room I'd just left, and the trap door at the top was swollen shut by the winter rains. Cramming my body up into the darkness, shoving against the unyielding door, I suddenly flashed on the wizened face of the man I'd killed the night before, seeing it more clearly now in my imagination than I ever could have seen it then. With a groan, the trap door broke free and opened.

I hadn't felt any burning on my forearm, but I checked it anyway. I was relieved to find there was nothing there. Even the residual bruising was almost gone. I stepped up into the steeple.

Under the bright sun, to the north, the mountains had soaked up the rain and were so fertile and so vividly green, they almost overloaded my vision. The Pacific was to the south here—not the west—and across the highway. Under the remaining clouds, the ocean—vast, indifferent, mesmerizing—was the exact shade of the slate on the church's roof. A breeze brought an acrid smell to my nostrils; someone had poured asphalt sealer over sections of that roof. I doubted it had done much good. Except for O'Ryan's place, the only buildings visible in any direction were miles away, almost to Santa Louisa.

Past those buildings, past Santa Louisa, was San Cristobal. There, where the traffic lights interrupted the highway, was the giant Moreton Bay fig tree Ann and I slept under when we were hitching around the country together back in 1970. That was just after I'd gotten out of Leavenworth for forgery, and before I decided to return to school and finish up on my degree. We'd gotten dropped off there on the hottest day in a decade. Out in the sun, the whole world felt like the inside of a parked car. Yet under the enormous branches—the smallest of which was too large to wrap my arms around—the better part of an acre was sheltered from the heat. There was even a faint breeze. Day soon evolved into the finest of nights. And for Ann and I and all the other long-haired travelers who gradually assembled there, the tree became a haven of leaves and starlight and each other's company.

Ann had found a simple brass ring underneath that tree—heavily tarnished, maybe a long-lost fitting from somebody's backpack—and slipped it on the third finger of my left hand. Nowadays I wore it on my right.

Back down on the second floor, I had a long, loosening soak in the tub, washing my hair, savoring my thirst, anticipating the beer I'd have when I was finished. The water—just as hot as I could stand it—rose until it drained into the overflow.

Getting out, drying off and looking for something to wear, I decided I might as well unpack. That took about a minute and a half. I had no hangers left after having hung up O'Ryan's donations, so everything went into various drawers of the scratched-up mahogany bureau—obviously it had come with the place. Still, it was probably worth more than all the furniture I'd owned back in South Bend put together. At the bottom of my gym bag was the plastic folder that held my last two twenties in traveler's checks. When I'd left South Bend, I had nothing but what was in my wallet and the traveler's checks I always kept in the glove compartment. The checks had originally been purchased in my real name. But since I could cash them by signing an indecipherable signature that matched my normal indecipherable signature on the check, I felt reasonably safe using them.

The folder with the checks was empty.

Shit!

I checked my wallet. Two singles and a personal check made out to my real name that I didn't dare cash—no traveler's checks.

I was stunned. It was like losing a thousand dollars.

I rifled through all my pants. The only paper I found was the crumpled note I'd written to Maria last night. I flushed that down the toilet.

Shit!

I counted up my change: a buck seventeen. Plus, the two singles in my wallet. Which reminded me. Picking up the wallet again, I removed the personal check, plus my real driver's license, which I'd slipped behind the one that "proved" I was Stephen Witowski. The real license was four years old—in the photo I still had longish hair. I'd already destroyed all my credit cards. I'd never gotten any in Stephen's name; I could have, and then run them up without paying, but—even beyond the ethical and legal issues—it would have seemed like slandering the dead.

The check was for two hundred twenty-five dollars; I'd sold my Gibson guitar last week so I'd have something in my pocket after putting everything else I could raise toward our big drug score. It would be safer to flush the check and the license. But you never know what might happen—I'd certainly established that. I stuck them under the newspaper lining the bureau drawer.

I checked my right forearm once more. Nothing there. I had no intention of leaving; I doubted if even pigeon shit or eunuch piss would dim my desire for Victoria. But if for some reason I did have to run, I'd have $3.17 to fund the rest of my getaway.

CHAPTER 11

Seven or eight bottles of Heineken were scattered throughout the well-stocked refrigerator. I drank the first one right down, but took my time on the second, wondering when Victoria would be back. I found a copy of that morning's *San Cristobal News-Herald* on the sideboard, next to a small stack of *Wall Street Journals*, all still in their mailing wrappers. The *News-Herald* had no mention of a body being discovered—not yet anyway—or even of someone reporting seeing one in a local wash. I did notice the rents in the area were outrageous, and nobody seemed to be doing much hiring. The national unemployment rate had reached nine percent, and in California it was almost ten.

I also called the San Cristobal library and found out they didn't carry the *South Bend Globe*. Dell and I were too small time to make the Chicago papers. I was tempted to phone South Bend again, but I dreaded doing it. Maybe I was afraid of what I might find out. I told myself I'd be better off just keeping my head down for now. Besides, it would be idiocy to call Dell and Paula's. And with all the breaking up and moving and dying and just drifting away, it was amazing how few others I felt like I could call in that city. Or anywhere, I suppose.

At five minutes to six, I picked up my beer and walked through the den into what had once been the nave of the church. Now it was Victoria's living room, a single high-ceilinged story stretching to the front of the building. In the center hung a massive chandelier. The hardwood floor was spotlessly clean and polished to a high gloss.

And then there was the mahogany. Mahogany crown molding that must have been a foot wide ran around the tops of the walls. Every window was framed in mahogany. A number of mostly empty mahogany bookcases were nestled beneath the windows on either side. And on the near wall, a fireplace with an ornate mahogany mantel had been added to the upraised area where the altar would have been originally. Even at a distance, I could see that much of the wood was nicked and scuffed and faded in places from years of exposure to the sun. Still, it wouldn't have come cheap. Not in dollars. Not, I would imagine, in terms of what any number of women may have had to endure so it could be there.

I settled into a recliner on the raised area, then picked up the remote control and switched on the TV. A couple of minutes of a Charlie's Angels rerun, three commercials, and the local news appeared. No bodies were mentioned. The weatherman was expecting rain, a lady in Santa Maria was expecting quintuplets, and some group up in Modesto was expecting Christ.

I ended up eating alone, making a meal out of an apple, a banana, and a whole lot of individually wrapped slices of American cheese that—authentically enough—tasted like the air in East Chicago. Though the deal with Victoria was for room and board, I would have felt uncomfortable grilling up one of her steaks. Besides, cooking for just myself seemed like too much trouble.

Outside, the on-again off-again clouds broke once more. The last light of day cast colored patches on the floor at the far end of the nave where the windows were stained glass. With no idea when Victoria might return, I was at once tired, restless, anxious and bored. In spite of the remote control, the TV only got one station. I've got my pride; I'd rather have her catch me sneaking through her bedroom than watching a rerun of *My Mother the Car*. But I needed something to do.

On the other side of the fireplace, boxes and crates were stacked up against the wall like building blocks. Next to them, an entire bookcase was filled with vinyl records: all, I discovered, in rough chronological order. A few from the fifties—main stream pop like Sinatra, Tony Bennett and Broadway scores. Then, starting with *Sgt. Pepper*, most of the major rock albums from the late sixties and early seventies, along with a good selection of more obscure artists like Fever Tree and Tim Buckley. Except for the Eagles' *Hotel California* and three disco albums—one of which was the obligatory *Saturday Night Fever* soundtrack—there was nothing from the last seven or eight years.

I pulled out an Argent album I hadn't heard since 1970. Unfortunately, the high-end stereo components lying nearby hadn't been hooked up. And I figured I was a lot more likely to blow something up than to assemble them correctly.

Looking for something to read, I dug through a stack of magazines: *Cosmopolitan, Vogue, Psychology Today, Prevention*, a single copy of *Fate*. I read an advice column in one of them, I'm not sure which. One reader was apparently living with the Marquis de Sade and terrified of losing him to another woman. Another inquisitive soul wanted to know how many calories there were in a cup of semen. The answer confidently provided was 47.6 calories, without any mention of where or why someone might obtain an entire cup of semen.

Next to the magazines was an open box full of Victoria's books, many of them on beauty, diet, or fitness—some on the level of popular science, some holistic, some just plain bullshit. She had eight or nine different diet plans there, at least six variations on *The Power of Positive Thinking* and enough exercise books to incapacitate the Pittsburg Steelers. I always wondered who bought this stuff. One of the last songs I ever wrote was initially called, "Fucking Our Way to Fitness," then "Loving Away Our

Love Handles." Nobody recorded either version. Maybe it should have been a book.

Digging down into the box past the level of self-help like Schliemann excavating Troy, I struck romances—a goodly supply—all with titles like, *Love's Rosy Passion,* and *Flaming Hearts of Lust.*

The cover of *Wild Irish Ardor* featured a young woman with red hair and an upturned nose. When I was in junior high, girls with upturned noses drove *my* ardor wild; I can't for the life of me figure out why. Near the bottom of the box, I found something called, *The Witches' Hammer.* It sounded like a novel, but it was—theoretically at least—non-fiction. I did learn that the devil had an icy penis that came to a sharp point. And I thought *I* had problems getting women into bed.

I settled on a novel called *Once Is Not Enough* and took it back to the recliner. The night closed in, isolating my little circle of light like an air bubble in a chocolate pudding. The big room became cozy, though whenever I got up, each step was echoed by the tinkle of the chandelier.

At some point, I dozed off in the recliner and dreamed more dreams of death and terror.

About eleven or eleven-thirty, I was out in the kitchen, shaking off my dreams and looking for a snack, when the front door opened and thudded shut. The chandelier chimed along, as two sets of footsteps crossed the living room floor.

A man spoke, his voice a deep round rumble, "It *is* a big job. Though it has possibilities."

"It's a good investment," Victoria answered. Adding with a laugh, "At least so my attorney tells me."

"Where would you like me to put your purchases, my dear?" *My dear?* Who the hell was she dating, Prince Philip? Somehow the voice sounded not only self-assured, but dignified, even handsome. Still, from the tone it was clear they were just getting acquainted.

"I'll take them. You just sit and make yourself comfortable. I'm afraid I'm just beginning the remodeling. I guess I should have stayed in a hotel while the work was being done, but the nearest decent hotel is way back in San Cristobal."

High heels clicked in four-four time, as she marched into the den and then through it into the kitchen, closing doors behind her.

"Hi," I called, glancing up from the refrigerator and for some asinine reason, feigning surprise.

"Shhush!" A finger went to her lips, raising a small bag marked, "Elaine's, Rodeo Drive," along with it. Her other hand held two larger bags, and she deposited them all on the table. "I'm not alone. Any calls?"

"Not a one." I had no idea answering the phone was part of my duties. And why were we whispering?

"Could you take these upstairs for me and put them on my dresser? I picked up a few things in L.A." Spreading her arms, she pirouetted like a model, swirling the simple black dress she was wearing. "What do you think?"

She made the dress look pure, classical, the way it must have looked in the fondest dreams of the designer. I nodded approvingly.

"Thank God for charge cards," she said, as if in explanation. "I splurged. Got my hair done, too. Don't worry," she patted my arm, "We'll be in the money again before the bills come."

What I was wondering about had nothing to do with the price of the dress.

"The books from the attic that I separated out are on the table here," I whispered.

Quickly, she clicked around and bent over them, bracing herself with one arm on the table, exposing the tops of her breasts. Tan and surprisingly generous—like the graceful contour of her legs, the highlighted curve of her cheeks, and the arch of her well-tended eyebrows, they seemed perfect natural forms. Money was as much a part of her appearance as her slim, full figure or her deliberate and precise features. But the effect was elegant, not crass. Like the Parthenon in the moonlight. Or the Hope diamond on black velvet.

"Well," she admitted after she'd poked through the titles, "I never really expected much."

"That's what you got."

"Listen, I've got to get back to my friend out there. You know how it is with these big-time captains of industry—can't entertain themselves at all." She gave me a little half hug and a quick kiss on the cheek. "I'll see you in the morning, all right?"

After she was gone, I could still feel the pressure of her hand on my back, the brush of the fabric covering her breasts against my shirt. And above all, her warmth. My body was flushed from the touch, as if I'd been infused with her heat, a veritable Flaming Heart of Lust, I suppose.

I toted the packages upstairs and set them on her dresser. Elaine's, Montclair's, Oleg's: all the stores were in Beverly Hills. I'd known the rich at Harvard; I hadn't thought much about them one way or the other. Neither wealth nor family prominence had any standing academically; and socially in the sixties, my friends and I rated each as somewhere between novelty and original sin.

Back in my room, I undressed and got into bed.

"I want you, Mercedes Lady," I whispered out loud, like an incantation.

The bed clothes felt hot. I got up and cracked a window. It wasn't the money. I didn't care if she never had a cent. But beautiful and emanating wealth whether she had any money or not. Victoria was a woman who could have any man she might choose. It was as if, getting her, I'd be as good as anyone, in spite of everything. An instant success. Even a fleeting relationship would be like a ballplayer making the major leagues, however briefly. Or a songwriter having a hit single. And no hitless songwriter ever looked down on a one hit wonder.

I lay there, wide awake. At one point shortly after midnight, the phone rang and was quickly answered, but no other noise came from downstairs. After a while, I turned on the cracked bedside radio softly. By the 1:30 a.m. sports report, Victoria still hadn't come upstairs to her bedroom. Was she still down there with him? I hadn't heard the front door shut, but at least she hadn't brought him up to bed with her. A business executive, "a big-time captain of industry." She may have been lonely, but a woman like that was never going to stay lonely long.

And then I heard it. It would have been impossible not to. The police siren. Followed by the opening chords. Victoria and her friend had hooked up the stereo and the intro boomed through the entire church. I knew the song right away, though for the twenty or twenty-five seconds of the intro, I kept thinking that they couldn't possibly be playing that particular song. Because there are actually a number of rock songs that feature a siren. Then R. Dean Taylor began to sing his only U.S. hit:

"Indiana wants me. No, I can't go back now."

The song ended charmingly enough with the hero—a killer—surrounded by police and then a hail of gunfire.

Then, just in case I had somehow missed the message, Victoria played it again.

TUESDAY, MARCH 23

WHERE
THERE'S
A WILL

"You can't depend on your eyes when your imagination is out of focus." – *Mark Twain*

CHAPTER 12

When I got down to the kitchen the next morning, Victoria was talking to her "Bald and Fat is Where It's At," friend, Humpert, on the pantry phone, telling him about having her hair done at a shop in the Beverly Hills Hotel and complaining about the quality of the complimentary champagne and hors d'oeuvres. A customer with one too many face-lifts had warned her that liver pate was bad for the skin and nobody in the place had recognized Victoria's dead husband's name.

"No big deal. It's not like I didn't know RAM was passé," she said. "All those self-important RAM ass kissers up in Sausalito with their Rolex watches and wheat grass enemas, knocking themselves out to protect nothing. You've got to know when it's time to move on."

A kettle of water was steaming on the wood burning stove. I found a cup and poured in the water before dumping in the freeze dried Maxwell House. Though I'd spent a good part of the night considering what my options might be, I had no idea where I stood now. Obviously, Victoria knew I was wanted in Indiana. *No, I can't go back now.* My first instinct had been to grab my $3.17 and take off in the middle of the night—maybe even before the record had finished playing. But if Victoria was planning on turning me into the police, she was unlikely to have decided to say it in a song. Obviously, we'd be having a conversation this morning, and I had no idea how that conversation would go.

Now Victoria was telling Humpert about the man she met when she stopped off at the Oxnard Hilton for dinner on the way home. Since she was making no attempt to keep me from hearing, I sat down and listened.

"I mean I *was* all dressed up and it *was* early... No... But I no sooner entered the bar than he comes up and offers to buy me a drink. I should have just cut him dead, of course. But he did have a look about him. So instead, I explained in some detail just exactly how flattering it is to be taken for some pick-up in a bar... Right... Well, they damn well better. After he apologized—and apologized—it turned out he was the head of a big investment firm down in Century City. He was out of town and all alone and just trying to be friendly. You know how it is."

I nodded to myself. I knew how it was. He was trying to get laid.

On the phone, Victoria agreed to something and giggled. I was stirring and kneading the floating Maxwell House into the hot water, sending grainy brown streams over the sides of my cup. It wasn't pretty. The investment executive had been attentive and flattering. An impressive dresser. And cute—in his early fifties, but distinguished looking—a touch gray and obviously well off. He bought her dinner, and she let him drive her home in her Mercedes.

"He claimed to have an appointment in Santa Louisa today. And besides, it's always so much nicer to be driven by a man... No... No, I meant a real man." She chuckled.

She listened again for a moment, then replied, "No. But he *was* one captivated suitor, I'll tell you. As it was, I let it go farther than I intended. He was so nervous." She whispered something into the phone, then laughed and said, "You know better... No... I took him to a motel fairly early. Actually, I was glad to see him go. I have no idea how he'll get back to Oxnard."

Though my status was clearly up in the air, I was glad to hear he left.

The coffee stayed a little lumpy, but I drank most of it as their conversation continued. Apparently, there was a trick to freeze dried coffee which I hadn't mastered. Finally, Victoria said happily, "Yah, well I just wanted you to know." Then she hung up and returned to the kitchen.

"And there he is, the man of my dreams," she said.

"Morning, Victoria. I guess we need to talk."

"We've got eggs, bacon, toast, whatever that cute little stomach of yours desires. Oh, and I want to apologize."

"You do? For what?"

"The music last night? We got carried away. He was nice enough to hook up the stereo. We had to test it, and he really wanted to hear that song. We'd had a couple of drinks and I'm afraid I forgot you were here. It might have been a little loud. Hope we didn't wake you."

"What song was that?" *As if I didn't know.*

"Who knows? Standard stuff, I think. 'I love you, I miss you.'"

And now the cops are filling me full of lead. Standard stuff.

I nodded and sipped my coffee. What were the odds; he'd just happened to want to hear that particular song? The only thing that made sense was that she was playing with me. But why would she? And it made even less sense that he was the one trying to send me some kind of a message. Could it possibly have been just a coincidence?

"Anyway," she said, "sorry if we disturbed you." She couldn't have gotten much sleep the night before herself, but she looked vibrant. I was worn out. She was wearing shorts that said, "Dior," and a tee shirt bearing the logo of the San Francisco 49ers.

"It's a football team," she explained. In my morning funk, I must have been staring at her chest. "I have a friend who used to play for them."

I got interested in the last of my coffee, and nodded again uncomfortably. When she asked how I liked my eggs, I told her, "over easy," just as she dropped the bacon on the skillet and it started crackling. If she didn't hear me, she didn't ask again.

Quickly, the smell of breakfast thickened the air. On the counter in front of the blender were—among other things—walnuts, peas, broccoli, and bananas. Victoria had obviously been busy early; the resultant mixture was greenish and speckled.

"I do want to thank you for doing such a great job separating those books yesterday," she offered as the sizzling died down.

I didn't know what to say to that. I was just glad I'd gone to Harvard so I had the necessary skills to recognize dates prior to 1930.

"Guess what I found last night?" she asked, like a child pulling out a savored secret.

"True love."

Her laugh was more the kind women make when they think you're cute—which I've never been—than the result of my magnificent wit. But that was probably the kind of laugh I wanted to hear from her anyway.

"Not even close," she said.

"Well, if it was in the living room, it was probably a business executive."

"After he left. In the basement Zandie's Last Will and Testament." From her expectant expression, I was obviously supposed to be overwhelmed. I didn't make it, but she went on anyway. "I was leafing through some of his old books downstairs and there it was. Take a look."

She pointed to a couple of books on the table. One of them was the volume of Pliny's Natural History that I'd brought down yesterday. The book underneath it was bound in worn leather and had no title on its spine.

"Inside," she instructed as I picked it up.

Between pages seventy-eight and seventy-nine, someone had stuck a single sheet of paper, folded in quarters. Brown and aged, it looked almost burnt around the edges and creases. I removed it cautiously. Beneath it, the title on page seventy-eight of the book read, "Planting

Ritual: Invocation and Potion for Harvest Bounty." The title had been underlined and starred in long-faded ink.

Gently—as if I were untying a knot of spun sugar—I unfolded the sheet of paper.

"Be careful now," Victoria warned, her hand raised as if she'd thought better of letting me handle the document. A few crumbs of paper slid out onto my lap.

The writing was in an old-fashioned, elaborate script.

"'Last Will and Testimen,'" I read out loud. "Close." The spelling improved in the rest of the manuscript. I read it to myself.

Visions of my death creep up on me, and I compose this will so none may benefit from my passing who does not love me, or who wishes me ill.

Our cherished home and whatever possessions and gold I may have are to go to my Yolanda and Katherine, or those who may have taken their places assisting me at the time of my demise. They may grant or deny whatever awards they see fit to any or all of the other ladies of the house.

The business may continue or die with me. I care not. Within my church or scattered like the ten lost tribes, I know that no man born of woman could ever usurp my place in the lives, the hearts and the souls of my devoted conquests.

My alchemical laboratory and the library of reference inside it should be sealed away from the casual perusal of those who would not understand.

Most vitally, my grimoire, the assemblage of my secret knowledges, the effective spells and rituals I have scoured the known world for, should never pass to any who are unworthy. It shall be interred in that secret and secure place where only the most dedicated pilgrim who studies and searches may bring its truths back to light.

To be appreciated, it must be earned, never bestowed.

As for my mortal remains, it is my strong wish to cheat the greedy ground. Let me be enthroned here within the walls of this my home, my church, my palace, site of my greatest triumphs, surrounded by my finest ladies, with Rebecca—she who gave me life—at my feet, in that supposedly hallowed place which I have previously set aside. Or in a similar one, if, in their grief, my ladies should choose to prepare a more glorious secret resting place, where I may rot in the ultimate security of the grave for eternity, or at least that part of eternity necessary to return my borrowed flesh to dust.

Once I am buried and at my peace, like the wise Egyptian destroy this document and all other records of my location, save those in the souls and the hearts of my most devoted, who should guard that final secret, even unto death. For there are many in this mean-spirited land who—knowing not what they do—might defile my body with the greatest Christian fervor. And what might happen after my passing could be a horror that would yield my enemies a comfort they do not merit.

– Zandie

"I've heard of people who didn't trust banks," I said, "but never one who didn't trust cemeteries. Maybe he should have had his body hidden in a mattress. Or stuffed into a sock and buried in the back yard."

Victoria stared at me blankly. I was trying too hard.

"I guess he did have his enemies," she said. "He was openly contemptuous of Christianity and always bragging about his occult powers—though I don't know how seriously anybody ever took that. I spoke to my real estate friend earlier this morning—God, she was excited about the will—but she said Zandie's real problem was women."

I could relate.

"He was apparently gorgeous," Victoria continued. "Tall and graceful—just about irresistible. She said that, at first, that didn't bother the men in town. Most of them saw him as a harmless kook who provided a necessary service. He was no good at anything besides women, and in those days being good with women wasn't as highly regarded as being good with an ax or a saw, or with crops, or farm animals. So nobody felt threatened. And since he couldn't do anything of any practical value, they probably never believed his apparent contempt for everyone else was real."

"It sounds like there's a 'But' coming into the story soon."

"*But*," she said nodding, "after a while, I guess he started disgracing a better class of women. There were rumors of married women pining away for him, of town virgins fleeing the area in shame. Later there was even talk of women from the town who proved themselves to Zandie by secretly working in his house as prostitutes."

"Charming."

"Isn't it. I'm sure he had customers who would pay a special price for a go with their obnoxious neighbor's unmarried daughter, or the snooty wife of some local mucky-muck, even if she was a good deal past her prime. Of course, later the same women might end up in the dirt and stench of a basement crib, servicing drunken field hands for fifty cents a pop."

"And nobody did anything?"

She shrugged. "You know how it is with rumors. I'll bet those involved weren't doing much talking. Maybe, initially, people simply saw it as an isolated case or two—sympathizing with the husbands or fathers, or laughing at them, or both. But eventually, either the isolated cases built up, or else Zandie crossed the wrong person."

"And he got lynched."

"Exactly. Food's ready." She set a plate in front of me with three strips of bacon and two fried eggs.

"According to the will," I said, "there's supposed to be a library sealed up around here. Your friend would love that. Unless, of course, these instructions were never carried out. After all, the will was supposed to have been destroyed."

Pensively, Victoria poured herself a large tumbler of the greenish goop from the blender and sat down. "Good point. Of course, the will doesn't give away the location of his burial or anything. So there was no real need to destroy it, whether they carried it out or not. Wouldn't it be a kick to find that grimoire and see all his spells and rituals?"

"Sounds like it's either well-hidden or is long gone." I dug into my eggs. She sipped at her concoction. I didn't find the subject as exciting as she did. The yolks were powdery, and so was the bacon. Maybe it was too early for me to have much of an appetite.

Outside the day was bright and beautiful. But the ground was as soggy as a wet sponge. We must have had another storm during the night. I had a quick image of rain pelting down on the face of a floating corpse.

The land sloped down behind the church, so the back porch—an obvious addition—was a good four feet above the ground. Latticework enclosed the area underneath it.

"There are all kinds of tools stashed under there," Victoria said. "They're all used, of course, but as you can see from the condition of the house, not used often."

I smiled: my polite laugh wasn't in her league. She had me pull out a large claw hammer that looked almost new, a rusty pry bar, and an ax. Then we went inside and climbed up to the attic, pausing outside the door to the last room before the steps leading up to the steeple.

"My favorite room," she said. "Wait till you see what's inside." She gave me an exaggerated leer before throwing the door open dramatically.

The room was large, filled with odd angles and low sections of ceiling—and overpowered by its wallpaper. I walked over to get a good close look. Embossed red nudes cavorted across a silver background—satiny Rubenesque women pursuing muscular little men.

This stuff covered three of the walls. The fourth was simply painted white.

"Zandie's room," Victoria explained. "For some reason, it's never been redone in all these years. You would have thought The Ashram—if no one else—would have made it a priority. But they weren't here all that long, and I guess their prime concern was turning the basement into a dormitory so their little clones would have somewhere to live while they fixed up the rest of the place for the leadership. Or maybe they were afraid to come in here; I think they were mostly celibate. These plump little lovelies could have been too much for them."

Victoria explained that the wiring in the room had been short circuiting and it all had to be replaced. Judging by the water-stained cracks that webbed across the ceiling and down behind the wallpaper, that was no surprise. My job was to rip out the walls, tear them down to the studs. Eventually the room would be re-insulated and re-paneled.

"You want me to destroy these lovely ladies," I said, kiddingly.

"They're all too fat anyway. Besides what do you need them for when you've got me?"

Suddenly, without having moved, she seemed very close. The hairs on my arm tingled, as if a current charged the gap between us. I was breathing her perfume.

"Your friend next door thinks I'm quite the temptress," she said lightly, striking a mock dramatic pose and spreading her fingers across the back of my neck.

"Who?"

"The old man, of course. Who else?"

Now I was tinglingly aware of her arm across my back, of the touch of her hip so close to my crotch, her breast against my arm. What would she do if I kissed her right then, transforming a joke into fact? I could feel the sweat forming in the small of my back.

"I wish he'd told me," I tried.

"I'm surprised he didn't." She smiled, removing her arm and moving back—half a pace.

I took a few steps myself, as if I was checking out the room, but actually so I could breathe. Beneath my feet, the floor creaked loudly.

"Speaking of surprises," she said, "I suppose there's a small chance you could be in for one here."

"Oh?"

"This was supposedly where Zandie kept most of his money—walled up here in his room to keep it safe. Apparently, he didn't believe in cemeteries *or* banks."

I looked around. The walls were intact. "If anybody within five hundred miles actually believed that, the walls would have been taken down to the studs years ago."

"They probably were. If there ever was money here, I'm sure it's long gone and at some point the walls were just redone."

"Still, that sure looks like it was the original wallpaper. I wonder how it survived."

"Who knows? Anyway, if this was once the 'secret and secure place' where Zandie kept his money, maybe it's where his grimoire ended up as well. And anyone taking the money might not have bothered to take that."

"It's possible, I suppose." *Anything is possible.*

"If you do happen to come across it or any of his stuff, don't toss anything out. My realtor friend signed her lease yesterday. She's ready to start on her store. Anything we might find, she wants. Books of course. And I guess Zandie owned piles of jewelry; bracelets, amulets, stuff like that. Even a gold plated human skull he kept on his mantel. And if we do find that grimoire, the old girl would be willing to pay a lot for that."

"Really? She sounds a bit too anxious. Maybe you should consult an expert before you sell her anything. She might know something you don't. Maybe his things have some historical value."

"Not likely. Zandie was just some local loony. And he only died fifty or sixty years ago. His stuff isn't worth anything. But she wants it. And listen, anything she buys we'll split fifty-fifty. Fair enough?"

"Sounds good." *Speaking of money*, I thought, *this would be a good time to ask for an advance.*

"Fabulous. How are your finances right now?" Like she was reading my mind.

"Ah, actually, none too good. I seem to have lost or misplaced some traveler's checks and, well..."

"I understand. I'll get you an advance on your wages—all right?"

"You know—if it's no problem." I was a little embarrassed, like I was asking her for an allowance. "I'd really appreciate it."

"Of course." She glanced at a sleek, bejeweled watch that seemed more tea-with-the-Queen than tee-shirt-and-shorts. "I've got to run. Got an aerobics class in San Cristobal in twenty-five minutes. Miss one day and my body falls apart." She slapped a butt that seemed in no danger of incipient decomposition. Then she blew me a kiss and walked out.

I tore into the walls. It was heavy work, but in a way the destruction was fun, and my own body loosened up luxuriously as I worked up a sweat. The boards beneath the plaster were thin—many were rotten. They came out easily, though often the nails remained behind in the studs, and I had to pull them out separately with the pry bar. Digging through the plaster itself was the roughest part. I had to open the windows to keep from choking on all the plaster dust. It soon covered me from tip to toe.

The morning slipped away. Victoria brought me up a BLT, some chips and two bottles of Heineken, and we had lunch together, sitting on the dusty bed. More dry bacon, no mayo. I had the distinct feeling that she didn't have much experience with food preparation and was surprised she seemed to want to adopt that role with me. And of course, it wasn't her fault that everything tasted of plaster.

I'd read an article a while back that—in a reaction to the women's movement—women in many circles once again had to be able to cook in order to be considered "properly feminine." But being properly feminine didn't seem to be something Victoria needed to worry about.

Her own lunch came from the blender again. Apparently, she was on the tail end of the latest diet fad, concocted by "Doctor" Ernst Something-or-other, one of those dudes with a string of initials after his name, none of them M.D. or even Ph.D. By now, she was almost certain the whole thing was a crock. I agreed with her, though gently. I'd had years of exposure to popular diets, as an observer if not as a victim—my mother belonged to the Book-of-the-Month Club and used her membership to try them all. This one sounded like it would produce nothing but bad gas, though it was hard to imagine Victoria with gas of any kind.

We chatted about San Francisco. We'd both lived in the Bay Area—her in Sausalito just recently, and in the Haight back in '67, the once legendary Summer of Love.

"I would have thought you were too young for that," I said.

"Sir," she grinned, "you should know better than to ask about a lady's age. But, yes, I was young. Does that make me old now?"

"Well, you're obviously younger than I am. I was there myself shortly after that. Very briefly in the Haight, then in Berkeley."

I took another hit of the Heineken. It tasted of plaster too. Right after I'd graduated in '71, I'd lived on the streets of Berkeley—crashing here and there, sometimes in one park or another in my sleeping bag. Hanging out and occasionally playing other people's music, mostly in a coffee house called Peace of Ass on Telegraph Avenue. Not really working on my songs, but feeling very with it and very dashing—in a grubby kind of way. And very mature—sleeping with the forty-three year old wife of the coffee house's owner, discussing open relationships with her upstairs in their over-ripe apartment, while her husband went after teeny boppers I would have considered too young for me. She was my prize. Only much later did I look back and realize I was simply *her* teeny bopper of the month, and that she was aging and scared and beginning to grow facial hair.

"I used to play music in some of the clubs up there," I said to Victoria. "Some," meaning two—infrequently and mostly for spare change. "But actually, I was never much of a performer. I was better off writing songs than singing them."

"Oh really? You're a songwriter?" She sounded amused. Who could blame her? A few years before that, everybody wrote music or poetry, or painted. Especially when they were talking to beautiful women.

"No. Not anymore. That was a long time ago."

I took another sip of beer, though the bottle was empty and had been empty the last time I'd tried to drink too. Strange, I'd deliberately slipped my songwriting into the conversation, and now I was embarrassed to talk about it—the way I used to be when I was actually writing and failing.

From 1971 to '78, writing sporadically, I'd submitted songs to every major record label and many of the lesser ones, anguishing over every note and every word. And yet I kept it as secret as an adolescent's masturbation—shamefaced in the post office when the clerk commented on tapes bound for Warner Bros. or Columbia Records.

There were people back then who would have been willing to pretend, or even believe, that my rejection slips were badges of honor—medals in the war against commercialism. But to me, my failures always seemed more real as they became more public. And if someone asked what I did, I usually told them I was a bum. That worked just fine because people took it to mean that I was a free spirit as opposed to being just another middle class cipher.

"Any successes?" Victoria asked, inevitably.

"You don't make no money, you ain't no musician." That used to be a joke, something a friend once heard a father scream at his son in a music store.

"True," she said. And earnings did seem to be the most convenient guide for sorting actuality from pipe dream. Victoria delicately wiped her mouth with a napkin. "I used to be married to Terry Davis."

"Really." It was getting harder to look unimpressed. I swallowed the last bite of my sandwich along with the rest of my tales of my musicianship.

"He dedicated one of his albums to me."

It turned out she married him in '69 and divorced him in '71. During that time Terry Davis was one of the minor demigods in the musical pantheon. He wasn't Dylan or Lennon, but he'd toured with both and had appeared on their albums. And Lennon, at least, had appeared on one of his. His music had been idealistic, lyrical, and sensual.

"Must be tough being married to a man so many women wanted."

She laughed and said, "If they only knew," in a way that made me think perhaps the idol had a dick of clay. That helped my confidence; I'd already been starting to wonder if I could ever match up to someone like Terry Davis sexually. She also mentioned that—contrary to his image—he was extremely jealous. Once he even took a swing at his manager just for dancing with Victoria at a party. Still, feeling completely outclassed, I was happy to let our conversation drift on to other things.

"By the way," she asked later, as we gathered up the lunch's debris for her to take downstairs, "what are you doing tonight?"

I shrugged. "I don't know. I thought maybe I'd just relax—sit around, drink a little wine. Does the fireplace downstairs work?"

"I'm sure it does. That sounds wonderful."

Yes, it certainly did. On her way out, Victoria turned and gave me a little wave before closing the door behind her.

If I knew how to whistle, I would have as I started back to work. An hour later, I still hadn't found anything behind the walls, except for the evidence of a good-sized fire. Beneath the wallpaper, the inside of the outer wall was badly charred.

I'd worked up a good thirst. Fortunately, I still had some beer left, the remains of my second Heineken sitting on the floor near the bed. Unfortunately, when I picked it up, there was almost as much plaster dust floating in the bottle as there was beer. I put the bottle back down, and, as I did, I saw the white wall on the other side of the bed at just the right angle. A straight line, scarcely more than a shadow, ran across the wall just an inch or two above the height of the bed.

A patch in the wall.

I pulled the bed away. From a distance, in the bright light, the patch was almost invisible. Closer up it was a clear rectangular indentation, about six feet long, maybe a foot tall, starting from about a foot above the floor.

I moved the bed a little farther away from the wall so I could get a good swing, picked up the ax and swung with my full body—bases loaded, bottom of the ninth.

It wasn't a strike out, but it certainly wasn't a grand slam. Maybe a long fly to left that scored a run. The patch was dry wall, covered with a thin layer of plaster obviously intended to smooth out the difference in depth between the dry wall and lathe around it. Giving it my best Hank Aaron, I quickly knocked out three good size holes, opening access to the three areas between the studs behind the patch.

Out from amongst the spiders, spider webs, rat droppings, dirt and dust, I pulled a torn, possibly rat-eaten, gray bag, marked "Bank of San

Cristobal," as well as four quarters, a dime, three silver dollars with dates ranging from 1903 to 1921, and half a ten-dollar silver certificate bill from 1915. I cleaned out all three areas thoroughly. There was nothing else back there.

I quickly knocked holes in the plaster and lathe between all the rest of the studs on that wall. I did the same with what was left of the other three walls. All I got in those holes was another spider bite and scratches on my hand when I hadn't made the opening quite big enough.

Ok, maybe not a run scoring sacrifice fly. Maybe it was a pop up to the catcher. Maybe the runner on first got doubled up.

By this point I was so dry and thirsty I could barely swallow. I gathered up my treasure to take down and show Victoria, and to get a drink.

That's when I discovered I was locked in.

Triple play.

I hate sports metaphors.

———

I'd barely begun to bang on the door and yell—especially since, dry as I was, it took a moment for my mouth to generate any real sound—when I heard Victoria coming up the stairs. A moment later, I heard the key turning in the lock.

The door opened.

"I'm sorry, Steve," she said, not looking sorry at all. I brought you another beer." She was unarmed. There was nothing to prevent me from pushing past her and leaving, which was why I didn't. At least that was partly why.

"You locked me in! Why did you lock me in?"

She chuckled. "Would you buy it if I said I did it by accident? Force of habit? The key was in the lock, I just turned it without thinking?"

"Would you expect me to?" I'd seen no evidence Victoria was in the habit of locking doors, not even her bedroom or bathroom doors.

"Let's blame Humpert."

"Humpert? Humpert locked me in? Like a prisoner."

"*I* locked you in, Steve. You're hardly a prisoner. Do I look like I have to imprison men to keep them around? There's the door—so anytime you want to leave…"

"I'm not saying I want to leave, Victoria."

"Good."

"I just wonder why you felt the need to lock the door. Is it that you don't feel safe being alone with me?"

"Don't be silly," she laughed. "Humpert—he's my attorney—he's paid to be paranoid. There was at least a chance there was a lot of money up here. I don't really know you yet. You were up here alone. It occurred to Humpert that you could find it and hide it someplace else while I was downstairs. How would I ever know?"

Humpert might have suggested locking me in, but obviously Victoria thought it was a good idea. I suppose it made some sense. Thirst getting the better of outrage, I took a long pull on the Heineken. It was delicious, though I could still taste plaster.

"Well… Anyway, it turns out you were absolutely right, Victoria. This is where Zandie stored his money."

"You found it? But you didn't find the grimoire, did you?"

"No grimoire." Victoria might be cash poor at the moment but clearly, she had no real money worries, not if her first question was about the grimoire rather than how much I'd found. "If the grimoire ever was here, it probably was taken with the money."

"I doubt it was ever here." She glanced around at all the holes as if to confirm that.

"By the way, there was only one place in the whole room that was patched. So, whoever took the money knew exactly where to look.

Probably Zandie himself or one of his people. And my guess is they were in a hurry since they obviously didn't check to make sure they had everything."

I handed her the gray bag, the coins and the half bill. I'd forgotten how dirty it all was.

She looked down at her hand as if I'd just put a turd in it. "That's what was still here?"

"You're $4.10 richer. Actually $2.05, since half of what I find is mine, right?"

"It's all yours." She handed it back to me and wiped her hand distastefully on her designer jeans. "And this shows that it was a good thing I locked you in. Otherwise, I might be wondering if that really was all you found. By the way, while you were up here making us rich, I figured out the will. The grimoire is buried with Zandie. And I think I know where that is."

CHAPTER 13

I finished reading the will one more time and looked up.

"Don't you see it?" Victoria asked.

I shook my head. My fingers ached from the ax and the hammer and the pry bar. I wasn't sure my brain was working much better. Especially since rather than focusing on the will I was focusing on the fact that—in spite of her apparent lack of concern for money—Victoria never would have locked me in unless she thought there was some real chance I'd uncover Zandie's fortune. But Victoria wasn't stupid. Far from it. And obviously, long before then, someone—probably many someones—would have checked out the rumor that Zandie's money was hidden in these walls. How could she possibly have believed there would be anything left?

Unless there was no such rumor. Had she found some kind of information lying around the old church that no one else knew about? That would explain the wallpaper being intact. On the other hand, I couldn't see any reason for her to bother to lie to me about it.

I took a long drink of beer.

"I'm surprised you can't see it," Victoria said, obviously pleased that she could. "Here's what happened. My real estate friend called again. I read her the will. Remember the sensation the King Tut's tomb exhibition created a couple of years back? She thought it would be 'totally, totally, beyond wonderful' if she could recreate Zandie's final resting place—wherever it might be—for her shop window, perhaps even displaying the skeleton intact in the casket, surrounded by his artifacts."

"Tasteful."

Victoria chuckled. "I know. She got very excited over the phone. I could practically hear her heart pounding. She thinks it'll be a great merchandising gimmick, and she could be right."

Or she could be out of her fucking mind. But since my marketing expertise was limited to setting up cigarette displays in liquor stores, all I said was, "And she's got the money to pay for all this?"

"She seems to. But my point is that when I was reading the will out loud to her some of the phrases began to click."

"Like?"

Victoria gestured impatiently toward herself, "Give it back to me." I handed it to her, and she searched through it for a moment. "The grimoire shall be 'interred.' In that 'secret and secure place.' And then later he talks about his body being buried in a glorious 'secret' resting place. Where he can rot in 'the ultimate security of the grave.' The grimoire shall be interred in a secret and secure place. His grave is to be secret and the ultimate security. Clearly the grimoire is to be buried with him in his grave."

"Could be." *Or he simply had a limited vocabulary* and *used the same words over and over.*

"It's got to be. And I think I know where that is. Come on. It's down in the basement."

"What about all this?" I gestured at the mess around us. "And the wiring?"

"Forget it. We can do this anytime."

As she led me down the stairs, I said, "By the way, there must have been a pretty good-sized fire up in that room once."

"I know."

"I doubt if there's any structural damage, though."

What a moron. The whole building could have been nine and a half minutes away from total collapse for all I knew of structural damage. If some of the things I say sounded as stupid to me beforehand as they did afterwards, I'd have a whole lot less to say.

***

We entered the basement through the kitchen. After descending an L-shaped stairway, we headed down a dim and narrow corridor, and then turned, apparently randomly, at various other passageways. The place was a maze, filled with small, crudely-made rooms and cubicles—some with doors, some with just old cloth hanging over the openings. It seemed to be considerably larger than the church above it. At Victoria's insistence, I'd brought the ax and the pry bar. She was carrying the hammer.

"Zandie must have made a fortune with all these cribs," I said.

"I doubt they were all used at once very often—maybe after the harvest or during the county fair."

Surprisingly, the basement was warm and dry. The rooms were all dark, but amazingly clean. The Ashram had done its work well. We passed several loudspeakers freshly mounted on the walls. Near the end of one corridor was a modern bathroom, complete with clean towels and toilet paper.

"I've been doing some work down here," said Victoria, anticipating my question.

"And this is the direct route?"

"This is the only route. Zandie's sense of humor, I guess. At the far end of the next corridor though, there is a bulkhead that leads outside. The working-class customers used to enter through there."

"Why didn't we?"

"The Ashram took the bulkhead doors off. That was going to be the main entrance to their dormitory. When they left, it was easier to just nail everything shut than to re-hang the doors."

The walls of the corridors were all wood, usually bare boards, old and uneven, with gaps between them. In some sections, boards were missing altogether. There were no windows, and the bare bulb lighting was irregular.

The far wall of the next corridor was brick; the only brick wall we'd seen so far. About halfway down, a table, a large cauldron, and several bookcases filled the passageway. Before we got that far, Victoria opened a door and stepped into the first room on the right.

"This is it," she exclaimed. The small room stank of long disuse. Victoria pulled out a cigarette lighter and lit a half-melted candle set in a wall sconce.

"Holy shit," I swore, even before she had a chance to light a second candle.

Mounted behind an altar, the statue was of stone, painted red. It must have been nine feet high, and yet it was so wide it appeared squat. The body was human, male and naked. Faceted red glass eyes reflected the candlelight malevolently. The face was flat, brutish, and reptilian, except for the lips which were so delicate they were almost vulgar.

"What do you think?" Victoria asked.

"Well," I said finally, "it wouldn't work in just any home, you understand, but here... I like it. Does it come in blue?"

Then I realized that, though somewhat more human-looking, the reptilian face on the statue was very similar to the face on the serpent knife that had stabbed Victoria Sunday—fangs and all. Since I had no idea what, if anything, that meant, I decided not to say anything just yet.

"And look," she said, pointing to the lines carved in the wall beside the monster's head:

The evil that men do lives after them; The good is oft interred with their bones.

"'The good is oft interred with their bones,'" she exclaimed, like that explained everything. "I'll bet he's buried here. With his grimoire."

I hoped not. The floor was unbroken concrete. "In the walls?" I tried. The external wall was stone and mortar, the other three were brick.

"From what I can figure, the walls aren't thick enough. I'm guessing he's in the statue! That it's a sarcophagus."

"Oh." I think she was expecting, *Eureka!* I stepped over to the thing. "It appears to be solid stone. How would they have gotten him in there?"

"It's flat up against the wall. The back could be open. Put him in it, then push it up against the wall and seal it up. Granted most sarcophaguses, or is it sarcophagi...?"

"I have no idea." So, had I given up on the aphrodisiacal power of pedantry? Actually, either was correct, though *sarcophagi* was preferred. (I didn't say I gave up pedantry for life. Besides, Sarcophaguses sounded like a character on Sesame Street.)

"Granted most of them are horizontal, but don't you think Zandie would rather be in a commanding position for eternity instead of lying down?"

"Hard to say. We weren't that close. But if we're looking for Zandie's grave, there is an actual grave outside in the church. The one we sat on after...after we first met."

"He's not there. The will said he was to be buried inside the house. This is much more his style. Besides, look at that penis."

"It's hard to miss." Fortunately, it wasn't erect, but nonetheless old snake eyes here would have been the talk of any locker room in the world.

Victoria shook her head scornfully. "I know men and I know what they think is important."

She said this like she would have said it to another woman, maybe a nun who'd spent most of her life in a convent.

Then she said, "I'm betting this is Zandie's tomb."

———

There's a reason the expression "hard as stone" has become a cliché. And whatever had been used to seal the statue to the wall had hardened over the years to the point where I finally decided it was actually easier to chip away at the stone.

Victoria had asked me to start at the head. But after she left, I realized that if a body *was* inside, it might not reach that high in the giant statue. Which meant I might have to dig my way in a second time farther down.

I started at the groin. Not that I had anything against this guy's manhood or snakehood or whatever the term would be. There simply seemed to be a seam between it and his body. Apparently at some point, he'd undergone penile enhancement. The fastest way to the heart of this particular demon was in all likelihood through his genitals.

Still, though there was no electric light in the room, I could see I'd hardly made a dent in the seam by six o'clock when I finally knocked off for the day.

I made my way out of the basement, turning at every corner where a notch had been carved, then continued on up to the second floor. I didn't see Victoria, but I certainly thought about her—with anticipation—while I was soaking in the tub. Women were so wonderful. And so powerful. In my experience, almost every woman has a look during sex, which she never gives to anyone, anywhere else. And inside that look is something so pure, so mysterious and exciting, so benevolent and approving and sustaining, that having it directed at you is like earning the approval of the gods. For that moment you are bursting with value. You are desired.

It was a look I'd always coveted, perhaps at this point in my life more than ever. And to see it in Victoria's eyes... I wondered if I had a chance.

It took me several washings to get all the dust out of my hair, which was nothing compared to how long it took to get all the crap out of the tub after I was finished. I even found bits of plaster in my razor after I shaved.

I used Victoria's hair drier. I'd been told blow drying was bad for my hair, but it made it look fuller. I was getting prepared as if something was going to happen between us.

I padded over to the closet and tried to figure out what to wear. When I'd first gotten the Richmond Tobacco job, my wardrobe had been strictly thrift store and yard sale, augmented by Christmas and birthday gifts. When you dress like I did, people give you a lot of clothes. It's like if you don't bathe everyone gives you cologne. But in the three years I was on the job, my clothing had become at least a bit more *au courant.* I'd had enough problems with my sex life without trying to maintain a separate standard of dress from the rest of the world. I even bought a brand-new three-piece suit. The only thing I wouldn't buy were designer jeans—that and my refusal to litter quite possibly being my last remaining principles.

But—aside from what O'Ryan had given me—I had only five shirts and three pairs of pants with me. The jeans were filthy, and the dress pants looked like somebody'd been using them for a pillow.

I settled for the cords—a little big but not too badly wrinkled—and a blue stretch jersey I got from O'Ryan. It hadn't been that many years before that, as often as not, I'd kept everything I owned in a backpack and never thought about wrinkles. When I was thirty, my pack and I moved to Los Angeles. Stephen, the real Stephen, had just died—though

I still hadn't accepted the fact that he'd killed himself. It was beginning to dawn on me that I wasn't going to be a saint (given up at age nine), a major league baseball player (forgotten at fourteen), the guru/leader of a group marriage commune (I probably hung on to that, vaguely, until about twenty-two), or a major sex symbol of any kind. The names of my former classmates were appearing in newspaper articles about industry and government, and on the credits at the end of TV shows. I was doing my Christmas shopping at K-Mart—and working shit jobs like day labor or picking fruit or, more and more often, phone sales.

So, I found a job in a beer bar and started working up a demo album of commercial songs—disco was huge. I told myself and Helen—the lady I was trying so hard to be in love with—that this would be my last attempt to make it in music. And clearly any idiot could write disco. Maybe even an idiot who failed at writing jingles the year before.

Halfway through the initial songwriting, I got concerned with critical response, and eventually I managed to transpose my disco ditties into—as I once explained to Helen after three glasses of wine—"an allegorical exploration of the relationship between the individual and reality as reflected in a fictionalized eco-system."

That may not be why she left me, but I'd have left her if she said it to me.

Victoria still wasn't around when I came downstairs. I drank another Heineken and read the *San Cristobal Times*—a long article about their problem with "winos, vagrants and others," a group that was starting to be referred to as 'the homeless'"—but still nothing about a body. Since Victoria hadn't indicated what her plans were for dinner, I was reluctant to go ahead and eat by myself or even to start something for us both.

Still, time passed, and I was just about to slap a sandwich together when I heard water running—the tub upstairs.

A few minutes later a bell rang—the classic ding-dong of a doorbell. I headed over to the double doors at the front of the old church. Not only was nobody there when I opened the door, there was no sign of a doorbell. The bell rang again. I hustled to the back door, where I found Maria—not exactly all dressed up, but scrubbed and combed, and wearing what seemed to be just the faintest touch of mascara. She had on the white peasant blouse she'd bought in Jerome, the day before we'd made love.

"What's up?" I asked her through the screen door.

"Oh. Nothing." She shoved her hands into her pockets as if they were getting in her way. It made her hips look bigger. "Just dropped over to see what you're... Wow, what happened to your neck?"

"Oh," I couldn't think of a lot of innocent reasons for my neck to be bruised up. "It's a long story."

"I can't wait to hear it."

Well, right before I killed this guy..."I was tearing down a wall with a sledgehammer. A board bounced back and slammed across my neck. It looks worse than it feels." That last, at least, was true.

"I certainly hope so."

I let the silence grow.

Not inviting her in was awkward, but I wasn't going to do it. I liked Maria, but it would be unfair to let her believe something could develop between us. Besides, it wouldn't do for Victoria to think I had a girlfriend—two or three girlfriends maybe—but not one, especially not one who lived next door. And to come right out and say the kind of thing decent people never come right out and say, Victoria didn't appear to be a woman likely to get involved with the kind of guy who would see someone like Maria.

You can see why I started out by admitting that I was an asshole. And maybe, just maybe, that will keep me from pretending that I was something better than that.

After a long moment, Maria said, "You need to be more careful."

I nodded.

Maria tried, "So what are you doing now?"

"I'm exhausted—been working my butt off all day. I'm probably just gonna drop into bed early and crash."

"New boss a slave driver?"

"Aren't they all? It looks like she split around four o'clock," I found myself saying. "I just finished up a few minutes ago."

Maria nodded. Then for a few more seconds we simply looked at each other. I used to claim that while I may lie like hell to corporations and bourgeois institutions, I never lied to people. I used to claim that.

Maria shifted her weight from one foot to another. I needed to hurry this along. Victoria could be coming down any minute.

"I've got a bath running," came out of my mouth. "Maybe I'll drop over later if I get a little more energy. Tomorrow night might be better, though."

At that exact moment, we both heard the unmistakable sound of the bathtub drain being opened and the water gushing down through the pipes.

"I understand," Maria said, pleasantly enough. The calm resignation on her face made me think that maybe she really had figured it out. Still, when she left I was, for the most part, simply relieved.

About fifteen minutes later, Victoria finally drifted down, in pale blue pants, over a leotard with a frilly top.

"I'm going to make myself a salad, if you'd like some," she announced.

"Sure. Want some help?"

"Why not?"

As we worked together on the salad in the pantry, the snow-white cat appeared for the first time since Sunday.

"Get out of here, La Perdita!" Victoria demanded.

The cat ignored her and kept getting under foot. Victoria didn't have any cat food, so I put a saucer of milk and some tuna in a corner. The cat preferred to stay in the way, making Victoria and I brush into each other several times as we moved around in the pantry. I was starting to really appreciate La Perdita. I didn't even mind when it made me spill the salad dressing.

On the other hand, my efforts at conversation with Victoria were exactly that—an effort. Revealing little beyond the most basic info. She and I had both lost our parents. I was separated by half a generation from my brother and sister; she was an only child. At dinner, too, I did most of the talking. Distracted, almost dreamy-eyed, Victoria told me her work-out had taken more out of her than it normally did. The salad would have been better if we'd had more dressing.

We cleared off the table and at my suggestion crammed several days' worth of dishes into the dishwasher. Victoria seemed to have forgotten dishes had to be washed. By now, I'd pretty much decided she was used to having a maid.

While Victoria used the bathroom off the den—the den that used to be a sacristy—I grabbed some logs and some old newspapers from the bin by the stove, brought them into the living room, and started laying a fire.

Terry Davis's old lady. Jesus! I was lucky I'd found out before I'd dragged out some of the shining successes of my songwriting career, like, "Looking for the Good Times," the B side of a Mickey Hanson single of which twenty-five hundred copies were pressed by a soon-to-be-defunct company called—honest to God—A-1 Records. Mickey Hanson's big hit, "Fire in My Soul for You," had been seventeen years and several thousand gallons of whiskey earlier on Columbia.

A-1 Records. Christ!

The phone in the living room had one of the loudest rings I'd ever heard. It was one of those old black metal ones, with a round dial.

"I'll get it," Victoria called immediately, returning from the bathroom. "Don't bother."

She sauntered over and stood next to the phone as it rang for a second and third time. Then, after the fourth ring, she snatched it up as if she was afraid it might escape.

"Bob," she said after a moment. She looked over at me and screwed up her face comically, shaking her head, letting me know she had no idea who Bob was. Obviously, this was not the first time she'd gotten a call from someone she couldn't remember.

I finished laying the fire and sat back on my heels for a second. A long string of small couples was carved in the mahogany mantel piece. Naked couples—in far more graphic positions than the ones on the attic wallpaper. Had Victoria noticed them yet?

"Glad to hear it," she said, replying sweetly to something Bob had said, "And as long as we're on the subject, Bob, who *are* you?"

While he was answering she grinned at me, enjoying this. Then, "Club Gatsby? When?... I'm afraid you still have the advantage on me." That was certainly bullshit. There was no question who had the advantage here. "Really? I did? Was I drunk... No wait... That's all right, tell me something about yourself. Maybe I'll remember..." She laughed warmly, picking a candy out of the bowl by the phone. "God, you'd think I'd remember meeting a gynecologist... Oh, sure... The one with the helicopter. Of course! Certainly. I remember now."

She shrugged her eyebrows at me. She still had no idea who this guy was, but he'd never guess from the sound of her voice.

They talked on—too long for my liking—getting chummier and chummier. Agreeing on such vital philosophical points as the unimportance of financial wealth, the necessity of traveling first class, and the need for diverse investments. Then she said, "No, I've never been there, either... All right. But listen, why don't I meet you there. It'll be quicker and easier... All right. Bye."

She hung up the phone and hurried upstairs without a word. Thirty minutes later she was back down in a white dress, fully made-up and almost regal except for the bouncy way she ducked in to toss me a quick good-night on her way out. She said it in almost the exact same casual tone Helen had used years ago when she'd split to Mexico with that burnt-out coke freak, three days before I finished my demo album. Helen was my last real old lady. Back then I'd always scoffed at coke as a drug that made you feel better about yourself while making you act worse—like alcohol or speed.

I would have liked a line or two now.

A second later Victoria was back.

"There's an old Volkswagen out in the garage. The keys are in the glove. If you want to go into town, feel free." She smiled that thousand-watt smile and was off again.

Later that night, as I lay in bed alone, the weird whistling began again. Louder and deeper than before. This time I registered it as a Hank Williams style loneliness—you know, melancholy whippoorwills, tearful robins and weeping moons. I wondered how it would have sounded to me if Victoria had stuck around that night.

ASMODEUS THE DEMON SEDUCER OF EVE AND OTHER ANNOYANCES

"Reason is intelligence taking exercise. Imagination is intelligence with an erection."
– *Victor Hugo*

CHAPTER 14

Wednesday was overcast. I woke up at 6:45 anyway. The first thing I did was check my right forearm. It looked completely normal. The second thing I checked was the door to Victoria's room. It was open. I wondered if it had been open when I went to bed. After knocking gently, I stuck my head in. Either her bed was already made or still made, I couldn't tell which. Was I fooling myself—did I have any chance with a woman like that? Would she have gone out with someone else, if she'd had someone she wanted sitting right here, working on lighting a fire? Yet why pass up a chance to have some doctor drop a pile of money on her? She could stay home with me anytime.

The note was taped to the bathroom mirror along with a twenty dollar bill.

> Good morning, Steve--
> Hope you slept well. Go out and
> get yourself some breakfast—my
> treat! Take the VW. And if you
> get a chance could you pick up
> two pounds of liver and a small
> bottle of Glenlivet scotch on the
> way back. Enjoy.

And good luck with the statue.
Love, Victoria

I thought about asking Maria to join me—I felt bad about yesterday—but her car was gone. Just as well. Halfway to the Volkswagen, I remembered how bad the bruising on my neck looked; I went back and put on my turtleneck.

The VW was beat up, but amazingly clean. And it started right up. Rattling like a four-wheel castanet as it accelerated, and pulling adventurously to the left when I braked, it nevertheless settled into a well-disciplined cruise once it got a little speed. I made my way down the Pacific Coast highway—just one lane in each direction—wondering if the overcast was going to burn off, or if we were in for more rain.

The first building I came to was four or five miles down the road—an Arco station with a sign boasting of cold beer and snacks. A mile or two later, Santa Louisa was just a glorified rest stop, so I drove on into San Cristobal.

The Pacific Coast highway became Main Street as it cut through the heart of San Cristobal. So much of the downtown area had been cleaned up, rebuilt, remodeled, or restored, it looked as if it'd been hit by the white tornado from the old TV ads for Ajax All Purpose Cleaner. And as with a tornado, the process had been erratic. One or two buildings had been half restored, then abandoned. Isolated structures and even whole blocks had been missed altogether. Even in age and disrepair, some of the old buildings retained the style and sensitivity of a particular time. But most had never been anything more than utilitarian ugly in the first place.

The new shops and stores were stylish, sometimes striking. They were probably more functional, and even warmer and more inviting than the outdated ones. Yet from a distance, they were all a little overly immaculate; I kept thinking of Disneyland. Closer up, some of them had the flimsy, slightly tattered feel of a soon to be abandoned movie set.

I didn't see anything like a simple coffee shop. I was getting a headache. I needed to eat.

Up ahead, I spotted a man about my own age with a gray ponytail and mechanic's coveralls. I pulled over, leaned across the passenger seat, and rolled down the window.

"'Scuse me," I said. "I'm looking for someplace to eat."

"I'm gonna bust your buns if we're late for that appointment," he screamed at a second story window above a shop. "Fifty fucking dollars for a dental exam!"

The building looked new, but the shop, A Touch of the Transvaal, was already out of business. The side door slammed and a girl of nine or so burst out, hurrying toward him, but not anxious to arrive. He glanced at me suspiciously and grumbled, "Breakfast?"

It was 7:55 in the morning. "Maybe a coffee shop?"

He jerked his thumb over his shoulder.

"Thanks, Joe," I said. His face erupted into paranoia like a huge pimple, until I pointed to the name tag on his shirt.

"Up yours," he muttered as I pulled off.

I made a quick U turn back toward where he'd indicated. Twelve or thirteen years earlier, before Dell—the gentle giant from South Bend—had given up the plumber's union in disgust, he had taken a trip to L.A. as the bright young treasurer of his local. He could never get over how friendly Californians were, and for a long time after that, moving to California had been his dream. Now he wouldn't be going anywhere for maybe seventeen to twenty-five years.

I drove past a brassy, ferny restaurant and bar called, Hank's. A block farther down, I passed Club Gatsby and Snuffy's. None of them were open. A shop named, The Hare Affair, featuring a giant pink rabbit in the window, was holding a half-price sale on their sixteen-dollar men's haircut.

In spite of myself, I remembered Dell's voice on the phone the week before, when I called him from two doors down the street to warn him the house was surrounded by cops.

"Get it all down in one flush," I'd cried. I'd seen the men we'd sold the first lot to, shutting off his water.

"Fuck it," he said. "Too much money." Then he hung up. As I left, I could hear them clubbing at the door. Whether Dell flushed the coke or not, they had us for selling to them once anyway.

———

In Martin McMulligan's, a hostess in a floor-length dress handed me a huge plastic menu. The place was another imitation 1890s restaurant, like Hank's, seemingly not all that much different from Snuffy's or Club Gatsby or the imitation New York style bars I'd gone by earlier. I was willing to bet there was nobody named Martin McMulligan, but that was OK. There wasn't anybody named Steve Witowski, either. Not anymore.

The waitress was an almost pretty blond lady with a dark complexion dotted with old acne scars, and a uniform stretched tight across over-regulation hips. When I asked her what she recommended, she told me, home cooking. She was right. My Fiesta Omelet looked and tasted just like the picture on the plastic menu. Unfortunately, the toast was burned. I told her I was new in the area and asked her what there was to do in San Cristobal.

"Club Gatsby is really popular right now. The drinks are better at Juggler's, but nobody really goes there anymore. Snuffy's is starting to draw good crowds, but the food's lousy."

"Not like here."

She giggled—sweetly and flirtatiously. And it occurred to me that this would be a woman I could come on to. She might not go for it, but the approach would be acceptable. She wouldn't be offended, but neither would she be thrilled or flattered. At least on the basis of physical appearance, we were both about the same distance from the ideal. When I left, we gave each other big smiles. For me, accessibility in a stranger always adds to their sex appeal. Or imagined accessibility—I'd been mistaken more than once lately.

After stopping at a Safeway on the way out of town to pick up the liver and the Glenlivet for Victoria, I headed back.

When I passed the stop lights by the giant fig tree, I was relieved to see there weren't any hitchhikers on my side of the road. That wasn't just because of the derelict the other night with that weird knife. Things had changed since I was bumming around, and I seldom picked up hitchhikers anymore. Me, of all people, after all the thousands of miles I'd hitchhiked. Maybe I'd been hassled too often by people I'd given rides to, or maybe—like everyone else—I'd been put off it by the media, I'm not sure. Maria and I *had* picked up one on the trip out. She'd asked if I wanted to, and I felt guilty saying no.

Once in the car, he spent his time staring vacantly out the window, seldom speaking, and then only in a disconnected mumble. In Tulsa, we let him out; he definitely wanted to leave, though I doubt he knew where he was. He was another of what Maria had called, "the empty people," roaming around the country. Not the adventurers or the restless or the unemployed, temporarily down on their luck, but the already beaten, the discards of different eras. After the attack the other night, Victoria mentioned she'd known more than one prominent person who'd ended up that way. Most of them lived locked inside themselves, passive, and silent, though some spoke—at various volumes—like the playback of an erratic tape recorder. And some, especially when drunk or drugged up, could even lash out randomly—at someone like Victoria, at someone like me. Their fury was dangerous, but ultimately self-destructive. Society tolerated them only to the extent they remained inconspicuous.

I got home to find Victoria out working in the backyard. The sun had come out and fried off the clouds. She was wading through a tall thicket of weeds. In one hand, she had five or six envelopes. Every step or two, she reached into one of them, and then bent down to the ground, chattering to herself softly the whole time.

"I can't even guess," I said.

"Oh, Jesus." She shook her head with a self-deprecating laugh. "I must look pretty foolish, huh? Actually, this is a garden."

"Nice. You have no future in agriculture. Become a cowboy."

"It's worse than you think. I'm following Zandie's planting spell. The one that was marked in that book where we found the will?"

"And what's that supposed to do?"

"Fast growth, abundant harvest. You don't think it could work?"

"Anything's possible."

"Yah, when rocks talk, and alligators sing show tunes. I don't believe it, either. Zandie was supposed to be wonderful with plants, but I doubt if this was how he did it. Still, it's fun to play with. Like astrology. These seeds are for various herbs for cooking."

"Wouldn't it be easier to just conjure up a full meal, maybe a nice pot roast?"

She smiled. "These are exotic herbs. Expensive to import and difficult to grow—but if Zandie's spell did happen to work, it could easily turn into a multimillion-dollar business."

Really? I thought. *But it would give a whole new meaning to the term, Voodoo Economics.*

"If you think this is bad, the other night right before... before I met you... I told you I was at the beach. Well, I had another of Zandie's books, and what I was doing—this is embarrassing—I took off all my clothes. First, I made sure I was all alone, of course. Then I faced the full moon and dunked myself in the ocean—the mother of all life, as the book put it. A very cold mother, too. In the water, I swallowed this potion—mostly honey, oregano, and chives—babbled some words that were supposed to be from a lost prayer to some ancient god and felt like a perfect fool. Needless to say, my arthritis got no better."

"No wonder. That's not a spell for curing arthritis, that's a spell for developing pneumonia."

"Well, it failed at even that. I'm afraid our friend Zandie's a bust." She had her hair tied back, and now she brushed a stray strand from her eyes with the handful of envelopes. "You didn't know you were working for a crazy lady, did you?"

"I got the liver and the scotch you wanted," was all I said. When the people I knew planted seeds in among tall weeds, they were hoping to hide their marijuana, though Victoria hardly seemed the type.

"Good boy. You can keep the change." I had nineteen cents left, including my own money. Then she asked, "Did I get any calls last night?"

"Oh right, I forgot. Some guy named Charles called. Sort of strange. Demanded to know who I was. He said he'd changed his plans and was going to stay in San Cristobal through tomorrow night. He seemed to think I might not pass on the message. Gave his phone number three times. I wrote it on the pad near the phone." His jealousy had been flattering.

"You should have saved yourself the trouble. That was the guy that was here the other night. The guy that insisted on playing that 'Indiana Wants Me' song? Some people don't discourage easy, do they. Anybody else?"

"No." Now Victoria knew the name of the song? The other night, she said she hadn't known it. Or maybe she'd just forgotten it then. And

Charles had *insisted* on playing it? Could he have been the one that was on to me? Hard to imagine how that could have worked.

"How's the statue coming?" Victoria asked.

"Oh... Slow."

"You'll get it open. Listen, when we're finished working today, I've got some steak and some wine for dinner. Maybe we could have another fire. Make it real cozy."

"You got yourself a date," I tried.

She gave me a pleased smile. "How did the fireplace work last night?"

"Actually, I decided not to have a fire. It was a little hot. I ended up going out to a bar." Maybe I was becoming a compulsive liar, but on the spur of the moment it seemed better than giving her an image of me sitting around with nothing to do while she flew around in some rich womb wizard's helicopter.

"Really? Where?"

As soon as I reached for the name of one of the bars and restaurants I'd seen or heard about that morning, all the names were gone. "One of those places in San Cristobal," I said off-handedly. "Definitely are a lot of fine ladies in that town."

The lie felt at once transparent and painfully visible; it was like hiding behind a stolen aquarium.

"Fine ladies, huh? Do you think so?" she chuckled. "The ones I've seen seemed man-hungry and overly padded. But I guess I'm no judge when it comes to women."

———

Though I told her there was nothing to see, Victoria wanted to take a look at how I was coming in the basement. As we headed in, I asked her about her problems with O'Ryan next door.

"I know he slips a little in first gear," I said, "but he seems like a nice guy."

"Nice! God! He's vicious. I steer clear of him. I was in the supermarket one time, and he started screaming at me at top volume. I was afraid he was going to slug me right in the middle of the produce section."

Several bad jokes about melons flashed through my mind, but somehow they weren't the kind of thing you could say to Victoria. So, I settled for, "Embarrassing."

"Embarrassing?" She considered that for a second as we started down the cellar stairs. "Well, it might have been. But who cares what that shriveled up old fool, or, for that matter, what the good ladies at the San Cristobal Safeway think of me. Actually, it was almost flattering—the way he kept screaming about how I'd lured his naive young nephew from the bosom of his family. Everyone must have thought I was quite the seductress. Can you imagine?"

I smiled, uncertain how to handle that particular rhetorical question. Perhaps she seemed too sure of herself to compliment. Instead, I said, "When I talked to him, it crossed my mind that his nephew might even be imaginary."

"The 'nephew' was an ex-con named Lyle Cranick. *Lyle!*" she repeated with contempt. "I'd hired him to help out with the remodeling like you're doing. He arrived a couple of days before Humpert and I—right after I'd passed papers on the place. It's been about four weeks now. I guess over the years, O'Ryan—busybody that he is—always made it his business to keep drunks and vandals off the property, so not surprisingly, he and Cranick ran into each other. *Lyle* might have been a criminal, but he was relatively young—your age or a couple years younger—and very clean cut."

"Also like me."

"Don't worry," she said reassuringly. "When I get my money, we'll get you fixed up. You'll be amazed."

It had been an automatic joke, if not a funny one, the kind I used to make when I was a scruffy long hair. Victoria had turned it into a confession.

We turned down the corridor at the bottom of the steps, and she continued, "Anyway, instead of shooing Cranick off, O'Ryan offered to put him up for a few days. The water and the electricity were still off here. Cranick was a diabetic and needed to keep his insulin refrigerated, and the place was even more of a mess than it is now, so why not?"

"I've got a feeling there's an unhappy answer to that question."

"Count on it. At some point, the old man got Cranick confused with some long-lost nephew. O'Ryan had apparently bragged about all the property he used to own in San Cristobal, so *Lyle* probably played along. When Cranick discovered there really wasn't anything left, he pretty much lost interest. After I arrived, he naturally moved back in here. To O'Ryan, I guess that made me a corrupter of innocent young ex-cons."

"And what had this guy Cranick done?" *Just how scruffy was I?*

"All I knew was that he'd been convicted of extortion—a nice safe crime. Since he was obviously too cowardly to be dangerous, I took a chance on him. Somebody's got to give these people a break, right?"

I made a sound that could be taken for "I suppose so." But hiring ex-cons "to give these people a break" hardly seemed like a Victoria type of thing.

We turned a corner into darkness, and we had to grope for the light hanging from the ceiling somewhere toward the middle of the corridor. It took a while.

After she finally found it, I asked, "So what happened to Cranick? Why did you let him go?"

"He had the wrong idea about what was going to be happening here. The first night after Humpert left, I'd no sooner gotten into bed and closed my eyes than he comes marching in—stark naked, in a... shall we say, rather excited condition—and stands over my bed. I don't know who the hell he thought he was. I mean, it was ridiculous. He wasn't that bad looking, but he was a nothing. A real nothing. When I asked him what he was doing there, he said he was cold."

"Clever. And he expected you to invite him into bed?"

"Only men allowed," she laughed. And after that discouraging story I was encouraged. But the laugh was tainted with bitterness, and her right hand was clenching and unclenching anxiously.

"A couple of days later," she continued, "I came home and found him calmly seated in front of Humpert's TV. He'd found a video tape…a personal one. Of myself and a friend. I'd only made it for fun. For memories." She lowered her eyes demurely. "Cranick had played back enough of it to decide I was running a blackmail operation. And he was going to be the good, strong man I needed. In my operation and in my bed. Can you imagine? *Lyle Cranick?* Of course, I threw him out."

Her story finished, Victoria realized we'd been standing outside the altar room, so she stepped on in and lit the big wall candles.

"As you can see," I said, "all I managed yesterday was that small gouge. And I broke one of the points off the pick. I really doubt if this guy is hollow." I really didn't care; I was just tired of banging on him.

"I thought I told you to start on the head," she said, without commenting on where I had started.

"We've got a better chance of hitting the body going in through the middle."

She considered that. "Makes sense. But the head would've been quicker."

"Maybe. It's your money, but in the time this is going to take me, I could finish taking the walls down to the studs in that room upstairs and probably replace every broken window in the attic."

"I know. This is basically a waste of time but to be honest, it's aroused my curiosity. It's like a puzzle I'm trying to solve. And I did promise to help my friend with her store."

"Actually, I'm probably damaging the best window display we're likely to find her. Put this guy in the window, people are going to notice. She'd have to put some pants on him of course."

"I doubt she'd want to go to the trouble and expense of moving him over there. Can you get me a ladder? Maybe we can figure this out quickly. If the statue's hollow and we pop out one of those eyes, we might just have an opening into the inside. Maybe Zandie will be looking right back at us."

———

Or maybe not. Which was the way it quickly worked out.

"Let me go up," Victoria said, once I dug out a rickety old ladder and leaned it up against the monster. "You steady the ladder and pretend you're not looking at my butt." I had no idea whether that was flirting or an admonition. She climbed up—her butt in those tight designer jeans of necessity passing inches from my face.

I handed up the hammer. She dug the claw end into the space between one glass eye and the stone, gave a single good shove and the eye shot out. It hit the floor and wobbled across the concrete like a small, dying animal.

Victoria peered into the eye socket, then stuck a finger in as if her own eyes were defective.

"Oh well, it was worth a try," she said. Then she popped out the other eye. No opening there either. "I guess we'll have to keep doing it the hard way," she decided.

She handed down the hammer. I put it on the altar. The bottom rung of the ladder was missing. So, she came down as far as she could and turned for my help. With my hands on her waist and hers on my shoulders, I used all my strength to keep our bodies from touching as I lowered her. Then I released her immediately. I wasn't sure if that was what she wanted, but anything else would have been too contrived—too Hollywood. And too likely to generate some sort of comment. Still, after she was down, she did let our arms rest together for a long moment. Then she patted me on the back in a friendly, asexual way, reminded me we were having dinner together that night—as if I could have forgotten—and she was gone.

CHAPTER 15

After changing back into my plaster-covered clothes from the day before, I spent the rest of the morning working by myself, cutting into Asmodeus.

And yes, Asmodeus was the statue's name—as in "Asmodeus, Destroyer Demon, Prince of Horror, Seducer of Eve in the Garden, Flaming Source of the Line of Rebecca," which is what was carved into his pedestal. He sounded like a charmer. Asmodeus as was scratched on the weapon wielded by Victoria's attacker. Obviously, that was no coincidence. My guess was that the guy somehow stumbled on a knife belonging to Zandie someplace around the old church. Maybe he'd even broken in. Victoria said she'd left the back door unlocked the night of the attack, and it had been wide open later, on a night that hadn't been all that windy.

I still hadn't mentioned the connection between the knife and the statue to Victoria. I wasn't sure why. I simply had a vague feeling that she knew more about the attacker or the attack than she wanted to say. I also had no idea what Jehovah, Ahura Mazda or Huitzilopochtli had to do with Asmodeus or each with each other. Most likely the connection existed primarily in the mind of whoever had scraped the names onto the knife.

I'd given up on the groin and moved to a spot on the side where I'd noticed a hairline crack. Progress was a bit faster there. Still, the stone the statue was carved from—whatever it was—was as hard as steel. And it didn't chip, it powdered. A fine grit soon covered my face and hands. Everything I did around that place seemed to generate dust of one kind or another. Once Victoria passed by the doorway, lugging a sloshing bucket, explaining it was for the plants. A magic potion, no doubt, probably consisting of fertilizer and plant food.

By the time the gouge in the side of the statue had become a wound large enough for some Doubting Thomas to stick a hand in, I was hungry again; Martin McMulligan's omelets were less substantial than his prices. Time for lunch.

The toilet in the basement bath didn't work at all. The soap dispenser ran out after one small dab. I managed to eke enough water out of the creaky, reluctant tap to splash a couple of layers of dust off my hands, but all I could do with the dirt on my face was transform it into mud. Figuring to spare Victoria's fluffy white towels, I drip-dried on the way upstairs. I gave my hands a final shake as I got into the kitchen, unthinkingly splattering the freshly painted wall with dark spots, which I aggravated into larger gray smudges by wiping them with my filthy sleeve.

"Needed a second coat anyway," I muttered to myself.

"Shit," said a loud masculine voice coming from the living room.

"Shit!" I agreed, not talking about the wall anymore. For a lonely woman, she was awfully popular. Why did she need a cat?

And I really didn't like the two matched leather suitcases sitting by the kitchen door.

"All right, stop pouting," Victoria's voice ordered. "It's not your fault. We never really expected that will to hold up anyway. But now at least the jewelry will be ours free and clear. Beverly Hills is the place to sell it. Leo says he's been getting murdered on the prices overseas."

"Maybe you should have sent *me* to Cairo instead of Leo," the man said, as the voices approached the kitchen.

"Humpert, you'd have given it away. You can't bargain."

"I'm an attorney."

"I needed you here," she said. Like a mother tells a child to stop drawing on the walls, *Because I need you to help me bake a cake.*

The man who entered was tall and overweight, in early middle age, and hairless rather than just bald. His eyes were dark and slightly bulging—no eyebrows, no eyelashes I could make out. When he caught sight of me, an expression of distaste spread across his pale, well-scrubbed face. I *was* filthy.

"One of the darkies is out of the slave pen, Missee Victoria," he called, putting on an Uncle Remus accent. "Peers to me he tunneled out."

Behind him, Victoria laughed as if she actually found the guy funny. I didn't, but I smiled anyway—showing I was a good sport, I suppose.

"This is our Steve Witowski, Humpert. He's from back east. I told you about him. He's going to be helping us. And he saved me from a rapist."

"Oh?" said Humpert, apparently amused, giving Victoria a questioning, skeptical look, as if he doubted my heroic qualities already.

"Steve went to Harvard," Victoria said.

"Sure he did," replied Humpert. His even white teeth disappeared as he pursed his lips, pretending to inspect my grimy clothing. "That's a lovely outfit, Steve. You must be one of those rich, fancy-dressing Eastern society types we hear so much about. Witowski, huh? Weren't you second flute in the Auschwitz Philharmonic? You ought to make up your mind which minority you want to be—Jewish or black."

"Polish, actually, last time I checked." I was still working on the "*our* Steve Witowski" and "helping *us.*"

"Copernicus, Pope John Paul, Lech Walesa, and Steve Witokowski, huh?"

"Witowski," I corrected. I'd never realized how much attention the name Witowski was going to generate outside of South Bend. Half the kids I'd grown up with there had been Polish-American.

Humpert set down the leather brief case he was carrying and helped himself from the Glenlivet bottle on the table. The first traces of broken red veins had begun to mottle his cheeks.

And Victoria had been right about two hundred and forty pounds. His face was normal size, and his upper body—even though gently rounded—looked powerfully appropriate for his six foot plus frame. Most of the extra stuffing had shifted down below the waist. Inside his well-made three-piece suit, his strong shoulders were hunched. He didn't look like competition. He did look like he could get in the way.

He reached into his jacket and pulled out a neatly bound stack of letters.

"I don't suppose you'll be needing these now," he said, handing them to Victoria.

"You never know."

"There was another one," he said, pulling out a single envelope. "This one came to my office. From a Mr. Armstrong."

"Aha," said Victoria.

"Aha," echoed Humpert, as if he'd just presented her with a long-awaited check.

Taking out a cigarette from a pack of Benson & Hedges and lighting it, he leaned back against the table. Surprised it supported him, I busied myself with lunch.

"Has Leo discovered anything in Egypt?" Humpert asked eventually.

"How to run up hotel bills," Victoria replied. "The guy in the article was long dead. Sounds like it was a hoax anyway. Leo's gone to Denmark now to check out those other stories—only *that* guy's in a mental institution. But at least the jewelry market is better there."

"Leo will fit right in in Scandinavia, now that he's a blond."

"You're just jealous, Humpert."

"What is there to be jealous of? He looks ridiculous. Blond hair doesn't go with his coloring."

"You sound like an old lady."

"Sorry. Anyway, I'm sure he'll dig up something. He may be slow, but if there is anything there he'll find it eventually. God knows he's persistent enough."

Searching for the mustard, I didn't see if it was a look she gave him or a gesture she made, but he laughed. A moment later, he crushed out his half-smoked cigarette in one of those little pocket ashtrays—Richmond Tobacco used to give them away as a promotion. Then he said, "I'm beat. If it's all right with you I'd like to go up to my room and relax and maybe get cleaned up."

"Sure. Go ahead. We can go over the details of their proposal later."

"It'll only take a minute. Perhaps our hero here could give me a hand with my luggage."

With that, he picked up his briefcase and headed for the stairs, moving as if he were uncomfortable in his own body.

I was about to say something. I didn't like his tone, and I didn't like him asking Victoria instead of me if I could help—like I was a servant. But Victoria tossed me an understanding look.

"Ignore him," she said.

"And I would appreciate it," Humpert called down from inside the enclosed back stairwell, "if he washed off some of that manly sweat and grime before he handles my luggage."

Shaking her head indulgently, Victoria chuckled and started for the stairs herself. "Just wash off your hands a bit," she said.

"What?" I'd thought "ignore him" meant Humpert could carry his own damn luggage up the stairs.

"There's some good strong hand soap on the sink behind you there. Humpert's room is the one on the far side of mine." Then she was gone.

I knew where the soap was, I'd just used it right in front of them before making the liverwurst sandwich that was lying uneaten on the table. *What the hell, why be petty enough to make an issue out of it?* And, after all, I *was* an employee there. I didn't wash my hands again, but I did comb my hair—probably for Victoria's benefit.

Whatever Humpert was carrying in those suitcases must have weighed more than he did. No way I was going to make two trips for him though; I got a death grip on each case and manhandled them up the stairs.

On the second floor, Victoria and Humpert were standing in front of one of the doorways. They stopped chatting to watch me haul the bags through the corridor, banging them against the walls on either side.

"What strength! What power!" cried Humpert. "I can see why he was a hero. Those muscles, those bulging biceps—a Black, Jewish Adonis. Why... Good Lord, it must be...it *is*! It's Arnold Schwartzen... I mean of course, Arnold Schwartzen-African-American! Just set them down here, Arnold."

What a dipshit. I almost dropped them on his feet. Instead, I decided to act as if lugging them up there had been no big deal. Still, I was waiting for him to say something about the residue of yesterday's plaster that had rubbed off my pants legs and all over the sides of his luggage. Apparently, he didn't notice.

Behind Humpert, in the one corner of the room that was visible, meticulously crafted and painted model planes hung on wires from the ceiling. Beyond the end of the bed sat a large plaster pool—twin pools really, built on two levels—in which equally detailed boats were floating.

"When the pump's on, there's a waterfall," Victoria explained, noting my gaze. "Though actually, it tends to leak."

The wall behind all this was plastered with a collage so busy it took me a few seconds more to realize it was made up entirely of pictures of pretty little girls—some photos, some drawings and paintings. Not kiddie porn—all were fully clothed, most actually dressed up in lace and frills and bows.

"*Your* room?" I asked Humpert scornfully, pointing at the collage.

He made no move to shut the door as I almost expected he would.

"I admire purity," he said defensively.

I nodded, trying to look skeptically superior. This seemed like the dark side of O'Ryan's collection of pictures of Todd.

"So did Dickens and Shakespeare," he added haughtily. "I'd never expect you to understand."

"Right."

"I'm going in to rest now," Humpert said to Victoria. "Arnold here is doing nothing for my stomach pain."

"Is it getting worse—generally?" Victoria asked.

"I don't know. Maybe a little worse than it was last time I was here. It comes and goes. It was almost completely gone for a while."

"You should have gone to the doctor sooner."

"It's just a temporary thing." Gazing down at me pointedly, he added, "The doctor said I should avoid *little* irritations."

"Is he safe?" I asked as Victoria and I were walking away.

"Humpert?" She sounded surprised, puzzled. "Oh, you mean the room. He really does admire purity—that's it. He likes children and old people. It's everyone else he has trouble with."

"I thought I had his room."

She took my arm, giving it a squeeze. "That was Cranick's room when he was here. I didn't want you to get the idea I was constantly moving men in and out of here."

Nice to hear she cared about my thoughts on that subject.

Suddenly the hall filled with the sound of Gregorian chant. Humpert must have had a high-quality stereo in there.

I ate my liverwurst and went back to work, pounding my pick into the monster, unable to drive Humpert out of my head. The idea of that lard ass lying in there salivating over those pictures somehow made their very innocence obscene. Why did Victoria keep him around? I was disappointed by his very existence. Victoria's plan for dinner and a quiet night alone in front of a romantic fire would be a lot less romantic with him sitting in some corner, sweating. I kicked myself for not having come on to Victoria already, although I didn't know when I could have.

Distracted by my thoughts, I got much of the way through the side of the statue by the end of the day. If it hadn't been so securely fastened to the wall it would have toppled like a squat ugly tree—and still no sign it might be hollow or have anything inside of it.

I arrived back up in my room just as a furious honking came from out in front of the church. Leaning out of the window, I saw, as well as heard, a yellow cab, bleating like it was in pain and determined to inflict its suffering on anyone in earshot.

The horn quieted as Humpert appeared, carrying a small overnight bag that matched the two larger bags I'd brought up to his room.

"Airport!" he cried.

"All right!" I congratulated myself. Thinking that I damn well better make it happen with Victoria that night.

The lavender jump suit Victoria wore at dinner was attractive, but loosely fitting and less provocative than I would have liked. I was wearing my cords again. Most of the wrinkles had fallen out of my dress pants by now; but when I put them on, the bell bottoms felt like hoops, and I finally realized they were way out of style and probably had been when I'd bought them on sale two years before.

Washed and dressed and combed, I still looked disheveled. The light mist of hair spray hadn't helped. I was wearing underwear though. That wouldn't have happened during the sixties.

Dinner was some kind of casserole. Without wine.

"After that diet, it's certainly good to get back to real food again," Victoria said. I didn't mention the steak. Humpert's business trip had probably disrupted her planning.

We ate in the kitchen. Afterwards we headed into the living room. A plush new sectional couch stretched in front of the TV. Victoria sat in the recliner. I sat on the couch, as close to her as possible. Before I could suggest listening to some music, she switched on the damn TV, explaining that Humpert had hooked it up to the old antenna on the roof. She flipped the dial through the stations: two now came in clearly, one more was hazy but watchable.

"If we're still here when the estate is fully settled," Victoria said, "maybe I'll get a satellite dish."

"If you're still here? I thought you were remodeling this place to live here." And of course, there had been precious little remodeling going on.

"Oh, I am. For a while. But this area is hardly what you would call 'where it's at.' So, after it's served its purpose I'll probably just keep it as a getaway."

On the TV, fussy old Mr. Whipple battled to keep women from the forbidden delights of squeezing rolls of Charmin toilet paper—until he was caught secretly doing it himself. Those who claim the morality play is dead apparently don't watch toilet paper commercials.

Mr. Whipple gave way to the last part of a show I'd never heard of called *Lifestyles of the Rich and Famous*.

"Why would anyone watch a show that can't help but make them feel like an impoverished failure?" I offered after a few minutes of pornographic wealth.

"I love this show," Victoria said. "It's new. You just need to give it a chance. 'Champagne wishes and caviar dreams'—what could be better than that?"

"Speaking of which, how about a glass of wine?"

"I don't know. Maybe I've been drinking a little too much lately."

"Actually, a drink or two in the evening is supposed to be good for you."

"Hmm. I have heard that. OK, bring me a glass of Merlot. It's in the upper cupboard on the right-hand side of the pantry."

After I got the wine, I finished laying the fire I'd started the night before. Seeing what I was about, Victoria told me how much she loved fires. In the glow from the TV, her skin looked as coolly flawless as polished marble. Soon the flames were crackling away briskly, though I kept them from getting too big. It was still warm for a fire. I leaned back on one of two large throw pillows sitting in front of it. The flickering light gave the cavorting figures on the mantel the appearance of motion, until Victoria turned on the table lamp beside her and picked up a book.

"What are you reading?" I asked, craning my neck in her direction.

"Another one of Zandie's books." She held up the cover and read out loud, "*Death: the Pause Between the Heartbeats of the World.* That's sort of deep if you think about it."

I thought about it. The more I thought, the stupider it sounded. The TV talked to itself. A detective show. As usual, the hero was running around asking questions, and as usual the bad guys kept offing the people with the answers, one by one. No matter—the hero always found somebody else to ask.

"You know," I said, "if the criminals would just kill the damn hero in the first place, it'd sure save a lot of lives."

"What?" asked Victoria, peering up from her book. "Sorry I wasn't watching."

The fire burned low, but I kept it going. The night remained warm. The phone rang. Though she was sitting right beside it, Victoria again let it ring four times before she picked it up. The expectant expression on her face went flat when she realized who it was.

"No," she said, catching my eye and holding it. "You can't come over. A friend of mine is here... He's *also* gonna be here all week... No, next week won't work either. My friend and I are living together now." She winked at me. "Stay with your wife and kids... I *do* understand... If you want to, give me a call—I certainly can't stop you. But I'm not promising anything."

She hung up, explaining, "That investment guy from the other night—Phil? I've got to start hanging out with a better class of men."

She went back to her book, scanning more than reading, though occasionally something caught her attention. After she finished her wine, I tossed back the rest of mine and got us both a second glass.

"There's another cushion, if you'd like to sit over here by the fire," I tried. The other cushion was there because I'd put it there the night before while I was laying the fire.

"Here's something," she said. "In ancient Crete, they believed that if a woman fed her lover a cake baked with her menstrual blood, he'd be impotent if he tried to sleep with other women."

"Or even if he didn't. Whew!"

After that mood-setter, her attention shifted between the book and the TV screen. She nursed her wine and seemed unapproachable. Reminding myself of the way she'd suggested steak and wine and the fire for the evening, I couldn't puzzle out what she was trying to do. She certainly didn't seem shy. I went over and sat on the couch and watched TV myself. Yves Montagne and Marilyn Monroe were deciding they were in love after all.

"He's really cute, isn't he," Victoria offered.

"She's not bad, either."

"You think? I never liked her when she was around; she seemed so convinced she was such hot stuff. But now I realize she *was* special. I mean, every man in the world wanted her—presidents, movie stars, authors, athletes."

"It didn't help her though."

"Maybe she just never found the right man," Victoria said, which seemed surprisingly sexist. "She probably should have stayed with Jack Kennedy."

"I don't think that was an option."

"For the right woman, it would have been," she said, going back to her book.

Awhile later, continuing to read, she asked, "Have you ever been to Crete?"

Back to the ancient Cretins. "No," I said and that seemed to satisfy her.

Almost all my traveling had been hitchhiking and that had been long ago. In the last five or six years, I'd been relatively stable. *Relatively.* After my imaginary career as a songwriter had self-destructed, I spent a year in New York as a Journalism grad student at Columbia. I'd omitted my 1969 forgery conviction from my application and given myself an imaginary background as Promotional Director of a small, defunct Midwest chain of pet stores I called the Age of Aquariums.

A year at Columbia and I was bored with facts and objectivity. I figured if I was going to be bored and a solid citizen, I might as well go for the top, so I applied to Harvard Law. Since my jail time had come in the middle of my undergraduate days at Harvard, it couldn't be hidden. And since any lie on my application about my employment background could result in a revocation of my law degree even years later, I went with something approximating the truth.

They rejected me.

My own fucking alma mater. Such was the value of my honors degree from Harvard.

That's when I moved back to South Bend and found the tobacco job. (My resume for that was almost too good—I almost lied myself into "over-qualified"—even though I changed my B.A. from Harvard to Notre Dame) And except for an occasional trip to Chicago, I hadn't been out of Indiana in the three years since. Until now.

After another couple of pages, Victoria looked up from her reading. "This book claims ancient Crete was Atlantis, and that all kinds of wisdom and learning were lost forever when the civilization fell. Sounds fascinating. A friend of mine's over in Europe now. Maybe he should stop in there for a quick visit. Who knows what he might be able to pick up?"

"I've heard that Atlantis thing a couple of times," I said. "I doubt if there's anything to it. After all, Crete wasn't swallowed up by water, was it. As far as learning goes, I seem to remember they were masters in the art of indoor plumbing, but in that area—with the exception of that bathroom down in the basement—we're rapidly closing in on them."

Victoria inspected me for a long moment. "Is that what they taught you at Harvard?" she asked, her lips tightening in anger.

She paged quickly through the rest of that book and picked up another. The Monroe-Montagne movie ended, and an old TV movie came on about a female gymnastic team that worked undercover for the State Department, jiggling around the world in undersized leotards while foiling evildoers and falling in love.

The phone rang again. Drawing herself up and idly patting a few hairs in place—a primping gesture I associated with bad actresses, circa 1960—Victoria once again let it ring four times before answering. But this time her face quickly grew serious.

"I need you to leave the room," she said to me.

———

Out in the kitchen, I chomped on an apple and considered what was happening. I suppose every man likes to believe he has some specific edge when it comes to women. I knew one guy who after a few drinks at a party, would somehow manage to slip into the conversation that his scrotum was so large that when he sat on the toilet it dangled down into the water. Which was exactly as helpful to his sex life as you would expect it to be.

But we all want to believe we've got something. Like Dumbo's magic feather, it helps with the confidence, with giving you the courage to put yourself out there. As for me, long hair and general scruffiness didn't work anymore as they had in the sixties and early seventies, and I wasn't good looking. An old lover had once described my face as pointy—thin with a sharp nose and a sharp chin. Another had called my eyes, "a soulfully beautiful brown," but they'd also been described as beady. In college, I saw my edge as my reputation for intelligence—not to be confused with actual intelligence of course. That didn't work as well when you were considerably over thirty and spent your days putting up cigarette posters and filling up displays in liquor stores for $13,500 a year. There are times when knowing the plural of sarcophagus is just not enough.

Here's a weird edge. In an earlier era, there were at least a couple of women who slept with me largely because several other women they knew had slept with me. One of them was a particularly straight laced Christian, the sister of a friend I was crashing with for a couple of days. She actually asked me beforehand, "Why did Chelsea want to have sex with you?" Which wasn't the most flattering question I ever got. Later that night, when she snuck into my bed, she wanted to try things she said she'd never had the courage to ask anyone else to do. With most women I would have been flattered that they felt they could relax and trust me like that. With her it was almost insulting.

And there have been times, I suppose, when my sense of humor was an edge—at least as powerful an edge as that guy's damp, saggy scrotum.

What I would have liked to believe was my edge—at least among certain groups at certain times—was that people respected me. That's what I would have liked to believe. Maybe it was true at one point, but nowadays it was really hard to find any edge I could believe in. Dumbo had dropped the magic feather.

"Is everything okay?" I asked when Victoria called me back in. Meaning, *want to tell me why you asked me to leave?*

"Everything's fine. Would you like to smoke some dope?"

"Why sure." *This was it!* Though liquor seemed to have regained its position as the ice-breaker of choice in most circles, she was, after all, Terry Davis's ex. And pot was just fine with me. The first sex with someone was often easier when I was loaded. It got me enjoying it so much I stayed relaxed and natural.

"I'll be right back down," she said, and headed upstairs. Soon I heard a toilet flush, then nothing for a while. The fire glowed like my greedy soul. *Should I turn off the lights and the TV?* I wondered.

"Here we are," she said, reappearing in a furry, fire engine red bathrobe and matching slippers. Not even the zipper position was enticing; it was up as far as it would go.

"Another glass of wine?" I tried.

"I'm fine."

Casually, she sat down beside me on the couch, and we took turns sucking on the pipe. On the third hit, I got to coughing—romantically. I was out of practice at this, too.

"Whew," she said, sliding down in the couch after we'd finished. "Tension. Absolutely, the worst thing for you. And I've been so tense lately."

"How come?"

"Well... I guess I don't really know. Maybe I'm worried about Humpert. He's been getting sick a lot. The dope is just right tonight. I've got some valium, but that's not really good for you."

Soon she was lounging with her head resting against the back of the couch, her bare legs stretched out in front of her. In front of us. The robe fell short of her knees, and it gaped open several inches above that. I was trying to guess what, if anything, she was wearing under the robe. Probably something. Probably not uninhibited enough to be naked underneath. I remembered the crucifix she'd flung into the canal and wondered if she'd tell herself she was surprised if we ended up in bed together tonight.

The lamp was on and so was the TV, but the room took on the cozy flush of the fire. The dope made me comfortable and therefore confident, savoring the moment. Reaching behind

Victoria, I flicked off the lamp.

"There," I said.

She smiled, her eyelids drooping sensually. "Can I have a sip of your wine?"

"'Course." It was as if we were already lovers.

I handed her the glass, she sipped, moistened her lips slowly, but daintily, and passed it back. Our fingers touched. Her lips, glistening from the wine, parted slightly. Smiling contentedly, she snuggled down again into the couch, her legs shifting apart three or four inches, the bathrobe riding up a bit more.

I got up and set another log on the fire. Returning, I stood beside her, gazing down. She was paging through a TV Guide.

"Not a damn thing on the tube. Nothing at all," she said.

"Figures. Why don't we put on some music?" I flicked the TV off.

"Naw, I'm beat." she said rising briskly, "Time for bed. See you tomorrow."

Dumbfounded, I did get out a "good night" to her disappearing back. *What the hell*? Had I waited too long to make my move? After we were loaded, I'd sat there for another fifteen or twenty minutes without doing anything. Did she figure I wasn't going to? No, shutting off the light and the tube were obvious preliminaries. And earlier in the evening hadn't I asked her to come sit by me beside the fire? She was the one who'd chosen to sit by herself. Though that was before we'd smoked the pot.

With nervous energy, I paced across the floor of the darkened nave. Telling myself just what an idiot I was. Victoria was not only gorgeous, she was used to money and to men more successful than any I'd ever met. Why on earth would she want me? In spite of years of evidence to the contrary, at the drop of a friendly smile, I was still ready to believe a woman like that is hankering to go to bed with me. She was probably just being cordial to the hired help.

The electric candles of the gaudy chandelier overhead tinkled along with my steps. Yet maybe she *had* gotten tired. Suddenly. Or maybe she was going through a time when she didn't sleep with anybody. How recently had she become a widow? I might be lousy at getting women, but I was great at explaining why I wasn't getting them. The ideal excuse, of course, had nothing to do with me—there was precious little comfort in, "She finds me repulsive." I preferred to test all other hypotheses first.

Unfortunately, I was far better at developing these excuses than at believing in them. And in any case, I couldn't deal with my full repertory tonight; reviewing all the conflicting signals that had passed between Victoria and me had quickly twisted my confusion into a headache.

Unfastening the brass safety chain—a recent addition—I tugged open one of the double church doors. From out of the shadows, La Perdita dashed past me and was gone. I almost stepped on her.

Outside, the night was cool and clear, and wondrous with stars—in spite of the lights nearby at the junction of the two highways. An owl hooted. Across the way, every light was on at O'Ryan's. The TV was probably blaring away, too, the way it had been when Maria and I had finally managed to find the place the night of our arrival. I smiled at the thought of O'Ryan.

No, every light wasn't on. What was now Maria's apartment in the back of the place was dark. She was probably asleep, which was just as well. She could do without a visit from me. All the way out here, I'd spent the days considering coming on to her, and the nights becoming less and less interested—even as Maria was growing more and more interested. Our first night in the motel in Jerome, sleeping next to her in a double bed that sagged deeply in the middle, I'd made a half-hearted attempt. Confused about her husband, and in pain from her broken wrist, she'd turned me down and I was relieved.

Checking to make sure I still had the keys Victoria had given me, I stepped away from the church and filled my lungs with the night air. Though I hadn't smoked in over ten years, I suddenly wished I had a cigarette. It would have been better if Maria and I could have left Jerome after that first night, but the car wasn't ready. The second night there, we'd had a pizza and a couple of beers in the room. About ten o'clock, I went out to try to call Indiana from a pay phone; I only tried one number and there was no answer.

When I got back, Maria was in bed and asleep or feigning sleep. Though I'd hardly slept myself since leaving South Bend, it was hours before I drifted into a tense half-doze, constantly aware of our bodies rubbing against each other. At quarter to eight, I awoke exhausted, desperate for more rest, knowing we still had a long drive ahead that day, but horny as hell. Slipping into the bathroom, I beat off quickly—disinterestedly—for medicinal purposes only. And got back to sleep.

It was a couple hours later, 10:15, when I woke up again. Beside me, Maria was reading the paper. She'd brought me coffee and doughnuts as a surprise. The second surprise was that Maria was now naked beneath the covers. I tried, but nothing happened. She was hurt—she took it personally though I told her she shouldn't. Because it wasn't true, it cost me nothing to hint of an occasional problem with impotence. Three hours later, after dozing in the car with the hot sun shining on my crotch, I had her pull off on a dirt road by the Arizona-California border. I was still more tired than horny, but seeing how bad she felt, and feeling bad myself, I wanted to make it up to her. After I kidded her out of her reluctance, we climbed into the back seat and undressed. It really wasn't her—her skin was soft and moist, and the sensation of being enveloped by that full, soft body, should have been erotic.

At least, I got it up—not right away, yet reasonably quickly. I entered her immediately. But I'd cum that morning and the stench of urine in the backseat of the old cab was suffocating. *And* the corner of that painting kept digging into my hip. Just as Maria was beginning to get really into it, I felt myself going soft. So, I faked a quick orgasm and brought things to an abrupt conclusion. Afterwards, I drove for a while, then slept much of the rest of the way to O'Ryan's.

Over at O'Ryan's house now, a light came on in the back window. I watched it for a minute until it went off again. During a lull in the traffic, I heard something over by the road. A shadow far too big to be La Perdita moved among the bushes—probably just some poor soul looking for a sheltered place to spend the night. If it wasn't for Victoria, I reminded myself, that could be me.

———

As I got ready for bed, pondering Victoria's "tiredness," it occurred to me that she might just be having her period. Still, there were no tampons in the medicine cabinet and no wrappers on the top of the trash in the bathroom.

Though I'd worked hard that day, it was early, and once again I couldn't sleep. About two o'clock, I borrowed a sleeping pill from the medicine cabinet. I must have dropped off, but sometime later, I was aware of a light cutting through the pre-dawn dimness. Victoria was reaching quickly to close the bathroom door. In the millisecond before she stepped in front of the light, sending her body into shadow, I saw her face, frustrated, and hurt—confused—and as beautiful as any dream. The blood smeared across it and all down the front of her naked body seemed to have been deliberately, consciously arranged.

JEAN-PAUL MARAT, DICK THE BUTCHER, AND JONATHAN O'RYAN

"She bears a duke's revenues on her back,
And in her heart she scorns our poverty."
– *William Shakespeare*

CHAPTER 16

Thursday morning the door to her room was open and Victoria was asleep. Enough of her shoulders stuck out above the pink quilt to let me know she was naked. The pale morning light made her flesh appear dull, but there wasn't a trace of blood on her face or any of the skin I could see. I was tempted to pull down the covers, but that wasn't because I wanted to check for blood. If that scene last night wasn't entirely a dream, it was a half-awake flight of groggy imagination—probably planted by that cute story about the menstrual blood cakes. I should know better than to take somebody else's pills.

Quietly, I retreated. Something about her breathing or her stillness made me wonder if she was really still asleep.

I futzed around with breakfast, and it was after ten o'clock before I was down in the basement carving away at Asmodeus again. I'd just worked up a sweat when Victoria bounced in, wearing a bulky wool sweater.

"Any luck?" she asked. Her eyes were blood shot, but aside from that she looked well rested.

"This guy's pretty solid, Victoria."

She rapped her knuckles against the statue. I'd never noticed how strong and rough her hands were before. Surprisingly enough, she must have done a lot of hard work in her time.

"Maybe that's because Zandie's in there," she said. "With his secret knowledges."

"This doesn't really have much to do with remodeling."

"I know, but this Zandie thing's got me fascinated. I mean, look at this place—where's your sense of adventure? Besides we could use the money right now."

"Troubles with your settlement?"

"It's one of those business messes. I'm no woman's libber—when we were married, I just signed over everything to Fairchild. I never had anything to do with our finances. I guess I'm too romantic. Everything was ours, nothing mine or his. But after he died, it turned out that the house, our cars, everything—my money and his—belonged to the RAM corporation. *Everything,* including the jewelry and a few other trinkets that I've been selling to live on. Fairchild's last will left me half of his corporate stock, but now his son and his son's mousy little wife want me to settle for just the jewelry. They're threatening to have me prosecuted for stealing it unless I give up all claim to everything else. "

"They can't get away with that, can they? I mean, if it was an honest mistake?"

"God knows. I never even realized they knew about the jewelry. Humpert warned me not to take it, but, well, he's not the world's greatest attorney anymore. The RAM people all hate me—and my charming daughter-in-law walked in while her wimpy husband was trying to use his sweaty paws and his drooling tongue to 'console me in my grief.' Right after his father's funeral. I could certainly fight them, but it would be long and expensive. It could take everything I'll get from the sale of the rest of the jewelry and more. And it would be messy. Very messy. Half-truths, lies and innuendoes. God, would they love to drag my name through the mud. And if I don't fight—if I accept their settlement—I 'll still end up well off. Since I figured they might try something like this, I got a lot of stuff out of there before I left. And don't you worry, there'll be plenty to pay you with."

"I'm not worried."

"You know, maybe if it works out, after we fix this place up, we can do other old houses. It's time for me to develop my business sense anyway. You invest the know-how, I'll invest the cash. And we'll both do the work. Partners. It could be fun. What do you think?"

"I don't know—maybe it would be worth giving it a try," I said with less enthusiasm than I felt. Just to have her thinking of the possibility of a long-term relationship had to be helpful. And it would be much better to be her partner than her employee. Not that I actually had any know-how.

"Fabulous." She looked over at the statue. "You know, aside from the excitement and the money, I'll be just as happy to get Zandie out of the house if he *is* in here. Sometimes it does give me the creeps."

"If I cut much farther into the middle of this thing without finding him, I'll have passed the point where there's enough room left for a body."

She shrugged. "That's only assuming they buried him in one piece. Keep at it. And even if he's not in there, his papers might be. So don't forget the head."

Victoria left, and I heard her enter a room down the hall. Two hours later, working the hammer and a chisel that was growing duller by the blow, I popped through into the hollow core at the center of the statue.

"Goddamn," I muttered, "the thing *is* hollow." And there was room inside for a body. There just wasn't a body in there.

Unfortunately, the hollow core only reached as far as the neck. Zandie's papers were supposed to be buried with his body and his body clearly wasn't here. But—model employee that I was—I climbed up on the ladder and went to work chopping an exploratory cut into the serpent head, starting from an empty eye socket.

"STEVE!" The name boomed through the passages of the cellar. "STEPHEN WITOWSKI! This is your lord and master—or is it mistress." It wasn't mistress, but it *was* Victoria on some kind of P.A.

system. "I'm going out now. The bulletin is—I forgot to tell you—I called a hauling service and they're picking up our trash tomorrow morning. It's behind the house, around the far side of the porch. They want it out on the street. That is all. Have fun. And don't track dust through the house."

A moment later, Victoria ducked into the room on her way out and said good-bye again.

For the rest of the day, I dug into the head. If anything, it was even harder than the rest of the statue. And it was hollow. But it was also empty.

By the time I was finished, I was exhausted. I hadn't found Zandie. I hadn't expected to, though I think at that point I would have enjoyed running into the old dude—whoremaster, sorcerer, mock priest—especially if he was buried with a few mementos of his era. Rotting flesh could be alive with all manner of disease, but I figured his bones should be decayed clean by now.

Victoria had so much food in her kitchen, it reminded me of my mother's house, but I ended up simply slapping together another sandwich. The Heineken was gone, but there was Bud. Which Dell used to refer to as "Bud-er-than-nothing." Halfway through one, I remembered the trash.

The four metal cans in the back were crammed full to the brim. Balanced precariously on top of two of them was the heavy frame of a formerly upholstered rocking chair, with one rocker missing. Fortunately, a dolly was attached to one of the cans—without it I could barely have lifted any of them, much less hauled them out to the street. The dolly made the job possible, but not easy. It slid more than it rolled across the grass and stuck in the tiniest grooves of the old dirt driveway.

My clean shirt was off, and I was sweating and cursing by the time I got the chair frame out beside the last can.

"They'll never take that." It was O'Ryan, leaky fish bucket in hand.

"Huh?"

"They never take anything that isn't in barrels. You'll have to haul it out yourself. Then it'll cost you $7.50 to get in the dump."

"Seven dollars and fifty cents? I've been in dumps like that—probably has a two-drink minimum, too."

"That a joke?"

"Apparently not."

He gave me his best yellow-toothed grin. "That's what I thought. Anyway, if you want, I'll take it off your hands. Free. I could use some more furniture."

"Mr. O'Ryan, this isn't furniture. This is garbage. If you bring it home, I'm sure Maria will be happy to explain the difference to you."

His laugh reverberated through his thin jowls, giving him resemblance to a friendly basset. "I do understand about women. You can believe that. But I'll fix it up. It'll be *House Beautiful*. Just help me move it over to my place."

Much as I liked the old guy, I couldn't face lugging that piece of junk all the way over to his house, just so it could keep the rest of his rubbish company. While I tried to talk him out of it, he dug through the trash cans, unearthing other treasures and strewing the overflow everywhere, telling me repeatedly how much he'd appreciate me helping him carry the rocker home. Which ended up meaning that I carried it, but we moved at his pace.

"We'll just leave it outside till I can clean it," he said. But I was sure it would become a permanent fixture there, along with the ancient oil truck, a huge radio console and a one wheeled bicycle.

I started to go, but O'Ryan wanted to talk. He'd gotten a letter that day from that ex-con, Lyle Cranick, still pretending to be his nephew.

Cranick needed money and the old man was obviously thinking about sending it.

"As far as I'm concerned," I said, "there's no way you should send him anything. But the one you should talk to is Maria. Not me."

"Maybe what I have to say concerns you, too."

Apparently, he thought Maria and I were a lot closer than we really were, but I wasn't up for trying to explain that relationship. "We'll both go see her," I said.

He stuck his fish bucket inside his door, straightened his neat sport coat, and we walked around the side of the building, where the Chesterfield girl and a giant Coca-Cola bottle shared a wall.

"There's a connecting door inside," he explained. "More convenient, but I think it broke. You could probably fix it. I'll bet you're good at that kind of stuff. Todd would..." he paused, confused, blinking as if the sun were too bright. "He's just a liar." It was partially a question. "He doesn't know what he's talking about."

No one answered when he knocked, so, over my objections, he let us in with a key. The small kitchen might have been converted from a porch. Multi-colored notes—stuck up with magnets—dotted the metal cabinets. In the main room, Maria was asleep, fully dressed. The bed had been pushed up against the wall she shared with O'Ryan, explaining why the connecting door didn't work.

The room was sparsely furnished, but already cozy, with thistle in the vases and several plants. A reproduction of a Japanese woodcut, and prints of a Vermeer, a Rousseau and a Rouault were thumb tacked on the walls, along with a poster of John Lennon. I almost tripped over her easel, which was set up with one leg sprawling out into the doorway.

"We should let her sleep," I whispered.

"MARIA!" O'Ryan yelled.

She awoke, scratching at the skin just above her cast, in a much better humor than I would have been under the circumstances. Fifteen minutes later, she'd set out a pot of tea, a baguette of French bread, and a plate of cheeses—mostly for her uncle's benefit. I had a beer. Maria and O'Ryan sat on the bed. I was on the braided rug, listening to Judy Collins sing about Jean-Paul Marat softly in the background. Maria must have just picked up the record player second hand. She'd lost her stereo before leaving Michigan.

"Mr. O'Ryan," I said, after telling Maria why we'd come, "this guy who was pretending to be your nephew, his name is Cranick, Lyle Cranick. He's an ex-con, and he was only playing up to you because he thought you had money. This letter is just his final attempt to score. Victoria Fairchild, next door in the old church, told me all about the guy."

"You should hear what *he* says about *her*. I wasn't going to tell you—I don't like to speak ill of people—but I don't much care for her myself."

"If I had to guess," Maria said, "I'd guess you think she's a diamond-collared she-bitch that probably eats her young."

"No... Well, that *is* well put. Now let me think, please."

The frail hands began kneading each other in his lap. His face tensed, as if straining to dredge some heavy weight up from the muck just below consciousness. After a moment, Maria rested her hands on his, trying to relax and separate them.

"Don't send him anything, Unk."

O'Ryan turned toward me. "What do you think of her—across the way?"

"Victoria? She's nice—a bit status conscious for my taste—but nice. She's got no reason to lie about this Cranick, but he could have it in for her because she refused to go to bed with him, and because she had to throw him out." I left the circumstances unexplained.

"You're probably right," he said, a small smile easing his face. "And I think he's a liar anyway. I get confused sometimes anymore. And I need to go put my fish in the ice box."

"Before you leave," I said, "Victoria's got a buyer for any of Zandie's stuff that might still be in the old church. I don't suppose you'd know where there might be anything of his still stashed over there?"

"Zandie's stuff? Like what? I think that mob got most all of it when he disappeared."

"He disappeared? I thought he was hanged."

"You're right. They hung him. Definitely hung him. Zandie's confusing."

"How so?"

"Sometimes I remember how he was. And I have to think he was amazing, wonderful. People just loved him. So smart. So handsome. And—you know—charming."

"The type of guy who could have been anything?" Maria asked. "Who could have done anything?"

O'Ryan rolled his eyes and gave me a look like Maria had just told us she believed in Santa Claus.

"Sometimes I have to think he was an asshole," he continued, "the biggest asshole. The way he treated people...women, it wasn't right. It couldn't have been right. What was he trying to prove? Such a waste. It's very confusing when I think about him. Such a shame."

"I don't suppose you know where he was buried?" I asked before I noticed that the old man's eyes had grown moist.

"Why do you want to know where he's buried?" Maria asked.

"They'll never find him," O'Ryan said. "Not now. There are bodies in that old building though. I don't remember who. I should go. My fish."

"Of course," I said. "It's really not important. Please don't let it bother you. Victoria just wanted to know if he was buried somewhere in her house."

"It's not her house." Standing, he finished the greater part of his tea in one swig as if it were medicine and slipped the piece of cheese he was eating into the pocket of his sports jacket. "Bait," he explained.

"Maybe I should go too," I said.

"You stay," he ordered, putting a palsied hand on my shoulder like a benediction. "A good woman can turn your life around."

"Hey," said Maria, smiling. "I got out of the salvation business when I got rid of Al." But turning to me, she added, "Stick around for a while anyway."

"You're lucky," O'Ryan said to me. "In the Danakil tribe in Ethiopia if you wanted a woman, you had to cut off somebody's balls. You wouldn't have to kill the guy. But you had to get his balls—somehow—and give them to her like a present."

"That's kind of the way we did it in Indiana," I said.

O'Ryan just nodded. As he trudged to the door complaining about his elderly joints, Maria got out a container of stew and insisted he take it with him and give it a try.

"He's really sweet in his own way." She smiled when she returned, plopping down hard on the bed, everything jiggling. "His mind does flicker in and out though. I think he gets me confused with my aunt sometimes—my father used to tell me there's a strong resemblance—last night when I was sound asleep, he crawled into bed with me."

I chuckled. "And that's why the bed was against the door. Well, at least he's still trying—though at his age he must be pretty harmless."

"Don't be so sure." Halfway through her laugh she averted her eyes. Once again, we were on a sensitive topic—potency.

Outside it was dusk. Judy Collins finished, and Phil Ochs came on, singing about the pleasures of the harbor. Memories cling to music like they do to smells. For old time's sake, or from a macabre sense of the melodramatic, we'd played that album after the real Stephen Witowski's funeral. At the time, Dell and I and Paula and all the rest of us wanted desperately to believe he was murdered—to believe the C.I.A. or the F.B.I. or the dark agents of some corporate conspiracy had placed the rifle in his mouth. Had pulled the trigger. But deep down where the coldest thoughts flowed, I always knew not even Stephen was that important to any of those people. I always knew what had really happened.

Now I took a long pull on my beer, finishing it off. Maria lit an oil lamp. In prison, with his baby face, Stephen had been raped and fought over and beaten and he'd come through with his Jesus and Mary intact. No—stronger. Luckily, I wasn't as good looking as Stephen. I'd had it much easier. We'd gotten out within days of each other and celebrated together. That fall I went back to Harvard to finish up, but instead of returning to being the unofficial spokesman for the radical movement at Notre Dame, Stephen marched off to bear Christian witness against something or other—some Evil with a capital, "E." We lost touch long before his death eight years later. It was a fluke I even heard about the funeral.

"Al's coming out," Maria said abruptly. She said it as if we were lovers and she owed me the information. "Sunday."

"Al, your husband?" Al who'd broken her wrist.

"He's coming out for a couple of days for a job interview in Vantana. He's had it lined up for months, and he decided to go through with it. He never did want to move out here before he had a job."

"I thought the whole trip was originally his idea."

"It was. We talked about it all through his schooling. He was going to teach chemistry and do research, and I was going to be able to get out of that damn snow, and paint outdoors all year long. Like Van Gogh in Arles."

"Only without the hookers."

"Maybe just a gigolo or two. Anyway, the closer Al got to finishing, the vaguer he became, postponing the trip for weeks—months. Then he interviewed for an industrial position in Kalamazoo—Michigan—and I found out he'd turned down a teaching job at San Diego State. He's several years younger than I am, and he's never been far from home. In East Lansing, his mother and grandmother lived three miles away. And everyone was telling him about how much money he could make in the private sector."

"Are you two getting back together?" It sounded like she was about to Dear John me, which I was condescending enough to consider cute.

She pursed her lips and shook her head slowly. "He may think so. He said he just called to tell me he was bringing out some cookbook of mine he'd ended up with—one I didn't even remember I owned. But when he phoned my mother for my number, he told her our fight was 'really pretty trivial.'"

I had no idea how I was supposed to react to all this. "How's your wrist?" I asked. "Pretty trivial?"

She ignored that, as well she should, and the conversation moved on. The day before she'd gotten a bank and a men's store to agree to display some of her pictures. And this morning, she'd secured a license to sell at the Sunday art show at the beach in San Cristobal. This got us on the subject of painting. She knew far more about it than I did of course. That made it fun because our tastes, though similar, were divergent enough that she could challenge my assumptions.

To me, for example, Norman Rockwell was just Peter Max for Republicans. And I loved that she wasn't trendy or moronically hip. Just because Da Vinci and Van Gogh were ludicrously popular, that didn't mean they weren't astonishing. Later, I told her a bit more about my work at the old church and chopping away at Asmodeus. I considered making love to her. But I didn't.

CHAPTER 17

At one point, the rumbling voices and loud laughter downstairs stopped, and Victoria came up to my room.

"I brought you some Excedrin for your headache," she said sweetly.

She set the bottle on the night table, then sat down on the bed. She was still wearing the white dress. Fastening it earlier, before we'd gone out, I'd run the zipper up the long expanse of bare back, flesh never touching flesh. I hadn't wanted to tell her how beautiful she looked.

"I'm guessing you didn't like Club Gatsby," she said. She was wearing her usual perfume, but up close I could make out another smell underneath. The bar had been hot.

"I was mostly just tired," I said.

"Maybe we should have just spent the night at home."

That would have been my choice, but when I got back from Maria's, Victoria was dressed and dying to go out. Club Gatsby had been a dead ringer for Hezekiah Duffy's, South Bend's latest in-spot. As we walked in, I heard a patron coming in behind us exclaim, "The perfect bar. Glass, brass, and ass." Seeing the way everyone else was dressed made my jeans seem even dirtier than they were.

The lawyer—and of course it was the glass, brass and ass guy—had moved in on Victoria when I'd gone up to the bar to get us drinks. By the time I returned, they were already discussing her settlement case—which of course was important to her. And when eventually I'd wanted to leave, pleading a headache, she immediately offered me the keys to the Mercedes, and said she was sure Perry Mason wouldn't mind dropping her off at home later. I was sure he wouldn't.

Now, sitting on the bed beside me, Victoria asked, "Are you sure you're feeling all right?" With perhaps more concern in her voice than a headache warranted. Especially an obviously fake one.

"I'm fine. I just need to rest a bit."

"I've got to get back downstairs." Her fingers stroked my cheek. Warmly. "My lawyer friend is a RAM graduate—he thinks Fairchild was a great man. Christ!"

Leaning over, she kissed me on the lips—lingering just briefly—then sat back and ruffled my hair with a look that seemed to set us together against the world.

"I'll see you in the morning," she said.

I lay in the dark, grinning to myself—until I heard the boom of his obnoxious laugh echo up the stairwell. When they got to the second floor, Victoria was talking to him in that little girl lisp, that some women think is cute and sexy. I never liked it when it was done to me; done to him, I liked it less. But who left them alone together in the first place?

Someone stumbled hard against a wall. They entered her room, and the bolt clicked into place. Maybe he *was* better looking than I was, but not that much. And maybe five years older. His clothing looked like he'd swiped it from J.C. Penny's window. Which still made him a better dresser. A lawyer, sure, with his "my firm this and my firm that." And lighting her cigarettes for her; I didn't even know she smoked. And sure, he might have a good-size bank account. But no more—less in fact—than I would have had if I'd taken my damn honors degree and gone straight into Harvard Business or Law after graduation. (Assuming they would have accepted me then.) Back then, he was probably jealous of men like me—of the way we lived and the women we were with—while he was a glorified law clerk, doing anything he could to get some disappointed and disillusioned secretary into the sack.

An occasional muffled laugh kept me awake. And once he used the bathroom. I couldn't hear much else until later when there came a single, protracted cry, high pitched, and suddenly muted, as if she'd twisted her head into the pillows to smother the noise. So, Victoria was at least a bit of a screamer.

"First thing we do," I quoted to myself, "let's kill all the lawyers." I suppose it was a benefit of my overpriced education that while most people quoted that line as if Shakespeare thought offing attorneys was good idea, I knew he had Dick the Butcher say it to show how threatening, how lawless, how dangerous to society he was. The name "Dick the Butcher" might have been another clue. At the moment though, it didn't seem like a bad idea.

I didn't sleep until long after I heard the attorney's heavy footsteps clumping down the stairs.

A Venus Mantrap

"Women are cursed, and men are the proof."
– *Roseanne Barr*

CHAPTER 18

"Are you in there Victoria?"

Once again, I pounded on the metal door just down the hall from the altar room. Once again there was no answer. It was late afternoon, sometime after five o'clock and I hadn't seen her all day. But I was sure I'd heard her go in there sometime around three. And she hadn't left—the squeaking of that door was hard to miss, even over all the banging I'd been doing down the hall.

"Victoria!" The door was locked securely. "I think I've found where Zandie's buried."

In the distance I head a hum as if the weird whistling was going to start again, but it died out. Then from inside the room came a muffled, "What?"

"I've found the tomb. At least I've found *a* tomb."

The door squeaked open.

"Where?" Like a schoolteacher or someone's mother, Victoria had a pair of glasses dangling from her neck on a string. And she was sucking on one of her mints. Her eyes were bloodshot from last night, and her face was somewhat puffy.

"Wait and see. Come on."

She followed me down the hallway labyrinth, away from the altar room. The corridor down there was filled with stuff that must have belonged to Zandie. I wondered why The Ashram hadn't tossed it. Glass jars were stacked four and five high, all sealed and most filled with dust and seeds and things which according to the labels used to be everything from roses and hemlock root to newt's eyes and wolf's paw.

"Look at this," I said to Victoria, picking one up. "Tartar's lips."

"I know. Humpert and Cranick and I stacked all this out here."

"Here's one marked: 'baby's finger.' Fortunately, it's empty. Was he really that much of a monster?"

Victoria nodded solemnly, "Probably worse. Look at this."

She handed me a jar labelled, "Nose of Turk" which was clearly an actual shriveled up nose.

"Holy shit!" I said, putting it back on the pile and wiping my hand on my pants.

"Holy might not be the right word."

We stepped over a partially unrolled tapestry depicting a three-headed ram beneath an even larger and even more evil-looking bird with gory talons. Then we squeezed between a bookcase and a table filled with antique Bunsen burners, test tubes, beakers, and, of course, a crystal ball.

"Zandie's lab," I suddenly realized.

She nodded back toward the room she'd just left. "And it was bricked up just like the will said. We had to unbrick it—that's where I found the will in fact, in that book in his library."

"What else is in there?" It seemed odd she hadn't mentioned opening up the lab before.

"Nothing much. Now I use it for storage, 'cause it's got a solid, metal door and a good, strong lock. I guess I'm paranoid after what happened with Cranick breaking into Humpert's room and playing that video tape—I was so embarrassed."

"There's enough of Zandie's stuff here for two or three store windows," I said.

"I know. And I suppose she'd take this if she had to—but it's not what she really wants."

"Does she still want his books?"

"Of course. She wants to recreate his full library as much as she can. We've already gone through the ones in the lab. Obviously, there are a few others that were his scattered around the place. But the centerpiece of the whole thing is the grimoire."

"And she wants to recreate his tomb? Is she going to have any room for merchandise in this store?"

Victoria's laugh was forced. Maybe she saved her best fake laugh for others. "I think she's given up on recreating the tomb."

I nodded as if I was actually buying all this. What I was actually coming to believe was that—for whatever reason—Zandie's grimoire and at least some of his books were worth a small fortune. And that they were never going to end up in some store window—unless that store was a rare book dealer.

The last obstacle we had to climb around was a rusty cauldron too big for me to have lifted by myself. After ducking through a curtain, we turned right down the next section of corridor and passed the room with the P.A. on our left. It had once been a small kitchen, complete with another built-in ice box like the mausoleum for munchkins in the back hallway. Just beyond the P.A. room was the nailed-up bulkhead exit and yet another cubicle-filled corridor, running parallel to the back wall of the building.

That's where the old stone crypt was, inside the first cubicle, like a small house within a house. The crypt filled the room, leaving just enough space for the locked iron gate to swing open. Through the rungs in the gate, we could see the burial vaults on the inside wall.

"How did you find it?" Victoria asked.

"You'll never believe it. I'm surprised you didn't find it yourself."

"I never looked in here."

"Why should you? From the hall outside, it's just another crib for just another whore. But obviously the crypt was part of the original church—look."

I pointed to five names that had been chiseled into the stone to the right of the gate.

Rev. Harold L. Turley

Rev. Horace Arnsworth, Pastor 1856-1864

Deacon Terence T. Pettimann

Rev. Albert O'Ryan, Pastor 1864-1873

Rev. Martin H. Stockton, Pastor 1877-1879

Crude lines had been gouged deeply through each name. A crucifix was carved into the stone above the gate. But later a serpent had been more roughly carved around it in the form of a question mark and the name Asmodeus added underneath.

I made a sweeping gesture toward the crypt. "'In that supposedly hallowed place,' the will said."

"Of course," Victoria said. "It makes perfect sense. I knew there was a crypt, but I just assumed it would be empty."

"You thought the church crypt would be empty? Why? I can see it's been desecrated."

"My guess is Zandie would have said it wasn't desecrated but re-consecrated. With Zandie, everything was all about him and his conquests. And this old church was his temple."

"And he didn't want the ministers of another religion buried there?"

She looked at me as if considering how to respond. "The rumors were that he had a use for the bodies—in his spells and ceremonies. In any case, they were never found. But it was much more about who he *did* want buried here. And that was his downfall. For over forty years, the churches and those locals who despised him couldn't close him down. Not permanently anyway. Not even when Zandie's mother somehow set one of his girls on fire in Zandie's own bed. But eventually he couldn't resist disgracing a better class of women."

"You mean wealthier."

"Wealthier. Connected to more powerful men. He finally went so far that one of his own people turned on him. She told the San Cristobal mayor that not only were several suicides over the years because of Zandie—including a couple of theoretically-virginal debutantes and the mayor's own notoriously plug ugly wife—but that, after those good ladies were all safely buried in the town's cemeteries, Zandie had stolen their bodies. He re-buried them here in the crypt. Apparently he believed that having them near made him more powerful and his spells more effective. He actually built up a collection."

"Of dead women? No wonder they lynched him."

"No wonder. Though one story did have it that Zandie's own girls had already done away with him by the time the lynch mob arrived. And some people pretended to believe that. In those days, mobs might string a man up as quick as you please, but it was better to let others grab the credit."

"So the moral of the story is that it's better to let the dead rest in peace?" That sounded like a good idea to me. And a lot less work.

"Nobody's going to lynch us for digging up Zandie. Anyway, whoever finished him off, afterwards the town returned the bodies of the disgraced women to their original graves—whether their families wanted them back or not. No matter how disgraced they might be."

"Disgraced? The debutantes at least would have been unmarried. All they'd done was to have sex."

"Zandie owned them. In life and in death. He was virtually irresistible."

"And that was their fault?"

"That was their weakness. And yes, weakness is a fault. But my point is that all the graves here in the tomb would have all been opened and emptied shortly after Zandie was hanged. Somebody for some reason went to the trouble of sealing them up again. The question is, why?"

"Maybe someone—maybe The Ashram—simply thought it was more respectful or just tidier to restore the burial sites as much as they could."

"Could be. Or maybe you're absolutely right and this is where Zandie's buried. 'In that supposedly hallowed place' where he figured nobody was likely to look for him. Obviously, it shouldn't be hard to find out."

What was also obvious—increasingly so every day—was that Victoria had done a lot more research on this than just a couple of casual conversations with her real estate lady.

Why?

I couldn't find either a file or a hacksaw with the old tools under the porch, and cracking the padlock on the crypt with a pry bar turned into another major project.

"This is one time Lyle Cranick might come in handy," Victoria remarked after I jabbed myself in the thigh, trying to pry the lock apart.

"They teach locksmithing in prison now, do they?"

"No. But he did learn breaking and entering. That metal door on Zandie's old lab, the room I was in this afternoon? With the old-fashioned lock? Cranick opened it in five minutes; it took Humpert an hour and a quarter to make a key for it, and he's the handiest guy I know."

"Humpert is the handiest guy you know!?!"

"For your information, Humpert happens to be totally mechanical."

"He looks it. Does he run on batteries or do you wind him up?"

That she actually laughed at, which made me feel better.

"You know," she said, "when I first met Humpert, he was all reason and dignity—now he's all hunches and emotion. But the less logical he becomes, the more he seems to get into tinkering with his machinery—waterfalls, model planes and boats, and anything that even smells like it might be broken. He was the one who fixed up that old Volkswagen. Though God knows why he bothered. The Ashram had left it for junk. He also draws really well."

I gave a noncommittal "Humm" and returned to the lock. She put her back to the wall and let herself slide to the floor, surprisingly unconcerned about dirtying yet another pair of designer jeans.

"Phew!" she exhaled. "I'm beat. Tough night last night. Who needs it? Makes me feel ugly today." She hugged herself tightly. "I must be getting old, huh?"

"You've been through a tough time." She *was* starting to look stressed.

"What?"

"I mean the attempted rape and all." I turned to look at her directly. "How could it not shake you up. I've got this picture of you in my mind, tossing that crucifix into the river."

At first, she didn't seem to know what I was talking about, then it dawned on her. "That wasn't *my* crucifix. *He* put that on me."

"He did? Why?"

She shrugged. "A loon, I guess. You saw his knife. It was a dick."

"No, it was actually a snake's head. A serpent. It just looked like a dick."

"So many things do."

"The face on the knife was the same as the face on that statue in the altar room," I offered, watching to see how she'd respond.

She tilted her head to the side, considering what I'd said. "No," she said eventually, "It definitely wasn't. I don't even think it was a serpent."

"Remember the names I told you that were scratched into the handle of the knife. The last one was Asmodeus, which is the name carved on the statue."

"You mentioned three or four names, Steve. I really couldn't tell you what they were, but Asmodeus doesn't sound familiar."

"Jehovah, Ahura Mazda, Huitzilopochtli and Asmodeus."

"One was Jehovah. That's right. I have no idea about the others. Maybe the name on the statue was similar to one you saw on the knife and your brain plugged that into your memory as if that was what you'd actually seen. Remember how you thought that bruise on your arm was the rapist's face."

I held up my hands, giving up the point, both points actually. Not because I was wrong, but because there was no convincing argument I could make for either.

She gave me the full hundred and fifty watt Victoria smile. Reaching into a pocket, she pulled out a pack of Virginia Slims Menthol Lights and a lighter. "Cigarette?" she asked, like it was a peace offering.

"No. No, thanks."

"Are you sure? Though I guess Virginia Slims aren't very macho." Virginia Slims, the "You've Come a Long Way, Baby" cigarette, empowering women to equality in lung cancer. I always wondered what the women who bought them as a symbol of how far women had come would have thought if they'd known how many people in the cigarette business—women included—referred to the brand as Vagina Slimes.

But all I said was, "I gave up smoking ten years ago. If I had *one*, tomorrow I'd be back up to three packs a day."

"I gave them up, too. Though when I'm around somebody that does..." She lit one and took a deep drag. "Our legal friend last night bought these for me. It'll help take off the chill, anyway."

I stuck the pry bar back in the lock and began twisting again. "He seemed quite taken by you."

"A very eager suitor." She smiled again. "A line or two of coke, which I wasn't going to do any more either—too much wine..." The smile grew conspiratorial. "Our friend has a few scratches today he won't be able to show his girlfriend—not there."

I was taken aback by the sudden intimacy of the remark. And excited. I wasn't into pain, but it was encouraging to hear that Victoria was funkier than I thought and reassuring to hear that the dude from Club Gatsby wasn't going to be a permanent addition, even if she had chosen him over me for one brief night.

Five minutes later, the lock finally snapped. We eased open the iron gates—I expected them to creak dramatically, but they moved smoothly and silently—and we were in.

Two stone sarcophagi sat in the middle of the crypt. Three other vaults were set right into the back wall—one at eye level, the others below and to either side. Wearily, I plopped down on a sort of concrete easy chair that had been built-in, God knows why, against one wall. It had been a long day. In the morning, I'd cracked open the marble altar in front of Asmodeus fairly quickly, but then I'd taken it upon myself to finish opening the walls up in Zandie's room. There was far too much work in the crypt to start on tonight.

Slumped down in the concrete chair with my chin down and my arms on the arm rests, I told Victoria I felt like Abe Lincoln in the Lincoln Memorial. She said I looked like Tony Perkins in Psycho. Maybe I shouldn't have shaved off the beard.

As soon as we'd stepped out into the hall, the whistling started—loud, and painfully high-pitched, and coming, appropriately enough, from back inside the crypt.

I was fighting the tape deck of the stereo—a combination 8-track and cassette player—and as usual with electronic equipment, I was losing badly. Victoria had a cassette of a classic Moby Grape album I hadn't heard in years, but nothing was reaching the speakers. On the other hand, the 8-track player worked just fine. Except I hated 8-tracks, which frequently and noisily split songs in two. Plus, the single 8-track album she owned was some kind of a Tony Orlando and Dawn greatest hits thing, and I'd rather pour molten lead into my ears. Anyone would.

At one point, I got a brief blast of Moby Grape singing, "Eight-oh-five"—from the song "8:05"—just as the clock on the deck moved to exactly...8:03. Then the song cut out again. I hit a switch on the deck and suddenly Tony Orlando was singing "Knock three times" which I shut off as quickly as possible, just in time to hear someone at the backdoor. Someone who proceeded to...ring the doorbell. If you happen to be one of those people who believes that the universe speaks to me, I can't refute that, but I certainly don't have a clue as to what it's trying to say.

Trying to shut the machine off, I must have hit the wrong switch again, because as I was heading to answer the door, Tony broke into, "Tie a Yellow Ribbon Round the Old Oak Tree" which actually did make me want to tie a yellow ribbon—as tightly as possible around his neck. But that was cause and effect not synchronicity.

Rather than listen to any more of it, I hurried back and turned off the power. Which is when the person at the door actually did knock—five times.

Years after all this, I made the mistake of appearing on Fox News. The reporter was a blonde "Fox Babe" who had graduated Summa Cum Laude from Yale, but at that point in her career was apparently required to play an idiot on TV. Dripping with fake sincerity, she wrapped up the interview with, "Mr. Kennan—*Gavin*—as a person who has become all too familiar with the inexplicable, how do you personally explain God?"

"Explain God?" I said. "I can't even fucking explain Tony Orlando."

Fox never ran that part of the interview. Even aside from the profanity, my answer didn't make a lot of sense. Which I suppose I could argue was exactly the point.

***

The doorbell and then the knocking was O'Ryan.

"Is she here?" he asked as I opened the door. He was as neat as usual, with the chill of the night turning his normally pallid face ruddy and healthier looking. Under one arm he carried a large rectangular package wrapped in brown paper.

"No. Victoria's out somewhere. No idea when she'll be back. Want to come in?"

Glancing at his watch, he shook his head.

"Come on in," I said. "I've got a fire going."

"That's okay—I can't stay. My bones ache in this weather. You look terrible."

"Thanks. I shaved off my beard this morning." It had been years since I'd seen my face without it. My chin was weaker than I remembered, and I'd almost forgotten about that mole and what a pain it was to shave around. Still, I thought I looked better beardless. (Of course, I'd also thought I looked better when I'd grown it.) I definitely looked cleaner.

"You know somebody was walking around the side of your house as I came up," O'Ryan said.

"Out here? You're kidding."

"Some old tramp. He was muttering to himself." O'Ryan's blue eyes were clear. I believed him.

"I thought I saw somebody out there the other night myself."

He nodded. "Tramps. We get them more and more often out here. And they think the church is empty. Only this one was carrying a big old candle. You should have left the beard."

Great, I thought, now I was getting grooming tips from the captain of the Olympic ugly team. That uncharitable thought made me feel guilty enough to insist on getting him a beer. And he agreed to a small snack. I sat him by the fire and dug up a jar of peanuts to go with the Budweiser. When I returned, he'd eased back in the recliner, the large chair accenting his small frame. He turned on the TV—*Dallas*: cowboy hats, big hair and accents from *somewhere*, maybe the southwest part of Oz. But we both ended up quietly staring into the fire and the conversation tapered off naturally and comfortably. When O'Ryan did speak again, his voice was softer than usual, as if it had relaxed too.

"Maria tells me you're tearing the place up searching for old bones and things."

"Remember I mentioned that Victoria's got a buyer who wants Zandie's old stuff—apparently almost any of it."

"I remember. If you say so. That Zandie—he was something."

"How well did you know him?"

"I don't know. I dream of him. Sometimes I don't even know if he was real." But then his face lit up. "Before I met Mrs. O'Ryan, I had some good times myself in this house."

"Really?" That wasn't what he'd said in front of Maria.

"Some of the best. It was quite the place."

"I'll bet."

"Say you got hungry. There's a knock on the door of your room. And there's a meal, without you even ordering it. But it's just what you would have ordered. The same for drinks—even if you were a perfect stranger." He peered around into the shadows, as if trying to look back down the years. "Great old place, isn't it."

"Think it's haunted?"

"Haunted?" O'Ryan wasn't about to be patronized. "Course not."

"Zandie was supposed to be some sort of a sorcerer, wasn't he?"

"Maybe he knew a thing or two. He liked to pretend he knew a lot more than he did—half serious, half joking, half putting on a show for the rubes."

"Three halves," I pointed out gently.

"Exactly!" he said, as if that proved his point. "I've got his skull at home."

That was such a non-sequitur it took me a moment to realize what he'd said. "You've got *his skull*? Do you know where he was buried?"

"What?" Now O'Ryan did seem confused. "No, I've got his skull. I don't have...*his* skull. I've got the gold covered skull he used to keep on his desk. That's what we were talking about—the show he put on for the rubes."

"I thought he used to keep it on his mantel."

He twisted his face in thought. "Does it matter? But it's around somewhere. I used to have it anyway. Might not be real gold."

"You should check on that."

"Yah, I might." He looked at his watch again. With effort, he straightened up the chair. The beer and the peanuts were untouched. "I got to go. I bought Maria a present. She sold her first painting down in San Cristobal today. And she's always trying to feed me."

"So, what did you get her?"

"It's another picture." Getting up, O'Ryan grabbed the package. "Came with its own frame and everything. Hope she likes it."

"I'm positive she'll be thrilled." And she would be. Even if it was a Day-Glow nude with nipples like scarlet parasols, or a velvet street scene with windows and streetlamps that lit up when you plugged it in.

"You want to come over?" he asked. "Come on over and see Maria?"

"Some other time, OK?"

He shook his head, then stared right through my eyes. "You're younger than you should be at your age. I know—I was too. You've got too much to prove."

I laughed ruefully. "Believe me, I'm too old to prove anything."

"A wiser man would be wooing Maria. This Victoria isn't as big a deal as she likes to think she is, believe me. I know. When I was young I had so many women around me..."

If that was true, he must have been an extremely wealthy young man. Even with his mouth closed, two of his erratic teeth protruded from between his lips. Then I remembered "the best times" he'd spent in Zandie's whorehouse. I felt a jab of sadness for his dreams of the youthful glory that he must have had to purchase by the hour.

"I'm sure you did," I said.

"But Maria's aunt—unsightly as she was—was the most wonderful woman I ever knew. Taught me a lot. Saved my life. It was her store, you know." He gestured over toward his house. "That's how I met her. Wouldn't be the man I am today if not for her." He gave me a pointed look and added, "That's what a good woman can do for you."

"I may be beyond saving."

"You're not as far gone as I was, believe me."

"That's good to hear," I said, doubting that O'Ryan had been anywhere near the lost cause he now pictured himself to have been. "Still, I'm not sure if it's fair to put that kind of responsibility, that kind of burden on a relationship—on a woman."

"Fair's got nothing to do with it. It's not fair at all. I wish I'd been fair. But I wasn't a fair man. I wish life had been fair. She gave up her family for me."

"They didn't approve?"

"Shacking up with me—they never forgave her for that. Then—when we did finally get matrimonial—it wasn't in church. She didn't care what anybody thought of her. But she was a better person than any of them.

I could never be that good. Likely, I was a disappointment to her—but I tried. Do you know Herodotus?"

"Herodotus? The historian?"

"No, Herodotus, the singing cowboy." He screwed his face into an expression of amused tolerance. "Of course, Herodotus, the historian."

"I never actually read him."

"You ought to. Herodotus said—or wrote—I don't know, he probably said it too—that every year in Babylon they'd auction off brides. They'd start with the prettiest girls—who'd go for the most money—and they'd work down to the ones where the families would have to bid on how much they'd have to shell out to get someone to take them."

"So, if you were rich, you could get the bride of your dreams."

"And if you were poor, you could get a bride and some nice cash. And probably a few ugly kids."

"And the women got?"

"Fucked in more ways than one. Makes you wonder who comes up with this shit."

I followed him to the front door. He still hadn't mentioned what he wanted with Victoria. "Any message?" I asked. His face had clouded over. I suppose he was still back with Maria's aunt. "For Victoria," I reminded him.

"No. Oh, wait. Yah, sure. Tell her I said she was...a what-do-you-call-it...a Venus mantrap. Understand. A Venus mantrap." He said it matter-of-factly, but I had the feeling a tirade might be gathering like a sudden storm in the back of his mind.

Venus mantrap, huh? I thought after he left. Maybe if I played my cards just right, she might trap me. I flipped the TV off again, and went back to the tape deck, but with no better results. Worse actually, since now I couldn't get records to play either. Perversely, I decided to check through Victoria's albums again to see what I couldn't hear.

The only Terry Davis records she owned were three copies of his *Reflections of an Era* album. On the back cover Davis beamed at a fringe-covered Victoria with long straight hair.

I could remember the scorn with which my friends and I had greeted the liner notes under that picture: the moronic fake-hippie-ish clichés, even asking people to send a dollar to join the Terry Davis fan club and get "your official psychedelic membership pin." The music itself wasn't as bad as the liner notes—what could be? But Terry Davis fell by the wayside. In any case, tastes were changing. Long, flowing robes were beginning to look silly, and Davis's once "cherubic," or "enlightened" smile was now, "insipid" or "inane." Revolution and incipient heavy metal were becoming the order of the day. By the time Davis was reported dead of a drug overdose, it was merely a footnote to an already vanished time.

I put the albums back. Even if I'd gotten the stereo working, I wouldn't have played *Reflections of an Era*. For me to be nostalgic for the sixties—much of which were actually in the early seventies—would be like an Englishman yearning for the good old days of World War II. I'd certainly believed in the ideals—and, at the time, in the psychedelics—of the era, if not necessarily in what Stephen called "the ontological weirdness." I never expected salvation from the thirteen-year-old Perfect Master or the space brothers, or from the truths revealed by playing "Hang on Sloopy" backwards. Maybe you had to be there to understand, but strangely enough we had honest-to-God believed we were creating a new culture, a new society. Hell, from birth we'd lived in a world where everything from Tide to Spam to automobiles were "New and Improved" on a yearly basis. Why not a new and improved civilization, new and improved relationships, new and improved people?

Okay, maybe I had believed in some of the weirdness. And now, for some reason, I was very aware of the puckered scar in the middle of my abdomen like an extra navel, and I was filled with a sense of loss—like something a paraplegic might feel in coming across his old hiking boots.

I wanted to get out of the house. I wanted more than that, but I wasn't up for getting shot down in some bar. So, I just went for a drive in the VW. The Mercedes was still in the other half of the garage; Victoria must have been picked up by a date. I headed north to avoid seeing the fig tree. It was still early when I returned. Fortunately, there was still plenty of Bud in the house.

Once again, I awoke in the middle of the night, this time forcing myself awake. The dream fled instantly, leaving only a metallic tasting apprehension. I'd been drinking too much lately. Rain was pelting down outside, but the room was stiflingly hot and as dry as my throat. I got up to crack the window, and then, getting a drink of water from the bathroom, I thought I heard noises coming from Victoria's room. I walked over to her door, but all was silent except for the soothing scratching of the rain. Slowly, carefully, and as quietly as any sneak thief, I tried the doorknob to see if she was in. It turned, but the door was bolted.

SOME BODIES CREATE MORE PROBLEMS THAN OTHERS

"I want the world to see my body."
– *Marilyn Monroe*

"Sometimes I feel my whole life has been one big rejection."
– *Marilyn Monroe*

CHAPTER 19

The next morning, I awoke, not too hung over, but groggy. The room was full of sunlight, and Victoria was sitting—and bouncing—on the bed.

"Time to get up," she said, bubbling over and radiant herself.

Through the blankets I could feel her hip, firm and warm, moving against mine. I was already aroused; maybe I woke up that way. She may have noticed the conspicuous lump under the blankets before I drew my right leg up, tenting the bed clothes to hide it.

"Your coffee, Sire. Whoops!" Coffee dripped on the bed as she handed me the cup from the night table. Laughing, she took a second cup for herself and almost spilled that one, too. "And I've only got one set of sheets for this bed," she said. "Well, *salud.*"

"You spilled some on your..." I began, stopping as I saw the way her nipple poked through the damp spot on her top. When she looked down, a flash of embarrassment and irritation crossed her face and was gone.

"It won't stain," she said, producing a smile.

We sipped the coffee. It was bitter and lukewarm, which was probably lucky for her nipple. As usual, she asked about her calls. Someone *had* called, but they'd hung up when they heard my voice. Below her lacy tank top, Victoria was wearing bright blue shorts.

Nonchalantly, I combed my fingers through my hair. If she'd noticed I'd shaved off the beard yesterday, she hadn't commented, but she probably would notice how grubby a day's growth looked. And my breath was probably thick enough to paint with. I drank more of the coffee, hoping to mask that, anyway. Swirling a second sip around in my mouth, I put the cup back on the nightstand.

"You've been sleeping through a beautiful day," she said, giving my stomach a friendly pat. I'd seen women do the same thing to friends of either sex. But she let her arm rest there, and when she shifted her body, the arm trailed innocently across my abdomen—only an inch or two—but disconcertingly close to the tip of my hidden erection.

"Yah." At least, my voice didn't crack. "I should be getting at that crypt today."

Sipping her own coffee, she leaned harder against my side. Her elbow moved a fraction of an inch lower. It could have been an accident. She didn't know I had an erection—did she? My own arms felt awkward at my sides.

"I won't have you down in that dark basement today. It's too beautiful out."

Again, the arm moved—another natural adjustment. My dick jerked once, twice, in excitement against the increasing pressure of the blankets. I was afraid my condition would be revealed momentarily, and if that was going to happen, I'd have to come on to her before it did. Though in my mind I could still hear her contemptuously calling Cranick a nothing, better to be rejected—even harshly, even scornfully—than to look ridiculous being so aroused by just lying beside her.

The way my heart was pounding, I wondered if she could feel it where our bodies touched or even through the bed. I wished I was at least shaved and clean. Was she asking me to make a move? I waited, hoping she'd be forward enough to remove all doubt. If she wanted me to take her in my arms, why was she still holding that coffee cup in her hand? The damn thing was a regular chastity belt. I envisioned myself taking it from her and putting it down on the table. I envisioned it, but I didn't do it.

She put the cup down herself—the coffee unfinished—and yawned, stretching her arms wide. From that angle, anyway, her breasts were surprisingly large. Then she dropped her arm back down on the bed—right on top of my dick.

"Oh well," she said, completely oblivious. She had to feel it, pulsing beneath her wrist, even as I shifted away—desperately, awkwardly—taking her arm on my hip bone. I couldn't bring myself to touch her. Now, all at once, I was more afraid of not being rejected than of being rejected—of failing as a lover and really turning myself into a fool in her eyes.

"I guess it's time to get to work," she said. The hand was off now, and she stood up. "Don't work in the basement today. It's too nice. I need you to check out that grave outside anyway—the one where we sat that first night? Maybe Zandie's buried in there. And at least it's outside in the fresh air."

"The will said he was to be buried in the house," I managed somehow. As she herself had pointed out.

"You never know though. Maybe you were right—maybe those instructions were never carried out. At any rate, we should check out that grave sooner or later."

Several anguished minutes after she left, I leaped out of bed, dressed hurriedly, combed my hair and brushed my teeth—the cold water making my whole mouth ache—and went after her, resolved to finally make my move. No matter what. Ignoring the tension constricting my chest, I knocked on her door. It was locked, but she wasn't inside. Wondering if I could come on to her at the breakfast table, I headed downstairs.

I saw it before I reached the bottom of the staircase.

The nail—a spike actually—had been smashed through the face of the small plastic doll, pinning its head to the kitchen wall opposite the stairs. It was a Barbie, blond and naked, and a small pink pouch hung from a thinner nail piercing its abdomen.

I was actually shocked. The crushed plastic face was almost obscene—as if it had once been alive. A series of swirling curves had been crudely painted in black around the doll—small gray feathers were somehow stuck into the wall to form a circle around the whole mess.

"What the hell?" I muttered.

"What? Oh yah," said Victoria. "Guess we had a visitor last night. That appears to be the sole damage. Looks like Zandie wasn't the only one around here into black magic."

"That's black magic?"

"Or modern art. Could be either."

"Nothing was taken?"

"Nothing. Course, we'll have to repaint the wall. I must have left the door unlocked."

Or maybe I had. Then there was the window I'd left open to climb into the pantry. Had I remembered to relock it?

"You didn't hear anything last night?" Victoria asked.

"Not that I remember." I had woken up once during the night. Had I heard something?

The intrusion bothered me more than I let on, but Victoria stayed calm, like it was simply part of modern life. "And I've got secure bolts on both my bedroom doors," she said. We did agree we'd better be more careful in the future. She'd recently had new locks and chains installed on the front and back doors, and we were going to be sure to use them. We'd been lucky this time.

I walked over to check out the doll more closely. Whoever did it must have stood on a chair to get the thing up there—probably the work of a single itinerant lunatic. Possibly even the drunk that O'Ryan had seen prowling around outside the house.

I had no idea if this was some jackass's idea of black magic. If so, what did that mean? The man we'd killed—I'd killed—had carried a crucifix and wielded a knife shaped like a serpent, a symbol of the devil going back to Genesis and probably before. And the Barbie doll on the wall reminded me of Victoria.

I had a single piece of toast and went out to work.

CHAPTER 20

It was a gorgeous day and, come to think of it, a Saturday. The inscription on the low burial vault outside the church was weathered but still readable.

R.I.P.
Horatio
Cavendish
1787–1853

Sinner though he may have been in the service of
mammon, and widely despised, his expiating bequest
provided this land and the funds to build our Church,
to shelter a growing flock for generations untold.
May this blessed house attract
the congregation it deserves.

*"And again I say unto you, It is easier for a camel to go
through the eye of a needle, than for a rich man to enter
into the kingdom of God."*
Matthew 19:24

That was quite an inscription—basically, "Thanks for the money and the land, now go to Hell!"

The stone lid those less than generous words were written on opened easily, and without much trouble at all I was able to slide it off and let it drop onto the ground. Unfortunately, that revealed that this wasn't so much a burial vault with a coffin sitting right inside, as it was a low budget imitation of an actual vault—simply a monument covering a regular grave. Obviously the faithful wanted to provide something significant for Old Horatio—or maybe it was a requirement of the bequest—but hey, if they could save a buck, why not?

If I wanted to see if this was Zandie's grave, I was going to have to dig, though there was no reason at all to suspect that anyone other than the widely despised Mr. Cavendish was down there waiting to be dug up. This might be the biggest waste of time yet. But at least I'd found a decent shovel, and Victoria had come up with a nearly new pair of men's work gloves for me.

Soon I was working furiously, plunging into the heavy soil. The Barbie doll slipped further back in my mind as I took out on the earth what I felt like doing to myself for having blown it that morning with Victoria. *What a jerk!* She'd fallen all over me, and I'd done nothing. What must she think? I could only hope I could make up for it before Humpert got back and got in the way, or one of those other dudes locked her up.

Tonight. Without fail.

The shovel slammed into a rock and kicked sideways. As I paused to catch my breath, Victoria came down from the back porch. Still in obvious good spirits in spite of the doll and carrying herself with an athletic grace and ease I hadn't really picked up on before, she sauntered over to the thicket where she'd dropped those seeds the other day.

"Steve! Come here! Quick," she cried. "Look at this!"

Before I even reached her, I could see what she was so excited about. Interspersed with the dull brown brush and scrub were bright green plants of various size and shape, some with flowers of red or yellow—all new growth, and all at least a foot high. Victoria knelt down and pulled out one branchless stalk that must have been twice that.

"I can't believe it," she said, gazing up at me as if I had an explanation.

I couldn't believe it, either. And she really had planted herbs rather than pot. Could she have been serious about casting that spell?

"Is this some kind of joke?" I asked.

She was so fascinated she never even bothered to answer. But the earth around the plants was as hard and as untouched as the rest of the yard. No one had transplanted the herbs there full-grown—not that anyone would go to all that bother. All I could figure out was that the recent rains and alternating sunshine had made the weather ideal. And that she must have planted fast growing weeds.

For the first time, I noticed she'd marked the different groupings on small stakes: Cleopatra's Rose, Flowering Fennel, Cyprus of Cathay, Circe's Down. One or two of the names I'd seen on Zandie's jars. Was that where she'd gotten the seeds? At least, she hadn't planted Tartar's lips, which I had a feeling didn't refer to a plant at all.

When I went back to my shoveling, my body had cooled down. And as the ditch got deeper the ground got harder. After a while Victoria came over, a bundle of assorted herbs in her hand, and peered into the hole.

"No sign of our boy yet?" she asked. "Well, I've got to run."

"Okay. Hey, how about if I cook up that liver for supper. I've got a great recipe."

"Oh. Well, the liver's gone."

"Gone? When?"

"I forgot to get cat food again. I had to feed it to La Perdita."

"You fed La Perdita two pounds of liver?"

"The cat's a pig." She smiled. "There's still steak in the freezer though."

"Well, maybe I'll just grill that up. Are you going to be back?"

"I can't tell. We'll see. Try to finish this up today, if you possibly can. I don't want to spend more than one day out here with so much to do inside."

"Got it."

"Remember though, even if Zandie's not buried out here, you still might find something worth something. We know he liked to tamper with the church's graves. So, finish up, and I'll see you later."

She carried the herbs back into the house. Twenty minutes later I heard the Mercedes start in the garage, then drive off.

Preoccupied as I was with Victoria and our relationship, past and future, the hole was waist deep before I really began to consider what I'd be unearthing here eventually. What the hell was I doing digging up somebody's grave? This felt completely different from chipping away at old Asmodeus, where I'd never really expected to find anything.

Leaning against my shovel and complaining out loud to the earth and sky, I muttered, "My mother didn't raise me to be a grave robber."

"Too bad—it looks like you're good at it," O'Ryan answered from behind me. As I turned, he smiled benignly and asked, "What do you think you're doing?"

"Victoria wants to check and make sure your pal Zandie's not buried here."

"Where's she?"

"She had to leave."

"Did you tell her I called her a Venus mantrap?" he asked.

"No. I didn't figure that would do much for neighborly relations."

He considered this as he watched me dig. After a while, he said, "If I was Zandie, I wouldn't be buried here."

"No? Where would you be buried?"

"Some of his girls, they'd be here. Maybe a customer or two. Maybe the odd baby."

"Secret burials?"

"Some, maybe. But you got a body, you got to put it someplace. Zandie and his folks weren't getting into the regular church graveyards with the holier-than-thous. No chance of that. Some of those people were even against premarital interdigitation."

He waited.

"Okay, I'll bite," I said.

He chuckled. "Handholding. *Interdigitation.*"

"Got it. So where do you think Zandie might be buried?"

"He *might* be anywhere. Tell me again—what is it she wants with these old bones? Maria said, but I wasn't paying attention."

I explained the offer Victoria had gotten—or the one she claimed she had gotten anyway—and right away he wanted to know who would pay money for such "old crap." Which was interesting coming from a guy whose house looked like the world's crappiest thrift store.

"Zandie *has* really caught Victoria's interest though," I said. "She even tried one or two of his spells."

"She did? Like what?"

As skeptically as possible, I told him about the spell with the plants, and he walked over and checked them out.

"Thinking on it a bit," he said when he returned, "how would you know Zandie, if you dug him up? You think he had his rib cage monogrammed?"

It was a good point and after a cab pulled up to O'Ryan's place to take him to the store and he hurried off, I sat on the side of the ditch and considered it. If I unearthed a skeleton holding a copy of a book labelled *Zandie's Grimoire*, then no problem. Otherwise, I could dig the old S.O.B. up and never know it, leaving five other burial sites in the crypt to open up, and God knows how many other corpses buried in the field around the old church if Victoria heard about those. How many coffins would I have to sort through? And now she had me out here, basically just looking for "something worth something." What did that even mean? Other books of historical value that might have been buried with the dead, or the rings on their fingers? How about the gold in their teeth?

When I went back to the digging, it was with even less enthusiasm than before. After a while, I decided the ground was so dense and rocky that things would go easier with a pick. I headed back under the porch. Where I found—among other things—another ax, a couple of shovels, a rake, a hoe, a window frame, a threadbare automobile tire and a lot of old lumber. But not a pick. Since looking for a pick—which I did need—was better than digging up graves, I was as thorough as if I was hunting for diamonds.

That's how I discovered yet another grave. Sort of.

The marble slab, covering it like a tabletop, reached from the basement wall. It wobbled as I crawled across it, clearing off the inscription:

REVEREND HORACE ARNSWORTH
PASTOR 1866-1874
Groping alone through the darkness.
Struggling toward salvation?

It was the rest of one of the wall vaults from the crypt. Obviously old Horace had been interred before the back porch had been added to the building. A corner of the marble slab on top had broken off, creating a V-shaped mouth. Even now I could hear a faint intermittent hum from the slight breeze that funneled under the porch and into the stone vault. It seemed clear this was the origin of the ominous whistle we'd been hearing, which is what had led me to the crypt inside originally.

Since there clearly wasn't another pick under the porch, I decided to go down to the basement and get the one I'd left in the altar room. Even though it was so worn down it probably wouldn't cut through Cream of Wheat, taking the time to trudge down and retrieve it seemed a better option than heading right back to work.

I wasn't sure why grave robbing bothered me. By the way, I'm guessing that I've just become the only TIME Magazine *Person of the Year* ever to have used the phrase, "I wasn't sure why grave robbing bothered me." I doubt even Donald Trump ever tweeted that.

Still, I'd done worse. And, to me, aside from sanitary considerations, old bones were just old bones—animal waste pure and simple. After I died, if someone wanted to use my skull as a drinking gourd and my femur as a whiffle-ball bat, well, glad to be of service. And yet, the people buried in these graves probably hadn't felt that way.

I had no scruples about messing with the bones of a pimp who reveled in destroying lives. Though as I said, I never really expected to find Zandie in either the statue or the altar. On the other hand, in spite of the game of musical bodies that had gone on around that place, the grave I was digging up that afternoon was in all likelihood going to yield somebody, probably somebody like poor whistling Horace, "groping alone through the darkness, struggling toward salvation?"—question mark and all.

I think it was the question mark that got me. As a smart-ass seventeen-year-old, I'd delighted in explaining to my mother how the text of her divinely-inspired Bible had actually evolved almost randomly over the centuries: by addition and omission; by intent and accident. As if that mattered. Only four years later, after the cancer had slowly tortured her to death, I discovered from her sister how my babbling had troubled her faith.

I know: *asshole*, we've discussed it. It's a given.

I couldn't get the pick out of the altar room. The basement door in the kitchen was locked for some reason, thwarting my procrastination. Unfortunately, it was only quarter to three. Too early to knock off. I decided to go back and dig a bit more, but if I got down to the coffin, I'd simply uncover it and quit for the day. I'd leave opening it for tomorrow. Maybe Victoria would change her mind when it came right down to doing it. The thing was probably filled with filth and disease.

When I returned to the grave, O'Ryan was standing on the edge of it, waiting for me, leafing through a new TV Guide, sipping from a can of Tab. A small bag of groceries sat at his feet. He must have done his grocery shopping at the gas station down the road.

"Goddamn, don't do that!" I said as he started picking his crooked teeth with the detachable pop top from the soda can. Fortunately, he stopped.

"Exhibition baseball game on tonight," he said. "The Dodgers and the Giants. Baseball's almost as good as fishing. Want to come over and watch? Maybe see Maria?"

"Thanks, Mr. O'Ryan, but I'm going to be busy tonight," I said.

"You hope you will be anyway," he offered, putting the TV Guide and the Tab can back in the bag, apparently getting ready to leave.

"So, no story about weird mating practices today?"

"You mean like the one about the country where guys work for free and dig up dead bodies and hurt people and make total fools out of themselves and lose sight of who they are and give up everything they believe in just so they can get laid?"

"Hmm, there's something oddly familiar about that one. We aren't talking about Babylon again, are we?"

"The Whore of Babylon maybe. And it's not a mating practice 'cause it never works. Never." He picked up the bag and headed off, leaving me with "You be careful, Todd."

I gave him a wave, dropped back into the hole and started in again. Immediately I struck something hard, sending vibrations up and down my arms.

"Hey, how about lending me a beer or two for the game?" O'Ryan said, back at the edge of the grave. "I forgot to buy any at the store."

"Sure." I didn't think Victoria would mind, not really. But I must have had an exasperated look on my face, because before I even started out of the ditch, O'Ryan offered in a conciliatory tone to get the beers for himself. I let him, though actually I wouldn't have minded another excuse to break off work. I told him where they were, and he wandered off.

Thinking I'd struck the coffin, I got down on my knees to examine it. It was only a flat rock. Looking up and realizing I was at the bottom of an open grave, I got to my feet immediately.

I worked the tip of the shovel around the rock and eventually pried it loose. It wasn't easy. Then, as soon as I started shoveling again, I hit another rock—an even bigger one. To leverage this one out, I definitely needed that pick from the basement, dull or not. And I suddenly knew how to get it.

The basement had no windows, but I found what I was looking for just beyond the sealed-up bulkhead, on the side of the house serviced by the twin ruts that were as much of a driveway as the pot-holed and grass-riddled former highway out front was a road. I brushed aside a bush or two and there it was, right where it should be—the outer door to the built-in ice box in the P.A. room. The door was exactly like the one on the porch, but the latch on this one was missing.

With a scrape of wood on wood, the door came open, and I peered inside. The Ashram had even cleaned in there. On the far side of the compartment were three more doors. If one of them was unlatched I was in. Unfortunately, I had to climb inside to reach them. Entering headfirst, my body blocked out most of the light. The first door I tried was latched tight. So was the second. I worked myself farther in and had a brief image of being trapped, of the outer door somehow swinging shut and locking me inside. Fortunately, the third door came open easily, but I had to back out awkwardly and then turn around and slide through backwards on my stomach, so I could ease myself down onto the basement floor feet first.

Dull light filtered into the P.A. room from somewhere out in the corridor. Once my eyes adjusted, I could make out a modern sink and a small gas stove to my left, and—in the shadows on the other side of the room—the microphone for the P.A., a turn table, and a couple of squares that might be record albums.

I was climbing past the cauldron in the hall when I heard a thud—dull, yet with a hollow ring to it. Probably because of the way I'd spent the afternoon, I thought of the lid dropping shut on a coffin. Though it seemed to come from deep in the bowels of the basement, I froze—not entirely sure I hadn't somehow caused the thud myself.

"Victoria?" I called, expecting an echo, but far from it, the building seemed to gobble up my voice leaving it flat and feeble with no carry.

I banged my knee on a corner of the bookcase that jutted out in front of me. "Damn you!" I snarled—not sure if I was talking to the bookcase or myself.

Another noise—like a scraping—came from some indefinite distance. Silence filled in around me, as thick as the darkness at the end of the hall. The scraping could have been scurrying. The cat? Rats? I'd been bitten by a rat while working in the prison kitchen, reaching into a bin of corn in a poorly lit storage area. A prison doctor—the same one who had so inelegantly stitched up the hole in my gut the year before—had informed me rabies shots "*probably* weren't necessary."

A tetanus shot probably wasn't necessary when I stabbed myself with one jagged, beaten-up end of the pick as I tried to work it back out through the ice box. But a band-aid was. When I got back to the grave after finally finding one, I noticed Victoria's car was back—parked outside the garage. So, it probably was her down in the basement—just at the other end and unable to hear me.

Aside from dealing with that one large rock, the pick didn't really help my digging much. That was okay because by the time I reached the rotting wood of the coffin it was past five and time to knock off for the day.

I cleaned a bit more dirt off the lid, thinking of that evening and how to tie up Victoria before she made other plans. Maybe I could talk her into something cheap, like a movie. I'd have to get some of my advance first, of course; I wondered if Victoria had forgotten it.

The six names had been scratched more than carved into one small area near the bottom of the coffin lid—so faintly and carelessly that I almost missed them completely.

M. H. Stockton
T. T. Pettimann
H. L. Turley
H. Arnsworth
A. Eddings
H. Cavendish

So now we knew what had happened to the ministers' bodies that had been removed from the crypt. Apparently, they were sharing space with the original inhabitant, the previously unpopular, widely despised, Mr. Horatio Cavendish. Though I didn't know how much could have been left of any of them if all six had been crammed into one coffin. And I wasn't interested in opening the lid to find out.

By the time I climbed out of the grave, the trend with Victoria had continued. The Mercedes was already gone.

I ended up in a San Cristobal laundromat called WasherWorld with three aging bachelors and a shapely young mother with curly blond hair and baby carriage complete with an infant cute enough to star in a baby food ad. As broke as I was, I got a load done free by telling the attendant one of his washers had taken my money. For a quarter, I added a cup of bulk soap.

The young mother wasn't wearing a ring. And I imagined Victoria's face if she came home expecting to find me alone and waiting for her and found me with this woman instead—her baby at least momentarily out of the picture. But then I watched two of the bachelors crash and burn against the blonde's overwhelming indifference. I decided not to audition to be reject number three.

Watching my clothes revolve around the drier, I pondered her lack of interest, not as it related to me but more as an abstract philosophical proposition. Not exactly Plato or Descartes, but hey, different inquiring minds are concerned with different questions. Was she indifferent because her sex drive was diminished so soon after having a baby? Or because laundromat guys—guys approaching middle age who didn't own a washer and dryer—weren't appealing as potential candidates for lover, husband, stepfather or breadwinner? Or was it because she already had a candidate, someone who couldn't or wouldn't be there to help her with the laundry that night?

A couple of other possibilities actually did occur to me. But I dismissed them as being unlikely, using the principle of Occam's razor, also known as the Law of Parsimony, which Dr. Rogers once cheerfully explained to me over a joint as "Don't overthink it, shithead."

The woman's baby began to cry and after finding the rest room was locked with an "Out of Order" sign on the door, she discreetly began to nurse the child. Maybe it was my imagination, maybe it was projecting my own feelings, but immediately the atmosphere in the laundromat seemed to change. The sexual vibe vanished. The bachelors—and I—were just there to do laundry, the woman to nurture her baby: feeding him, washing his clothes.

Soon the dryer tumbled my laundry to a stop. I packed everything up—reasonably neatly—and headed out to the VW, bringing an end to the combination philosophical inquiry and fluff and fold.

It wasn't a particularly deep thought, but as I drove off it occurred to me that evolutionarily speaking, the purpose of sex was to create that baby. But what had been happening earlier between the woman and at least two of the bachelors—maybe all three, maybe me as well—had nothing at all to do with that.

Philosophically, I was out of my depth, but I had clean, almost dry clothes for a total of just fifty cents.

I returned to the old church about eight o'clock, disappointed but not surprised that Victoria wasn't already back. I found a bag of pretzels in the pantry and sat down with a beer at the kitchen table. I could wait for her till one or two o'clock if necessary. After that, it would probably be too late for me to have any chance with her that night.

To strengthen my resolve, I conjured up images of us together: Victoria at my side, hanging on my arm, wanting me—in restaurants, strolling down streets, driving through some indistinct town. Always we were observed. But not by Dell, he was in jail—a tender bruise on my mind. Stephen was dead, as were my mother and father. So aside from my older brother and sister, the onlookers to my triumph were just low-level friends, former girlfriends and acquaintances, and the world in general.

After finishing my third beer and far too many pretzels, I moved into the living room. Sitting back in the recliner, cycling through the three channels for something to watch, I realized that before I met Victoria, I'd just about run out of fantasies. For years, I'd always had one close at hand, especially at night to fill the hours when I couldn't sleep. As a child I was just as happy to lie there, imagining my future—either delighting God and my mother with a saint's death, or playing big league ball before an adoring world. I never really worked to attain either. In those days, it was as if I expected to get what I wanted simply because I was me.

Still, fantasies never did anything for me unless they seemed possible. In adolescence, nothing was possible right away, but everything was possible someday. And my dreams fought against my buck teeth and my gawky shyness and slipped out into the daytime to hasten that someday. I might have had a face that only Clearasil could love, but when my braces weren't stuck together with rubber bands, I was still capable of hints and innuendoes to my friends, of slips revealing mysterious assignations and fabulous unseen dates. And there were evenings spent roaming the streets alone, while those friends—some cuter, some more athletic, some tougher than me—were supposed to wonder who I was with. If I could get the reputation I wanted, I was sure the reputation would eventually create the reality.

When I finally got a real girl—or, more accurately, she got me—I let my friends catch me with her, but I did hide her existence from my father. Though I knew he would approve, I also knew his kidding would blow it all out of proportion in the face of the ever-present prospect she might disappear. Even worse, that kidding would reveal to her how little her prize beau was actually sought after. And as my Cousin Denise always said, "Nobody wants somebody nobody wants." Besides, my ego was too fragile to handle being a novice. It was easier playing a stud.

A beer commercial on the TV reminded me I'd finished the last beer in the house, which naturally made me want another. Unfortunately, no matter how thoroughly I searched the refrigerator, no beer appeared. Actually, I'd been lucky to have three. O'Ryan had forgotten to take the beer I'd promised him. He'd also somehow managed to forget his groceries—which, strangely, turned out to include a six pack of beer—leaving them on the kitchen counter. I considered taking them over to him and stopping in to see Maria—just for an hour or so for a little company. Victoria might be home when I returned. But when I looked out the window, their place was completely dark.

By 11:45, I was exhausted, and I decided if Victoria was out that late she was most likely on another date. And actually, it was with some relief that I headed up for bed around midnight.

Halfway up the stairs though, I remembered that morning and images of Victoria started percolating once again in my head. Victoria, her flesh warm, her hand dropping casually but accurately upon my dick. Victoria aggressive, passionate and demanding, undressing me and pulling me on top of her. By the time I got to my room, I was wide awake and fully aroused. I considered masturbating—something I did very seldom anymore. Instead, I brushed my teeth, climbed into bed and stared at the ceiling for a while.

The light in the bathroom came on. Immediately, the water was turned on in the tub. Loudly.

"Victoria?" I hadn't heard her come in.

Victoria appeared and bent over the tub. Her short red skirt rode up in the back, exposing, first, nylon clad legs, and then a pale blue swatch of her panties. Straightening, she reached up the skirt to the waist band of her panty hose. I nearly called out again to warn her I was there and awake—but I didn't. For a moment her hands rested there on her hips—her skirt bunched up around them. Seeming to catch a glimpse of herself in the full-length mirror at the end of the bathroom, she raised the skirt even farther, holding it at her waist, twisting herself this way and that, examining her legs—theatrically sensuous in nylons and high heels.

Slowly, she flexed and relaxed the backs of her legs and the muscles in her butt. Then even more slowly, she began to massage them. Her butt was small, scarcely the kind I'd always liked, but just then—small and round, and straining against the glaze of the nylons—I liked it a lot. I could hardly have liked it more.

The skirt dropped to the floor. She kicked off the heels then rolled off the panty hose, somehow without removing her panties, which I now realized were transparent. Gracefully, almost dramatically, she turned. Her short white blouse reached only to her waist; her dark blonde pubic hair looked more exposed than if she were naked.

Though I was sure my whole bed was in shadow, I closed my eyes a bit as she stepped forward toward the door to my room—I could still see her thighs working. I tried to keep my breathing natural. Instead of shutting the door, she stood in the doorway, the light behind her making her body a dark outline, slowly unbuttoning her blouse, deep in thought. The blouse came off. A shadow figure, she reached to the side to hang it on the back of the door, unclasped her bra from the front and draped it over the blouse distractedly before stepping out of her panties.

I held myself perfectly still, taking large breaths through an open mouth, but trying to do it silently. I wondered if she'd momentarily forgotten I was even living there. But either remembering or from force of habit, when she turned—briefly illuminating one long-nippled breast—she gave the door a gentle tug, pulling it shut behind her.

Only it didn't catch. And with agonizing slowness, it began to swing open again, exposing a section of the tub and the blue wall behind it. Just out of sight, Victoria was re-adjusting the water. I shifted to the side of my bed, even stretching out beyond the edge. A naked leg came into view, propped up on the tub rim. The leg disappeared, and in its place an arm braced itself against the wall. I could almost see the shoulder and the torso behind it. Then the arm was gone, and the leg returned, more of it exposed—all of it exposed. She might have been a collection of beautiful body parts stuck into my line of sight the way Saturday Matinee cowboys stuck up their hats above a covering wall to see if anyone would shoot at them.

Despite the white noise roar of the water into the tub, the creak of the springs as I left the bed halted me in my tracks. Suddenly no flesh was in sight and the water was turned down. Below my shirt, my erection stuck out in front of me. I inched forward—heart thumping—so inflamed that it was all I could do to remind myself not to step into the patch of light from the bathroom which reached all the way to the wall. I was at its edge when I saw her again, back to me, the crack of her butt disappearing behind the wall of the tub. Her body continued downward, then stopped. Between her arms and back, the swell of one breast was visible in the steam that rose from the water. Gently her fingers began to tantalize and caress it. Did I hear a quiet, velvet moan? Glistening with beads of water from the steam, her skin looked soft and moist. She sank into the tub, sliding her body backwards so I had to step back myself to keep her in view. Then she slid forward again. Arms hooked over the side, her legs came up and locked themselves together behind the faucets, as if behind a lover. Her lips parted as she eased her vagina beneath the massage of the water.

I don't know if I heard the yelling first or the frantic pounding on the front door. Startled, Victoria shut off the water and—with a voice that held more concern, more irritation, and far more scorn than it did passion—she looked straight at me and said, "Don't you think you better see who that is, Steve?"

CHAPTER 21

I'm not sure how long it took me to react. But I stood dumbfounded, staring at Victoria in the tub until the banging and the accompanying cries finally tore my attention from what had just happened and gave me something to do. Slipping on my pants over my rapidly dwindling erection and turning on every light I passed, I made my way to the front of the church. The living room clock read 1:05. Nice things seldom come pounding on the door at that hour. It made me wish Humpert was there with me instead of Victoria.

"Steve, open up! Hurry!" It was Maria. I threw open the door. Seeing her frantic expression and the way she checked back over her shoulder toward her house, I immediately pulled her in and locked the door behind her. Though barefoot, wearing only a dark tee shirt and those baggy white panties of hers, she was too agitated to be cold. I was carrying a hammer which I didn't remember picking up.

"What's all the commotion?" called Victoria from across the room behind us, her bathrobe wrapped around her.

"Please, Steve, quickly," Maria pleaded. "Call the police. He's still in there."

"Who are you?" Victoria demanded, suspiciously.

"She lives at O'Ryan's place—in the back."

"Since when?"

213

"Please," Maria cried. "He's still in there. A big dude, really big. He tried to force his way into my room—through the connecting door from my uncle's place. Where's your phone?"

Once again, I wasn't that anxious for the police to be called, but it was Victoria who spoke first. "Are you sure you weren't having a nightmare?"

"What!?!" Maria cried incredulously.

"Maybe your uncle has a guest," suggested Victoria.

"Maybe Cranick, his 'nephew,' *has* come back," I tried. "After all, that was going to be his room originally. Maybe he didn't know you were in there."

"This guy saw me. He was *forcing* his way in. The bed is in front of the door." Maria paused, then, with desperate patience, explained from the beginning, "I woke up. I heard furniture being moved around. And the TV was off. I called out and when I got no answer I cracked the connecting door open an inch or two. That's when he came after me. *Please*, where is the phone?"

"Maybe you should check it out first, Steve, before we phone the police," Victoria said, casting me a look heavy with significance. I had a hard time holding her gaze—but because of what had just happened upstairs, not because of what she may have guessed about my recent past.

"We've got to call them," insisted Maria. "And now!"

"Shut up, you silly female," snapped Victoria.

"Please, Maria," I said, putting my hand on her shoulder, unconsciously invoking our intimacy. "Not just yet. Let me check it out."

Though I had no great appetite for confronting oversized burglars who push around large pieces of furniture in the dead of night, I had less appetite for the police. Besides, burglars and home invaders usually don't stick around after someone's run off screaming to the neighbors.

All the lights were on at O'Ryan's. As usual the front door was unlocked. And as usual, the place was in shambles, though Maria seemed to have made a dent in the garbage content, and across the room, the stack of dishes by the sink was just beginning to rebuild. I surveyed the scene carefully. I'd called to O'Ryan loudly several times as I'd come down the old road to the house. The last thing I wanted to do was trap the intruder inside. I called out to O'Ryan again before moving away from the front door into the interior of the house. A couple of chairs and a lamp or two were overturned, but that was barely noticeable among the clutter.

Maria and Victoria arrived behind me, startling me visibly. Victoria offered me a flashlight and a look that might well have been contempt.

"No thanks," I said. The place was lit up like Yankee Stadium, and I was still carrying the hammer. "There doesn't seem to be anybody here. Where's O'Ryan?" The door to Maria's apartment gaped open four or five inches, but the bed on the other side hadn't been moved far. The only other rooms—a bath and a small bedroom—were almost fully visible.

"Must be a kidnapping," said Victoria, sarcastically. "That's what he gets for flaunting his wealth like this."

In O'Ryan's bedroom, the bed was unmade—totally unmade. All the bedding lay in a nest-like pile on top of the bed. Among the "collectibles" beside the bed were volumes three and seventeen of an encyclopedia that originally sold in supermarkets, a 1965 Almanac, a box of costume jewelry, and a warped copy of "After Bathing at Baxter's" by the Jefferson Airplane. No one was in the closet. In a display of paranoia, I even checked quickly under the bed, bracing myself on a wobbly night table and knocking off a bottle of sleeping pills and almost toppling a plaster of Paris bust of Andrew Jackson and a porcelain vase.

"Maybe it was a gang of international trash thieves," I said as I left the bedroom, regretting it when I saw the concern on Maria's face. *Where was O'Ryan?*

Then for the second time in the last fifteen minutes, I found myself peering into a bathroom through a half-opened door. Only this time the door opened inward instead of outward, and when I pushed, something was jamming it. Knowing what it might be, I felt a rush of adrenalin. My hand was unsteady on the knob. But I was nonetheless stunned when I slid my way around the door and found O'Ryan crammed into the corner behind it, his head battered and at an unnatural angle, dried blood mixed with his overly black hair. A single cockroach wended its way across his lips.

When I left the bathroom and put my arm around Maria—to keep her from entering and perhaps to steady myself as well—she knew immediately what I'd seen. I led her away from the bathroom. At the kitchen sink, she splashed water on her face, and I did the same. Through force of habit or something, I began washing my hands, though I hadn't really touched anything. When I realized what I was doing, I stopped.

"My God," Victoria said, emerging from the bathroom and coming up behind us.

"I'm going to call the police," Maria said as if we might try to talk her out of it even now. "I'll have to use your phone."

"Of course," I said, cold drops of water running down my neck onto my chest. The discomfort helped. "But I can't be here when they arrive, Maria. I don't even exist. You and Victoria found the body. All right?"

Maria nodded without saying anything.

Just then, I had a quick impression of movement outside the window in front of us, then light. A figure was seated in the rocking chair frame I'd brought over the day before, illuminated by a small flicker of flames around him. I had just enough time to register the bulky, red, fur-collared coat; the stubbly beard; the uneven clumps of hair. The staring eyes boring into me. Then, with an explosive *whoosh,* the flames engulfed him completely.

"That's him," cried Maria softly.

The smell of burned flesh was already filling the air as I turned to Victoria. Her mouth gaped open—her eyes wide, in shock and in fear.

She'd recognized him, too. The man I'd killed out on the highway Sunday night—the man I thought I'd killed—was burning to death in front of our eyes.

I dashed outside looking for a hose or some way to deal with what was now a fireball. Slowly, one of his hands dropped to the side, as if surrendering. The light from the blaze lit up the old oil tanker ten yards behind him. There was nothing that could be done but let the fire burn out on the concrete slab.

My right forearm started to ache.

I walked back inside just as O'Ryan began to moan.

GAY OR NOT, EVEN SOCRATES WOULD HAVE WANTED VICTORIA

"There is nothing safe about sex. There never will be."
– *Norman Mailer*

CHAPTER 22

It was raining—hard. Or the world was on fire. Or maybe both. There were women there, but their identities kept shifting. The dream was incoherent even for a dream, just a jumble with a free floating sense of dread.

I awoke hot on tangled sheets. From the light, it was late morning. I'd waited up for Victoria until past dawn. I'd been concerned about O'Ryan certainly, but I also needed to know about the police investigation. Did I have to lay low? Could I safely do it here? (Could I do it anywhere else without money?) When she'd finally gotten back, Victoria wasn't up for talking, and I was still shame-faced. I'd gotten only the bare facts. O'Ryan was alive—at least he had been when he was put into the ambulance. But the paramedics said he might not even make it to the hospital. Considering the severity of the injuries to his skull, they figured that was actually a blessing. To the police, it was a murder-suicide: Maria had identified the killer. No motive. Possibly a failed robbery. That was the extent of my conversation with Victoria. Afterwards, we'd both fallen into our respective beds.

Now I remembered my forearm and took a look. The ache that had started last night—after I watched the guy I thought I'd killed actually die—had turned into a mild stinging, then gradually disappeared. No face had appeared, and my arm was still clear.

"Morning, Arnold," called Humpert, appearing in the bathroom doorway wearing only a towel. Had he entered the bathroom from Victoria's room? "How's the little man?"

"Great. Absolutely superb," I said sarcastically.

Several dark bruises stood out against his doughy white skin.

Was he bald? That's what Maria had asked the night before about the burned man—just before O'Ryan had moaned. "I thought he was bald when I saw him earlier," she'd said.

"I understand I missed quite a barbeque last night," Humpert said now.

Humpert was bald and he was big. I remembered his room and all those pictures of little girls. Who knew what he might be capable of?

"When did you arrive?" I asked casually.

"Flew down from San Francisco on the early flight this morning." A flapping gesture sent the flesh under his arms quivering like the buttocks of an elderly stripper.

"Your practice is in San Francisco?"

"Practice? Victoria is my practice. I'm her *personal* lawyer," he said with pride. "Oh well, time to get clean. I usually use this bathroom. The old fixtures in the one by my room aren't what they used to be. And who knows how many generations of whores scrubbed off who-knows-what in that tub. You don't mind, do you Arnold?"

"Can the Arnold crap, Humbug," I said irritably. Even if Arnold hadn't been intended as ridicule—which it was—nicknames to me were like being touched familiarly. I didn't want someone I disliked doing it.

"Arnold and Humbug," he mused with a sigh that actually sounded genuine. "Quite a pair. Well, we better get used to each other; I'm back for the duration."

How wonderful. "Did you settle your case?" So I could get some money.

"Sorry again. I never discuss my client's business with her hired help. If you'll excuse me, bathing is *supposed to be* a private business."

He shut the door before I could reply, which was just as well. I was always fresh out of retorts around him. My face felt hot, though I hadn't blushed in years, and I wondered if there was any chance that last remark hadn't been as pointed as it sounded.

Victoria was downstairs on the couch watching the tube, the Sunday paper scattered around her. Between sips of coffee, she worried one corner of her lower lip with her teeth. Though she looked troubled, even wounded, the sunlight lit her hair in an almost triumphant halo, and her eyes sparkled as blue and bright as a Technicolor sky. Shaken, she was more beautiful than ever, possibly because the vulnerability was so obviously temporary—a momentary breach in her self-assurance through which I might crawl.

And sure enough, as I approached she stretched out an arm to me and pulled me down to her—a quiet hug, a kiss on the cheek—an expression of what we'd been through the night before.

I was still uncomfortable because of the bathroom scene, but she'd evidently chosen to forget it. And the flip side to my embarrassment was that she'd known I was watching her—for how long?—and had done nothing about it until Maria had banged on the door.

I sat down beside her on the couch and pretended to watch TV for a while. Victoria sank back into her thoughts. She raised her thumb to her mouth as if to bite the nail, then stopped, clasped her hands in front of her face and rested her index fingers on her lips.

"That *was* the guy from the freeway—the one who attacked you?" I said finally.

She gazed at me, lips pursed as if considering the question, before nodding. "He must have been crazy."

"At least I know I didn't kill him."

"He's dead *now*. I guess neither one of us is too good at recognizing death."

"I feel terrible about O'Ryan. If I'd have called an ambulance immediately…"

"It was only a couple of minutes. Doesn't sound like it would have made the slightest difference."

"When you were talking to the police…" I began, "did you…?"

"I never mentioned the other night. Or you. You aren't a murderer yourself, are you?"

"Cocaine. Tried one big deal and it fell through; I'm really more inept than criminal."

"It can get pretty rough, playing with the big boys."

"It was supposed to be a sure thing. A friend had been dealing small quantities for a while. He met two guys—at *his* connection's house—and later he sold them a gram. They turned into regular customers, and after a bit they wanted to make a big score—money was no object. So, my friend and I pooled our resources and sold it to them. The next week they wanted even more—much more. Dell and I scraped together every cent we could." I shook my head. Beyond my meager savings, I'd hocked my stereo, my tape recorder and my keyboard.

"And?" she prompted.

"And… we got the drugs, only when they came to pick them up, they came with the entire South Bend police department—including the guy who'd been selling it to Dell in the first place."

"Harvard, huh?"

"It wasn't the brightest thing I've ever done."

"How did you get away?"

"Fortunately, they weren't much brighter than we were. Dell and I had just bought this beautiful new digital scale and we'd given his old one to a lady a couple of doors down the street. Only just before the buyers were supposed to arrive, the new scale broke down. I walked over to borrow the old one back. While I was there I laid out a line or two to thank her."

"And she was a looker of course."

"Why do you say that?"

"That's why your friend gave her his old scale. That's the way it works."

I shrugged but Bea was a good-looking woman, no doubt about that. "Anyway, when I left her place to head back, Dell's house was already surrounded by cops with walkie-talkies and drawn guns."

"And you ran?"

"I ducked back in the woman's house, quickly called Dell to warn him, and headed back outside—leaving the scale of course. There were three police cars right in front of Dell's house. My car was directly across the street. Then the pickup truck parked just in front of my car pulled out and drove off. The cops didn't react at all. They were completely focused on Dell's place. So as calmly as I could, I crossed the street and—while the police were smashing down Dell's door and charging inside—I walked over to my car, jumped in and just pulled away. Then I just kept on driving."

"What happened to your friend?"

"Don't know. Haven't been able to find a South Bend paper. A couple of days out, I called some mutual friends, but as soon as they recognized my voice they got paranoid—told me I had the wrong number and hung up."

"So how much were you trying to make?"

"Aah, let's see, if we'd have pulled it off we'd have made about $15,000." Maxed out, we'd have made $9,559.00.

"Oh." A very deflating *oh*.

"It's a seventeen-to-twenty-five-year sentence in Indiana. Even small-time coke dealers have been getting fifteen to twenty years." Trying to give the crime stature, I'd made it sound more foolish—so much risk for so little. We were past the era when being a fugitive was in itself romantic.

The phone rang. Victoria picked it up, and I picked up a section of the paper. The newspaper wanted me to know there were twelve peachy ways to pamper my peonies—and they didn't even have Zandie's secret recipe for plant growth.

Victoria told someone that, "in that case," she'd have Humpert take a load of her lesser treasures down to L.A. that afternoon for possible sale. Good.

After she left the room to find Humpert, I dug through the rest of the Sunday paper. As current as the news section was, it could have been printed on Wednesday.

I was giving La Perdita some milk when Victoria came back downstairs, wearing a pair of yellow shorts and a matching top. Though it was still only March, the weather had suddenly turned hot and sunny enough for the beach.

"I'm on my way to the store," she said. "Anything you need?"

"As a matter of fact, ah, I could use a couple of things. But I'm out of money."

"Really?" she sounded surprised.

"Unfortunately." I hated asking people for money. "Anyway, if you could let me have some of that advance we were talking about... Well, I'd definitely appreciate it."

"Of course," she said, touching my arm. "You should have said something."

"Well, it wasn't all that critical. I only just ran out. And it's not that I need anything right this minute, but..."

"Of course. Be sure to tell me when you need money. I'm going to need most of my cash for groceries and all, but..." She dug out a bill from a purse inside her pocketbook and handed it to me—a ten. "If I can I'll give you some more when I get back from the store. And I'll get you the rest of your advance as soon as possible. In the meantime, I'll try to keep the pantry stocked with everything you need. All right? I'll see you later."

For the next couple of hours, I lazed around the house. Even if it hadn't been Sunday, I wasn't up for doing any work. Especially since the next job was opening the casket I'd uncovered the day before. I did get a hammer and remove the doll from the kitchen wall. Inside the pink pouch nailed to its stomach was a small brass bull, a jagged piece of blue glass, and several slips of paper covered with indecipherable hen scratching.

I thought about Humpert. Before leaving O'Ryan's the night before, I'd wiped my fingerprints off as many surfaces as possible. What others might I have removed in the process? And no one had informed the police that the man who'd gone up in flames had definitely not been bald like the man Maria had seen in the house.

After a while, I went for a drive. I ended up in downtown San Cristobal, where surprisingly enough the Hare Affair—pink rabbit and all—was open for business. Their haircuts were still half price and on impulse I went in. A young woman in bright red lipstick and pleated shorts was polite and chatty and still gave me the feeling that I always get in such places—that I didn't belong there. I didn't. The eight dollars for styling and blow dry—no wash—left me two bucks for the tip, which left me nothing. What the hell—I had all the food and drink I needed at Victoria's, and she'd promised me more money. I left the Hair Affair with a new style: a shorter haircut, made up of individual locks of hair which could go anyway they wanted without spoiling the neat yet casual effect. By the time I got home, at least two of them already looked like cowlicks.

No sooner did I get back than Humpert pulled up to the front door of the church in a black Lincoln with a bright red Avis logo on the license plate holder. Humpert himself looked like last month's guacamole. I wondered if his stomach was bothering him. I helped him maneuver a number of large oil paintings into the trunk. Fortunately, we wrapped them in blankets first. Even trying to be careful, Humpert banged them around clumsily, scraping two of the frames badly.

With Victoria's sound system working again, Humpert somehow found a radio station that played Gregorian chant. Though distracted and subdued, he was much more civil than he'd been earlier, almost friendly, pensively humming along with the music. He spoke of Victoria, with a solemn deference that reminded me of my mother discussing the Pope.

"Men love her," he said, picking a mint out of the bowl by the telephone, then actually offering the bowl to me. "But women hate her because she's so beautiful."

The final oil painting was a powerful portrait of Victoria as a brunette. We slid it into the back seat along with a couple of American Van Lines boxes of china which had never been unpacked.

"Victoria insists," Humpert said, "that her hair grows faster since she started taking vitamins. Now she has to get it touched up every month, whereas before it seemed as if it was staying blonde almost by itself. Do you think that's possible? For vitamins to make hair grow?"

Since he was bald and I was getting there, at first I thought he was trying to be funny. When I realized he was serious, I told him vitamins might be worth a try, just as if it were understood that beauty secrets were a specialty of mine.

CHAPTER 23

One of the two TV stations that came in clearly was an independent that relied heavily on old movies. As I switched it on, Sean Connery was entering his hotel room to find a gorgeous woman he'd never met waiting naked in his bed.

Great, a movie I could really relate to.

Humpert was banging around in the kitchen. Tonight had to be the night with Victoria. I'd been brooding over it all afternoon, trying to put myself in Victoria's place. Actually, I'd already waited too long; last night in the bathtub she'd known I was watching her, *wanting her*. I'd have to invent some excuse for not having had the guts to do anything about it for all this time. It was going to be tough to play the Sean Connery role—the experienced man of the world—but Victoria wasn't likely to have anything to do with an adult male who acted like a superannuated adolescent, more adept at leering and drooling than making love to an extraordinary woman like her. Maybe I could say I'd been afraid of getting involved. And last night I had only just decided I could no longer resist her when Maria had arrived, banging on the door.

Appropriately enough, just then the doorbell rang at the back door. A moment later, it rang again.

"Somebody's at the door," Humpert cried from the kitchen, within a few feet of the back door.

I said nothing.

"It must be for you," Humpert called, when the bell rang for a third time.

"Well, could you get it?"

"I'm not *your* servant!" he shouted, lumbering up the back stairs.

It was Maria, and she'd already started back down the porch steps by the time I got to the door. Sport that I am, I invited her into the kitchen and offered her a chair. Wearing a print dress and just the faintest touch of lipstick, she could have used some sleep, but she seemed to be in control.

"Would you like something to drink?" I asked.

"No, I don't think so."

"How's your uncle?"

"Alive. Sort of. For now. Minimal brain function. His face is all misshapen. And there's something wrong with his spine; he's got some kind of a swelling on his back, like a hump. At first, this intern tried to tell me it was congenital—as if maybe I simply hadn't noticed that my uncle was a hunchback. Now they think it's an accumulation of fluid that may be putting pressure on the spinal column and paralyzing his body—though I don't suppose it matters with his brain gone."

She put her elbows on the table and started massaging her temples.

"I'm sorry to hear that. I really liked...really *like* your uncle. And I'm sorry about last night. About your uncle—and about not being able to stay."

She waved it off.

"You've been doing a great job with him," I went on. "The last couple of times I talked with him he was sharper than I was. I'm sure just having you around meant a lot to him."

"He was off and on. Our last night together—last night I guess, it's hard to believe it was just last night—he'd bought me a present, a gorgeous reproduction of "The Potato Eaters." But later he forgot who

I was again. He got so gallant. I think he thought he was on a date." She sniffed the air. "Is that your dinner on the stove?"

"No, one of Victoria's friends is cooking up a batch of flamingo feces."

She got up and checked the pot. Her eyes were moist. "Menudo," she said. "With the delicate and lively odor of wet sheep."

I kissed my fingertips like a French chef. No wonder Humpert had problems with his stomach.

Maria smiled. "Breathe through your mouth." She looked upward at nothing in particular, as if she was working out what to say next. Then, "Al arrived in Vantana today. That's what—forty-five miles down the coast?"

"Something like that."

"I started cooking a pot roast, thinking I'd make dinner for him and get my mind off last night. But then I called to invite him—and of course I told him what'd happened. He was just trying to be protective, but he insisted so strongly that I come down and spend the night with him at the Holiday Inn that I realized I wasn't up for dealing with him at all. Not yet. So, I never even mentioned dinner. Anyway, now I've got this half-cooked roast. One of the problems with no longer being a vegetarian is that meat doesn't keep as well as soy burgers. I was wondering…you know…if you'd like to come over tonight. I've got wine. And chocolate cake…"

The fingers sticking out of the end of her cast were fumbling with a saltshaker.

"You two *are* going to be getting back together again?" I asked, hoping to ease myself out of this and cause her as little pain as possible. I had plans for tonight.

"No. I don't think so."

"I'm sure you will," I said, ignoring her tone and trying to be friendly. Just friendly.

"I don't want that. Not right now." She put down the saltshaker and pinned me down with her eyes. Simply and without melodrama, she said, "I don't need *any* big serious relationships just now. But I could use a friend. And maybe a little extra-friendly cuddling once in a while."

I let that go. Instead, I said, "That guy in the fire—that was definitely the man who tried to break into your room?"

"Who else would it be?"

"No one, of course. But you did say at first that the man who went after you was bald."

"I thought so. But it was just a quick impression; I didn't get much of a look at the guy. The police—deputy sheriffs actually—weren't concerned. After the fire, it was all they could do to determine his sex, never mind his hair line, but the theory is that my first impression was correct—that he *was* bald—but with the shadows from the fire and his head back, it just looked like he had hair."

"Possible, I suppose." *Wrong.* I'd gotten a good look before the flames completely engulfed him—not to mention when he was trying to strangle me up close and personal that night on the roadside. He wasn't bald, but unless I was prepared to go to the authorities there was no point in saying so.

"It wasn't like on Columbo or Quincy or some show on TV," Maria said. "The cops seemed to be almost enjoying themselves—and nobody was snooping around suspiciously, examining microscopic clues. Besides, who cares if the guy was bald or not? It was either the murderer in the fire or somebody who'd borrowed his coat. It would be hard to mistake *that.* Of course, there *could* have been two or three people running around the place wearing the same coat." She chuckled sadly. "Maybe it was a uniform?"

"The bad taste gang rides again." I wasn't going to mention her use of the word, "murderer." I suppose emotionally, she was preparing for her uncle's death.

"Ugly, maybe, but that coat was expensive."

I let it drop. Her identification was probably correct. Coats could be exchanged, but if that guy wasn't the one who'd broken in and assaulted O'Ryan, why did he pick then and there to set himself on fire? Then again, why did he do that even if he was guilty? Shame? Remorse?

"At any rate," she said, "I could use a nice cheery meal tonight. How about you?"

"Definitely." I'd been hoping I could slide off the subject. "Unfortunately, The Boss has already made plans for a big meal this evening."

"Menudo!?!"

"That's just for her friend Humpert. She's out shopping now—Sunday dinner and all. So let me take a rain check."

I asked a few questions about her husband, though I already knew most of the story. Their problems went back a long way. Little things, like managing the apartment building, which interfered with her work, while he studied away from home in the school library. Bigger things. The two years they'd lived together before marriage had soured his mother on Maria. And Al had gotten it into his head that she'd lost the baby they'd wanted because of an abortion she'd had before she'd met him.

The final blow up on the trip had been about nothing: why he'd sold her stereo at their moving sale but spared his color TV. But by midnight he and his color TV were back in East Lansing.

I wasn't completely listening to what Maria was saying. I felt like I'd done something wrong, though there was certainly nothing wrong in choosing which of two possible relationships to go with—and with Victoria it was now or never. Maybe it was just because of what Maria had been through, and because I was the closest thing she had to a friend out there. Or because I'd lied, if harmlessly, to spare her feelings—or my own. Or maybe it was because I actually liked Maria more than Victoria;

I certainly felt more comfortable with her, and we always had much more to talk about.

I ran through the broken syllogism in my head:

My affection for Maria was greater than my affection for Victoria.

My desire to fuck Victoria was greater than my desire to fuck Maria.

Therefore, I was choosing Victoria.

Obviously.

Socrates was a man.

Men are idiots.

Therefore, Socrates would have picked Victoria too. (Gay or not.)

Quod Erat Demonstrandum.

"Why do you suppose he did it?" Maria asked abruptly.

"Probably crazy," I answered when I figured out she wasn't talking about her husband. And perhaps crazy *was* the reason: I'd finally run into a real-life homicidal maniac, right off the Six O'clock News.

"But sane enough to put an end to himself when he realized what he'd done?"

"Or so far gone we couldn't even guess what he thought he was doing."

A car rumbled down the driveway and pulled up beside the porch. A horn blew twice. It was Victoria with a Mercedes full of groceries.

"Get Humpert and get all this stuff put away," Victoria called as I approached the car.

I deposited a couple of bags on the kitchen table before yelling up the backstairs for Humpert. Before I got the name out of my mouth, the water started running into the bathtub upstairs.

"He's always taking a damn bath when you need him," Victoria complained from behind me. "You can handle it, Steve."

"He took a bath this morning."

"He takes a lot of baths."

"If he'd drop a few pounds, he wouldn't sweat so much."

"Humpert hardly sweats at all. Baths just help him relax. Besides, he cares about his appearance," she said lightly. "There are those who would do well to follow his example. Bathing's not just a spectator sport, you know."

Humpert's very line. They'd obviously discussed it. This time I *was* blushing. I could only hope my face wasn't nearly as red as it felt.

"You should talk, Steve," injected Maria, coming to my defense. "On the way out here, Victoria, it seemed like he was always in the shower. He even found a gas station with one."

She gave me a playful smile. I tried to force one in return. To cool off and relax after having sex in the back seat that day, we'd taken a shower together in a truck stop. The single stall had been outside but secluded behind the station—until a family with a little boy and two little girls had pulled around back looking for the rest rooms. *Maria* had been embarrassed that time, blushing all the way down to her navel.

"Steve never told me you two were old friends," Victoria said evenly. Turning to me, she added in the same tone, "Before last night, I didn't think you knew anyone out here at all. Not a soul. Now it turns out, not only have you got a friend living right next door who you never even mentioned, but the two of you actually drove out here together."

"I told you about Maria picking me up and giving me a ride out here."

"No. You just said you hitchhiked—you did hitchhike?"

"Of course."

"But you said you didn't know a soul in California."

"I didn't—not when I left Indiana."

"Men!" Victoria exclaimed to Maria, sitting down at the table beside her in front of the bags of groceries. "God knows what the big secret is. But what brings you over this afternoon?"

"I just dropped by to invite...you people over for dinner. But Steve tells me you're already planning a big meal."

"Me? No. I'm not planning a thing."

I picked up the two bags I'd set down on the table only moments before. "I thought you said you were going shopping for a big meal," I offered lamely, moving toward the pantry, neither of the bags big enough to hide behind.

"Are you kidding?" She looked at me strangely in a broad way that said: *she looked at him strangely.* "I wasn't planning on anything except going to bed early. Why don't you go over to Maria's... You two have fun."

Even aside from making me look like a moron, this was not what I wanted to hear from Victoria.

"You're both invited," Maria said, fiddling with a fork now, and sounding like she no longer really wanted either one of us. "But it's not going to be any big deal."

"I'd like to," said Victoria, "but I'm just too exhausted. But don't let me stop you two."

"I really think I'm going to be too tired as well, Maria," I called from the pantry. "I'm fading fast. But let me take a rain check, OK?"

"Sure. Of course."

"Well, anyway," Victoria said to her, "I'm glad we got a chance to meet, though I'm sorry about the circumstances last night. We'll get together soon, I'm sure. You're going to be living here for a while, aren't you? Or is something happening with the property now."

"I don't know. It's too soon..."

"I can't understand it," interrupted Victoria. "What possible motive could anybody have for attacking that crazy old man?"

"That crazy old man was my uncle," Maria replied tightly. "And he never harmed a soul in his entire life." It was hard to tell if she was mad at Victoria or me or both, but she was obviously mad.

"Well," said Victoria with a humorless laugh, "that would make him unique among mankind wouldn't it."

"No. I don't think it would. But then I'm sure you know a lot more about men then I do."

"For obvious reasons," Victoria said, looking Maria up and down, her expression worthy of Mozart listening to *Louie, Louie.* "Some of us don't have to pick up hitchhikers for company. At least I've known all my men by name."

"You require I.D., do you?" Maria asked, angry and flustered. "Do you take checks as well as major credit cards?"

"You little bitch!" Victoria got to her feet, her fists tight at her sides.

I stepped back into the kitchen, ready to separate them. "Hey, you two, now..."

"Victoria, I'm sorry," Maria said, her voice thickening with emotion. "I don't even know what I'm saying. The stress and the lack of sleep must be getting to me. I really am sorry."

Victoria's face relaxed. "I understand. Forget it. Hey, look at Steve. He was terrified we were gonna kill each other."

"And maybe him, too."

Everybody pretended to laugh.

"I've got to get Humpert out of that bathroom," Victoria said. "I'll get him down here yet to give you a hand, Steve. You haven't made much progress, and he knows where everything goes."

Calling for Humpert, she went up the stairs. As her voice and footsteps faded, the silence between Maria and I grew. I felt I should apologize; I wasn't sure how.

The menudo simmered. Loudly.

"I've really got to go," she said, finally. And she left without bothering to look at me.

CHAPTER 24

Humpert left for L.A. with the paintings sometime late that afternoon. Since I had no real grounds for my earlier suspicions about him, his very absence helped to alleviate them. Besides, my thoughts were occupied with Victoria—or, more accurately, Victoria and me. At dinner, which did turn out to be a big meal, with salad, baked potatoes, veal cutlets, and a very solicitous Victoria, I caught myself—like Lucy Ricardo or any other fifties situation-comedy wife—waiting for Victoria to react to my new hair style. Like Ricky Ricardo or any other fifties situation-comedy husband, Victoria never noticed. It is not necessarily a blessing to recognize your own foolishness. Neither Victoria nor I mentioned what had happened with Maria.

The beginning of the evening was a piece of deja véjà vu. Victoria sat in her chair, with a glass of wine, watching another old movie and paging through another old book. I was on the couch, sipping scotch. About 7:30, Victoria glanced up from the TV as it went into a tire commercial.

"I wish somebody would call," she said.

Unlikely—I'd taken the precaution of knocking the pantry phone off the hook.

"I thought you were tired," I said.

"Actually, I am," she said laughing. "I guess I'm just a woman who needs to have a man around her."

I wondered if I qualified. I had no idea how to interpret the signs; I'd probably have more luck sifting through the entrails of dead chickens. Running over my list of positive signals from Victoria, I'd told myself again and again that she was obviously interested. Unfortunately, I had a second list too. Although shorter, it was composed entirely of her actions in crucial situations which seemed designed to keep me away. Each rebuff had an alternate explanation. But then again, so did each enticement.

"What's that you're humming?" she asked.

"Oh, nothing." I wasn't about to tell her that it was from my half-assed attempt, in the wake of *Jesus Christ Superstar* and *Tommy* to create a rock opera based on *Hamlet*.

"It doesn't really go with the movie," she said.

"Sorry." It hadn't really gone with *Hamlet* either. Set to music, things kept turning out funny. No way in 1973 America that "Who would fardels bear?" was anything but a laugh line. So, I gave it up, missing my chance to be the man who brought the world *Hamlet, the Musical Comedy*, and leaving the field to Mel Brooks and *Springtime for Hitler*. Still, I guess my subconscious was at work again, because the lyrics to the melody I'd been humming were:

"And thus the native hue of resolution

Is sicklied o'er with the pale cast of thought..."

I thought about Victoria in the bath last night and shifted uncomfortably, glancing over at her as if she could read my thoughts. That was on both my lists, pro and con, and also in a separate category by itself. The memory of her naked was a strong inducement to act, but even more so was the desire to remove the taste of that humiliation from my mouth and to correct the impression she must have gotten of me.

On the TV, Grace Kelly asked Cary Grant whether he wanted a leg or a breast. She was serving him chicken at a picnic. And at the time that was considered a daring line. So much for sex in the fifties.

I shifted position again. I'd put on my dress pants—for lack of much else to wear—and after that big meal they were too tight. In a maneuver that would have fit right into a fifties film, I used the movement as an excuse to edge down the couch closer to Victoria's chair. Cary Grant would have done it better. I decided to let the situation take its course in the early hours and make my move around 9:30 or 10:00, if nothing had happened spontaneously or semi-spontaneously by then. Much later than that and Victoria might be off to bed, perhaps wondering what the hell was wrong with me. Nine-thirty or ten would be about right, I thought, and that took some of the immediate pressure off.

On the TV, in what I first thought was a scene from the movie, two identical blondes in bathing suits strolled by a series of leering males, as the jingle invited me to double my pleasure, double my fun—with Doublemint gum. Subtle. In innuendo at least, we'd come a long way baby from the fifties.

Victoria looked up from her book. She seemed to pay more attention to the commercials than the movie. A moment later she chuckled and said, "So, Steve, it sounds like you've been holding out on me. Are you and your friend next door close?"

"Maria? No. She just gave me a ride." I told Victoria about Maria and her husband, mentioning that he was now out in California, and concluding, "There's nothing going on between Maria and me."

"Still, it sounded to me like she might be interested in starting something."

"I know."

"I think she's nice—and fairly attractive, too."

"Uh huh. She *is* nice." But somehow "nice" here was like the blind date with the "great personality." Guiltily, I added, "She's got beautiful brown eyes... I just didn't want to give her the wrong impression. Plus, I felt like a quiet evening at home."

"Sounds good to me." Victoria glanced over to see what was happening on the TV. "It's a shame she doesn't fix herself up."

"Attracting men isn't the most important thing in Maria's life."

"A career girl?" Victoria said scornfully, adding with surprising bitterness, "Trying to find fulfillment as an assistant manager of a Woolworths or an advertising copywriter or some other moronic job that a man would at least have the good sense to despise."

"Maria's an artist. She makes her living from her paintings."

"I was chunky myself when I was younger—very young. Everybody can't be beautiful. But she could at least make the best of her appearance. Then she might be able to get men interested in her without having to be so aggressive."

"I like aggressive women," I said, more a potential hint than a defense of Maria. "Don't you think women should be as free to make their desires known as men?"

"A woman should never have to chase any man. At least, not any man worth having."

Who and what were we talking about here anyway?

"You don't believe in equality for women?" I asked, trying to generalize the conversation.

"I don't believe in equality for anybody," she said heatedly. "Who in this world is equal to anybody else? I'm not looking for a man who is my equal; I'm looking for a man who's better than I am. Who is stronger, and more intelligent. Someone I can belong to."

What are you, a cocker spaniel? is what I'd actually said the last time I'd heard that particular line of sexist nonsense, probably ten years earlier. But why was she giving me her requirements in a male? To challenge me to match up to them? Or to show me how I didn't? At any rate, I couldn't just jump on her right after that speech, and especially not after we settled on opposite sides of a gaping silence. I was hardly Raymond Fairchild or Terry Davis. Hell, I wasn't even Stephen Witowski—not really.

Was the very idea of me coming on to her ridiculous? I wasn't looking to get laughed at, to be humiliated. And I did have to live with this woman, at least for a while.

I got up a couple of times over the next hour or so, once to start the fire, once for another scotch. About nine o'clock, I went to the kitchen to refill her wine, and I noticed I was tapping my teeth together nervously. Returning, I stood by her chair, self-consciously, making very small talk about remodeling the house, until I heard myself babbling about how weird it was that Zandie collected the corpses of his old lovers. Since that came out sounding much more gory than romantic, and since I was getting nothing at all from her I saw as encouragement, I backed off.

By 9:45, I was grinding my teeth, not tapping them. Victoria was back absorbed in her book, flicking her tongue over her lips—not sensually, but rapidly—her own nervous mannerism. The TV was showing Bob Newhart's current situation comedy: wise wife, neurotic Bob, and a cast of assorted wackos. Victoria and I had been silent for the last half hour.

At three minutes till ten, I told myself I'd make my move by 10:30. I wished she'd break out the dope or at least that she'd been drinking more. A program came on about a Southern California detective with a high-end sports car and an even more expensive wardrobe of casual clothes. He was six foot four, blond, with a perfect body and better teeth, and nothing of mine looked as good as anything of his. Victoria pronounced him cute, then watched the show intently. If she'd ever wanted me to make a move on her, she may well have changed her mind by this point. I certainly would have if I were her. During the mid-show station break at 10:30, I kept telling myself, "now," only nothing happened. After that, I figured I'd better wait until the program was over. My opinion of myself was not exactly growing by leaps and bounds.

If only I could touch her naturally, things could flow from there, but the three feet between her arm rest and mine was a chasm with no easy bridge. While I was racking my brains for a natural lead-in, the detective on the damn TV threw the beautiful young client against a wall, shielding her with his body as bullets from a speeding car danced around them. The sound of the gunfire had hardly died down before they were clinging to each other passionately. Equally predictably, the scene dissolved into a commercial.

"Good spot for an ad for bullet-proof condoms," I tried.

"What?"

"Nothing. Just being silly."

I leaned back on the couch, feigning relaxation like a third grader in a dentist's chair.

How could I reach Victoria without the benefit of machine-gunning thugs? Once again, she had her wine glass poised in front of her. The indications were not "go."

Maybe she's having her period tonight, I thought, and mentally groaned because I'd instantly reminded myself of Period Pete Pretzger. Pete had earned the nickname our freshman year. A nineteen-year-old virgin who'd gone to Catholic schools his whole life, he was uncomfortable with women, but beyond desperate to lose his virginity. His cousin went to Radcliffe and kept fixing him up with blind dates. He'd leave the dorm with high hopes and come back dejected—and trying to rationalize what had happened, more to himself than to anyone else. He must have used the "having her period" excuse once too often, because at one point a movie reviewer in the student newspaper, *The Harvard Crimson,* started ranking violent movies like *The Wild Bunch* on the Pretzger scale, so named because "more blood has apparently been lost by women on dates with Period Pete Pretzger than during the entire Franco Prussian War."

On the TV, Detective Beefcake saved the woman's missing brother from the mob and the show ended. I was paralyzed. Just to move, I got up and jammed a superfluous log on the fire, heading straight toward Victoria on my way back.

Damn, she was beautiful; her features were so precise, so delicate.

"I'm gonna get some water—want some water?" I asked, ignoring the nearly full glass of wine in front of her. I barely knew what I was saying.

I paced around the kitchen, telling myself, "tonight, tonight," and searching for composure. My face was hot, my heartbeat echoed in my chest.

What is going on here? I wondered. *Who am I?*

Back in the living room, the news came on. Last I'd heard, Pete Pretzger—fucking Period Pete Pretzger—had become a corporate raider and was dating the love interest from the last Superman movie.

The kitchen door opened. Victoria tossed me a perfunctory, "Night, Steve," and headed up the back stairs.

By the time she was out of sight, I was furious with myself. All the times she'd ever touched me or smiled flirtatiously rushed into my head. Yesterday, she'd jumped into my bed, "accidentally" going for my cock more than once. And last night...last night. That strip-tease through the open bathroom door.

Tomorrow Humpert would be back and even if he wasn't, with all her dates and phone calls, who knew when I'd ever get the chance again? At that moment, she was everything I'd ever wanted and never had the courage to truly pursue.

Why was I so terrified?

I honestly didn't understand it. I paced the kitchen until my inability to even try to get something going with her became more depressing and discouraging than the possibility of being rejected. *What was one rejection more or less?* Suddenly I was charging across the room and then climbing the stairs—on my way to her, blocking out all consideration of the consequences.

"Feel like making love," I whispered, testing the words. Or maybe I should walk up to her bed and ask, "Mind if I join you?" as casually as possible—a man of the world—as if to say, if she was in the mood, it would be fine, but no big deal either way. A good safe approach. It never worked, but it was safe.

I knocked the moment I reached her door, afraid if I hesitated I'd never do it.

"Yes." Not: *Come in.*

"It's just me." Who else? I paused but got only silence. "Can I come in?... I want to talk to you."

"What about?"

"It's no big deal," I said, committed now, opening the door as I was speaking.

I'd expected she'd already be in bed with the lights out, so I could cross the room, sit on the bed and touch her gently, all under the cover of darkness. But the light was on, and she was standing in front of me, in bra and bikini panties—two sheer pink nothings—her hair disheveled from removing her blouse over her head. She just stood there, one hand on her outthrust hip—as if she were alone—the expression on her face neutral, maybe even bored. And I knew I had no chance. Had I always known it?

"It's just that I was thinking," my fucking voice actually quivered. A pounding in my ears drowned out my thoughts. I crossed to her on automatic pilot, my gait was stiff and disjointed.

I took her bare arm, pulling her toward me. Behind her, the eight-by-ten photo of herself on the bureau mirror seemed ready to snicker. She came to me—musky with perfume—heavy with reticence. When my lips went to hers, hers barely moved. My arms closed around her back. I was getting hard already. My tongue tried to enter her mouth but ended up running across her cheek as she twisted her head.

She gave a small, off-hand laugh. The taste of her make-up soured my mouth. The pink sheets had already been turned down on the waterbed—the one with the mirror in the ceiling.

"Listen, I'm not into this, all right," she said redundantly, evenly, firmly. Not a question, but an embarrassing dismissal—prom queen to class geek. She clucked me under the chin so sharply I wondered if the fingernail drew blood.

"All right," I said.

At one time, I might have pressed her for a reason before departing. Now I just wanted to get out of there before she gave me one. I could have handled a standard, "I'm involved with someone else," or a half-hearted, "I'm not into sex right now," or even, "I just don't feel it with you." But what I was afraid I might be hearing was just exactly how ludicrous she thought the idea of sex between us was.

Stumbling down the hall into my room, I locked the door behind me and dropped onto the bed.

"Oh shit." The entire evening returned to me in gradually increasing waves of humiliation. And at its end, Victoria had stood there—her nipples and her pubic hair clearly visible through her sheer pink underwear—stood there the way she'd stand in front of a young child or another woman. Or a eunuch. Not uncomfortable or awkward—neither displaying her body, nor making any move to cover it—in no way conscious of it, or of me as a male. As if the situation, even as I approached her, was devoid of sexual overtones.

I groaned.

Forcing myself up off the bed, I closed the door to the bathroom tight. If it had a bolt, I would have locked it. She might take another bath before bed. There had been nothing non-sexual about her last night.

"Fucking cock-tease," I hissed. How could she treat me like that? I was a person, too. Had she been leading me on since I'd arrived just to get me to work for her and to keep me working?

"Fuck her." I wasn't sticking around for long, and I was damn well getting every cent that was coming to me before I left.

Fully dressed, I lay there, stewing, for thirty minutes, maybe an hour. Then down the hall, her door opened, and instantly, idiotically, I was sure she was coming to apologize or to explain. Once again, I could see myself as desirable and perhaps even desired—a man who sleeps with women, who women are open to and obliging with. It was all a misunderstanding, or maybe there was some kind of problem. She wasn't really so cold and unfeeling: *Steve, it was just that I was so tired tonight; some other time, who knows?*

I knew I couldn't have misinterpreted so many signs, couldn't have been so wrong about what was real and what wasn't. The footsteps padded right by my room and down the backstairs.

"Bitch!" I hissed.

That book I'd found in the living room—*The Witch's Hammer*—had attributed witchcraft to the power of carnal lust and declared such lust to be insatiable in women. Whoever wrote it should have seen Victoria tonight. Of course, women who wanted other men have always been seen as insatiable witches. How they're seen if they want *you* depends on who you are far more than who they are.

But nobody wanted me. Not anymore. Another song idea I'd once tried had been for a novelty number called "Cashing in My Sex Stamps." The idea being that sex stamps would be like Food Stamps that the government could issue to the old, the lame and the infirm, the failed and the extraordinarily ugly—anyone who couldn't get sex on their own. At the time, I never expected to become a sexual welfare case myself. The song hadn't worked. I could never get the proper balance between pathos and humor into the lyrics. Much like my life (he said, pathetically).

When eventually, I heard Victoria coming back up the stairs, I didn't get excited, but I did switch on the lamp beside the bed. And the radio, too, when I remembered the light probably couldn't be seen under the door.

Long after she'd returned to her room, I undressed and got ready for bed. I'd probably been grinding my teeth because a couple of them ached a bit as I brushed them. That reminded me that, to Freud, teeth falling out was a symbol of castration.

"They'll probably all be gone by morning," I muttered.

MONDAY, MARCH 29

SOME PEOPLE JUST WON'T STAY DEAD OR HOW NOT TO DEAL WITH THE SONG OF THE SIREN

"Murder is always a mistake—one should never do anything one cannot talk about after dinner."
– *Oscar Wilde*

CHAPTER 25

Once again, the crowbar slipped when I tried to wedge it between the heavy lid and the body of the sarcophagus. Once again, it scraped shrilly across the thick stone and once again I barked my knuckles.

"Shit! This is worse than that damn statue."

We were working in the crypt because Humpert "wasn't into playing in the dirt" of the outside grave and neither one of us saw much point in opening a coffin filled with multiple sets of moldering remains, none of which were likely to be Zandie. I was hoping Victoria wouldn't insist.

"Let's try it together," Humpert said, raising himself from the concrete seat on the crypt wall, and picking up another pry bar. Decked out in a snow white, army surplus jump suit, he looked like a balloon in the Macy's Thanksgiving Day Parade.

"It's suffocating in here," I said and went out into the hallway for a breath.

The air was heavy and close today, even down in the basement, and inside the crypt it felt contaminated. Now that we were really about to discover some old bones, I was acutely aware of the filth and decay, the putrefying flesh we were likely to uncover. This would be worse than Ready-Rooter, the first job I'd taken after I dropped out of journalism grad school. I'd been broke and in debt, but even after all the day labor and bottom of the barrel jobs I'd had, it had taken me only six hours of wading through the overflow of other peoples' toilets before

I finally realized why my father had busted his butt to help send me to Harvard—so I wouldn't have to be a Ready-Rooter Man. And here I was four years later doing something much worse.

"Come on Arnold, let's get going," Humpert called.

"Up yours." *Just let someone around here open their mouth about my work habits.*

I hadn't seen Victoria that morning to talk to her about when I could get my money. According to Humpert, she was out on a date at the beach—with some dude she'd picked up hitchhiking this morning, for chrissake. Gregorian chant rumbled through the crypt—Humpert singing along, his Latin entirely imaginary.

"Could you knock it off?" I asked, re-entering the tomb. At least Ready-Rooter undeniably made the world a better place in which to live—unlike grave robbing. Granted I needed the money—and I intended to get everything I was owed—but what I was really kicking myself about was that I'd gotten into this to get next to Victoria. As if this was a brilliant way to compete with those lawyers and authors and rock stars.

After we'd been at it another hour or so, Humpert seemed to tire.

"Why don't you go upstairs and get us something to munch on?" he asked. "A little salami, perhaps."

I didn't want any salami, but since his tone was, for him, pleasant, and since it was a chance to breathe a little clean air, I decided it wouldn't hurt me to get him some. And I did end up finishing off a good size piece on the way back from the kitchen.

After he ate his salami, washing it down with some coffee from his thermos, we returned to work in silence, prying at the heavy stone lid. Humpert was clumsy, though determined, and as strong as a draft horse. Finally, with a great heave, we broke the lid loose all the way around.

"My hand!" Humpert screamed. "Get it out!"

I have no idea how he managed it, but his index finger on his right hand was wedged into the crack we'd opened between the lid and the body of the sarcophagus. Though the finger didn't come out easily, when it did, it wasn't bleeding, and it didn't seem broken. It was, however, already starting to darken and swell.

Back upstairs, he washed it and iced it while I watched. I couldn't take that lid off without him. He got himself some more salami and a can of Heineken from somewhere—all I'd seen in the refrigerator was something called Ace Beer. As a defense against conversation, I picked up the paper.

The story was on the second page:

ATTACKER SETS SELF ABLAZE

The story recounted the facts in the case, adding:

> ...Jonathan O'Ryan is on life support in critical condition at Saint Elizabeth's Hospital in San Cristobal and is not expected to survive. Using a Med-Alert tag worn by the assailant, police identified him as Lyle Cranick, 37. The identification was confirmed by prints from one finger and one thumb, and by partial dental charts, though many of the teeth were missing.

Cranick! *Lyle* Cranick! O'Ryan's "nephew," Victoria's attacker. The ex-con Victoria had hired to help with the remodeling. Was it possible she hadn't recognized him either during the original attack by the highway or later at O'Ryan's? Across the table, Humpert was awkwardly cutting the salami with his left hand.

What would he look like in that bulky red coat? Maria had only a glimpse of the man forcing his way into her bedroom?
I quickly finished the rest of the article.

Cranick was only recently released from Vacaville State Prison after serving five years for extortion. Police theorize that after assaulting O'Ryan and stumbling upon Maria Delgado during the botched robbery attempt, Cranick doused himself with gasoline from an oil truck abandoned on the premises and set himself on fire. Remorse and fear of being returned to prison are cited as possible motives, though Detective Ralph Stamat said, "It was a PCP case if I ever saw one." An autopsy will be performed Wednesday or Thursday but is expected to be inconclusive due to the condition of the body. No other suspects are sought.

Lyle Cranick's criminal career dated back to 1963 when, at the age of 18, he served time for filing a false police report claiming to have been sexually molested by a Catholic priest in 1957 while serving as an altar boy. The prosecuting attorney called it "the most outrageous, disgusting and ridiculous slander I've ever heard."

Flipping the page, I pretended to read a story on a new shopping mall for San Cristobal.
"Time for my stomach medicine, anyway," Humpert announced. "That's good for pain."
Ponderously, he headed up to his room. That morning I'd discovered the packet of letters Humpert had brought Victoria. The top drawer

to her bureau had been open. I'd peeked in thinking she might keep a diary. I'm not proud of it, but I was almost desperate—it was like a sickness—for some understanding of what she'd been thinking about me the last few days. The letters were still bound and unopened, and addressed to Victoria Langford, not Fairchild, at a San Francisco post office box. Judging from the return addresses they'd all come from soldiers and prisoners.

I knocked impatiently on Maria's door. She answered slowly.

"Can you come over to the house right away?" I asked, sounding a bit breathless.

"Why?"

"I want you to take a look at somebody. It may be the bald man who really attacked your uncle. So be prepared and don't let on. Just say you came over to borrow some tea."

"Huh?" One syllable—skeptical, irritated.

"Please, just come."

CHAPTER 26

Back at the old church, I slipped in through the front door. When I entered the kitchen, Humpert looked up, saw it was me and popped open another Heineken. I heard Maria's car rattle up even though she didn't pull down the driveway. I remembered her husband had bought the heap through the mail. Because she could change the plugs and points of their last car, he'd considered Maria practically a mechanic. When the doorbell rang, Humpert looked at me, unmoving. I was going to get it anyway.

Maria gave me a faint smile, then didn't say a word as she followed me into the kitchen.

"So, what brings you over?" I asked.

"I just stopped by on the way into town."

"Anything I can do for you?"

"Unh-unh, not really."

Maybe we should have spent a bit more time on the cover story. Fortunately, Humpert was ignoring us. Maria's glance at him was perfunctory. She tossed her kinky black hair over her shoulder, and stood—arms folded over her heavy breasts, one thick leg leaning against the wall—obviously less the casual visitor than a person awaiting a summons. Reluctantly.

"Oh," I said. "Let me introduce you. Maria this is Humpert, and vice versa. I'm sorry Humpert, I don't know your first name."

"Anthony. How do you do, Maria?"

"Fine. How are you?"

They were both fine. And as their eyes met—nothing. Maria scanned the room, her cast tapping against her leg, obviously waiting to be shown the attacker I'd told her about. Humpert examined his finger and kept ignoring us. *Another perfectly good theory shot to shit.*

I couldn't just stand there indefinitely, so I invited Maria into the living room, supposedly to tell me about her uncle.

"That wasn't the man?" I asked unnecessarily, as soon as we were out of earshot.

"Him? No, of course not." She sat down on the couch.

"If he was wearing that big fur-collared coat? Without it Cranick wasn't all that big."

"Cranick?"

I was too worked up to sit, but keeping my voice low, I explained about Cranick, including the attack on Victoria; I didn't go into my cowardice.

"Are you fucking kidding me?" Maria said though she seldom talked like that. "So, the body in the flood control wash, that was you?"

"Well, it wasn't...."

"You know what I mean. You and your friend, Victoria, were responsible for it."

"Except last night the body came back."

"I noticed—he assaulted my uncle. Then he came after me."

"Maybe it was Cranick. But maybe it wasn't."

She made a dismissive noise. "Your pal Cranick was obviously homicidal. He'd written my uncle asking for money. When he didn't get any, he probably decided to just come and take whatever he could from a helpless old man."

"So why didn't Victoria mention she knew him—either time?"

"Nobody wants to get involved, right?" she said pointedly. "Maybe that, or maybe she figured if she admitted knowing the guy she dropped over the bridge, she might be more likely to end up charged with something? Who knows? And as for Humpert—he's as hairless as a ball bearing. There would be no question he was bald. The man I saw had some hair; I *got the impression* he was bald on top. You know—typical male pattern baldness. And he was big, but coat or no coat, he wasn't as fat as Humpert."

Defeated, I plopped down beside her on the couch, feeling silly. She was probably right. This wasn't TV. The attempted murder, like life, was probably as mundane as the police figured it to be, devoid of plots and conspiracies. They weren't even bothering with an autopsy until Wednesday or Thursday.

"Is that all you wanted to see me about?" she asked coolly. I still owed her an explanation for having hidden her existence from Victoria. All I had to do was think of one. One that wouldn't hurt her.

I asked about her uncle. She said he was about the same. It was just a question of time. Still, with no healthcare proxy, the hospital wasn't going to remove him from life support. They already had two lawsuits pending. The large lump on his back turned out to be tissue, but it also appeared to be shrinking. Not that it mattered.

Maria let the conversation die.

"I hope you didn't get the wrong impression over here the other day," I began. "Frankly, the reason I didn't mention you to Victoria was that I was uncertain about what you and I were doing, and I didn't want to look like a fool if you went back to your husband or took up with somebody else."

"Al and I are finished. Though if he does move out here we'll probably stay friends."

"Are you going to tell him about what happened between us?"

"I'm undecided. What do you think?"

"The truth is always best," I said, lying again, I suppose. Would anyone confirm the suspicions of a badly deformed blind child that she was physically repulsive?

Our knees touched. Reflexively mine, maybe hers too, jerked away, then we let them rest together. She smelled clean, like Ivory soap. I was conscious of her body next to me as softer and more comfortable than the sofa we were sitting on.

"I felt like shit today," I said. "I wanted to see you." I realized this was true even as I said it. I also realized I wanted her to want me. I needed the reassurance. I also realized that wasn't fair to her.

"I read your note," she murmured, turning to face me.

"What?"

"The one you left that first night at my uncle's, telling me why you were leaving. I spotted it right after I woke up. Before you got back and spirited it away."

This wasn't a shock. I knew she suspected something, and she'd never asked me why I was so desperate to avoid the police after her uncle was hurt.

"Obviously, you intended to leave back then," she continued. "I wondered why you stayed, when supposedly California was no longer safe for you. I even worried that you might be getting hung up on me; I guess that was pretty silly. And it was touching how concerned you were in the note that I might get in trouble for helping you. That didn't bother you when we drove across the country together."

"You were safe. I was only a hitchhiker. We weren't lovers then."

"Are we lovers now?"

I took a deep breath and let it out slowly. "I don't know."

"We aren't," she said calmly. "When I met Victoria, I understood why you stayed. That was fine. We still could have been friends, you know. We both could have used it. But I don't need any bullshit. I'll see you later."

It sounded like she wouldn't, not if she could help it.

CHAPTER 27

As Humpert and I both put our backs to it, the lid to the sarcophagus shifted with a wrenching of stone upon stone. Humpert must have pushed too hard—it was unlikely to have been me—and the lid tottered, squealed once more, then toppled off the far side, slamming into the cement floor with an explosion that reverberated through the tomb. The sarcophagus itself was empty.

"My ears will never be the same," I said.

"They never were the same. Your eyes don't match, either."

"Hilarious."

The second sarcophagus was easier to uncover than the first, but it was empty, too. After we got it opened, Humpert picked his way wearily around the pieces of the first lid and, with a discouraged sigh, eased himself down again on the concrete chair. Pulling a silver flask from a zippered pocket, he took a long pull, then offered it to me. Though I was hardly devastated by the lack of rotting flesh, it was a friendly gesture, and my body was getting used to all this drinking, so I accepted. Automatically, I wiped the neck with my fingers, a reflex left over from childhood.

"Don't worry," said Humpert, unoffended. "It isn't contagious."

"What's not?" The whiskey was as smooth as Victoria's cheeks.

"Whatever it is I've got." He was chewing his words. He hadn't had that much to drink. "I get stomach aches. And I get tired."

Remembering the bruises on his body, I asked him if he'd had his blood checked. The guy next to me in the prison hospital had leukemia—and black and blue marks all over his body. I passed Humpert back the flask, now less than thrilled about sharing it.

"I've been checked for everything. Even Victoria was checked—to be on the safe side. Turns out it's just some minor stomach disorder—more painful than serious. I guess I'm getting old."

"There's a lot of that going around."

Figuring I might as well get the job over with, after a few minutes rest I picked up a pry bar and started on the top wall vault. The inscription on the capstone, "Reverend Horace Arnsworth" was heavily scratched over. At one time it seemed to have been painted over too, and something painted underneath it, but—to paraphrase a document we found later—paint adheres to marble as easily as righteousness adheres to the spirit, and it was long since gone.

I tried to hammer the pry bar between the headstone and the crypt wall, but a heavy sealer secured them together. Nothing was easy around this place.

After about fifteen minutes, Humpert seemed to recover, grabbed a hammer and pry bar of his own and went to work on one of the lower vaults. The small stone room rang with the high-pitched pounding. We ended up stuffing toilet paper in our ears, but that didn't help all that much.

Eventually, I worked the capstone free and lowered it to the ground with sore fingers. Once more the cupboard was bare. The empty vault had an old dank smell mixed with brief eddies of clean air. A small patch of dull light shone against the darkness at the far end. Obviously, this was the vault under the back porch.

Obviously. I kicked myself. The thin, cracked slab of marble that covered it up there could have been opened by a strong child. I lifted the capstone and replaced it—for some reason I felt like I should—though it was badly chipped around the edges.

The vault Humpert was working on was nowhere near open. And we were both in danger every time he slugged the pry bar with the hammer. He was a lummox when it came to gross movement, but when he put down the hammer, you could see the dexterity that built all those models. Though the injured finger stuck out in a crippled point, in even the simplest motion—unscrewing the cap from his flask, unwrapping a stick of gum and popping it into his mouth—the rest of the long, thin, almost delicate fingers trailed through the air with an elegant exactitude. And I was willing to believe they were as strong as the rest of Humpert.

———

By 4:45, I was tired and Humpert was exhausted, so we knocked off. It was too early for dinner. Instead, we switched on the TV and vegged out, watching a Mary Tyler Moore rerun.

By the time the news came on, Humpert was sitting back in the recliner, his feet up, and, for some reason, his shoes and socks off. He was working a crossword puzzle in the paper and making a serious dent in a good size pour of scotch. I could actually see the pulse fluttering in the thick blue vein in his neck. Once or twice, one foot twitched. When he spoke, he was chewing his words again—worse now. He looked beyond tired, and the alcohol probably didn't help.

On the news, a story came on about a missing fourteen-year-old girl from Compton. She'd just been found keeping house in San Diego with the thirty-seven-year-old man who'd been her English teacher the year before.

Humpert put down the puzzle and glared at the TV. "They ought to castrate him," he said bitterly. "I'd be happy to do it."

"Ok. I guess we all need a hobby."

He shot me an irritated glance then turned back to the TV, but the news had moved on to a story about leaky breast implants.

Humpert said, "When my sister, Selena, was thirteen, my mother was diagnosed with stomach cancer. For the next four years Selena devoted her entire life to caring for her—and taking my mother's place caring for the family. No cheerleading, no proms. Virtually no discretionary time at all."

"That is rough," I said.

"Yah, rough. Very discerning."

"Was she a lot older than you?"

"About two years. But she was a natural caregiver."

"Lucky for you. Maybe not for her."

He took another pull at his scotch. "I recognize that. I could have done more."

"Not for me to say."

"You're fucking right about that, Arnold." The Arnold was slurred. "Anyway, that's not the painful part. I had a friend, Joey Ambrose. Sometimes we'd hang out after school or on weekends. Once in a while he'd eat with the family, or I'd eat with his. One time I came home from skating with some other friends, and he was already there inside the house. No big deal. He said my sister had made him a sandwich. She was like that. Caring for everybody. The day after my fifteenth birthday another friend came up to me—not a friend really, more an asshole, the kind of asshole that would get off on telling you that another supposed friend of yours had been bragging to any guy who would listen about "butt-fucking this pig in her dead mother's bed" and that the pig he was bragging about was your sister."

"And the guy doing the bragging was Joey what's his name?"

"And to think I underestimated your keen grasp of the obvious. But that's not the painful part either."

"Which is?"

"The painful part is that even after hearing about this, no matter what else she heard, no matter how Joey treated her, my sister couldn't stay away from him; whenever he snapped his fingers she was there."

"She was young. We've all been young."

"She was a rare and special creature," Humpert said wearily, "a rare and special creature who allowed herself to be transformed into just another piece of ass. Henceforth, I became extraordinarily glad to discover I could have no children of my own."

I wasn't sure I saw the connection. But I said, "Actually, I've considered having it done to myself. But the change is so permanent... Still, as far as having a family goes..." I shrugged.

"Victoria is my family," he said.

"You've been with her for a long time?"

He nodded, closed his eyes briefly, then opened them again. "Whereas most attorneys have achieved baccalaureate and doctorate degrees before admission to the bar, I was merely apprenticed to a lawyer." His tone had grown formal, perhaps to try to counter the effect of the alcohol. "Henceforth my academic training was limited to classes audited without benefit of enrollment. Consequently, in letting me act as her personal attorney, Victoria demonstrated a confidence in me of which I can only strive to be worthy."

"Well, you've got the lingo down. Whereas and henceforth and consequently."

His smile was almost friendly. Then suddenly it was as if something in him collapsed under its own weight. His body seemed to shrink like a defeated erection, and when he continued, his voice was a thin wire—taut, yet simple, small, and exposed—and his eyes were focused on his feet.

"Victoria probably told you," he said, "three weeks before she first hired me, I'd smashed my car into a bridge abutment. At the hospital,

I never let on it was deliberate. Victoria saved me, gave me a reason to get out of bed in the morning."

I had no idea what to say to that. His earlier comments—maybe keyed by exhaustion or drink or a combination of the two—were one thing, but I'd never expected this stark honesty. Even before this last revelation, I'd wondered how badly he'd resent me the next day for what he'd revealed. I felt like replying in kind to show that I understood.

But before I could say anything, he added, "I would die for her in a second. And I would kill anyone who I thought might hurt her. No injunctions, no restraining orders, no lawsuits, no lawyer horseshit. I'd just fucking kill them. Dead."

I nodded in acknowledgement but when I looked over his eyes were closed. Within seconds, he was snoring. But then he snorted loudly and shook himself awake.

"I didn't tell you the most significant part of the Joey Ambrose story, Arnold. That happened after I decided I'd had enough of the son of a bitch. That's when somebody—the authorities never discovered who—jumped him one evening and used a cordless power drill to drill through his left testicle. Unfortunately, the drill bit was both rusty and dirty. Filthy actually. It was three weeks before the infection killed him."

Victoria arrived a short while later, her hitchhiker in tow.

His name was Peter Sisley. He was scroungy, with sandy hair, washed out blue eyes, and a prominent English nose. Instead of the public beach, Victoria had taken him to the more secluded area used for nude bathing. And now he kept making leering remarks about always wanting to be exposed to the best pieces of California and pretending to complain because Victoria had insisted on them being off by themselves. Victoria had two hands and one breast pressed against his arm and was laughing much too loudly.

I didn't like Peter. Under the circumstances, I might have had difficulty finding anything to like about Jesus Christ—though the crucifixion might have seemed like a good idea. I didn't like Peter's "fabulous" accent. I didn't like his habitual blink or his Adam's apple that bobbed up and down as he explained to Humpert and me he was writing a book as he hitchhiked across the country.

"It's going to be the true story of America," he said. "Not the one the history books tell."

I've freely admitted to being an asshole, but Peter was a moron.

I didn't like the piece of scotch tape which held one side of his wire rim glasses together, and I didn't like the crescent shaped stud he wore in his ear. And when Victoria mentioned something about his intelligence, I felt as if he was poaching on my territory. Before I could tear into him, Victoria started to whisk him off upstairs so he could "take a nap."

"Could I speak to you for a minute, Victoria?" I interrupted. "Alone. It's important." I still wanted to talk to her about my money, but the subject of Lyle Cranick had now taken precedence.

"Sure," she said, sounding irked. A residue of sand still clung to her bare legs. "Just let me show Peter to my room."

When she returned, she looked down at Humpert asleep again and said, "How's he feeling?"

"Tired."

"Any calls?"

"No. Why didn't you tell me it was Lyle Cranick who attacked you that first night, and Lyle Cranick who burned to death over at O'Ryan's?"

For a moment, she continued to gaze down at Humpert as if he might have the answers. Then, she fit herself into the corner of the couch and faced me.

"A lady has to have her secrets, Steve. You weren't ready to know. And I wasn't ready to tell you."

"I don't understand."

"Exactly right. But you will. And I'll start your education by explaining why I had to kill him."

She said that calmly.

CHAPTER 28

"It's not so bad being a murderer. A murderess," Victoria said. She ran her hands through her hair, tousling it. I wondered if she knew it looked better like that, as if she'd just climbed out of a warm bed. "We all do what we have to do to survive. I hired Cranick from an ad I'd placed in a few newsletters. I was looking for a prisoner or somebody in the service, someone who needed a helping hand. I was careful not to let him get the wrong idea—Humpert did the final interview in Sausalito. Gave him all the details of the job and sent him down here. And Cranick *was* handy. His letters from prison had seemed timid and weak-kneed, but I wasn't searching for a leader of men. Also, I knew about Zandie, and Cranick claimed to be an expert in what he called, 'the paranormal.'"

"What that meant," grumbled Humpert, letting us know he was awake, "was that he was a superstitious fool who believed in goblins, ghosts, witches, and all manner of unseen silliness—including things no one else had ever even heard of. And he was terrified of all of it."

"'Cranick's panic,' Humpert used to call it," Victoria offered.

"Trust Humpert," I said distractedly, still struggling with Victoria's admission.

Humpert straightened his chair and crossed his legs. His words were clearer now. "Cranick carried a list in his wallet that he was always updating of what warded off what. So he could easily check which beasties were afraid of mirrors or of the Tibetan talisman he wore around his neck, and which were destroyed by water or sunlight or silver bullets or Latin prayers or the incantations of Armenian gibberish he'd learned from his maternal grandmother."

Victoria chuckled, "Humpert told him to put the whole list by the phone next to the emergency numbers for the police and fire departments—for easy reference next time we were attacked by werewolves."

"He was a worthless faggot," snorted Humpert, just when I'd almost started to begin to think about possibly liking him. Maybe.

"Please, Humpert," Victoria chided with a smile, "some of my best friends are gay. Isn't that what you're supposed to say, Steve? Though actually none of them are."

"At least as far as you know," I said.

"Agreed. But really, what's the point of a man who doesn't want to have sex with a woman?"

"Exactly," Humpert intoned. "Genetically, they're of no use to the human race."

Now, this particular dumb-ass remark had absolutely nothing to do with Victoria murdering Cranick. But it was the inverse of one of those random thoughts I'd had in WasherWorld. Or maybe it was the converse. Or the contrapositive. I really had no idea what those terms meant anymore—if I'd ever really been sure. But it did seem connected. And I was annoyed.

So I said, "You mean because evolutionarily speaking, the purpose of sex is to have children. Is that what you're saying?"

"Exactly," he repeated. "To propagate the next generation. And advance natural selection."

"By that token," I said, "what's the point of *anyone* who doesn't want to have children? Or any sex act that can't lead to that. Seems like a lot of people are spending a huge amount of time and energy pursuing the pointless."

"Yes, it does, doesn't it," Humpert said smugly, as if I'd just made his case.

"What is the point of this discussion?" Victoria demanded. "Besides, Cranick definitely liked women. No doubt about that."

Humpert snorted. "After all those years in prison, he was probably an equal opportunity copulator—men and women. Maybe that was part of the problem."

"Maybe," said Victoria, "Or maybe he was just more of a man than I gave him credit for."

It had grown dark, and she reached behind me and switched on the lamp. Her hand came to rest on my leg above the knee. Then she picked up her purse, taking out some Chapstick, applying it thoughtfully.

I was about to try to drag us back to the small matter of murder, when she continued unprompted.

"After Cranick found the video tape of me and my friend—after I convinced him I wasn't a blackmailer and that no one was ever ashamed of making it into my bed, I sent him packing. It was a week later when he attacked me out by the highway. But he looked awful—dirty and emaciated and just beat up. He not only felt I'd rejected him, he also seemed to believe his physical condition was my fault—that I was some kind of evil spirit. He was the most superstitious man I ever met, and he was no longer in his right mind. After hanging that crucifix around my neck, he tried to force me to suck on that penis knife. Serpent knife? Whatever." She shuddered. "When I wouldn't, he tried to stab me. Though I'm sure he never intended to let me live anyway. That's when you came along, Steve."

"But Cranick didn't die that night," I said.

"No. I wanted him to, I guess. But I knew he wasn't dead when I gave him that shove off the bridge. I hoped it might kill him, and I thought it probably had. Is that terrible? I still worry that somebody driving by might have seen me do it."

The shadows from the soft lamp highlighted the tiny scar by her mouth. Brushing some sand from her thigh, she smiled sadly, shyly, and so sweetly and so vulnerably it tore at my gut. I wanted to take her in my arms. In spite of everything, her beauty seemed so elemental, so basic. As if it were the standard of beauty—some Platonic ideal—some absolute that I would have recognized as beautiful before I'd learned the Lord's Prayer or the names of the characters on Howdy Doody.

Ok, leave it to a Harvard education to make even a hard-on pretentious.

"Was that so terrible, Steve?" Victoria repeated.

"It's probably just human," I said.

"But *he* wasn't. He didn't seem like it anyway. He was a nightmare. Friday night he came back again! Like some creature from some horror movie that just wouldn't die. He was in the house when I came up from Zandie's lab. I saw that doll nailed to the wall, and then he was coming at me, dirtier and crazier than ever, carrying this huge candle—and this *was* shaped like a phallus—with blue stones embedded in it. God knows where he got such a thing."

"Probably a special at Dicks-R-Us," Humpert mumbled, his eyes closed again.

"I tried to reason with him, but he ignored me. He'd apparently even put wax in his ears—to protect him from the siren's enticements, he said."

"How'd you get away from him?" I asked.

"Fortunately, he wasn't gay. He started chanting some new spell he'd dug up. Said it would make him the master of any woman. Sexually and otherwise. I was just lucky he didn't come after me with a knife again. So, he mutters his stupid spell, and I just pretend to go along—take him up to my room—even bring a bottle of wine." She shivered; with the sun going down, the temperature had dropped quickly.

Humpert groaned and shifted position—he was back asleep again. Victoria got up and got a blanket from the den, draping it over him, giving him a kiss on the cheek, then returning. She sat down closer to me. When she sighed again, I could smell the staleness of her breath.

"And then?" I prompted. "With Cranick?"

"Well, he had two—no, three—glasses of wine. He really believed I was under the power of his stupid spell. It was easy to slip a couple of sleeping pills into each glass. They didn't seem to affect him, so the last glass had three, maybe four. I knew he was going to kill me when he was finished with me. Still, I never expected him to die. I didn't want him to die. Right after the first attack I did, but I was past that. But obviously he did die—though it was hard for me to believe. He died in my bed. Then Saturday night, a friend of mine—Leo, you'll probably meet him soon—Leo took him to O'Ryan's and lit the fire."

<hr>

The muffled voices of Peter and Victoria filtered in from Victoria's room. Lethargically, I took off my working clothes, figuring I'd get cleaned up then go down and get something to eat. The shade on the window was up, and it occurred to me I might be visible from the highway. Nobody was really interested in my naked flesh, but I pulled it down anyway. My arms were so tired they ached; my legs felt as if they were swollen. And I was a bit stunned by what I'd just heard. I lay down on the bed to rest for a moment.

I knew I should go back downstairs. What was the point in lying there, hoping not to hear the tell-tale sounds from the next bedroom? In an act of will power, I got up and shut the door to the bath, putting a room and two walls between us.

I slipped back under the covers. What did Peter have that I lacked? He wasn't good looking. He was no big shot. Blue eyes, but watery blue in my opinion. Blondish hair. His teeth were nicer. I might have seen too many commercials, but I actually did wonder if it was my breath. Maybe Victoria just wanted to be free now and didn't want to be involved with someone living in the same house. Maybe I should have come on to her that first night before I'd arranged to live here. Still, tonight on the couch, we'd seemed closer than ever before.

Once again that weird whistling noise started ringing through the house—softly this time—but it faded out almost immediately. It occurred to me that if I'd have left the capstone off the vault, it probably would have fixed the problem.

I flipped on the radio. The music was tinny and distorted, by one of those new wave groups I knew nothing about. I shut it off and closed my eyes for a moment. *Leo.* Another name. Leo, who'd been in Europe, selling Victoria's jewelry. Fortunately, at her request, he'd returned to L.A.—prices were better in Beverly Hills, and now, after giving up on the rest of the estate, she had formal title to the jewelry.

Saturday, after Cranick's death, Leo had flown up from L.A. to help her. I got the impression she wouldn't have trusted Humpert with the job. Victoria had picked him up at the San Cristobal airport.

She freely admitted she never seriously considered calling the police and trying to explain.

"I thought we'd stash the body in one of the burial vaults in the old crypt," she told me. "That's why I sent you out to dig in the backyard. Only while Leo was carrying the body through the basement he rounded a corner and there's O'Ryan, probably looking for his 'nephew,' but staring off into space. Leo crashed into the old man before I could stop him. It was instinct. He used to play in the NFL. O'Ryan hit the ground, and his head smashed against the cellar floor. He never even knew what hit him. We couldn't find a pulse. Like you, we were sure he was dead."

The rest had been mostly Leo, and he must be a prize.

"I was so upset and sickened I had to leave," Victoria explained. "I've been having trouble thinking clearly sometimes lately anyway. I can remember hearing you calling my name from the other end of the basement."

But she told Leo that sooner or later—probably sooner—the old man would be missed. After all, he was a fixture in the area, and even if he seemed to have no close friends or relatives—or so Victoria thought at the time—the local ranchers all knew him, not to mention the cab company, the county sheriffs, the Highway Patrol, and the mailman. Plus, there was always the chance that someone might have driven by and seen me digging a grave-sized hole out in the back that afternoon. Better he should be found at home than turn up missing.

"I left," she explained. "I just got into the Mercedes and drove and drove. That fake murder-suicide was Leo's brainchild. I had no idea he'd be so foolish. Of course, neither one of us knew the girl was living there, but still—if the police hadn't been as stupid as he was..." She shook her head. "And we can only hope the body was too crispy-crittered to give them an accurate time of death."

"Or to reveal that he actually died from an overdose."

"Right," she said uncertainly, as if somehow she hadn't thought of that.

"Leo went after Maria too. Would he have killed her as well?"

"No, God no, of course not. He's not a murderer. He just wanted to scare her off."

Maybe. Maybe not. "She'd seen him."

"She got a glimpse of him. A big guy in an ugly red coat. So, he put the coat on Cranick's body. He was lucky he wasn't wearing his new blond wig—she couldn't have missed that, believe me—or he'd have had to stick that on the corpse as well. Would have served him right."

"Uh huh, that certainly does seem like an appropriate punishment," I said dryly. "I mean, since it's new and all—and blond."

"He was protecting me, Steve. I won't fault him for that. What happened to the old man was an accident. Leo was simply trying to work things out on the fly."

"So, he set the fire and ran. He was lucky we didn't spot him."

"Damn lucky. I'm sure he never expected Maria to get help back there so quickly. At least he was smart enough not to try to head over here."

"Where did he go?"

"He got to spend a cold night walking the beach in his short sleeve shirt. The next day he phoned from Santa Louisa, and I had Humpert drive him to L.A. along with a few more things to sell. That's when I had to tell Humpert what had happened. It shook him badly. In fact, his condition has been deteriorating since then."

My bedroom was hot, with a dry, desert warmth. I felt feverish, but the Santa Ana winds were blowing, and the temperature had simply risen sharply again. Opening the window seemed to help.

I'd also asked Victoria about the face that had appeared on my forearm.

"Wasn't that something—incredible detail," she said shaking her head with wonder, admitting she'd seen exactly what I'd seen. "Looks like some spell Cranick stumbled across somewhere actually worked—most likely he found it here. Maybe that powder he threw in your face during the fight came from Zandie's lab and that did it. Maybe triggered by your guilt. Have you had any other symptoms?"

I just shook my head. *Guilt?* The guy was trying to kill me. Beyond that, I didn't know what was worse: the face being mostly my imagination, the result of psychological trauma, or the face being real, like some kind of weird stigmata. Was it possible some stupid spell of Cranick's or Zandie's actually worked? I just didn't buy it. If that face was actually there—if what I thought I'd seen was real—it was some parlor trick Cranick had pulled. More likely, that powder was some kind of drug. If Victoria had actually seen it too, maybe it was the drug plus the power of suggestion.

Maybe.

Was I satisfied with any of those explanations? Not at all. But they were the best I had at the moment.

But even beyond that weirdness—that had happened to either my body or my mind or both—at this point, we had one dead, one dying and the number of attempted murders depended upon how you classified them. For example, was Leo really hoping to scare Maria off when he tried to force his way through the connecting door, or was he planning on something more sinister?

Looking back on that night from the distance of all these years, it makes absolutely no sense to me that I didn't just get the hell out of there. Granted, I had no money. I still hadn't gotten the advance Victoria had promised. Granted, I was a fugitive. But when it came right down to it, the real reason I stayed was that—hard as it might be to believe—I once again thought I had some kind of a chance with Victoria. And I wanted her as badly as I ever wanted anything. Or rather I wanted her to want me too as badly as I ever wanted anything—which was an entirely different thing.

My last conscious thought that evening before I drifted off was that I was extraordinarily lucky that sometime in that death and destruction I hadn't been confronted by cops with questions I wouldn't be able to answer.

At least not yet.

I awoke a few hours later. I'd kicked off the sheet that had been covering me, and I was chilled from the cool air blowing across my sweaty body. It was too hot with the window closed, but much too cool with it open. Soon my stomach remembered I'd forgotten dinner, and getting dressed, I quietly made my way downstairs. It seemed late. The house was asleep. Peter's backpack sat by the foot of the stairs. It was open, and the unmistakable aroma of cat shit rose from inside it. The phantom La Perdita strikes again. I was beginning to like that cat.

A light shone through from the living room. When I ducked in to see who it was, I found Victoria lying across the couch, her bathrobe wide open, a fully dressed Humpert sucking on one of her breasts while she stroked the back of his head.

Christ, she *was* fucking everybody!

A thin trickle of yellowish spittle appeared at one corner of Humpert's mouth. Before I could retreat, Victoria glanced up and smiled at me, just like a Madonna.

A Day at the Beach and an Evolutionary Dead End

"Clothes make the man. Naked people have little or no influence on society."
– *Mark Twain*

CHAPTER 29

Tuesday was a scorcher. In the bathroom, I found a large set of false teeth in a glass—obviously, Humpert's too-perfect set. A little cash was taped to the mirror with a note:

> For your breakfast.
> Love, Victoria

Thinking of the friendly, almost pretty, blond waitress who waited on me before, I returned to Martin McMulligan's. I did get the same waitress, but today she had trouble tearing herself away from a tow-headed twenty-something at the counter in an "I'd Rather Be Sailing" tee shirt.

I sent back the frigid omelet. And I had to ask three times for my toast, eventually using a tone that matched the sullenness of her expression. When she finally delivered it, she leaned across the table—scooped-out neckline and all—and I glanced down and found myself staring at the better part of two tough little tits. Straightening up, she made a production out of pulling up the front of her blouse, all the while sneering at me like I hung around playgrounds waiting for little girls in dresses to hang upside down from jungle gyms. The toast was colder than the omelet, but I kept quiet. Our relationship was established: I wanted to look at hers, but she had no use for mine.

Sauntering back to the guy at the counter, she whispered something that made him laugh. And when he swung around to look at me, she giggled and half-heartedly tried to stop him. His handsome, outdoorsy face was smugly amused: the face of a man who took female breasts—especially such ordinary ones—for granted, and neither wanted nor needed to look.

I didn't even bother to ask for the juice that came with the breakfast. I hate grapefruit juice anyway, and it looked like that was all they had. Leaving enough at the table to cover the bill and a decent tip—resisting the temptation to stiff her—I left.

When I got back, Victoria and Humpert were discussing Beverly Hills and some rich dude there, who Humpert claimed was "several miles beyond smitten" when it came to Victoria. She didn't disagree.

"Morning, Steve," she said. "How was breakfast?"

"Fine, I supp…"

"Listen, my love. You worked Saturday, and the weather's going to be absolutely perfect today. Why don't you and I take the day off and go down to the beach? Just the two of us. I've packed a lunch. I've even bought you a bathing suit. We'll find some secluded little spot and have a picnic. It'll be great. I promise."

Her eyes went wide as she talked, and her face was as warm and friendly as her words. She promised all right, but I could never tell what she was promising. Peter's backpack was gone. And so was he. Maybe he'd slept in her room the night before but so had I one night. Had she had sex with Humpert? Her expression with him on the couch last night had been more indulgent than erotic. I let her talk me into the beach—once more she promised it would be great—and hurried upstairs to use the bathroom.

I shaved. I brushed my teeth. I even took a quick sponge bath. I debated over washing my hair, but I figured I'd look pretty silly having just washed my hair on the way to the beach.

As I was drying off, I noticed the hamper was open. On top was a filmy white negligee. I held it up. I've always thought a woman's night clothes told a lot about her; Stevie Wonder could have seen through this thing. After starting to leave, I changed my mind and went back and dug out the panties that went with the negligee. They were just as flimsy, except for a slightly thicker cotton crotch. I felt I had to know what she was into before I made a fool of myself coming onto her again. Had she had sex with Peter? With Humpert? Both? Neither? Gingerly, I checked the crotch for dampness, then turned the panties inside out and examined them.

OK, and then I sniffed the damn things—though from a distance; I didn't want a nose full of someone else's cum. I was relieved not to find anything. The smell was perfume and woman. Once again, I felt like a sneak thief, but I felt a whole lot worse a second later when I tossed them back into the basket and saw Humpert standing in my room, smirking.

"I was just..."

"I know. Looking for something to wear, no doubt. Better a panty wearer than a panty sniffer." He shook his head, laughed once and left, lumbering down the hall to his room.

The public beach where we parked the Mercedes was too crowded for Victoria. Carrying the picnic basket and a beach umbrella, I followed her between the sea and the cliff face and around a promontory. I wore my jeans, self-conscious about the small tight speedo I had on underneath. But considering Victoria had bought it for me, its size was encouraging. Not far up the shoreline, we squeezed behind a barnacle-encrusted boulder, into a small, secluded cove carved out of the cliff and filled with soft sand.

"People hike up and down the beach," she said, "but nobody ever comes in here—complete privacy." I told myself nothing was going to happen between us, yet a pleasant nervousness was stirring in the backs of my knees.

After we laid out our blanket, I set up the umbrella. She took off her cover, slowly, over her head, leaving her arms up when she'd completed the motion, almost posing. It was worth it. The two-piece bathing suit shone white against her surprisingly deep tan—a stylized "V" on the bottom, and a top that gaped open between her breasts as she moved. Not that she was planning on doing any swimming. What appeared to be Chinese coins dangled from each ear, and as usual, her make-up was perfect.

Lying down with just her face under the shade of the umbrella, Victoria watched me as I undressed. My own bathing suit was getting tighter. Then her eyes focused on the scar puckering my stomach. I'd been gaining weight lately, and the extra flab made the jagged hole look bigger and uglier.

"What's that," she asked, making a face. "Ugh."

"An accident," I answered. Which was probably true. The real Stephen and I had never really expected to go to prison. Starting with phony draft cards for public burnings and phony hearing notices to tie up recruitment depots, we'd progressed to a sophisticated identification package for draft resisters and army deserters. I made them in Boston, and he distributed them in Indiana. But on a very small scale—pissing on a forest fire was what Dell had called it. And even after the government stumbled across us, they probably never would have been able to prosecute us—much less convict us—if we hadn't admitted everything, publicly declaring we weren't going to let them compromise our ideals and force us into lying.

Obviously, I looked at the world differently then.

We were convicted in Federal Court and brought back two weeks later for sentencing. Stephen and I were never into violence, him because of religious convictions, and me for what I pompously labelled "pragmatic Teilhardian reasons." (Trust me, you don't really want to know.) In any case, the idea was to stop the slaughter, not expand it. But the times they were a-changin', and some idiotic, self-styled guerrillas who nobody even knew decided they were going to free us.

On the courthouse steps after we'd been sentenced to three years apiece and were being escorted to prison, a long hair in a khaki jacket shouted, "Death to the pigs! Free the people!" I remember thinking, *what is this, some made for TV movie? Nobody really talks like that.*

His first shot hit my guard in the shoulder. Then from three feet away, the gun drew a bead on the crumpling man. The idea of stepping between them was to prevent the jerk from firing again. Instead, I cleverly managed to catch the second bullet in my abdomen.

The whole episode was captured on film by a local TV crew. It was featured on the nightly news on all three national networks and PBS. Two of them carried a brief comment from Stephen, still at the scene in handcuffs, tearfully praising the strength of my beliefs which allowed me to sacrifice my life for a stranger—even someone who would do me harm. As perceptive as Stephen normally was, he couldn't have been more wrong about that. *He* could have sacrificed himself, coolly, deliberately, but as for me, I hadn't had time to weigh the consequences one way or the other. I certainly hadn't expected to die. Who knew the "Free-the-People" idiot would shoot with me standing there?

For about twelve hours I was a national hero. Big cheers. Nixon sent me a telegram and so did John Lennon—that one I kept for years.

Everything was forgotten long before I got out of Leavenworth two years and two hundred and three days later.

"Why don't you oil me?" Victoria said now, handing me a black plastic bottle of Hot Tropics Super Tan.

I squirted some lotion into my hand, rubbing it between my palms, warming it. It was dark and gooey.

"Chocolate cum," smiled Victoria.

I was startled, almost shocked—not by what she had said, but because *she* had said it. She smiled, undid the top of her bathing suit, and flipped over on her stomach—without apparent effort keeping everything covered. That reminded me that she hadn't suggested we go to the nude beach today—to my relief and disappointment.

The middle of her back was the most neutral part of her body I could find, but when I started applying the lotion, she closed her eyes and purred, "Mmmm, chocolate cum all over my body."

I didn't know if I was ready for this. Was it finally my turn?

My touch was tentative at first, restricted to her shoulders and arms. They soaked up the lotion the way the shingles on the old church absorbed paint. My bathing suit kept tightening.

"Your neck is so tense," I said, beginning a massage there.

"Feels good," she murmured.

With that, I straddled her, pretending to be absorbed with working the knots out of her neck, while in fact concentrating on the firmness of her butt against my thighs. Surreptitiously, I readjusted my bathing suit, trying to ease the savory pain. The suit was so small my erection poked out the top. Forcefully, I returned to Victoria's back, pushing her breasts against the blanket and the warm sand below. Her skin was virtually unblemished, though a spot or two was drier and rougher than the rest. I worked down the back of her ribs, the tips of my fingers drifting inside the bottom of her suit where it gaped open a quarter of an inch, then sweeping upward to explore the sides of her flattened breasts. I was breathing through my mouth.

Trying to relax and to find a position where my suit was less restrictive, I slipped off her and went to her feet: spreading lotion, rubbing her calves, the backs of her knees, her calves again, then gradually, very gradually, lest she stop me, working up her thighs—retreating lower and to the outside of her legs—but always returning, slowly moving up and inward.

She didn't open her legs, but she made no move to close them either. Without forcing the issue, I wanted to work a hand between her thighs; the tiniest shift in her position would do it. I moved up to the flesh exposed by the high cut of her bathing suit, then dropped all pretense of spreading lotion and began massaging her butt. After a few moments her legs spread. I teased her, letting my fingertips glide ever closer.

"How about doing the other side," she said, drowsily. Then she rolled over, without bothering with her top.

Her breasts—like her butt—though not oversized, were amazingly full for such a trim body. The areolas were large, dark coronas, but her nipples weren't extended.

She opened her eyes. Shading them, she saw my erection, and with an amused, but enigmatic grin said, "Some little man is having trouble keeping his mind on his business."

That was annoying. Victoria wasn't the only one who liked being wanted. "I'll be glad to stop if you're not enjoying it too," is what I should have said. It's what I would have said a few years before. Instead, I simply gave a small, almost embarrassed smile, like an old man caught cheating at solitaire.

I spread some of the cream on her stomach, and she closed her eyes again and gave a contented purr. Since this seemed to be a tacit approval to proceed, I went to her breasts, oiling and teasing—the nipples stiffened, but just slightly—before quickly sliding off them. I oiled each leg separately, raising it, rubbing lotion all around it, caressing the tops of each thigh with both hands, letting a finger trail across the crotch of her bathing suit—though as lightly as I did it I wasn't sure she could feel anything through the material. Her legs spread easily now. Inside the warm smell of the suntan cream and the burn of the sun on my back, I was inflamed. I bent down and licked one nipple, tasting the suntan oil and something else. Then I licked the other before rapidly trailing my tongue down across her belly, sticking it deeply and suggestively into her navel. And getting a load of the "chocolate cum" on my tongue. It didn't dampen my excitement. The cord at the waist of my suit was digging into my dick; I actually wondered if I might not just cum, myself. She lay stock still. I wanted to see her desire, but felt vindicated, absolved by just having her accept mine. She'd wanted me all along. I knew it. Her reasons for putting me off had nothing really to do with me.

"All right—that's enough," she ordered coldly, immediately letting me know she hadn't been into it, she'd simply been humoring me as one would humor an over-excited puppy. "Thanks for the massage. I'm going to take a nap. I've got a lot to do tonight."

Without bothering to put her top back on, she turned over on her stomach. I sat there as stunned as if I'd just gotten up on stage to sing and seen the whole audience walk out. Everything had seemed so close. She couldn't withdraw from me so quickly. After a moment or two, I began rubbing her butt again—first softly, but then, almost immediately, more firmly, desperate to earn a response. Did she purr again? I slipped my hand between her legs.

"I've told you I'm not into that," she said immediately, as irritated now as she was cold before. "Jesus, you probably got lotion all over my suit!"

I sat there, tracing nothing designs with one hand in the sand, thinking, *fuck you, I'm not begging anybody to get laid.* I went for a swim. When I came back, she was entirely in the shade, apparently asleep. I wasn't hungry, but I kept munching away distractedly on the trail mix and the submarine sandwiches we'd brought, and by the end of the day I'd devoured virtually the entire basket of food.

On the trip home, Victoria was in good spirits and never seemed to notice that I was only responding in monosyllables.

"You know I'm flat broke," I said finally, belligerently. "I'd like to be paid for what I've done. You've got your settlement."

"Most of what I've got is jewelry that has to be converted into cash. And besides, I hired you for three weeks. I told you I'd pay you when the time was up. And I will."

My recollection of our deal was that she'd pay me when she got the settlement. I was on the verge of starting an argument; I would have, if it wouldn't have been so pathetically obvious that the money was not what was bothering me just then. And you can't really berate someone for not wanting to sleep with you.

Besides, what had she really done? Given me a job, touched me a few times in friendly fashion, accidentally left the bathroom door part way open—and then she'd been understanding enough not to jump all over me when she discovered me sneaking around in the dark like a peeping Tom. Today, after giving me the day off and inviting me to the beach, all she'd done was ask me to oil her back. And I had kept going after she'd asked me to stop, which was really unlike me and made me feel even worse.

I rolled down the window of the Mercedes, and let the wind blow into my face. Had she actually led me on, or had I just become another one of those jerks so desperate to believe in their sex appeal that every time a woman said hello they thought she wanted to leap into bed with them?

In all likelihood, Victoria never had the slightest interest in me sexually. It might have never even occurred to her as a possibility. The last couple of years there seemed to be a lot of that going around.

Telling me she had something to do, she dropped me off at the house.

"Straighten up," she called as I started away from the car. "You walk like you've got a dumbbell dangling from your neck."

What's it to you? I wondered.

CHAPTER 30

That evening a light was on at Maria's. The only car out front was her old Checker cab, but a man answered when I knocked.

"Yes?" he asked suspiciously, peering through the screen. He was slender, in his mid-twenties with short dark hair and glasses that made me think of Buddy Holly. Was this Al, the husband, the ferocious breaker of female bones?

"Sorry to bother you. I wanted to see Maria." As an afterthought, I added, "For a second."

"Maria is hanging pictures this evening in the Bank of Cabrillo," he said stiffly. What I first thought was a bit of a Texas twang was actually a slight whine. "She won't be back till late. Who shall I say came by?"

"Just Steve from next door."

"Is there anything in particular I can tell her you wanted to see her about, Steve? Or are you simply horny again?"

The last sentence was spit out so quickly I wasn't entirely sure I'd heard him correctly. I said, "It's not important."

"I'm sure it's not."

"Excuse me?"

"I mean, what *is* important to a man who preys upon women in their most vulnerable moments? Who's happy to insert himself between a wife and the husband she's chosen as her partner for life. All for a few selfish moments of gratification."

I nodded. I didn't need this tonight. "Okay. Well, I only wanted to tell her the swelling has gone down, the sores are closing up, and the doctors no longer expect my dick to fall off. Tell her that penicillin will probably do the job for her too. Unless, of course, she's allergic to it."

I walked away before he could respond. Good to see that in spite of my own problems I could still take the time to fuck up somebody else's day. And, of course, that performance would make Maria's life easier, too.

"Asshole," I heard from behind me. An opinion which of course I wouldn't argue with.

When I got back home, Victoria called me into the living room, where she was sitting on the couch with yet another man. This one—in his late twenties, I suppose, and appropriately cute in a Disney movie kind of way—had a thick head of curly blonde hair and a blinding smile, which he didn't bother to use on me. His clothes reminded me of that TV detective with the million-dollar wardrobe the other night. He and Victoria were both drinking wine. If I had the alcohol concession around this place, Victoria could keep what she owed me.

"Are you staying in again this evening, Steve?" Victoria asked.

I was ready to say, of course I was staying in because nobody had given me any money. But noting the way that guy was looking at me, I suddenly didn't want to seem so dependent.

"No," I said. "I've got a date." I didn't want him thinking he was grabbing Victoria away from me, either.

"*You've got a date!*" exclaimed Victoria. "Fabulous. Who? Your little friend next door? The chubby one?"

It was nice to know I wasn't the only asshole around here tonight.

"No," I said. "A lady I met a couple of days back. I've got to go."

"No," insisted Victoria, with the transparent gaiety of a Tupperware saleswoman. "Come over here and tell us all about it. And I've got something for you. Actually, though, you can tell me when I get back. I've got to go upstairs for just a moment. Hang on."

"No big deal, Victoria," I said to her back as she left. "Just somebody I met."

"Well," said Cubby or whatever the hell this guy's name was, "I'm sure the young lady doesn't think of herself as no big deal."

I went over and picked up the glass Victoria had left and took a drink. "You're right," I said reasonably. "Maybe you could give me a couple of hints on how to treat a lady, since I can see you're doing so fucking well."

I had a good word for everyone tonight. Who said the Age of Aquarius was dead.

"Now listen..." he started.

"No, I mean it. Look at your clothes. It's just like the ads say: they're really right now—today. My clothes are all yesterday—a few are even the day before."

"Or the day before that." He laughed as if this were a particularly clever retort. But his fingers began drumming on the chair arm.

"But those clothes of yours—is that the forties or the fifties look? Or maybe the thirties? I mean, what could be more *today* than a thin copy of a style that was stupid fifty years ago when it was brand new. At least, these," I offered, tugging at my thrift store shirt, "are *genuine* old clothes."

"Obviously. What is your problem, man?" He put down his glass and stood. The man had great posture. And four inches on me. He also had the build of an athlete, though one that was starting to go to fat. I wondered if he was going to hit me. He probably should have.

"Nothing, *man*. It's your privilege if you want to look just like everyone else." Everyone else with a million-dollar wardrobe, that is.

"What's it to you?" he demanded, boxing me in with impeccable logic. What *was* it to me? I shut up without even bothering with any of the more fashionable anti-fashion clichés. The ones we all make about the obvious absurdity of slavery to those fashions we don't follow. The ones my friends and I used to hear when we were all wearing shoulder-length hair, granny glasses and army jackets. The ones I used to mouth myself—first, when everyone started dressing like we did. Then, more caustically, when everyone moved onto something else.

He sat back down, and we both tried to pretend we were alone until Victoria reappeared a couple of minutes later. For obvious reasons eager to get out of there, he was across the room and at her side as soon as she came in.

"Just a second, Leo," she said.

Leo. Who'd done in O'Ryan. Accidentally. Under the soft light of the living room, I would never have guessed he was wearing a wig. I suppose I was lucky he hadn't clobbered me, though he couldn't keep decorating old houses with flaming bodies indefinitely. As he followed Victoria back into the room toward me, he limped—so slightly I might have been imagining it. I wondered if that was why he was a *former* football player.

Opening her purse, Victoria bestowed a ten-dollar bill on me. "For tonight," she said. "I realize it's not much for a date, but I'm really scraping bottom right now."

"I don't need it," I lied moronically.

"You said you were broke. Take it." She tucked it in my shirt pocket. I almost tossed it back at her. But I *was* broke.

"Some people here try to act so proud," she said.

"Some people here are a tad jealous, I think," Leo said as they left the room.

"Steve?" She was amused. "He may have a little crush, poor thing." And then she whispered something I didn't catch but hated anyway.

As soon as I got what I'd already earned, I was out of there. And Victoria and I were going to have another talk about when that was going to be, first thing in the morning.

———

I drove in to Club Gatsby that evening, and as expected I didn't find a deeply meaningful relationship, get laid, or even find somebody who could call me once or twice and be alluded to in front of Victoria.

The women—none of whom was half as attractive as Victoria—were gathered in groups of two and three. They were outnumbered by the men five to one and checking out the exceptionally attractive and well-dressed men around the room, I could see I wasn't close to being in the top twenty percent. Not that it mattered; I knew from the start I wasn't going to approach anyone that evening.

Eventually I ended up sitting at the bar. The fiftyish man on the stool beside was easily the oldest person in the club. He had a cigarette that trembled badly in his hand and an Eastern European accent. He told me he was a high school biology teacher.

"Just the man I need," I said. "I was having a discussion the other day with a... well, you couldn't really call him a friend."

"Au contraire. I can call him anything I like. This, my friend, is America. I have my Second Amendment rights."

"I think the Second Amendment is about the right to bear arms."

"Exactly. If your friend doesn't like what I call him, I can shoot him. This is America."

"Can't argue with that."

"Exactly. Or if you do, I can shoot you."

"Back to biology."

"Please."

"Evolutionarily speaking," I said, pointing to the dance floor and to the room in general, where the more successful members of the species were pairing up, "what is all this about?"

"Evolutionally speaking, the male is sexually aggressive so that his genes might survive, ensuring his success as an individual."

"So, you and I . . .?"

"Forget it—evolutionary dead-ends. Because the female decides among the competing males to see which genes get to reproduce, thus selecting for the species. But there is a problem."

"That's for sure."

"Aside from the fact that you and I are both going home alone tonight—the species might be very happy about that, cleaning up the gene pool and all—the problem is that mankind and ultimately womankind are now selecting mates primarily on the basis of appearance. Which means in a relatively short amount of time the world will be populated by gorgeous morons."

"Maybe someone should alert the President," I said.

"He's one of them! At least he was during his procreating years."

After another drink, he muttered, "If God is everywhere, why am I sleeping alone?" Which I thought was a great title for a country western song. A moment later, he peered into the mirror behind the bar, as if he'd spotted something particularly interesting. "Now that's an attractive couple," he said.

Victoria and Leo had just entered. They were looking around as if they'd lost something.

I swung around on the bar stool as Victoria walked up.

"Have you seen Humpert, Steve?" she asked.

"No."

"He left a note saying he would be here. If you see him, send him home."

She started to turn away and I swung back to the bar. In the mirror, I saw Leo appear and say something to her. They both laughed. Then Leo stepped up beside me.

"By the way," he said, meeting my eyes in the mirror and grinning unpleasantly, "I understand you're afraid of old bones. Don't worry, I opened that coffin you dug out and finished your job. No grimoire, no papers, no nothing, just old bones. And nothing to be afraid of."

"Really? Hmm. So, you're saying your rigorous education in Exercise Science from the University of Football never got around to explaining just how many diseases you can catch from human remains." Neither did my Ivy League degree, but I pretty much majored in pretending to know what I was talking about. "I hope you wore gloves and a surgical mask."

The smile disappeared. His jaw clenched as he considered this unhappily for a moment. Then he tried, "It doesn't matter. The bones had all been cleaned."

"Of course they were. Zandie probably subscribed to one of those weekly bone cleansing services that were so popular in the 1920s."

"There wasn't a speck of flesh or even a scrap of old clothing anywhere. Just five spotless skulls and a coffin full of completely clean bones."

"Well then, as long as they were sterilized too you should have no worries. Though I'd just as soon you didn't stand quite so close." I took a sip of my drink, then said, "And five skulls? There were six names written on the coffin."

"Five skulls, asshole." He raised a fist, spread the fingers to indicate five and made it a fist again. "You can dig them back up and count them if you want."

He stepped back, then he and Victoria disappeared into the crowd. I guess the missing skull explained where Zandie's gold plated skull came from. I turned back to the bio teacher—the closest thing I had to the date I'd told Victoria and Leo about. But he was deep into an argument about supply side economics with the guy on the other side of him. In the mirror, I could see the guy was wearing an *Atlas Shrugged* tee shirt under a sport coat and flashing a Rolex watch so fake even I could spot it. When I finished my whiskey, I managed to sneak out without seeing Victoria or Leo.

Rather than drive home, I wandered aimlessly down Main Street. In a block where several streetlights were burnt out, an older woman hesitated to come toward me—her fear reached me even if she hadn't. I crossed the street to let her relax.

Farther down, drunken long hairs with backpacks and sleeping bags mingled with winos with shopping carts—pushed into a tiny corner of town between the highway and the railroad tracks. Several of them were nodding out on junk. I was spare-changed twice, in spite of the signs in the store windows warning against it. Next to what was probably the last flophouse in San Cristobal that would rent a room for what welfare would pay, I stepped over a damp spot on the sidewalk leading from a doorway where a solitary soul sang tunelessly to no one. In front of me, a young man with eyes like frosted blue glass and an ugly boil reaching toward his mouth, paced in a circle. More of Maria's empty people—"campers" to Ronald Reagan.

I sped up my pace, threatened the way a fireman might feel threatened by a visit to a burn ward. Randomly, I turned a corner, trying to slip out from under the feeling that sometimes descends on me, the feeling that life was something to survive, something to be endured, to be gotten through. That if I just made it to the end without committing suicide like Stephen or going insane or ending up like these poor souls, then I'd won. The feeling wasn't rational—not unless Jesus was standing at the finish line distributing prizes—but there it was.

A few blocks away on another side street, I found a bar where the drinks were half the price of those at Club Gatsby. The only woman inside was a bar maid with stringy black hair and dark fuzzy sideburns. She wore a beer-stained bikini above and below a dumpling belly and advised me that the girls who worked there sometimes flashed their tits if you tipped them a dollar. I didn't.

I ordered a bottle of Dos Equis. I knew enough not to trust what was in the bottles of supposedly name brand whiskey behind the bar. By the time she returned with my beer, I felt bad about rejecting her tits, and I let her sell me a copy of a nudie newspaper called, *Hot Flashes* that featured her picture. She wanted three dollars and accepted two—not perhaps great bargaining on my part since the price on the cover was a dollar fifty. I'd thought looking at it might motivate me to go out and meet someone, but the amateurish photos were ludicrously unsexual. The rest of the tabloid was filled with strange want ads, letters from readers describing sexual adventures—all either astonishing, ridiculous, or impossible—and two full pages soliciting more letters and photos for future issues.

The bar maid's photo was a badly reproduced polaroid her boyfriend had submitted.

"What do you think?" she asked tentatively a few minutes later.

"I think I'd like you to autograph it for me."

"Seriously?"

"Absolutely. So people will believe I actually met you."

The huge smile that got me was definitely worth two dollars.

I was nearly finished with my beer when she headed over to the beat-up old juke box and punched in a number of selections. The first one that came up was Bobby Vinton's "Roses are Red"—a song which, in my opinion, no true music lover can listen to without wanting to puncture their eardrums with an ice pick, a song which made me yearn for the relative genius of Tony Orlando and Dawn. There was no telling what horrors might follow. I drained the last of the Dos Equis from the bottle, waved a quick good-bye, picked up my autographed newspaper and headed back to the V.W.

By the way, "Roses are Red" sold well over a million records. Tony Orlando sold over thirty million. As I mentioned, my best effort, "Looking for the Good Times" was snapped up by something less than 2,500 discriminating souls, the vast majority of whom, in all likelihood, were actually interested in the A side of the record, "Come on, Baby, Dance the Ugga-Bugga."

As I entered the kitchen, I realized for the first time why the smell of the church had always seemed so familiar. It was the stuffy, overheated odor of my grandmother's house on the morning after her death.

The sounds were coming from the basement, muted by the kitchen floor—faint music, strange calls and cries, all punctuated by a thudding beat. I tried the cellar door, but once again it was locked. What were they doing down there? It was Victoria and Leo, I assumed. And Humpert, too?

The cries became a backdrop for a low rumbling like a chant and then gave way to what sounded like rhythmic gasps and moans. Whatever it was, it was obviously being amplified by the P.A. If I hadn't fastened the inside latches of the basement ice box—against burglars or whatever—I could have checked it out that way. Obviously, it was none of my business. But the locked door and the odd semi-sexual sounds were a strong enticement. After all, Victoria had rejected me and apparently no one else; I was still in the market for a good, impersonal reason.

And then I remembered. I had Cranick's keys! Were they the keys for the church, or for something else?

They were still in the top drawer of my bureau. Clever to kill a man—or to think you've killed him—and keep his key ring. Those keys should have told me right away that the man who attacked Victoria wasn't any deranged vagrant, sleeping by the freeway or trying to bum a ride. I'd beaten around long enough myself to know vagrants didn't carry key rings. What did they have to lock?

I half expected the new-looking, old fashioned style key to be the one I needed. But the basement door had a modern lock. The third key I tried turned the bolt easily.

A final swelling groan from the basement was followed by a variety of metal clicks. Quickly but quietly, I hurried down the steps. Then, as I wound my way through the corridors toward the P.A. room, the smell reminded me of Good Friday services when I was a kid. A flute began to play gently. And voices—young and female—started speaking in unison. Besides English, I've only had a year of college French, and the tiny bit of Latin I picked up as an altar boy, so I'm no expert. But this language—calm and inexplicably chilling—was like no other I'd ever heard anywhere. Gradually the unison dissolved once again into individual gasps and sighs, almost—but not quite—sexual.

Still, maybe I expected to discover some kind of orgy, I'm not sure. I did expect them to be down in the P.A. room—until I rounded a corner and saw Humpert and Leo, naked in the glowing torchlight of the altar room.

They were on their knees, backs to me, facing the altar. Several tiny spots of what appeared to be blood congealed on the floor right before the doorway. Ducking back as far out of sight as possible, I peered around the corner from the shadows. Leo was holding up a huge flaming pentagram at the end of a pole. Humpert swung an incense burner, thickening the air with fragrant smoke as, on top of the altar,

Victoria stepped into view. Blood was smeared across her bare breasts and thighs—but smeared in the shape of symbols and strange letters. A black hood covered her face, but I would know that body anywhere. In her hand, she carried a short, viciously curved sword, dipped in more blood. The female cries from the P.A. ended, and Humpert and Leo reached toward Victoria—as if entreating, even venerating her. Slowly, deliberately, she raised the sword above her head. My knees trembled. Nothing seemed real behind that smoky haze. For a heartbeat, she hung suspended—the image of a conquering, flesh-devouring deity about to strike. Her shriek echoed in the silence as she ripped the hood from her head. And, once again, turned and gazed straight into my eyes.

"Shit!" she swore.

———

Victoria sat down on the edge of the altar, beside the hole I'd cut in the top. Then she began to laugh bitterly. "This is ridiculous. You might as well come in, Steve. As usual, I see you hiding there. Come on in and take a look at how three grown people spend their time."

Tentatively, I stepped into the room, avoiding the blood on the floor. The P.A. hissed and ticked intermittently with the sound of a record that had finished but kept turning under the needle. Beside Victoria on the altar, sat two large cruets, one empty and one holding about an inch of brownish red liquid.

Humpert noticed me gazing at the cruets. "Blooood," he moaned in his best theatrically spooky voice.

"Liver," Victoria explained. "The liver you picked up for me."

"The liver you fed to the cat," I said.

"I'm not going to feed liver to that cat. I'd wanted it for Humpert, to build up his red blood cells. Then I stumbled across this ritual in one of Zandie's books. It called for blood, and that liver was the only blood handy. The ritual didn't work the first time I tried it—of course. But since it also called for assistants and herbs which I didn't have, when the herbs grew and Humpert and Leo returned, I figured what the hell, I'd try it again." She shook her head. "I wanted to use La Perdita's blood this time, but she got away."

I thought Victoria was joking about the cat until Leo added, "Damn cat scratched the hell out of me and ran off. We were halfway down the basement stairs, and I damn near fell down the rest of them."

"Maybe you need more practice handling pussy, Leo," said Victoria, climbing off the altar. "I hope the damn thing starves down here. Some familiar."

"So what was the purpose of . . .?" I began.

"I got her at the pound," she explained impatiently, thinking I was asking about the cat rather than this bizarre spectacle. "Some of the rituals I wanted to try called for a familiar—an animal that various helpful spirits supposedly can inhabit." She rolled her eyes. "Anyway, I've had it with this nonsense."

"Maybe . . ." began Humpert.

"Maybe nothing. It's nonsense," she declared with rancor and just a tinge of hysteria. She turned towards me. "It's supposed to give you a glimpse of whatever it is you're seeking. We finished the whole ritual. We got nothing."

"Still, Victoria . . ." Humpert tried again.

"Except for the one trick with the plants, everything in the books we have is garbage. We aren't going to find Zandie's grimoire, and we aren't going to find the ceremony I need anywhere else—not in Egypt or Crete or Denmark or anywhere. And it doesn't matter. Because I *don't* need it. I'm fine now. Before I was just too timid."

"All right, but let's . . ." began Leo.

"Time for bed," said Victoria, marching out past us, still naked.

"So, what's the ceremony she needs?" I asked with extreme skepticism.

"Fuck you," said Leo.

Wet Dreams and Nightmares

"Some Girls Get Roses, Others Just Pricks."
– Unpublished song by *Gavin Kennan,* aka *Steve Witowski*

CHAPTER 31

"How was your date last night?" Victoria asked innocently, walking into my room without knocking. Fortunately—I suppose—I was fully dressed and combing my hair. Her eyes were bloodshot, her skin sallow, and her carriage weary, yet she looked awfully good to me. And she was obviously wearing nothing under her thin robe.

"She couldn't make it."

"One of those last-minute things, huh? A late-night dental appointment—or an emergency oven cleaning?"

"Actually, her mother died." *Her mother died?*

"What?"

"Suicide."

To avoid taking tests and turning in papers on time during college, I'd killed off my own mother once or twice, along with a girlfriend or two. It always worked. Nobody would lie about a thing like that. In those days, I'd called it beating the system. This was before I'd known anyone who'd actually killed themselves.

"Rough," Victoria said, with a stubborn note of disbelief in her voice, as if the whole idea of me having a date was still ridiculous. "I found a sleazy little magazine on the kitchen floor this morning and threw it out—full of naked fat girls. Is that what you needed money for?"

"I only bought it because..."

"You actually *bought* it? I thought maybe you found it in the trash somewhere."

"The barmaid at Melvin's was selling them. She had her picture in it."

"Melvin's? The place on Chapala Street that says, 'Bikini'd Beauties' in the window?" From her tone, she might have been talking about body lice.

"The beer's cheap," I said pointedly.

"I'll bet magazines weren't all she was selling, and she was probably cheaper than the beer. Or maybe that place is only for lookers. Why don't you just go down to the beach? Or maybe instead of giving you money to waste at Melvin's, I should just let you watch me bathe once in a while. That would be harmless—and cheaper, too. Would you like that?"

"I've seen it. And I wasn't all that impressed."

"You looked mighty impressed to me," she laughed. "As I remember you could barely breathe you were so impressed." She patted me on the cheek.

"Shee-it," I said as if that was ludicrous. But I said it too late.

"By the way, how the hell did you get into the basement last night? That door was supposed to be locked?"

"Really? It was? Is there even a lock on the damn thing?"

"There is and it's a damn good one. But it's not much good if people don't actually lock it. Humpert's really starting to lose it."

Up close, I imagined I could smell the residue of the blood on her skin. "Listen, Victoria," I said. "This isn't working out between us. I should go."

"Go? Why?" Her surprise sounded genuine. "Because I don't want to sleep with you?"

"No, it's not that. Not really. But we're simply not getting along. Maybe it's the sexual tension between us—maybe not—but it doesn't matter. We're not getting along."

"Sexual tension? What sexual tension?"

"Maybe it's me. It's no secret I want to sleep with you—I have for a while." It was a relief just to say it—honesty was easier now because it certainly was no secret. "At first, I wasn't going to do anything about it because of...because of us living and working so closely together."

Total honesty was more than I was up to.

"I'm sorry, Steve. I'm just not attracted to you that way—not at all."

I tried to hold my face impassive. Though this was obviously no surprise, the confirmation still hurt. "I realize that. And that's why we're having trouble getting along."

"It's my fault? I thought we were getting along fine."

"It's nobody's fault. Maybe it's mine; it's hard to get past it when someone you want finds you repulsive."

"Why can't we just be friends?" she said inevitably.

Great. I couldn't even get a contradiction on "repulsive."

"Besides," she added, "I thought this was a business arrangement."

"Maybe you should just pay me for what I've got coming, and I'll get out of here."

She thought for a moment, then said. "I don't want you to go, Steve." She put her hand on my arm. "Why don't we both just think about it for a couple of days. Then if you still want to go, I'll pay you off. All right?" Her gaze was warm.

Oh, well. "All right. A couple of days."

"Fabulous. Now give me a hug."

It may have been a friendly hug to her, but it lingered, and I became too conscious of her breasts tight against my chest, and the heat of her abdomen against my damnably growing erection.

"You *are* attracted to me, aren't you." She smiled, not backing off a millimeter. "Poor baby, maybe I should try to look ugly for you."

"No big deal." She was enjoying this too much. I was about to add: "I'm attracted to a lot of people," but I changed it to, "I'll survive," so as not to hinder any progress I might be making. *Hope springs eternal.*

"Good," she said, kissing me on the cheek and hugging me even tighter for a second before stepping back and peering down at my erection. "I'll try not to make it difficult for you. And I won't throw away any more of your magazines."

Then she patted me on the butt and walked out.

I went down to the kitchen and made myself some breakfast. Okay, I was repulsive, and she didn't want me. But what was she supposed to be thinking over in the next couple of days? And the hug? I'd stick around. I needed the money—I was more paranoid of being broke than I'd ever been in the past. But I probably could have insisted and gotten paid off right away. To be honest, I was staying to play out the run, to take a chance on even a pity fuck—because she felt sorry for me or because she didn't want to lose my labor. I always used to say that I wouldn't want to have sex with anyone who didn't want to have sex with me, but Victoria had made no bones about not *wanting* to have sex with me and was only slightly ambiguous as to whether or not she *would*. And here I was.

While I was eating my Raisin Bran, Victoria came down and went into the den. When I was finished, I went in and asked her if she wanted me to go back to the vaults in the crypt—hoping she wouldn't.

Seated behind the desk, she looked up from what she was reading and rocked back in the chair before speaking. "No. Humpert finished off the wall vaults yesterday—no Zandie. No bodies at all for that matter. And no secret knowledges." She lifted a finger toward her mouth as if she was going to bite a nail, then stopped and stared at the finger as if studying it for the answer. The muscles tensed in her neck and around her jaw.

"Want me to start back in on the remodeling?"

She shrugged. "The remodeling doesn't matter. Actually, it doesn't even matter if I don't find the grimoire. Still, it's got to be here somewhere."

I saw what she'd been reading now—Zandie's will.

"I know it's with him." She tapped the pages in front of her. "It's got to be. Only where?"

"Is it that important?"

"No. It isn't. I'm just trying to decide whether to give it up or to keep searching. I could be in Beverly Hills now. I should be."

"You're not going to remodel this place?"

"Humpert had suggested I remodel the place to get back some of my investment. I overpaid for it in order to get The Ashram out of here. And I did—or I had Cranick do—a few things to make it more livable. I should have stayed in a hotel. But I came here—I bought this place—to find Zandie's grimoire. And not to sell it to some real estate lady. I told you a little white lie or two so you wouldn't think I was crazy. But if we can find it, Steve, the knowledge—the power—in that book will do a lot more than just make us both rich. And you can believe that."

I nodded noncommittally. Twenty years earlier, she *might* have seemed crazy, but twenty years earlier no one like Victoria would have said what she'd just said—at least not out loud. Since then, I'd heard any number of equally unbelievable claims from allegedly sane and rational people and nodded in the same way. After all, we lived in a world where the First Lady of the United States consulted with an astrologer on scheduling presidential trips and speeches.

I once knew a woman who insisted on the lights being out during sex because she was haunted by her grandmother's ghost, and she couldn't cum if her Granny was watching. The following year that woman graduated from Harvard Law on her way to becoming an extremely successful U.S. Attorney.

Victoria's eyes widened with sincerity as she murmured, "All I can do for now is to ask you to trust me. Can you do that?" And I did think of that spell she'd put on the plants.

"Let me see the will," I said.

Perched on the edge of the desk, I read it through, slowly and carefully—at least I did once I forgot about making a show of reading it through slowly and carefully.

"Again, there's no way to know if these instructions were ever carried out," I offered when I'd finished. "If they'd have followed all of them, the will itself would have been destroyed."

"That could be an oversight. It must have been chaos around here, with Zandie having been lynched, and the whorehouse being shut down. Remember, his lab was bricked up just like he ordered."

"Uh huh. And the equipment inside was intact?"

"It certainly was," she said eagerly. "All those glass beakers and instruments and things and none of them were broken."

"Then maybe it was bricked up *before* the lynch mob arrived. Zandie may have done it himself if he was afraid of trouble. And then there's the language of the will. It may or may not be significant that he mentioned his grimoire being interred in a secret and secure place, then called his grave secret and secure. We're just guessing that those are clues. Just because the hiding place and the grave are described with a couple of the same words doesn't mean they're the same place."

"But he said the grimoire was 'interred.' And look at this." She stood up, leaned across the desk and took the will from me carefully. She searched through it for a moment. "This line here: 'where only the most dedicated pilgrim who studies and searches may bring its truths back to light.'"

She looked at me expectantly, hoping I'd agree she'd just proven her case, then said adamantly, "It's hidden somewhere—somewhere it can be found by searching and studying. Those have to be clues."

"Even if they were, even if he intended for it to be buried with him, suppose the mob got it first. Or one of his girls decided to keep it."

"I'm certain it's with the body. It's got to be." She didn't sound so certain. She handed me the document and sat back down. Her shoulders were slumped, her breasts drooped slightly—but excitingly. Once again, imperfection made her seem more accessible.

I skimmed through the will one more time, and that's when I found it. Everything clicked into place.

"Victoria," I said, "I know where he's buried."

Evading her questions, I asked, "Are Leo and Humpert around?"

"Upstairs."

"Better get them."

She hesitated momentarily, then went to the back stairs and called them down. Leo appeared in a sweat suit without his wig. He was panting, but if he'd been exercising, he hadn't worked up a sweat. When Humpert arrived—puffing on a cigarette that obviously annoyed Leo—I took them down to the basement.

Humpert knocked over a rack of test tubes as we wove our way around the equipment outside the room that had been Zandie's lab. But if there had ever been anything in them it had evaporated long before. When we got to the crypt, Leo informed me with disgust that everything in there had been checked and if that was all I had, he might as well go back to his workout.

"Where's Zandie?" Victoria demanded.

"Inside." I motioned for them to lead the way.

Humpert let out a sigh, and they all exchanged skeptical glances, but they went in. Inside the crypt, only the top vault was still covered.

"And that's the one you opened yourself, Steve," said Humpert. "So, where's Zandie?"

The lower vaults yawned empty, their shattered headstones littering the floor along with the broken sarcophagi lids. A sledgehammer leaning against one wall gave evidence of Humpert's dainty touch. The smell of dust mingled with that of decay.

"According to the will," I explained, "Zandie wanted to be laid to rest 'surrounded by his finest ladies,' right? Maybe that simply meant he wanted to be buried somewhere in the old church—in effect surrounded by the women who worked there. Or maybe the finest ladies he wanted to be surrounded by were the local women who'd supposedly died for his love. Whose bodies he'd stolen and collected here."

"If *they* were those finest ladies," Humpert said, "the mob took them back and re-buried them where they came from."

"But Zandie didn't know that when he wrote the will."

"*Obviously*. But maybe that's why he wasn't buried here. Because, *as you might remember,* we've already checked and..." Humpert paused and made a sweeping gesture, taking in the vaults and sarcophagi, "he *isn't*."

"You're right. Because..." I matched his pause, enjoying my moment. "He wasn't actually buried at all."

They all stared at me blankly.

"The will didn't say to 'bury' him. It didn't even say to 'inter' him. The will said they were to 'enthrone' him."

I sauntered over to the concrete chair—the concrete throne. I kicked away some rubble that was leaning up against it. A circular indentation had been recessed in the base the throne was sitting on. Set in the indentation was a brass plate. I bent down and wiped it off, but I still couldn't read it.

"Go get a flashlight," I ordered Humpert. He looked to Victoria for confirmation. She nodded and he went.

When he returned, they all crowded around. I switched on the flashlight and flashed the light on the name.

REBECCA

Not what I was expecting. But before the comments had even begun, I lowered the flashlight and bent down a little farther. It was below the brass plate, carved into the concrete along the bottom of the base. The script was so flowery I'd originally taken it for a decoration.

I read out loud:

E.S. ZANDIE—KING OF HEARTS

Then—in control for a change—I commanded, "Break it open."

CHAPTER 32

And the throne *was* hollow.

But it was also empty.

"Brilliant!" Victoria spit out, visibly upset. "It's not his damn throne. It's not his damn tomb. It's his damn chair. It would be like being buried in a Barcalounger."

She stormed off with a crack about my "claim" to have attended Harvard, as if it had been a transparent lie she'd humored until then. Leo looked as if he wanted to strangle me. The concern on Humpert's face was shattered by a sudden coughing fit. It sounded as if dust from the crypt had lodged in his lungs.

Since nobody was working, I just sat in my room, reading *Rumanian $ucce$$ $torie$*. Getting another brainstorm at one point, I dashed back down to the basement and checked out all the compartments in the built-in ice box. That was probably a stupid idea. No Zandie of course. Still, afterward, I went through the one in the back entryway, too. Success!

Later, I walked across the highway down to the ocean, following the path beside the flood-control wash. The only other people on the beach were two attractive young women, sunbathing in matching white bikinis. They looked to be about college age. One glanced up at me briefly. As far as I could tell, the other never even looked up. In my tight crimson speedo, I felt like an aging exhibitionist, so I pretended they weren't there either and kept my distance. Eventually they headed out, passing closely enough for me to realize they were only about sixteen. I should have felt fatherly.

After I left the beach, I got dressed, hopped in the VW and just drove. I still had a quarter of a tank of gas, but in San Cristobal I pulled into the gas station just past the giant fig tree to use the men's room. Traffic slowed to a crawl there anyway because of the stop lights. That was why the spot used to be so popular with hitchhikers.

The time Ann and I had spent there back in 1970, we'd no sooner stashed our stuff under the tree than we were joined by another couple: a tall, graceful dude and a lady with an elegant, expressive face who looked about twelve months pregnant. They were obviously thrilled by the impending baby and by each other. As the evening progressed, more and more hitchhikers joined us. Some we'd already seen or met or shared rides with coming down the coast. Some we'd meet again farther on. Some we'd never seen before and would never see again. People from all over the country. In those days, we never knew we were a fad. We'd thought of ourselves as the seeds of a new world-wide community. And virtually any long hair in a car would pick up any other. Of course that was before everyone had long hair. One couple had an old school bus they drove up and down the coast as if they were on a route, picking up hitchhikers and smoking weed. Just after dark that bus pulled up at the tree and twelve more folks joined us.

Several people had guitars, many of us contributed a little pot, most had some extra food or some money to contribute for wine. Ann and I didn't need any pot and only a sip of wine for the taste. We were tripping—we'd split a little acid we'd been given by the people we'd stayed with the night before. More than that, we were discovering we were in love.

As the sun had set, the pure, sweet sound of a recorder arose from some place indeterminate, like a delicate scent in the air. An evening of songs—tripping. They were laced like colored banners through the branches of the enormous tree. An evening of making love in the shadows—Ann above me, beside me, beneath me, delicate, strong, passionate—as a soft soprano voice sang the album version of Terry Davis's *Living and Dreaming*. On one side of us, the rhythmic breathing of the ocean. On the other, the more irregular current of the highway, waiting to carry us away the next morning. The thick, low hanging branches of the tree sheltered us all from the wind that night—as they'd sheltered us from the sun during the day—a roof that let in the starlight.

In front of the tree, the city of San Cristobal had placed a plaque with "Fantastic Facts" about the tree's massive dimensions. We'd made fun of it at first because those dimensions weren't entirely nature's work. Strong cables linked and supported many of the sagging branches, allowing them to reach such huge proportions. A smaller plaque revealed that the cables had been strung by the city, giving nature a hand. On acid, I eventually decided that those cables were not only appropriate but desirable. And it seemed to me that the colored, musical cables that joined all of us together were even stronger.

Turns out that was a hallucination.

As twilight approached, I went out and sat on the old church's front steps. The Santa Ana winds blew hard—and hot as dragon's breath—raising a dusty haze. After a few moments, Victoria joined me. She had yet another old book in her lap. A popsicle stick marked her place. It was the first time I'd seen her without makeup. Not that she wasn't still beautiful, but it was as if her anxiety had been exposed in the tense lines around her eyes and mouth. She opened the book, but didn't look down into it. Her fingers fiddled with the popsicle stick.

"I've been having bad dreams lately," she said. Was this a semi-apology for the way she'd been acting?

"Me, too. It's amazing we sleep at all, what with O'Ryan and Cranick and spending all our time digging up graves."

"I think Humpert's dying. He doesn't know it, but I think he's beginning to suspect. The doctors can't figure out what's wrong with him. But they don't think it's serious."

"Then what makes you think he's dying?"

"I don't know. I just feel it." She cleared her throat. It sounded as if she were holding back tears. "Zandie could do things. He could. I know it. Maybe he didn't understand what he was doing, but with all the spells and rituals and ceremonies he dug up, he stumbled on one or two that could really make things happen. Strange things."

"Like?" I asked, thinking this was like asking my law student friend why she didn't just ask her dead Granny to leave the room when she wanted to have sex. It was usually better to leave ghostly Grannys and similar dogmas alone.

Victoria shook her head. Her smell on the arid breeze reminded me of the taste of a woman's mouth when she was having her period. Victoria was afraid. "We won't know unless we find the grimoire. The grimoire is the key. I don't really need it, of course. But it's got me crazy. I've gone to every fake medium in the county. The last one looked more like a surfer girl than a psychic. Her claim to fame seemed to be one glass eye and the ugliest lipstick I've ever seen." She gave a sad little smile. "In the back of my mind I almost believe that if I'm very, very good, the book will turn up, like a present from Santa Claus."

She made a noise that was half laugh, half sigh, and flipped her popsicle stick out into the yard.

"I'm a desirable woman," she said out of nowhere. "An extremely desirable woman. Everyone wants me."

"Everyone doesn't want anybody."

"Bullshit. I can get anybody. *Anybody*. Men dream of having me. Of marrying me."

"Is that so?" I said, irritated. Who said that kind of thing? "To be honest, Victoria, I haven't been exactly overwhelmed by the men I've seen hanging around you so far."

"If that isn't the limit," she mused, almost to herself. "Now I'm being criticized about the quality of my men by an itinerant failure who spends his time with his nose in jack-off magazines and other people's underwear. Who can barely manage to get into the sweaty bloomers of the neighborhood lard ass."

"Maria's worth four of you. She's also one hell of an artist."

"Well, at least she has a *career*." The distain in that word was astonishing. *The child may be hopelessly slow, but I hear she can feed herself.*

"And you're doing a whole lot better than I am? Boffing Humpert?"

She simply shook her head at my stupidity—not even bothering to glance over. "Humpert couldn't boff anybody, even if he could find somebody silly enough to let him. He's a watcher. *You* should be able to relate to that. I know you like to peep."

I knocked the book out of her hands. It flopped down the stairs, the cover ripping partway off, one of the stitched sections falling out. Maybe it was a substitute for hitting her. I needed a reaction.

"And what are you, Victoria?" I yelled. *So, she wasn't sleeping with Humpert after all.* "I'm not so sure you aren't all show and no go, yourself. I see all the men coming around, but I don't see any of them coming back. Maybe when it comes right down to it, you can't get right down to it. Maybe you're as frigid as you look."

In her fingers, Victoria still held a yellowed piece of a page from the book. It was trembling. In the dim light, her eyes were a darker blue, and shining with fury. Her clenched jaw hollowed out her cheeks, aging her. She could have been forty-five.

Slowly she got to her feet. Then, pouncing like a cornered animal, she was upon me, her fingers twisting into my hair, yanking my face toward hers. I was aware of the pores on her face, the faint hairs on her upper lip, the slight bunching of skin that someday would become wrinkles.

"You fucking worm!" she cried. You know who wants me? Rich men. Important men. Gorgeous men. Successful men. Men who could have any woman they want, want me. This very minute, one of the most powerful men in the world is waiting for me in Beverly Hills, *dying* to make me his wife. I should be insulted that you could even imagine I might want you. That you could even dream of having a woman like me. Not that you could handle it if you did."

With a push, she let go of my hair. I didn't know what to say. Because she was right. I was completely and totally out of her league. And I was also ashamed of myself for the frigid crack. Talk about the classic male idiocy: *If you don't want to sleep with me, you must be frigid.* She *was* a stunningly beautiful woman; and to be honest, every man who saw her probably did want her. It was hardly her fault she couldn't want them all back. And from all recent evidence, I was an easy guy not to want.

Trying to phrase an apology, I went down and picked up her book, holding it together to make the damage appear as minimal as possible. My face was damp with sweat, and my shirt was clammy against my back with the heat and the tension.

Victoria stood above me—rigidly—a statue of a goddess.

"I'm sorry," I said, offering her the book. "I was out of line. I don't really think you're frigid." Someplace, though, in the back of my mind I was hoping she'd still try to prove to me that she wasn't.

"*You'll* never know," she said with a contempt I could hardly help but share. "You just stick with the Maria's of the world. You can probably handle that."

I didn't feel that I had the right to accept second-class citizenship for Maria as well as myself, but all I said was, "I could do worse."

"*You* probably could."

We sat there together silently as it grew dark. I don't know why. After a while, a car bounced down the old road in front of us. Another Mercedes, an ugly brown one. From inside came the sounds of Top Forty radio, mixed with high pitched, but male, laughter. The car went by, then stopped and backed up. A moment later, Maria got out and headed toward the church. Then her husband got out and followed her. He stumbled and laughed loudly. He'd been drinking.

Several yards from the steps, Maria seemed to notice us for the first time. "Oh...Victoria? Steve? Hi... Al... Al and I were just wondering if you might like to come by for a drink."

"We're having a celebration," said Al. "We're going to have a baby. Maria's pregnant. And I got my new job."

"So much for your great piece of ass." Victoria's whisper probably just missed being audible to Maria and Al.

I began to beg off and Maria started to accept it. But Al—who I wouldn't have thought would be all that eager to see me after the night before—insisted. And to my amazement, Victoria accepted for both of us, telling them we'd be over shortly.

They drove off, and Victoria went in to freshen up. That turned out to mean full make-up, nylons, and a mini dress which for her was blatant. As we crossed over to Maria's, Victoria broke the silence only once, to ask what "the career girl's" husband was like.

"Why?"

"No reason. Just making conversation."

"He's the salt of the earth," I said, knocking on Maria's door. "Perfect, if you don't mind an occasional broken arm."

"You don't react well to violence, do you, lover? If it was up to you, I'd have been slashed to pieces that first night. And you should have seen your poor little face when you first caught sight of me last night on that altar. God, you'd have really died if you'da known the blood we were using was human."

She clucked me under the chin—once again, stabbing me with her fingernail. And Al answered the door.

While I was still chewing over that last crack, Al and Victoria decided we should go out, so we all piled into the turd-colored Mercedes. Victoria made a fuss over the car—ignoring the four inch gilt lettering on the side reading, "Vantana Chemical International,"—and Al described the salary and benefits of his new job. On the way into San Cristobal, Victoria sarcastically suggested we try Melvin's Bikini Bar.

We ended up at Juggler's, a restaurant on the wharf. Getting out in the nearly empty parking lot, we could hear the waves lapping at the pilings. The water around us was dark and smelled of low tide. I thought of blood and putrefaction—though by then I'd decided that Victoria probably got Humpert and Leo to cut themselves to provide the blood the night before, maybe mixing it with a little water. They'd have done it for her. If it was anything more dramatic, she never would have told me the blood was human.

It was quite a bit of blood though.

"Why don't you girls go ahead and get us a table in the bar," Al said, pulling me over by the low railing at the edge of the wharf. "I just want a quick word with Steve."

Maria looked distressed. In spite of Al's glasses, his squinty face, uncertain chin and thin body, I had a quick vision of myself ending up in the water below. I'd have to swim through the stench to the shore. Victoria would have a great time with that.

"Steve," he said quietly. "I love my wife. I never realized how much I loved her until it looked like I was losing her."

He seemed more sober now. Leaning on the railing, he kept running his free hand through his short black hair as if it used to be longer, saying, "I got crazy for a while, real crazy. I drove her away. I don't blame you for what happened between you two, not really, and I'm sorry about the way I behaved toward you. I only blame myself."

"Well, I'd like to apolo…" I started, but he waved it off.

"I understand, Steve. It's none of my business, but Maria told me about your problem. To be honest," he added, embarrassed, "I forced it out of her. You saw how I was last night."

I couldn't see why my being a fugitive had even come up between them. Then he told me that I had nothing to be ashamed of, and that it happened to everybody occasionally, and I realized he was talking about my supposed impotence. I'd forgotten all about it.

"And I suppose Maria's not the prettiest girl in the world," he said apologetically, horribly. And like that was his fault.

"It had nothing to do with Maria," I insisted quickly. "It was me."

The conversation continued in reverently hushed tones, as if a person had died, not just my dick. Though Al was obviously relieved, he wasn't gloating; he even told me about his own occasional potency problem.

"There's this one fantasy that usually works for me," he confided with a shy eagerness. "Would you like me to tell you about…?"

"That's okay, Al." *I'd rather have a family of kangaroo rats munching on my scrotum.* "Thanks though." I almost felt guilty for my lack of impotence. And yet, it was all I could do to keep from blurting out that it might be his problem, but it certainly wasn't mine.

"If you don't mind me asking," he said, "are things getting any better? With Victoria?"

A gust of warm wind blew my hair out of place, exposing my bald spot. Al couldn't have been more earnest in his imitation alligator shirt and his new Sears jeans. Across the harbor, the rigging of sailboats clanked and lights squirmed upon the water.

"Sometimes yes, sometimes no." The lie tasted guilty and pleasurable. It was the first time in my life I'd claimed to be sleeping with a woman when I wasn't. Welcome to adolescence. *Shit,* I thought, remembering the way Stephen and Dell and I used to make fun of the guys who did that back then, stretching their credibility over half the girls in Emerson High. Now I tried to tell myself I'd only lied to show that Maria and I were a thing of the past, that I'd moved on, and to confirm that my "problem" was not just with her. That's what I tried to tell myself. But I knew better than to believe such a liar. "Generally, it's getting better though," I concluded.

"Glad to hear it," he said. "And I hope you two are as happy together as Maria and I intend to be."

"Victoria and I aren't really together. I mean, we're not really a couple. She dates a lot of men... We're both free agents really."

Behind his glasses, he blinked. Then he cocked his head to one side as if he was trying to hear better.

"Really?" A new respect, and an almost childlike wonder. "An open relationship, huh? That's great. I wish... no... Not really. I'm going to be a father now. A child needs the stability of a solid family."

"Sounds like you're excited though, about becoming a dad?"

"I really am. My own father was a lout; thought he was a real estate tycoon. He was always someplace else. He'd do anything for a buck. The last time I ever saw him I was nine. On one of his rare visits home he gave me the fatherly guidance that—with all he'd made and with all he had—the only two things worth anything were old whiskey and new pussy."

"Lovely."

"Worse, he repeated it two hours later at the dinner table in front of my mother, her mother and my two sisters. You can see why my mother divorced him. We've got to get back to the family in this country: parents, grandparents, even great-grandparents. A child needs roots, don't you think? The deeper the better."

"I suppose."

He started telling me about his family history, which he could trace only as far as his grandparents. Then he wanted to know about mine. I tossed off a couple of generalities and headed for the restaurant, answering his follow-up questions as briefly as possible. I'd never been interested in my own mostly Irish-American ancestry until it had been too late to find out.

My mother's parents died before I was born. My paternal grandfather's main ambition was to be left alone—perhaps with an occasional beer. My grandmother—thick Galway brogue and all—was actually born on the South Side of Chicago. She worked fourteen hours a day, raising her family and cooking and cleaning for what she called the gentry, hoping her children could someday rise to their level. With her help, my father progressed through Indiana University and Harvard Business School, from a Norman Thomas socialist to a proud Republican stockbroker, busting his butt to provide everything for his family, including a sixteen room house-on-the-hill he struggled to afford, with no servants but his wife.

Unlike Al's father, mine worked his whole life for his family. Like Al's, he seldom saw them. He despised "do-gooder liberalism." His ambition was to join the Nixons and the Goldwaters, the aristocracy of "practical intelligence" that he believed should rule the country, almost as if by Divine Right. He ran for state senator, state assembly, and city councilman. Though proud to the point of bigotry of his Irish heritage, he was too much of an elitist for the electorate. And no matter how successful he became in business, he never quite shook the sense of loss inflicted on him by a populace he didn't respect.

My mother, on the other hand, took care of the house and raised three children whose ages spanned fifteen years—I was almost exactly in the middle. She was deeply religious. Before marriage, she'd worked with "special" children for the Archdiocese, and had considered becoming a missionary nun. It was because of her that, as a child, I talked about becoming a priest. Because of my father perhaps, I was a bit of a hustler, at least when I wasn't playing baseball: selling greeting cards, candies, and magazines door-to-door; putting together snow-shoveling and lawn-mowing routes. As I entered my teens, J.F.K., an Irish-American Catholic talking idealism, ran for President. That hooked me on politics—at least temporarily combining the hustling and the religion. And my father and I started getting farther and farther apart, and more and more combative.

Then the sixties happened.

In a hail of laughter, a party of eight people pushed out of the restaurant just as Al and I were about to step in. He held the door for everyone, smiling though one of them almost knocked him over.

At a tiny drink table across the room, Victoria was surveying the crowd with a bored expression. Maria stared out the window at the bay. She must have shifted her position three times as we approached. Her beer was untouched.

As soon as Al and I got our drinks, Al proposed a toast.

"To our new friends," he said. "And to the child who's coming to join us."

"And to the mother and father," I added. Breaking Maria's hand might have been unforgivable, and it probably was, but she'd said it was the only time he'd ever touched her in anger and before that he'd barely even raised his voice to her. We all screw up—even in major ways—and I wasn't as ready to judge Al as I once would have been.

"How far along are you, Maria?" asked Victoria, as we put our drinks down.

"Six weeks."

"Then it happened before your trip out here. I mean... nowadays they can tell if you're pregnant just about right away, you know. Of course, it had to happen before you and Al split up, didn't it."

Maria nodded, but she and I looked to Al simultaneously. His smile had grown rigid, as if—chemist or not—perhaps he hadn't known how rapidly they could now determine pregnancy.

Absently, he fumbled in his pocket and pulled out a cigarette. I threw a warning glance in Victoria's direction, but her eyes were on Al, too.

"Mind if I have one, Al?" she asked as he put an English Oval up to his lips. I'd never seen her smoke a cigarette stronger than a Virginia Slims Menthol Light.

Instead of offering her the pack, he pulled out a single cigarette, handed it to her, then slid her the matches. Victoria inhaled the harsh smoke easily. Between quick, nervous pulls on his beer, Al cast a furtive glance toward his wife. When he finished off the drink, he immediately slipped over to the bar to get another.

"That was really stupid," I hissed at Victoria. The English Oval was sitting in the ashtray smoking itself.

"What?"

"You know what. Why don't you just ask who the father is?"

"What are you talking about?"

"Just let it drop, Steve," whispered Maria. "She didn't mean anything."

At the bar, Al paid for his beer and took a drink. He returned his wallet to his back pocket, then, thinking better of it, switched it to his front pocket as if he was afraid of getting his pocket picked in the seven steps between the bar and the table.

Victoria went on as if she didn't notice Al's approach, "Of course, I didn't mean anything. Steve couldn't possibly be the father... Unless," she added suspiciously, "unless maybe your dates are a little off. You two aren't trying to pull something on that poor guy, are you?"

"Maria?" Al's voice was remarkably controlled. There may have been just the slightest tremor around his upper lip.

"If it wasn't your child," said Maria with great simplicity, "I have no reason to say it was."

Al's face softened. I wanted to change the subject before Victoria opened her mouth again, but I wasn't sure what to say.

"It's all my fault," Victoria said. "Come here and sit down, Al."

"Maybe we should call it a night," I said.

"Nonsense," Victoria replied. "We came here to celebrate. We can't leave on a note like this."

"It's all right, Steve," Al said. His movements thickened with drink, he pulled back his chair from the table and sat down, crossing his legs with elaborate casualness. "I know you couldn't be the father. I'm just not used to anyone else being with Maria. But things are different than they used to be. We'd split up; she had a right. I mean, I wasn't exactly a monk, myself."

"No one would expect a man like you to be," said Victoria, patting his knee.

Al brightened. "Damn straight. And if it's all right for me, it's all right for her, too."

"Although it *is* different for a man," said Victoria.

"It's no different for a man, Victoria," I said. "Normal women need sex, too." I tried not to stress the "normal," in spite of my irritation.

"The great expert on women," she said, shutting me up.

"Can I ask you something, Victoria?" Al ventured.

"Whatever you like, Al."

"Does it bother you? About Maria and Steve? Especially with you and Steve having sex problems of your own. I mean, Steve told me about his..."

"What!?!" she exploded, searing me with a look of cold fury. Trying to stop the blush from rising, I probably made it worse.

Victoria took a moment to collect herself, and then she spoke with a terrible calm, tapping Al's knee as she made her points.

"The only sex problem Steve and I ever had was him trying to grope me after I fell asleep on the beach. He *works* for me! Look at him. I don't get that desperate."

Conversation had stopped at the nearby tables. I couldn't believe this was happening. I could feel the eyes—especially Victoria's—like spotlights on a fleeing convict.

"Did you tell them we were sleeping together?" she demanded.

I wanted to tell her to quiet down, but I couldn't even bring myself to look at her.

"No...not really," I said softly. "I told him I couldn't get it up with Maria. To make it believable I let him think I sometimes had the same problem *even* with you."

The emphatic, "even," didn't halt the sharp slap across my face, nor the back of the same hand as it returned.

"You may have a problem getting it up with Maria, but *nobody* has ever had that problem with me. You tell this man right now that you've been running around with a hard-on ever since we met."

Playing with the ring of water from my glass on the plastic surface of the table, I felt like I'd been waiting for this moment—like this was the day of reckoning for all my sins.

"I'm a liar," I said, without looking up. "I don't have a potency problem. And the only problem I've ever had with Victoria is that she was smart enough to have nothing to do with me."

"Whose baby is that, Maria?" Al shot.

"I told you whose baby it was." Her eyes were moist, but her voice was harder than his.

"You also told me he was impotent."

"She told you the truth," I said. And she had. Though I had gotten it up once with Maria, not only had she used her diaphragm but I wore a rubber. And I hadn't stayed hard long enough to cum. There was virtually no chance I could have impregnated her. "This whole thing is my fault. I apologize to all of you. I suppose I'm not much of a person."

"For once I agree with you," Victoria snapped. "Al, would you please drive me home?"

CHAPTER 33

We all went home together. Beyond humiliation, I tried to explain my "impotence" on the way. The truth sounded like another lie, even to me. Al was obviously preoccupied and drove right past the church to Maria's. I think he was planning on dropping us all off and heading to his hotel. But Victoria told him she had something she wanted to show him, so she took his arm and they walked back to her place. I stayed at Maria's to apologize. Which I did, several times.

Then Maria apologized to me for telling Al about what had happened—or hadn't happened—between us.

"He asked if we'd slept together, then got crazy when I admitted we had," she explained. "I knew today I'd probably be telling him he was going to be a father, and I didn't want him to ever have the slightest doubt the child was his. I knew it would eat at him for the rest of his life. Especially because we wouldn't be together."

"And did you tell him that?" I asked, surprised. "That you wouldn't be together?"

She nodded. "He just didn't believe me. Not with the kid coming and all. His kid."

My bones creaked as I lowered myself down on a cushion. I noticed a well-worn copy of *The Bloody Chamber* was tucked into the bookcase between *The Art of Sensuous Massage* and something by Krishnamurti. Only her favorite books had made the cut coming out from Michigan, so most of the others were on painting and painters. Above the bookcase, Maria had hung one of O'Ryan's White Rock signs. In this version, the White Rock girl was thin and tall, and she was still topless. Maria had hung only one of her own paintings: a strikingly powerful study of an old woman of indeterminate race who reminded me of my grandmother. Not a cookie-baking grandma from a Hallmark card, but a woman with the strength to claw out a life for herself and her family in a sometimes unfriendly country.

Maria put on Phil Ochs again, rattling the old speakers. The evening after Stephen's funeral, listening to Phil Ochs, so well-intentioned, so *relevant*—so irrelevant, perhaps even pretentious, as the world moved on to *Saturday Night Fever*—was when I decided to go to L.A. and make the disco album.

"Al's never had a beautiful woman make a fuss over him before," said Maria, flopping down on the bed. "Besides me, he's only had one girlfriend—when he was a senior in high school. And she dumped him for a Marine who was never even around."

We were both silent for a moment. Then she mused, "I wish I'd brought out my dog. Though I guess it would be too crowded in here."

"You could move into the main part of the house."

"Uh-huh, I suppose I will, eventually. Assuming..." she sighed. "Don't know what I'll do with all that stuff in there. I got to spend the afternoon digging around in it today. The insurance people at the hospital needed to know my uncle's Medicare number and if he had any other insurance. But try to find anything in that jumble."

"Some of it might be worth something, I suppose."

"I doubt it. Al wanted a few things that he thought might be cool. Nothing of any real value. I told him that if my uncle didn't make it then..." once again, she let her voice trail off.

"How is your uncle? Any change?"

She shook her head. "It's so strange to think he's hurt so bad because he looks better than he did before it happened. The deformity in his back is all gone now, and all the wrinkles and lines in his face have relaxed. Like a corpse, I guess," she added sadly.

A half hour later, Maria—who was obviously exhausted—had dropped off to sleep. As I headed for the door, I realized that the small table in what passed for a kitchen area was covered with a strange jumble of stuff—most likely the things that Al had picked out as "cool." The most prominent was a human skull covered with the tarnished remains of what I would bet was gold plating. So O'Ryan did have the skull Zandie had kept on his desk or his mantel or wherever.

But that wasn't what caught my attention.

Because just behind the skull was a rack of knives with handles in the shape of serpent heads. Six knives, each identical to the one Cranick had used to stab Victoria that night by the highway. Six knives and one empty spot on the rack. I picked one up. Crudely carved in the handle was the number five and listed underneath, "Aton, Itzamna, Baal, Asmodeus."

One by one, I checked the other knives. Each had a number from one through seven—with three missing of course, since I'd throw that one into the flood control wash. Below each number were four words. The first three were unique to each knife, though the ones I recognized all appeared to be the names of gods and spirits from various religions. The final name on each knife was my old pal, Asmodeus.

Just as I replaced the last knife in the rack, Al stumbled in without knocking, singing. He seemed surprised to see me, but not upset.

"Victoria wanted me to check out her tap water," he offered, unasked. "To see if I thought her well might be polluted. I'll have it tested but I'm sure it's fine."

"Everything about Victoria is fine," I muttered.

"Whatever." Al glanced over at the bed, noticed Maria was asleep and lowered his voice, too. "I just dropped in to say good-night to Maria. I'm on my way back to Vantana. Busy day tomorrow."

"No, Al, you stay with your wife. I'm leaving anyway. I'm sure she wanted to talk to you. Believe me, what happened between her and I was nothing."

"Right. Nothing to you. Victoria told me how Maria chased after you, how at first you wouldn't even admit that you knew her. So how am I supposed to feel when I discover my wife is barely good enough to be one of your one night stands? You must have thought it was really funny tonight when I told you how much I still loved her. Is she too fat for you? Too ugly? Who are you to be ashamed of having slept with the woman I love, the woman I married? Who are you!?!"

He spat out the last words, not quite at normal volume but no longer hushed. So much for not being upset.

"Nobody. I'm nobody."

"Victoria..."

"Victoria is a bitch!"

"Why? Because she told me the truth, or because she wouldn't have any part of *you?* In any case, it might interest you to know that Victoria and I have a date tomorrow."

That was his exit line. I let him go and waited until I heard his car drive off before I headed home.

"Good night, Steve," Maria called sadly as I opened the front door to leave.

———

All the lights were off at Victoria's, and I practically snuck in. I intended to see her just one more time—tomorrow, when I would take whatever

I could get of the money that was coming to me and get the hell out of there.

But the minute I entered the bathroom, the light in her room flicked on.

"Steve! Get in here. Now!"

She was sitting up in bed, wearing a thin negligee. The light from the bedside reading lamp cast shadows on her face, giving her a double chin and deepening every budding wrinkle. It also outlined one breast through the thin fabric. The nipple pointed downward. In such harsh light, her hair, disheveled around her face, appeared dull and coarse.

And of course, as I approached the canopied bed, I was becoming aroused.

"Listen, stud," she hissed, "under no circumstances are you ever to even hint to anyone that you and I have slept together. Do you understand?"

I nodded, thoroughly ashamed.

"Answer me. Do you understand me?"

"I understand you."

"I mean who the fuck do you think I am?"

"I think," I said wearily, "that you are a cold unfeeling cunt."

The anger that flashed over her face was transformed almost instantly into something else, something I didn't recognize that was both wounded and vicious.

"And what are you, stud? Huh? A ball-less pussy? You can barely work up the nerve to touch a real woman, but that doesn't stop you from running around telling all your little friends you're screwing her. Right now you're standing there sneaking peaks at my tits. You're not even man enough to really look. You want to look...here!"

She ripped open the front of her nightgown. A button popped off and almost hit me. One breast was fully exposed, sagging, nipple dark, almost black, lengthening even as I watched. The other, still partially covered, was lightly puckered with stretch marks. I was getting hard. In spite of myself, I wanted her like I wanted life—maybe, at just that moment, more.

"Look at you," she laughed. "If you were ten times the man you are, you might make it to the level of some slimy little rapist, lurking in a dark alley. Do you want to rape me? Do you want to prove what a man you are?"

"I'm not into sleeping with anyone who isn't into sleeping with me," I said, repeating my old mantra.

"Then what's that erection doing there?"

"Maybe it's a tribute to the beauty of your soul."

"You think you're any better?" Her breasts were trembling, her breathing heavy, but no heavier than mine. "What about what you did to that poor little fat thing next door?"

She flipped a switch on the wall by the bed, but nothing happened. "Maybe," she continued, "maybe we should see what you can do with a real woman, stud. You called me frigid earlier. Maybe we should see who's frigid here."

"What?"

Her hand found my belt buckle, pulling me toward her.

"You heard me. Fuck me. Come on, fuck me!"

Both hands were at my belt, and, with easy strength, she dragged me down on top of her. Just as quickly, she was on top of me, straddling me in cold blue panties. Her breasts swayed beneath the open sides of the negligee. Her hands tore at my pants and underwear insanely, working them both down around my knees.

"Slow down, huh," I sputtered, unable to keep an edge of panic from my voice. This was too much, too fast.

"What'sa matter? 'Fraid of the big bad lady?"

Throwing off her top, she arched her back. The light played around the contours of her stomach and breasts. I'd wanted her for so long, fantasized about this very thing so often. Her eyes were gray steel, with a dry, vicious gleam. She tore open my shirt.

"You don't know who you're dealing with here, stud. Men have died to be with me. Do you understand. *Died!* Willingly. Come on!"

Her breasts brushed over my chest: hot, almost singeing my skin. Sweeping down, they teased my jerking cock. Then, abruptly, surprisingly, her lips closed over the head, her tongue already working. Swirling, sucking. Enveloping. Hot. Moist. Instantly, I came into her mouth. She sucked me dry as my body convulsed, then spit the cum into my face with a contemptuous laugh, her breath the odor of burnt hair.

"Over before you even started," she sneered. "I guess it's fair to say you leave the ladies wanting more. Or any. If I ever wondered what I was missing by not fucking you—which I didn't—the answer is pretty clearly, NOTHING!!!"

Switching off the light, she turned her back and within minutes was either asleep or pretending to be. My wet dream had come true—as a nightmare. I couldn't believe what had just happened. For Chrissake, I wasn't a fourteen year old kid anymore.

I lay there, and my mind immediately slipped into excuse mode. It had been a long time since I'd been with anyone like Victoria—the kind of woman that every man and a lot of women wanted. Long time? I'd never been with anyone like that, but it had been a long time since I'd even been close. Unfortunately, that excuse didn't cut it.

If you fail in the major leagues it's no compensation at all that you had a great career in the minors, I thought bitterly. *And lately my career in the minors hasn't been exactly impressive either.*

I pulled my pants the rest of the way off and removed my damaged shirt, realizing that I'd just classified Maria and Helen and Ann, and every other woman I'd ever been lucky enough to be involved with, as minor league—when of course the only thing actually minor league about them was their choice in men.

I still had my own cum all over my face, so I went into the bathroom and washed it off. All I could think of was how delighted I would have been the night before, if I'd known how soon I would be walking naked from Victoria's bed.

She was still turned away from me as I climbed back in next to her. My mind was constricting into ever-tightening knots. I had to erase that image of myself as a loser from Victoria's eyes and from my own. The burnt-hair smell about her was even stronger now, yet I was so stirred by lying up against her that I was hard again immediately. It did occur to me that I was so aroused so quickly that what happened before might happen again, but I told myself that was physically impossible. Besides, no matter what, it would have to be better than the last time. Gently, I ran my hands over her back. Her skin was hot and in places surprisingly dry, almost rough. Whether that was the reason or not, my caresses seemed herky-jerky, and I couldn't help feeling inept.

I snaked my arm around her body. As before, she didn't respond as I massaged a breast. Kneading it firmly against her ribs, a trickle of warm fluid escaped into my palm. *Holy shit*, I thought. *Is she lactating?* I dried my hand against the sheets, then kissed her on the back. I was about to take her in my arms and turn her toward me, when she rolled over on her own and gave me a fed-up sigh.

"You can't stay here," she said, staring at me through the darkness. "Go sleep in your own room. You've got work to do in the morning."

"Please?" The word just escaped. I couldn't believe I was begging for another chance.

Her second sigh was even more disgusted than the first. I gathered my clothing and slunk out of there.

THURSDAY, APRIL 1
AHAB

"It was as though in those last minutes he was summing up the lesson that this long course in human wickedness had taught us—the lesson of the fearsome...banality of evil."
– *Hannah Arendt,* "Eichmann in Jerusalem"

CHAPTER 34

I awoke the next morning already depressed, feeling discarded and worthless, though it was several seconds before I remembered why. The room was as stifling as any Chicago August. I lay in bed, my thoughts foggy from too little sleep, running the scene in Victoria's bed the night before over and over again in my mind—a thousand times, a thousand different excuses. If I'd just made everything move a little more slowly... If she hadn't taken me by surprise... If my attitude had been more forceful, or more passive.

I'd tried to make myself out as so worldly, so sure and experienced. Such a winner, a success socially, if not at the moment financially. A man desirable and desired. But Victoria had seen through it all as easily as she'd seen through my treatment of Maria. She'd known from the first she could manipulate me and my bullshit, and she had. And last night she'd known I was going to fail. There'd been no question in her mind. Her uncharacteristic aggression would have been born of her utter contempt. She wouldn't act like that with anyone whose opinion she valued in the slightest. To her, I just was a buffoon, an unattractive poser. Naked blood-covered dances, passion-free sexual aggression, it really didn't matter how she acted in front of me.

I dragged myself out of bed and turned on the shower, but ended up slumped down on the toilet seat, watching the water beat against the side of the tub. Suddenly, I realized I was once again humming a tune I'd written years before. The only lyrics I remembered had something to do with "peering down into the empty chasm of my life." At nineteen, that had simply been an affectation in purple prose. Now it seemed significant that I'd hit upon such a phony and pathetic way to express just how phony and pathetic I was—my whole life every bit as phony and pathetic as my pursuit of Victoria. The fifteen year old virgin who pretended to be a popular, experienced lover. The honor student who sometimes posted notices in classrooms calling off classes he hadn't prepared for. The fearless, crusading, romantic draft resister with a safe student deferment who never in his wildest dreams actually expected to go to jail.

And those were my successful years. Things went downhill from there.

Groaning audibly, I stuck my head under the cold water. Victoria was right; I'd never been anything but twenty-four-carat fake. It was as if I'd always unconsciously understood that if anyone figured out who and what I really was, they'd want nothing to do with me. I wasn't Victoria's equal. I wasn't even close.

The shower was so cold it hurt. Masochistically, I didn't add any hot water. Dressing in last night's clothes—the shirt had a small tear and a button missing—I started downstairs. As I walked down the hall, I felt like dropping to the floor, rolling up in a fetal position, and sinking into the ugly red carpet. Halfway down the stairs, I remembered I'd forgotten to brush my teeth. What the hell, I decided, I wasn't going to be impressing anyone, anyway. Might just as well blow them away with my breath as my personality.

When I do pathetic, *I do pathetic.*

Just then, Victoria's voice came from the kitchen. "There's no reason why we shouldn't."

Humpert muttered something I didn't catch.

"I haven't decided yet if I should take Steve with us or not," she said. "But don't worry, either way there'll be no repetition of the Cranick episode. The days of half measures are over."

"Take me where?" I said, stepping into the kitchen, just as her last sentence registered.

Slumped in her chair, Victoria was still naked, except for a fresh pair of panties. To hold her gaze—or at least to look like I was—I focused on the bridge of her nose.

"We're leaving for Beverly Hills tomorrow," she said. "I fully expect that within a very few days of our arrival, I'll be asked to become Mrs. Harrison Armstrong. Just as soon as his divorce is final."

"That's THE Harrison Armstrong," Humpert injected proudly, glancing up from the book he'd been leafing through. "The former CEO of GR&T? The ambassador?"

He explained that Victoria had met Armstrong at the Desert Inn in Las Vegas shortly after her husband died. As soon as she had Armstrong thoroughly captivated, she'd had to go away on "urgent personal business." Which meant coming here.

"Absence makes the heart grow hornier," commented Leo, his stomach straining against the tiniest of bathing suits.

"You're assuming" smiled Victoria, "that somewhere in all that greed and ego and pompous bluster my darling Harrison actually has a heart. Still, he's used to getting whatever he wants whenever he wants it. When a man like that has to wait for something, he values it more."

I kept my face impassive. Like a great many people, I'd heard of Armstrong. California agricultural money—lots of it. He had a gift for generating PR, among other things leading the fight against the farm workers union. A few years back, he'd bought his twenty-four year old son a NBA team. Armstrong had been on the periphery of politics for many years, usually as a contributor. And I had a vague recollection that he'd been made an ambassador during the Nixon Administration:

probably to Monaco or Liechtenstein, or someplace else where a man whose expertise was in his wallet couldn't do much harm.

"So you're pulling out," I said. "Without the grimoire. Not with a bang, but with a whimper."

"Much like sex with you," cracked Humpert.

After they all laughed, he added, "Sorry, Steve," which surprised me. A thin blond fuzz on his cheek indicated he hadn't shaved in a few days. His finger was still swollen and black and blue from catching it under the sarcophagus lid. If anything, it looked worse.

"There's still plenty to be done today," Victoria told me. "We've got to go through all the rest of the books, just in case one of them might have some spell or ceremony that turns out to be what I need. And I want you to give the whole building one last going over—check anywhere a book could be hidden. I won't be selling the place, but I don't want to be coming back here either if I can avoid it."

"So, you'll be able to pay me off then?" Though I didn't know what she meant by the remark about finding the spell she needed, I no longer cared.

"We've got moving to do," said Victoria. "This is only just the start."

"Victoria may have a place for you with us in Beverly Hills," Humpert offered as if that should delight me.

"Shut up, Humpert," she snapped. For the first time, I noticed a large patch of scaly skin, like a bad heat rash, on her shoulder.

"I signed on for here, that's it."

"Why don't you go get us some coffee, stud?" Leo asked.

"Get your own coffee."

"Testy little thing, isn't he?" he said.

Victoria turned to me, her breasts swaying wearily. Her face was slightly blotchy, and the faintest tremor animated the flesh around the tiny scar on her face. Twice, she flicked her tongue rapidly over her lips the way she did, though now it reminded me of a lizard or a snake.

Idiotically, I thought if I could fuck her just once really well, fuck her so she cried my name in passion, then I would have accomplished all I ever needed and everything would be all right.

Ahab in quest of the Great White Pussy. Beyond idiotic.

"I told you I would take care of you, Steve," she explained patiently. "Didn't you believe me? Look at Leo and Humpert. They want for nothing, and they never will. Neither will you. But you are going to have to earn my trust. Do you understand?"

The phone in the pantry rang.

"Let me fix you some brunch, and we can talk," she said, standing up and coming over to me. "*Alone.*"

She moved even closer. "If you quit, you won't ever see me again, will you?" Then she reached her tongue out and licked across my lips from bottom to top.

The phone rang again. To get out of there, I went to answer it.

It was Maria. She must have just gotten her phone installed.

"I'm on my way to the hospital," she said. "But I just found something, and I thought you might be interested in taking a look. I was over at my uncle's again, trying to figure out where he might have kept his Medicare info, when I happened to notice an old porcelain vase sitting on his night table."

Behind me, Victoria padded into the pantry. She looked cold in spite of the heat of the day, and, barefoot, she walked as if her feet hurt. She had something in her hand and flashed me a smile. I swung back to the phone.

"There was gray dust on it and around the base," Maria said. "It turned out it wasn't a vase, it was an urn. A burial urn, filled, or rather partly filled with somebody's ashes."

Victoria stepped up behind me, embracing me with one hand while the other placed a newspaper clipping on the counter in front of me. Maria's voice continued in my ear:

"But what I thought you might be interest..."

"Maria, I'm sorry, I've got to go. I'll talk to you later, okay?"

Victoria had just whispered in my ear that my name was Gavin Kennan and that I was wanted in Indiana for murder.

"*Indiana wants you,*" she sang as she left the room. "*No, you can't go back now.*"

CHAPTER 35

The newspaper clipping explained that the murder they wanted to prosecute me for was that of Dell Abramson. The story was from the *South Bend Globe*, dated March 25.

SEARCH CONTINUES

Police today continued their search for Gavin Kennan, the alleged drug dealer wanted in connection with the recent drug raid at 828 E. Blaine Street in South Bend. The raid resulted in the death of a second suspect, Dell Abramson, 35, who according to police was fatally wounded by members of the special narcotics unit after pulling a gun on the officers. District Attorney, Harold Belinski, announced Wednesday that Kennan, who allegedly fled the scene of the bust, faces first degree murder charges stemming from his alleged involvement in a felony which resulted in a death.

Dell was dead.

The paper went on to claim that police had confiscated five ounces of high grade coke. (We'd had seven ounces, and it wasn't all that good even before we'd cut it.) The estimated street value was ridiculously high, even for seven. After a few sketchy details of Dell's life, the story returned to me, giving me undue credit for leading the "South Bend Six, an anti-war forgery ring," noting my year and a half in federal prison, and mentioning I was an employee of the Richmond Tobacco Company. Someone had underlined the next section.

According to the Richmond's personnel office, on his employment application, Kennan claimed to be a Notre Dame graduate. A spokesman for the University said they had no record of anyone by that name ever being enrolled there.

If someone had dug a little further, they would have discovered that on the same application I'd claimed to have spent the years since my graduation working my way up to the position of Promotional Director for Abramson Enterprises, Dell Abramson, President. Richmond Tobacco's background check consisted of calling the number I'd given them and having Dell tell them in that deliberate, Gary Cooperish way of his, that I was the best salesman that had ever worked for him. He would have said anything to get me out of the converted garage that served as both his home and the offices of his struggling plumbing and heating business. He was also broad-minded enough to lend me his wife for the second interview. Richmond Tobacco didn't hire single men. Single men were too unstable. Since at that point I was over thirty and had never in my life held a job for more than three months, I could understand that. Dell was dead.

Dell was dead.

Almost as an afterthought, the last sentence in the story noted that Paula Abramson, Dell's wife, had been arrested, but had been released and wasn't going to be charged. Stapled to the back of the clipping was my old driver's license, the one I'd put in the bureau drawer, identifying me as Gavin Kennan.

I dropped into a kitchen chair, got up, and sat down again. I didn't want to deal with this. Dell was gone. Like Steve. That gone. His gun had been real, but, though the police couldn't know it, he'd never have used it. *Never.* Not Dell, that gentle giant of a man, who now—in sudden, jarring retrospect—seemed more like a boy. It was more like he—like *we* were just playing at being big macho drug runners. You shouldn't die for that. There had been no warning it was that serious a thing.

And I was wanted for murder.

"Steve! Let's go," Victoria called from the living room. "We've got a lot to do today."

The second time she called, I went in. I was still holding the newspaper article. She took it from me, crumbled it and tossed it into the trash.

"That's between you and me. Don't mention it to Leo or Humpert, especially not Humpert.

Oh," she said, "I almost forgot. Have you seen today's *San Cristobal News-Herald*?"

She handed me the paper, folded open to highlight a letter to the editor.

ANTI-WAR FELON RIPS REAGAN

To the Editor:

The Reagan administration continues its effort to throw 485,000 people—including any number of Vietnam veterans—off social security disability benefits.

For anyone who hasn't noticed, the sixties are over. The country has awakened from dreams of the Great Society, from dreams of the Age of Aquarius, to a cold, harsh Morning in America.

It's a new era, presided over not by a visionary statesman or an enlightened guru, but by a corporate spokesman who earned his spurs on the Warner Brothers backlot fighting ersatz Indians and Nazis; and on the rubber chicken circuit telling the wealthy the commies were coming for their Rolexes; and in Sacramento battling students and hippies and welfare mothers and, of course, cutting funds for education and the poor.

So it's no longer "Ask not what you can do for your country." And it's certainly not "Love Is All You Need," if it really ever was. Nowadays it's tax cuts and "Where's mine?" And while we generate unimaginable budget deficits for the largest peacetime military build-up in the history of the universe—nobody wants the commies taking our Rolexes—we economize by tossing the wounded and the debilitated out onto the streets like so much litter.

Sincerely, Gavin Kennan
San Cristobal County

Editor's Note: *Gavin Kennan served time in Federal prison for his activities as the leader of the notorious anti-war group, the South Bend Six.*

"A well-written letter, Gavin," Victoria said, "though I couldn't agree less with the politics. And it probably wasn't the smartest idea to use your real name. Radical ideas like that do draw attention. Lucky you've got a safe place to hide with us."

"You write well, Victoria, though you might work on the run-on sentences." The catch in my voice destroyed the attempt at indifference.

"It was Humpert. He's good at speaking for other people. That's what attorneys do. Still, one puny 'ersatz' and a couple of semi-colons was hardly enough to reach the appropriate level of pomposity of a Harvard grad like yourself. Or was it Notre Dame? Or perhaps Leavenworth?"

"He didn't send the newspaper the address?"

She shook her head. "Just San Cristobal County. He gave them a bit of your history as an excuse for not being more specific. Also, of course to let them know just which Gavin Kennan was haranguing them. And I know you like to get credit for everything you've accomplished."

"You realize if you keep me with you you're harboring a fugitive—a murderer."

Victoria put on an expression of mock surprise, and in a fake syrupy voice said, "But, Your Honor, you can't possibly imagine that awful ol' criminal told us what he'd done? Why, he even gave us a phony name." Returning to a normal tone, she added, "Speaking of which, Humpert's known about you and Indiana since right after my investigator first called me. Still, as an attorney, he's squeamish about harboring a fugitive anyway, so I'd just as soon he didn't discover that fugitive's now actually wanted for murder. Anyway, time for you to get busy. I'm going to try to reach Armstrong again."

She was still trying to get through to Armstrong when Al arrived, obviously uncomfortable to see me there.

"Get us a couple of glasses of wine, Steve," Victoria ordered. "Then disappear." This was a test. She wouldn't have used that tone on a slave. "Oh, and tell Humpert to place that call to Beverly Hills for me. Tell him to keep trying."

By the time I returned with the wine, "timid" Al was already pressed up against her on the couch, kissing her feverishly. Seeing me, he made to break off, his face flushed with passion, not embarrassment.

But Victoria guided his head down for him to kiss her on the neck. The cold smirk she was giving me loosened into a conspiratorial smile. She rolled her eyes to the heavens and shook her head almost imperceptibly. So now Victoria and I were comrades, together, watching this silly dude make a fool of himself, wanting her. I wondered if this was how Humpert felt; a passive observer, yet superior to the men he watched jumping through Victoria's hoops. Another motion of her eyes told me to go.

Over the next few hours, the reality of Dell's death gradually spread through me like poison. Now I was sure I remembered being startled by a car backfiring as I'd driven away from the drug bust. Backfiring twice? Had it occurred to me it might be shots? I certainly hadn't knocked myself out to discover what had happened after I'd fled. After I'd run. Was I avoiding what I didn't want to know? Trying for the big score had been my idea.

My left forearm began to burn with a now familiar sensation. I unbuttoned and pulled back my shirt sleeve in time to watch Dell's features begin to appear in the gray scale of various shades of bruising, swelling into a cameo of his face.

CHAPTER 36

In spite of Victoria's purported passion, Al left early. I stayed out of everyone else's way, pretending to be searching through the books for the grimoire and/or a spell I couldn't be less interested in, shuffling through a lifetime of memories of Dell and I—and Dell and Stephen and I. Especially, for some reason, all those hours we'd spent tripping together, twelve to fourteen years before, in what Stephen called, "a communion of acid"—finding the hidden meaning in rock 'n roll clichés, planning a new world—even the evening before we were all going to jail. The evening Stephen introduced me to Ann.

Victoria poked her head into my room, once again without knocking, sometime after seven.

"Come on down for dinner," she said as sweetly as a new bride. "I made you something special."

White linen covered the kitchen table. It wasn't fully dark outside yet, but the interior light was provided by two beautiful silver candlesticks. In spite of everything, the sight of Victoria, in white harem pants and a matching blouse, rekindled in me the nonsensical idea I'd had earlier—that making love to her would make the world all right again.

It wouldn't do much for Dell though, I reminded myself.

"Actually, Steve, I misjudged the timing," she said. "Why don't you relax, grab yourself a beer. Dinner will be a couple of minutes yet."

I wasn't really up for another Ace Beer. So I wandered out into the living room, thinking I'd watch TV. I plopped down on the couch preoccupied, and never switched on the tube.

It was sometime later that the doorbell rang.

"Get that, will you, Steve," Victoria called. "I'm tied up with dinner."

Again, she was ten feet away from the back door. But in the hierarchy of things that mattered to me just then, that was about as far down as it was possible to be. I'd have been more concerned with say, who on earth would actually purchase something called Ace Beer, or why Elvis recorded "Queenie Wahine's Papaya," or for that matter, with who put the bomp in the bomp bah bomp bah bomp.

By the way, "Who Put the Bomp (in the Bomp Bah Bompa Bah Bomp)" spent twelve weeks in the Billboard Top 100. It made it as high as number seven.

The bell rang again. "Get the door, Steve! It's for you."

I trudged past Victoria—who was not cooking but sitting at the kitchen table—and into the entryway, I could see someone standing on the other side of the back door. I threw it open before I realized it was a cop.

———

"Hello," she said.

"Hello." *Are you fucking kidding me?*

"I'm Deputy Galloria. Are you...?"

Victoria was walking up behind me. "Thank you for coming, Deputy. I've got a problem I think you can help me with."

So, was this it? Was Victoria turning me in? My first thought was to run. But there was nowhere to run. Deputy Galloria had delicate ebony features but an air of earnest professionalism: no makeup, military posture. I wondered what would happen if I tried to overpower her.

"I recently hired Steve here," Victoria said. "I'm a woman alone and I do have to hire temporary help from time to time. You never know who you might end up with."

"Is there a problem, ma'am?" the deputy said, eyeing me. If my face looked anywhere near as guilty as I felt, she was probably ready to put a bullet in me. Her right hand actually did flex and move closer to her baton. Overpowering her might not be that easy. And weirdly enough, it felt like it would be cheating. But I was facing a murder charge.

"A problem?" Victoria echoed. "Oh, no, officer—deputy. Steve's a good boy. Aren't you, Steve? But I have had issues in the past. So the reason I wanted you to drop by was that I thought that perhaps in the future when I needed to hire someone, I could have the sheriff's department run a background check on them. Let me know they're safe. Not Steve of course. No need to run a background check on Steve. Steve's as safe as a little puppy. He's actually a Harvard graduate. They probably only produce white collar criminals. Or is it Notre Dame you didn't graduate from Steve?"

Relieved and annoyed at the same time, I met the deputy's gaze, rolled my eyes and gave a little "I can't believe this shit either" shake of my head. She seemed to be trying to decide if Victoria was serious.

"Ma'am, we don't do that for private citizens. They could have told you that when you called the station. I'm sure there are private services you can hire."

"I would pay of course, officer."

"We don't do that, Ma'am. And we don't like having our time wasted either."

"Of course. I understand. Well, I'll let you go then. I'm sure you have parking tickets to write."

The deputy sighed and started to turn away.

"Deputy Galloria?" I called.

"Yes?"

"If you'd like to shoot her," I said. "I'd be happy to swear it was self-defense."

"Good to know," she said.

———

"I'm sorry, Steve. But please don't let that spoil our dinner. I just needed to impress upon you the importance of proving to me that I can trust you."

"You made your point, Victoria. I only hope that what you were doing wasn't as obvious to Deputy Galloria as it was to me."

"The meter maid? I wouldn't worry."

"Did you tell her my last name?"

"Which one?"

"Either."

"I just left a message for her to drop by. And she thinks your first name is Steve. You're safe with me."

———

The special dinner turned out to be stew, in individually covered bowls. As Victoria served my wine, I could see the coarseness of her skin and a few tiny blackheads on the side of her nose. But I already knew she was beautiful, and I'd seen all the evidence I ever needed to see about how desirable she was. A few blackheads couldn't shake my faith.

"Humpert and Leo are both busy," she said. "They won't be bothering us."

I sipped a spoonful of the broth from the edge of the stew. It was warm rather than piping hot, so I started to eat.

After a moment, I said, "So, Victoria, if I don't do what you want, you're ready to turn me in to the police."

"You wouldn't make me do that, *Steve*."

"But if you have to…"

A cocked eyebrow served as her response. Then, "Things might happen that could make it easier for them to find you."

"I want to leave tomorrow. I need my money."

"We need you a while longer."

"How long?"

"Who can say? I'm hoping you'll choose to stay of your own accord. Of your own free will."

I grunted derisively. "I'm not the only one around here who might be vulnerable to a charge of murder."

"Those crimes have been solved. The police aren't going to believe anything *you* have to say." She tasted her stew. "You still want me, don't you?"

"Does it matter?"

"What you want? Not much." She smiled, not unkindly. "I don't sleep at night. Not usually. I don't need to. Sometimes I lie awake and wonder about the fantasies I've inspired—the wet dreams. Or I think about someone like Harrison Armstrong, a rich and influential giant, who may be tossing and turning, lusting for me at that very moment. That's power over souls. The power of Circe, the power of Helen of Troy."

"Great. I wonder what Helen looked like at sixty?"

"What did Circe look like? At sixty or a hundred and sixty." Victoria leaned back in her chair, peaking her fingers in front of her like some chairman of the board type. "Or in my case at ninety-seven."

I stared at her for a moment. "Right." I wasn't in the mood for inane jokes. "Well, let me say that you're fairly well preserved for someone who was born in 1885."

"Born? That's probably not the word. And to be honest, the date is just my best guess. But one of the spells that should be in that grimoire is the spell Zandie used well over ninety years ago, right here in this old church...*to create me!*"

"Do you actually expect me to believe that?"

"Believe it. And over those ninety-seven years, men have been giving up more and more to be with me, more and more. As tribute. Gladly. Cranick gave up his very life."

She smiled, and a sick chill ran through my body.

"You're out of your fucking mind," I said.

And that was when she reached into her napkin and tossed something over at me. It landed by my stew—the shape both odd and familiar. The shriveled lower half of a human ear. A crescent shaped stud pierced the lobe.

"Peter," I said, stunned. "The hitchhiker."

"Peter," Victoria confirmed. "And speaking of Peter, if the meat in your bowl of stew is a bit chewy, it's because you're eating his dick. Peter's peter. I don't play games here, asshole. Don't you."

I could feel the vomit rising in my throat as I dashed from the room, as if getting to a bathroom on time mattered.

"All right, I guess I do play some games," Victoria called after me, with a laugh. "You didn't really eat his dick. I just overcooked the beef. Sorry."

CHAPTER 37

The cold tile of the bathroom floor pressed against my cheek. Victoria's admission about what I'd actually eaten had come too late to keep me from vomiting. In between the violence of the purging and the realization of the homicidal insanity I was living with, I'd actually found myself calling the name of the God I hadn't believed in for twenty years—the residuals linger on long after the faith is gone. This was the woman I hadn't given up to the police even after she'd admitted what had happened with Cranick and with O'Ryan.

Outside the open window in the yard below, Leo and Humpert were talking. Most of it was about nothing, but someplace in there I focused in on Humpert's voice.

"How can I tell her? Armstrong's her dream man. I don't know if she can take it."

"You mean you don't know if you can take it. She has to be told. They're all her dream men at first, the important ones. How long does that ever last?"

A few moments of silence and then Humpert spoke again. "Is she threatening him?"

"Who?"

"Steve?"

"Wonder wimp? What difference does it make?"

"In the old days, she didn't need threats. Not with you, not with me. Threats won't work with a man like that; they'll scare him too badly." I heard Humpert take a deep breath and slowly expel the air from his lungs. "Do you think she really is losing it?"

"Don't be ridiculous. You know what happened to Cranick."

"The second time."

"And you *saw* what happened to that hitchhiker. She's more potent than ever." Their voices seemed to be fading, as if they were moving away.

"But why does it happen more and more frequently? And now they're even dying. It frightens me."

"Doesn't everything? But you always watch, don't you?"

"Don't you?"

As they were walking out of earshot, Leo said, "Anyway, we've got to tell her."

How long I lay there I don't know. It wasn't that I kept vomiting or that I was incapacitated. I think I lay there simply because I had no idea of what else to do. The room had grown quiet. And dark. As if a blackness loose in the house had entered through the locked door. Finally, I pulled myself up, rinsed out my mouth and rinsed off my face, and left the bathroom.

Victoria was still seated at the kitchen table, but the lights were on and the candles were out. The dishes had been cleared, and the ear was gone. Humpert was standing beside her.

She'd been crying. I guess he'd told her whatever it was they had to tell her about Armstrong. In any case, it soon became clear Beverly Hills was off. And now she was more determined than ever to discover Zandie's secrets.

"Even if the information we need isn't here," she said to Humpert, "Zandie got it from somewhere; we can find his source. Besides Egypt and Crete and Eastern Europe, he spent years down in the jungles of Mexico—the Yucatan Peninsula. That's got to be where he picked it up. So that's where we'll head."

For just an instant, Humpert cocked a hairless eyebrow skeptically. Zandie'd been in all those places—and probably more—so of course he had to have gotten whatever it was he got in Mexico? It didn't make a lot of sense.

"Lay a fire in the living room, Steve," Victoria ordered. "I've got company coming. And chill a bottle of Chardonnay and uncork a Cabernet Sauvignon. The Gallo though, not the expensive stuff. This one would probably be just as happy with Ripple. After that, stay out of sight but don't be hard to find. Maybe just go to your room and rest. Tomorrow will be busy. I still want to be packed and out of here by noon, and we've got a lot to do."

I didn't respond and she looked at me carefully. "Is there a problem?" she asked. It was more a threat than a question.

And now they're even dying, Humpert had said.

I held her gaze for a moment then said, "In the words of the immortal Screaming Jay Hawkins, 'I don't care if you don't want me, I'm yours.'"

"'I Put a Spell on You,'" she smiled, quoting the name of the song and making a comment at the same time. "Good."

So, Mexico it was going to be. Just like that. She left the room and I did what I was told, without asking any questions.

A half hour later, Victoria was composed and made up and back in the living room. Someone knocked on the front door, and I was dismissed.

I closed the kitchen door behind me and went up to my room loudly enough for her to hear. Humpert was off someplace. I hadn't seen any sign of Leo since I'd come out of the bathroom.

Quickly, I gathered up my things, leaving behind only the glass bottle of whiskey. I nearly took a pull off it for my nerves, but I needed a clear head.

The window had been recently painted. And though I'd cracked it three or four inches almost every night, when I tried to open it further, first it wouldn't budge, then it gave way with a screak a dead man could hear. Even so, the opening was barely wide enough to force my bag through. It hit the bushes below like a baby falling from a roof. Ducking away from the window, I listened for voices or footsteps below, but none came.

I was trembling as I slipped on my old jacket and made my way down to the kitchen—armed with the feeblest of excuses about going out for air if I'd encountered anyone. Fortunately, I didn't. Maybe they thought I didn't have the balls to take off. I left the keys Victoria had given me conspicuously in the center of the kitchen table—as if to say I was going in peace. I realized I had Cranick's keys in my pocket as well. I tossed those in the trash. There was no particular reason to do that. But there didn't seem to be any reason to keep them.

That was a mistake—a bad one.

I snuck around the side of the building and dug my bag out of the bushes, wondering about Humpert's assessment of my courage. Was I leaving because Victoria hadn't frightened me enough to make me stay, or because she'd frightened me so much that staying would have been unbearable? If someone had walked around the corner of that house; Humpert, or Leo, or Victoria, I have no idea how I would have reacted.

I made my way toward Maria's, moving as quickly and as quietly as I could. Maria's house would be the first place they'd look for me. I wanted to make sure she got out of there and stayed out until they were gone.

Part way across the field, I checked back over my shoulder and saw to my relief that the light had come on in Humpert's bedroom. Then I stumbled over a can, accidentally kicking it across the concrete in front of the old store. A flash of fear shot through my body like an electric shock. Victoria had me that spooked.

Urgently, yet softly—as if somehow they might be able to hear me back at the old church—I knocked on Maria's door. Once again I checked behind me, and noticed for the first time that the car parked in the church driveway was Al's shit-brown Mercedes—probably deliberately parked where Maria might see it. *He* was the company Victoria had been expecting. And I'd left him with her, unsuspecting.

The light was on in Victoria's bedroom.

I pounded louder.

"Oh, hi," said Maria. She reached back and then handed me something through the door. "Here. This is what I tried to tell you about—this manuscript. It was on his bedroom table under the burial urn. I haven't had much chance to check it out, but it does look fairly old."

I took it automatically—maybe ten to fifteen pages, the whole thing folded like a letter—and brushed in past her. I kept moving, through the swinging kitchen door into the bedroom, as if I was less vulnerable farther from the door. I was explaining as I went.

"Al is over at Victoria's. You've got to call him. Make up any excuse, but get him out of there immediately. They're crazy! They're the ones who killed Cranick and hurt your uncle."

At first she seemed confused, stuck on the idea Al was seeing Victoria. It took me a long moment to get her to focus on the rest, and when I finally did, her immediate reaction was that we should call the police.

"And tell them what exactly? Besides, by the time we get them up here from San Cristobal, it could be too late. Even if it isn't, we won't be able to back up a charge of jaywalking much less murder. And we'd have alerted Victoria that I'd talked and that now you were on to her, too. You've got to call and get him the hell out of there. Now!"

"Why would they hurt Al?"

"I have no idea. Why did they murder a random hitchhiker—and who knows who else? It's like the Ralph Lauren version of the Manson family."

I gave her Victoria's number. We'd already wasted too much time. "Make up a family crisis and get him out of there. I'd do it myself, but they'd never let me talk to him. Hurry, please! Even letting them know that you know he's there could keep him safe."

Her eyes blinked several times as if something was clicking into place. Then she repeated the phone number back to me and brushed through the swinging door back into the kitchen. I could hear her dialing a rotary phone.

"And don't tell them I'm here," I added, shifting my weight from foot to foot. We had to go.

Nervously, I flipped through the pages in my hand. They were gritty with ground-in ashes, human ashes Maria had said. I was about to put them down and wipe off my hands when I registered that the familiar, old-fashioned handwriting was Zandie's—though it seemed to have deteriorated somewhat. I turned back to the first page:

> It has been five years since my house has fallen. It is all over now. All my aspirations. Everything. As for myself, I have deteriorated to the point where I am clearly no longer the man I was back then. To be frank, I'm beginning to understand that is not entirely bad.

Over on the stool by Maria's easel was the urn. So O'Ryan had Zandie stashed in among his junk all along. The porcelain urn must have been an irresistible target for the old pack rat. I should have guessed he would have taken anything worth taking out of the long-abandoned church years before—though who else would have considered this to be something worth taking?

My girls have wandered off, unharmed, almost heroes to the upstanding citizenry. The drunken mob that closed my house stole whatever jewelry I was forced to leave behind, uprooted my plants, and, for reasons known to none but the inebriated, set fire to my bed and my wardrobe. I survived only because my loyal Katherine showed them a soot-covered skull and some random bones in a fire pit and led them to believe that—while none of the girls would admit anything for fear of prosecution—I had already been destroyed and my body disposed of.

I suppose the soot covered the gold plating on the skull nicely. And when the vigilantes reclaimed the bodies from the crypt, they apparently never realized that Mrs. Toban had lost a bone or two, which, I am certain, she will never miss.

Katherine also produced my infamous book of spells for the mob to burn, which they did with delight, superstitiously believing that would destroy my knowledges. I call them knowledges but in truth they were mostly impressive gibberish, along with two or three tricks with mind shadows. The hors d'oeuvres we used to generate cravings for whatever food we needed to sell, for example. And the spell that could cause a small garden to thrive. There was also the tedious ceremony I used to make the church itself moan weirdly when the wind blows. I do not recommend that one, as I was never able to get it to stop.

Still, for what little it is worth, I will recreate them all on these pages, along with the details of the one genuinely powerful ritual that was to be my glory. The one that birthed Nephil, my creation, a demon in human form, a small, ugly, insignificant psychic parasite, which, once in this incarnation, truly believed itself to be a human female. She who I used to call my Venus man-trap, the flower that devours.

So this was where O'Ryan had gotten that odd phrase.

Perhaps it was vanity to ever believe she would return to me. From her creation, Yolanda called her, "La Perdita," the little lost one. She may be even more lost now. Like a child, her earliest days may be cloudy or even forgotten. But she must remember at least her last year or two here. And she could never forget me—her father, mother, mentor and first love, all in one.

It was as if Zandie was confirming Victoria's insane story from the grave. Not that I actually believed it. The most logical explanation was that she'd uncovered some other version of this story and was crazy enough to accept it. Maybe she'd found it in the old church or maybe it had turned up even before she'd come here. Maybe that was why she'd come in the first place. The one thing she was right about was Zandie being buried with his secret knowledges, or what was left of them. Like the prize in a cereal box, the pages had been hidden among the ashes in the burial urn.

I heard Maria hang up the phone, rather loudly. Once Al left, Victoria was bound to notice I was gone. We had to get out of there. I picked up my gym bag. Maybe I'd have Maria drop me at a rail yard. Hitchhiking seemed too risky, but if I could hop a freight train, that would at least get me out of the area.

"Your uncle's the only man I know who would ever check to see what was inside a burial urn," I called. Which was when I noticed the gold lettering on the urn, "E ECC."

I stepped back into the kitchen. "Hey, did you...?" The front door was open and Maria was gone.

"Shit!"

CHAPTER 38

When I got outside, Maria was more than halfway to the old church. The lights were still on in Victoria's bedroom. I had to stop Maria. That place was high on the list of locations where I didn't want to be. Very high. Especially if they were about to find out I'd told Maria all about them.

"Maria!" I tried. "Maria!"

When she didn't turn around, I broke into a run, yelling louder than I should have. She must have heard me. Her form blended with the blackness of the church. A moment later the back door slammed.

I was still holding Zandie's manuscript as well as my bag. I tucked the pages into the inside pocket of my jacket. I told myself to get out of there; Maria had Al to help her now that she was inside. But, reaching the back porch, I dashed up the steps. Maybe I could catch her before she got to Victoria. Even if I couldn't, if she had enough sense to keep her mouth shut, maybe I could pass her off as nothing but a jealous wife.

I heard her muffled cry even before I reached the second floor. Leo had grabbed her in front of Victoria's bedroom door and was holding her easily with one hand over her mouth. The other hand held a gun.

"Good timing, Steve," said Humpert, coming up behind them with a gun of his own. "You were supposed to be watching this anyway."

"We just didn't expect you to bring a date," Leo said, pushing Maria down the hall.

"Why show her, Leo?" Humpert asked.

"Why not? I'd say our boy here has already blown everything wide open. Do you want to let her go?"

Leading me roughly and awkwardly, but not unkindly, Humpert followed them into his own room. Leo opened a door revealing a walk-in closet and a window cut in the interior wall which must have corresponded to the huge mirror in Victoria's bedroom. Obviously, it was a one-way mirror. We stood at it four abreast.

Victoria was naked, stretched out on her waterbed, and Al—naked as well—was curled up at her feet in a fetal position, but with an erection.

Humpert reached over and flipped a switch.

"What shall we have you do now?" Victoria's voice came through in an electronically amplified stream. "Crawl across the floor on your belly? Beg? What other tricks can you perform?

My friends Leo and Humpert are watching, and they love tricks. Did you really think a woman like me would give herself to someone like you, like some common slut?" She flicked his erection with her toe. "You still want me though, don't you. And maybe you've earned a touch. Come on up here and give me a little hug. Come on."

In spite of her words, and in spite of the fact that we'd obviously come in at the end of an extensive process of humiliation—perhaps an instant version of what I'd gone through—Victoria's smile was inviting. So inviting, that after she took his face in her hands, Al uncurled slowly, like a beaten puppy, and rose to his hands and knees. She lay back voluptuously. Hesitantly, he touched her side, and gasped as if he'd been burned. I actually expected him to jerk his hand away, but he didn't. Instead, like an arthritic old man—his body beaded with sweat—he gradually pulled himself on top of her. His eyes, open wide, darted around in their sockets; ashamed, desperate, and yet still filled with want. Victoria was relaxed, smiling scornfully. He made no attempt to enter her, but their flesh pressed together all along the length of their bodies.

Suddenly, he yanked back his head. His mouth twisted open in a silent, tortured scream—spittle dripped from a corner, sizzling into steam when it hit her skin.

A golden haze seemed to emanate from the juncture of their bodies, slowly thickening and spreading throughout the room. Through the haze, Victoria's face now looked rapturous and unimaginably beautiful. Beautiful beyond fantasy. Beautiful beyond sanity. Like the face of a demented god.

It was terrifying. And my mind dredged up a quote—more likely a misquote—though I'd never been entirely sure what it meant: *Beauty is a mysterious and terrible battlefield where God and the devil fight for the heart of man.*

The haze thickened, turning from golden to a putrid yellow.

Writhing mindlessly, Al's body seemed to wither before our eyes. And I realized the haze was actually smoke coming from small flames flickering between the two bodies. A sudden flash of heat came at us like a noiseless explosion—along with the cloying stench of rotting flowers.

We shrank back from the glass. Washed by the jaundiced light, Leo and Humpert took on a pig-like look of depravity. I suppose I did, too. But the heat was gone as quickly as it had come, the haze already dissipating.

And Maria was back across the room, heading for the hall.

Leo caught up with her just as she smashed up against the locked door to Victoria's room.

"Wait," he said, as the horror on her face seemed to solidify.

We didn't have to wait long. Humpert and I caught up to them—the gun once again digging into my back. The lock on the door clicked. The door swung open. The scene on the bed came into view, and Maria's face crumbled, slowly at first, then gaining speed like an emotional avalanche.

There was no haze. No smoke. No smell. Nothing was burning. Nothing had been burned. Al slouched against the pillows, virtually unrecognizable, his formerly pale skin now ruddy as if seared from the inside. His head rolled back and forth to no particular rhythm. His slack-jawed face was skeletal, his eyes vacant. A small sore, already crusty, gaped open on one temple, and he was bleeding around the eyes. Dark hair was sprinkled across the pillow behind him.

Holding the door open, Victoria smiled radiantly, a normal American beauty, no more, no less. She stood to the side to let us in. "You should see your faces," she said to Maria and I. Her hair was a wild mane, her naked flesh glowed and her eyes were vibrant.

Traces of blood showed on her teeth and her lips.

"You sucked his blood?" My voice didn't sound like my own. "You think you're a fucking vampire?"

"Vampire?" She laughed. "Sorry to disappoint you, Steve. The blood's mine."

"Bad gums," Humpert explained. "Or something. We're not sure why it happens when...when this happens."

A soft cry escaped from Al like the air escaping through a pin hole in a blow-up doll. As if in response, Maria let out a small moan—a small moan that couldn't have been more tortured if her soul was being wrenched from her body.

Victoria laughed again, more pointedly, but less confidently.

"You were right anyway, Steve," Maria said in a monotone. "She *is* a monster."

A cloud passed over Victoria's face. "*You were right, Steve,*" she mocked. "Where did *she* come from? Is that where you were, Steve? I wanted you to see this."

"You wanted me to see...what...?" I asked, beyond confusion. "What is it?"

She grinned proudly. "Actually, I'm not sure," she said, walking over and plopping down on the bed. "It's only been happening this strongly for the last ten or twelve years. I feel this sudden surge of contempt and then..." She patted Al's thigh.

With a start, like a man shaking off a bad dream, Al began groggily checking out his surroundings without recognition. Then he pulled himself off the bed. Victoria gave a signal and Humpert went over and helped him get dressed. They were both awkward, and Al grumbled incoherently, but he didn't resist. His clothing hung off him. He looked like he'd gained fifteen years and lost twenty pounds. Still disoriented, like a derelict who'd stumbled into a strange house, he staggered out the door.

"He doesn't know what hit him," offered Leo, moving us aside to let him pass.

"At first it only happened after I'd been involved with someone for a long while," Victoria said. "But nowadays it seems to occur quicker and quicker."

"It seems to depend on the person," injected Humpert.

Victoria shook her head. "It only happens after I lose *all* respect for them."

"So this is why you came searching for Zandie's secrets?" I asked.

"No. Not at all. The last year or so I just got the urge to find out where I came from. Maybe I did wonder once if this... this might be a symptom of something wrong with me. But now I realize that I was right all along; this is just part of who I am, another power I've grown into."

"And what you're doing to them doesn't bother you," I said.

"*No.* Not anymore. Not in the slightest. It's not really my fault."

"She's like a touchstone," Humpert explained. "She may uncover their lack of quality, but she can hardly be held responsible for it."

"If you think about it," Victoria added, "the contempt I feel for these people just mirrors their own. No matter how much I may have once respected them. No matter how successful they may appear on the surface. And afterwards they just wander off harmlessly."

Maria shook her head as if as disoriented as her husband. She muttered, "'Venus mantrap.'"

"What? Where did you hear that?" demanded Victoria, startled. Her breasts swung full and heavy as she leaped off the bed to confront Maria.

"Hear what?" Maria's eyes sought mine, not sure now of what to say or not to say.

"Where did you hear that expression?"

"I mentioned it to her," I said. "'Venus mantrap. The flower that devours.' Humpert called you that one time."

"What!" cried Humpert indignantly. "Victoria, I never, I swear…"

"Humpert never heard that expression in his life."

I worked my teeth against each other visibly and tried to look guilty without overdoing it. "Maybe it was, 'Nephil,' he called you."

The name drew a blank. Victoria continued as if it had never been spoken.

"Venus mantrap was what Zandie used to call me," she explained with excitement and bitterness.

"Did you find the grimoire?" Humpert asked me.

As blatantly as I could, I shot Maria a "keep quiet" look. She was impassive.

"You found the grimoire—that's it, isn't it?" Victoria cried, seizing upon the idea immediately, almost reverently, a sense of wonder spreading over her face. "That's it. And you never told me; you were going to keep it for yourself."

"Shit!" I exclaimed. The *shit* sounded bogus to me, but it hardly mattered now. They'd already convinced themselves. Now I had a single card to play, and I'd better play it well.

"I just discovered it tonight," I said. "I don't have any use for it. Set us free and I'll tell you where I hid it." I moved my left arm imperceptibly against my side, reassuring myself that the pages were still in the inside pocket of my jacket.

"Fabulous. Hand it over and you're both free."

"Come on, Victoria," I said.

"I'm supposed to set you free first." She snorted derisively.

We bargained like that for a while, but obviously we didn't trust each other. And even more obviously, no matter what she said, Victoria never intended to let us go.

———

Though Leo emptied my gym bag onto the floor, confirming my aborted flight, Victoria was looking for a full-size book and never thought to search Maria and I. Taking his cue from a thousand movies and TV shows, Leo was ready to "make them talk." But since the most likely place for me to have stashed the book before returning was Maria's, Humpert thought it would be a lot easier to just have a look over there first.

"Why don't we stick them down in the basement while we're doing that?" he suggested to Victoria. "We can lock them in Zandie's lab. Then we can all search."

"That makes no sense," insisted Leo. "The book could be anywhere."

"If I can have a word, Victoria..." Humpert pulled her off to the side for whispered conference. Leo looked on like a fullback being replaced on fourth and inches. Then he began playing with his gun, training it on various parts of my body and pretending to pull the trigger.

As soon as the conference ended, he jumped in again. "Victoria, I guarantee I can make him talk."

"I wouldn't guarantee it," I said. "Unless you can convince me you're not going to kill us once I tell you where the book is—and I'm more than a bit skeptical on that particular subject—I'm never going to tell you." I wasn't nearly as convinced of that as I tried to sound.

"It could take a while," Leo said. "But you'll tell me. And I can work on your girlfriend too. That might speed things up."

"No torture," said Victoria to my relief. "Not yet. I'm not ready to give up on Steve. Not just yet." She came over and put an arm around my shoulders—normally something a man does to a woman rather than vice versa. Leaning her naked body up against me, she cupped my penis with her free hand. "First, we look next door. And we let Steve think about what he wants to do with the rest of his life. And how long he wants that life to be."

Unbelievably, I was starting to get hard. Victoria felt it. She gave me a little squeeze and a knowing smile and stepped back.

"All right," she said after a moment. Carefully watching my reaction, she added, "Tear that place apart over there. I'll do the same to Steve's room here, just to be sure. In the meantime, lock them down in the lab."

As Leo and Humpert started to lead us out, Victoria grabbed my arm, "Are you sure you don't want to trust me, Steve? If we find the grimoire without you, it will be too late. You'll never leave that basement."

"It's yours if you let us go," I countered. "How about if you take us to some public place, a restaurant or a hotel lobby? I'll tell Leo where he can find the book. When he brings it back, you can free us."

She ignored me—instead she turned to Leo. "Speaking of hotels, did you get through to Beverly Hills again?"

He nodded, examining the spot he was scratching on the back of his gun hand. It was already raw. "There was no mistake. The marriage was in Las Vegas yesterday. And it *was* Nancy Palmer from *The Morning Show*. Humpert got it right. Armstrong's personal assistant had me on hold for twenty minutes before he even took the trouble to confirm it.

I almost missed..." He waved the gun at the bed. I knew what he almost missed. The phone must have been tied up when Maria tried to call to warn Al.

"If we don't find what we want, and quickly," Victoria said, jabbing her finger at me in sudden anger, "we're coming down to that basement and getting just as goddamn unpleasant as we have to get in order to make you talk."

I realized that. I also realized that one way or another we were going to end up dead.

CHAPTER 39

So down we went to the basement. Much of the way, Leo kept the barrel of his gun against the back of my neck, but it was actually redundant—his hand was clamped around my upper arm like a vise. I couldn't believe the strength of these guys. Up close, his teeth looked like they were as false as Humpert's, and he smelled of tobacco.

Outside the lab, more equipment than ever was piled up in the corridor. I thought I heard La Perdita meowing in amongst it.

"Hold them out here for a minute, Leo," Humpert said. "I want to make sure there's nothing inside they can use as a weapon."

"Right. Since all we've got are these pistols, we'd be in big trouble if they happened to stumble across a bazooka or a nuclear warhead. We've been over every inch of that room. There's nothing left in there that's going to do them any good."

"It doesn't hurt to check."

A few minutes later he was back, carrying a battered toolbox in one hand and a couple of thin iron rods and a pack of matches in the other.

"Good work," Leo said. "Maybe they'd have built themselves a tank and driven to freedom."

"Or jimmied open the lock and left."

"There's only one way out of this basement. And that's past us upstairs."

Still, once they deposited us inside, Leo himself spent several minutes looking through what was left of the dusty equipment on the few remaining tables and shelves scattered around the room. He left with three or four gizmos that looked as harmless as the rods Humpert had taken.

Humpert started toward the door, then hesitated and turned back to me, as if he had something he wanted to say but wasn't sure how. After a moment, he said, "I'm sorry, Arnold—Steve. I really am. We're just trying to survive here. We aren't bad people. We really aren't."

I nodded. "I understand, Humpert. I really do. You're a good person. I'm a good person. The problem is that poor Maria got caught up with us good people, and she's going to end up every bit as dead as if she was murdered by someone who wasn't nearly as good as we're both so certain we are."

He caught his lip between his teeth in a gesture he might have gotten from Victoria. "Got it, the banality of evil—Hannah Arnold. You're not the only one who's read a book. But is it evil to be who you really are? To do what you have to do? Is a tiger evil? Is a virus? If you think about it..."

"Fuck you, Humpert!" I yelled in a rush of anger. "This is not a goddamn academic exercise. You can't reduce this to some bullshit philosophical question. This is my fucking life! And Maria's life! This is death! And it was Hannah Arendt. Her name wasn't Arnold. It was Arendt. My name isn't Arnold. It's Steve."

"Actually, Arnold, your name is Gavin."

<hr>

Humpert slammed the heavy iron door shut. Then the lock was thrown with a solid *clank*. The old-fashioned lock wasn't as large or as menacing as the lock on a dungeon in some old movie. But it did look like it was most likely the mate to the thick, old fashioned style key on Cranick's key ring.

The one I'd tossed in the trash upstairs.

CHAPTER 40

"*CLYDE MURPHY, THE GOSPEL SINGING COAL MINER, WITH HIS WIFE, WANDA AND HIS DAUGHTER, JUANITA! NOW! ALL YOUR FAVORITES!*"

It was so loud we were both jolted. Then, as the volume was quickly reduced, we realized we were hearing a radio station over the P.A. It flashed loud again, "*A ONCE IN A LIFETIME OPPOR...*" before sinking way down to a level that was just loud enough to make out over the ambient hum.

"What's that all about?" Maria asked.

"I have no idea. Hard to believe any of those three are big fans of Clyde Murray, the Gospel Singing Coal Miner."

"Murphy. Clyde Murphy," she said.

There seemed to be an issue with names that night. "Sorry. I didn't realize you were a fan."

"Never heard of the guy, but the sound is still ringing in my ears."

Maria wrapped her arms around herself as if for warmth, and we spent a quick couple of minutes making sure there was no possible way out. The room itself was as windowless as the rest of the basement, illuminated at the one end by a bulb dangling from a cord and at the other by a reading lamp next to a chaise lounge. Given everything that was piled out in the corridor, I was surprised by how much assorted equipment was still inside.

Humpert's paranoia had given me one idea. I checked the hinges on the iron door. They *were* on the inside. But the heavy hinge pins probably couldn't have been pried out with a jack hammer. There was nothing left in the lab that would even begin to move them.

Victoria had filled the walls with portraits on poster boards, but the various surfaces behind them—long ago painted with man-headed birds, bull-headed men, snakes, Egyptian ankhs, and innumerable other weird symbols—were of solid rock, brick and mortar.

Since leaving didn't appear to be an option, I needed a place to hide Zandie's manuscript that was more secure than the inside pocket of my coat. Just past the chaise lounge was a video set up: a TV, a video recorder, a camera on a tripod and a shelf full of video cassettes. I stashed Zandie's manuscript in among the cassettes. At least Victoria wouldn't find it on me by accident if they started to torture me. And it would be close by if—when—I couldn't take it anymore.

In the background, the radio murmured, "Did you ever wonder why all your favorite TV preachers have such amazing hair? Do you think it's just a coincidence? Or could it be a gift Jesus bestows on those who offer the most to Him? Now you can find out. With just a small offering of..."

Which reminded me.

I turned to Maria. "By the way... Leo? The big blond guy? Think big, bald guy. Male pattern baldness. Today he's wearing his wig. But he was the one who assaulted your uncle and went after you."

She thought about it for a moment, then the realization spread across her face, and she nodded.

I hadn't caught the amount Jesus wanted in order to provide a head of amazing televangelist hair. I did wonder what he would charge to get us the hell out of that basement.

I filled Maria in on most of what she didn't know. I included the murder charge against me. She had trouble believing that faces had appeared on my arm, so I showed her the one of Dell, greatly faded but still clearly visible. *Were these things lasting longer?*

"Do you believe it now?" I asked.

"I don't know what I believe. That woman...what happened... what she did to Al. I don't believe any of it."

"Neither do I. The problem is that it all seems to be true."

And all the while, my brain was racing through our possibilities—or the lack of them. I used to be good at talking my way out of trouble—though that was years ago. Still, there had to be a way out of this. There always was.

Or almost always.

Pacing, I walked by two mirrors and a banner that read, "Miss Southern California—1951." But most of the wall space was covered with those poster boards, mostly portraits of men with a few paragraphs of text. Over in one corner of the room, someone had converted an old table into a drawing board. On it, a selection of pens in a large assortment of colors stretched out above a portrait that covered a third of a poster board. Similar to the portraits mounted on the walls, this was of Peter—the hitchhiker—and beautifully rendered. What in person had seemed pretentious and haughty—the tilt of his head, the loft of an eyebrow—now seemed ennobling and visionary. The tense uncertainty of the mouth, which to me had spoken of an underlying fear and insecurity, now offered evidence of a poetic vulnerability.

On the right side of the poster board was his name—Peter Sisley—and Tuesday's date. In the same fine calligraphy, the artist had begun the story of Victoria's relationship with Peter, copying it from a nearby draft in Victoria's handwriting. The drawing showed real talent, if no respect for reality. It took little imagination to figure out it was the work of Humpert, who somehow worshipped purity and Victoria at the same time.

I went over and checked out a few of the other portraits hanging on the walls. Apparently, the place was a trophy room of Victoria's lovers.

"They're in chronological order," Maria called, already examining the poster boards across the room. Adding with astonishment, "But they begin in 1892."

On the right side of each portrait was an account of the relationship often extending to a second poster board, and occasionally—for the more illustrious and longer relationships—to a third. Many of the boards had photos—of Victoria with the individual—that were mounted underneath the portraits. Walking around the room and spot checking them, I saw Victoria, dressed and coifed for 1971, but otherwise looking much the same, leaving a courtroom with Yippie protest leader, Ted Chadwick. And Victoria with a bouffant, a J.F.K. button and a youthful executive-type in a tux.

Farther on, she was a platinum blonde, wide-hipped, and big breasted, in a low cut fifties evening gown, getting out of a Rolls Royce in front of the Copacabana nightclub in New York. The silver haired man behind her in the photo and depicted in the drawing was Chauncey Adams, a fading English actor who had killed himself sometime in the mid-fifties. Pictured at a U.S.O. bond drive, in 1942, Victoria had an Andrew Sisters' wrap around hair-do, a stronger nose, and was dancing with a Colonel with a chest full of ribbons.

I came up to where Maria was staring at a poster board with a fading photo of Victoria as a flapper, sitting on the lap of a substantial-looking gentleman in a crowded speakeasy.

"What *is* all this?" Maria said, shaking her head. "Obviously, these photos are fakes. Or taken at costume parties or Halloween?" It didn't sound like she completely believed what she was saying.

"If they're fakes, they're astonishingly good ones. Do you see that heavy-set guy in the background, the one that people in that part of the bar are looking at?"

"Uh huh, he kind of looks familiar."

"That's Babe Ruth. And the guy whose lap she's sitting on in the photo, the guy whose portrait is above it on the poster board? It says it's Joseph Force Crater?" I scanned quickly through the words written under the portrait just to be sure. But I'd read an entire book on this guy several years before, and I recognized the face with the sharp nose and the slicked hair parted in the middle. "Judge Joseph Force Crater. Judge Crater. Maybe the most famous missing person of all time. At least until Jimmy Hoffa."

I hustled back to the portraits from the seventies, then added, "No Jimmy Hoffa at least."

"Here's one I missed before," Maria called a bit later. "Take a look at the photo. It was a hunting party, everyone lined up behind a dead elephant. Victoria's at the far right, next to the skinny, older gentleman with the pith helmet. But check out the guy at the other end, the guy holding the gun with his other hand on the elephant."

"Teddy Fucking Roosevelt?" I exclaimed.

"I don't think that was his middle name. But it's definitely him."

We went around the room, looking for the most part at the attached photos. And not only were the portraits all over the walls, there were several good-sized stacks of them that there hadn't been room to mount.

"Could these possibly be real?" Maria asked eventually.

"I have no idea. I'm not sure which is crazier, the idea that the photos under these portraits might be real or the idea that Victoria went to all the trouble to fake them. And sure, five or six of the photos have famous people in them, but if they were fakes wouldn't they all include somebody famous—or at least a lot more of them? And people who were more famous: One of the Beatles or Bob Dylan rather than Terry Davis. Clark Gable or Cary Grant rather than Chauncey Adams. Why on earth would you fake Chauncey Adams?"

"I have no idea. Why would you do any of this?"

"She's always where it's at, though," I said.

"In with the in-crowd. Queen of the zeitgeist. Or trying to be."

"Right. Not always at the top, but as prominent as possible in whatever's the dominant hierarchy of the day."

"But what about the changes in her appearance?" Maria wondered. "That's more than fashion. More than style. Some of it's that, of course. And some of it may be cosmetic surgery. But many of the changes are subtler. And in the earliest color photos her eyes are brown."

I nodded. Without ever seeming to change that much, in both her features and her body type, Victoria always seemed as close to the feminine ideal of each of the differing eras as she now was to that of the 1980s. Maybe closer. Except for the very earliest photos. Seeing off a sailor on a crowded pier during the Spanish-America War, looking about twenty-four, she seemed plain and somewhat less attractive than the women around her. A few years earlier than that, on the poster board dated 1892, the photo showed a homely young girl standing next to a seated gray-beard in front of a horse-drawn caravan with "Notions,

Cloth, Elixirs, Etc." written on the side. Though far less attractive, the young girl did look very much like Victoria.

We hadn't really been reading the commentaries but now we decided we should.

"Let's read them in order," I said. "Moving up the years."

"Are we saying we believe this is real?" Maria asked.

"Crazy as it sounds, I'm beginning to have trouble believing it isn't."

The gray-beard depicted in the oldest portrait turned out to be a traveling peddler. Like the other men on the earliest boards, he only rated a few lines of text. As the men grew more prominent, the form of the accounts standardized. Most began by detailing, often reverently, the wealth or importance or power of the particular husband or "suitor"—Victoria's word, used repeatedly—as if she was re-living the initial glow of the relationship.

The next sections seemed designed to prove how much this mighty man valued Victoria—actually gloating over flowers and gifts, and over small sacrifices and accommodations that were made for her sake, even those which anyone else would have considered normal. Going beyond that, several men gave up the idea of having kids. In other cases, friends were put aside, and "unsuitable" dreams were abandoned, as were children from former marriages. In one instance, a mother was cut off completely. In 1928, Victoria seduced the wealthy widow of a prominent steel baron and forced the woman to announce her homosexuality to the local papers, as "a symbol of her love." Without, of course, mentioning Victoria.

"This guy was a banker," Maria said, reading another one. "She had him shaving his entire body two, three times a day. She insisted on it, then ridiculed him for doing it. She left him for being too wishy-washy."

"Wouldn't you?"

"I suppose so."

As we read the accounts, moving up through the years, the humiliations grew greater, far greater, and far more often sexual. By 1940, her men and occasional women had undergone a full catalogue of degradation. Usually, the more important she believed them initially, the more she put them through before she came to despise them. And her ostensible disappointment and disgust over what they became seemed to hide a strange satisfaction.

"She must have an uncanny instinct for putting pressure where people are the most vulnerable," I commented.

One husband mutilated himself, another jumped from the Chrysler Building in New York. Amazingly enough, few walked out on her. Or if more did, she didn't commemorate them. And though Victoria obviously had a much lower regard for women than men, a disproportionate percentage of those that left her were females, as if paradoxically she had more difficulty gauging their wants and needs, a harder time captivating them. By the sixties, she stopped getting involved with women altogether.

The few souls that did leave her were castigated. It always confirmed her suspicions that they'd never loved her in the first place. Oddly enough, these people were also idealized. And even with them—perhaps especially with them—Victoria always stressed what they *had* done to win her.

"Listen to this," Maria said. "'As Otto slithered over me, slobbering on me—a pathetic scum I'd once considered so much my superior—I was seized by an indignant fury. I crushed him to my chest. It was as if our bodies were forcing themselves together in spasms. Small fires flickered in the gaps between us, and Otto's eyes rolled up into his head. When it was over, he was as wizened as if he'd been through weeks of a serious illness. Several of his teeth had fallen out. He seemed unaware of his surroundings. A great thirst had come over me, but that night my milk flowed better than it had in four years. I was extremely frightened by what had happened. Humpert determined it was a weakness in Otto.'"

When it happened again, three years after that, she was not so frightened. After a few more times, she described a lover wanting her so much she could easily keep him hard even as the flames consumed him and turned him into "an empty shell—but an empty shell with a stiff dick. He might not have known his own name, but he still craved me."

I said, "This is the woman—the creature—I left Al alone with this evening when I ran off. I'm sorry, Maria."

"You said you never knew it was Al until you were at my door."

"I knew it was somebody. I knew she was deadly. Either insane or..." I gestured at the portraits around the room, "whatever this is. And I knew there'd be a lot more people alone with her eventually."

———

We found the story of Fairchild, Mr. RAM, the self-help guru. Victoria hadn't caused his death, though she had left him, a sick man, unattended for over twenty-four hours. The relatives had already hated her for the way she'd treated him, and Victoria had been anxious to avoid a messy public fight even at the risk of losing the estate. That's why, against Humpert's advice, she'd copped the jewelry.

The poster board on Cranick related somewhat the same story Victoria had told me earlier. Cranick was hired as a possible replacement for Humpert, whom she seemed to believe was dying. Then Cranick discovered her new video recorder and tried to blackmail her. "Clearly, he was too strong and too self-willed. So, all at once, I tried to turn him into a suitor and then make the flames come. I tried to force it." It had appeared to work, to leave him a hollow shell; she didn't discover it was incomplete until he attacked her. He was the only one who had ever come back:

> He was completely crazy that night by the highway. I really don't know if I would have been able to turn him around and finish taking him if Steve Witowski (Gavin Kennan) hadn't bumbled into us. But days later, when Cranick snuck into the house to attack me again, ludicrous and terrified, mumbling those stupid spells of his, I seduced him easily and took him naturally.

And obviously with great relief. So, it hadn't been sleeping pills she'd used on Cranick, but seduction Victoria-style. Afterwards she kept expecting him to get up and stumble out, as he hung on for hours in a coma-like state.

> I called Leo to help me get him out of there. By the time he arrived, Cranick was dead. I was upset at first. But soon I realized that such is the way of the world. Some must dominate, and some must be dominated. And if Cranick happened to die from it, it was because he was already a nothing.

The old lab was dusty but—since it was a lab—it had a sink with running water. Marie let it run clear before cupping her hands and taking a drink.

"Yecch," she said. "But no worse than the water over at my uncle's. Or anyplace else around here for that matter. So at least we won't die of thirst."

In the background, the radio played softly, barely noticed. The programming seemed to consist entirely of ads for odd religious products, churches, cults and movements, the kind of ads you'd expect to find on a religious station that broadcast nothing but ads. At one point, I may have even heard an ad from The Ashram—selling as a sacrament "the exact strain of peyote that had turned Professor Richard Alpert into Baba Ram Das." My guess was they'd left the tuner on that station, and Humpert or Leo had just flipped the radio on tonight for noise rather than content. But why?

Maria took another drink then shook the excess water from her hands. "I don't suppose there's any chance she'll let us go after she gets Zandie's manuscript?"

"This room was always locked before. Would she have let us see all this if she was planning on letting us live?"

"Maybe. If it's all B.S. and it's her way of frightening people. Or, in some bizarre manner, of showing off."

"Weird as it is, does it feel like B.S.?"

"No matter what, you're hardly about to run to the police," Maria said.

The unspoken question was, what about her? Would Maria be safe if we could incriminate her in something as well?

"They can do anything to us they want to do," she continued. "Anything. If they want us to tell them something badly enough, sooner or later we're going to tell them."

"We're going to have to make the best deal we can before it gets down to that."

I walked over and dug the manuscript out from among the video tapes. Sitting down on a corner of the chaise, I began reading.

CHAPTER 41

I started reading from the beginning but soon moved past what I'd read before.

... And she could never forget me—her father, mother, mentor and first love, all in one.

I must admit the creature, Nephil, was a misstep. She was my creation, in theory the spawn of Asmodeus. Yet, I had hoped to create a male, a son, a follower and a descendant to help spread my name and amplify my power.

The ceremony is explicit. Initially, Asmodeus is summoned—from Hell or someplace very like it, I assume. Then "under his watchful gaze," employing seven separate knives, the flesh is ceremonially stripped from seven corpses, arranged in the form of a serpent and saturated with a potion consisting primarily of the residual flesh boiled from the bones.

At the climax of a tedious sequence of incantations— invoking far too many deities—the celebrant allows a living serpent to puncture one of his or her veins and chants, "This is my body, this is my blood," seven times as the hot blood throbs out and is—it is supposed—transformed into the seed of Asmodeus, penetrating and impregnating that rotting mass of flesh.

Thus, the demon is incarnated.

Of course, I thought, *how else would you do it? Simple and straightforward, and completely insane.* I was almost afraid to keep reading.

Thirteen days and thirteen nights later the transformation into human form is complete.

Why it works is a mystery. That it works is beyond dispute. Though I have some insight into these knowledges, true understanding adheres to the human mind no better than righteousness adheres to the spirit.

Be that as it may, to create a male, the ritual calls for the flesh of seven men. I had six: five moldering nicely in the old church crypt and another serving no particular purpose buried out in the churchyard.

On any given Saturday night, I was also host to a basement full of drunken, transient fieldworkers, clutching their fifty cent pieces, waiting their turns at discounted delight. One could scarcely imagine a better assemblage of potential number sevens. Still, I doubt any would have volunteered, and valuing personal principles as I do, I have never been entirely comfortable with murder. Most particularly, when it comes to paying customers.

Therefore, I decided to proceed using the remains of only six males. To augment and enhance the mix, I sprinkled in some of the ashes from my Rebecca, the very woman who had used this same ritual to bring me into being all those years before. It seemed most fitting.

Too late, I realized Rebecca—the nearest thing I will ever have to a mother—may herself have been an incarnated demon. She was certainly unique among women. In any case, those few ashes must have overpowered the remainder of the fleshy mixture, and Nephil was birthed in female form. Though in reality, when it comes to male and female, the creature is neither—or perhaps both.

I was of course as disappointed as Henry VIII or any man who dreams of a male heir and finds himself with a mere female. It was especially frustrating because my Rebecca—a true believer in a way I will never be—had insisted in the notes I'd found that Asmodeus only grants the necessary boon of his participation once in any individual's lifetime.

My one chance had only yielded a female, and not even a comely female. Though possessing the aspect of a young woman of sixteen at her creation, she looked enough like the ill-favored Queen of England—this was during my anglophile period—that I began calling her Victoria.

Not being the Queen of England, this unalluring Victoria seemed destined for failure even as a woman: unlikely to lure a truly worthwhile husband on her own; likely to require an infusion of wealth even to capture a much lesser soul.

Such was my sad lot.

Victoria did improve in appearance—marginally—over the years, and I did grow somewhat attached to her, in spite of her sex. When she somehow actually managed to charm that itinerate peddler into taking her away, I was surprised by how much that stung.

Now, in the five years since my downfall, Penelope, my new helpmate, has impressed upon me that Victoria's departure—like her gender—may have been at least partially my fault. As understandable as my disappointment was, I will grant that I may have taken it out on her more than was warranted. Realizing that, perhaps I could even forgive her for having purloined a few fistfuls of my walled-up cash. She actually took a rather restrained amount.

So, I can understand her taking the money—at least in my better moods. It takes money to live. Victoria's appearance being what it was, it may have even taken money to get her into that peddler's decrepit wagon—into his sordid and bug-ridden bed. What I refuse to understand is why she took the time and trouble before leaving to gratuitously betray me to that idiot mayor—generating the mob that stormed my business hoping to take me down and yearning to string me up.

Would I like to see Victoria again? My answer would be yes, I would—and no, I would not. She is after all, my only child, my creation, perhaps my greatest. But she was also an ungrateful Jezebel who deserted me—captive, I assume, to her uncontrolled lasciviousness—and a Judas who went out of her way to betray me, in all likelihood simply for spite. The fangs of the snake pierced my flesh to give her life. But to quote the Bard, "How sharper than a serpent's tooth it is to have a thankless child."

Yet, there is another line that stays with me, one I stumbled upon while paging through the bible of the children of Abraham in search of esoteric secrets. I may not have it entirely correct, but I remember it as:

"On her forehead was written the name Mystery, Babylon the Great, Queen of Harlots and Mother of Abominations—a woman drunken with the blood of the saints."

As homely and weak and ineffectual as Victoria was, I cannot understand why she makes me think of those words and those words make me think of her. Or why—in a world massively devoid of saints—as time goes by and my faculties and memories fade, I sometimes find the connection between those words and Victoria almost terrifying.

THE RETURN OF ZANDIE

"Sometimes paranoia's just having all the facts."
– *William S. Burroughs*

CHAPTER 42

For some reason they didn't come for us that evening, allowing us to go over the full manuscript several times. I even read the sometimes gory—almost always bizarre—point-by-point details of the various rituals. Even after what had happened to Al, Maria was still unconvinced by any of it. I think she still half-expected to discover the whole thing was some kind of hoax. But as for me, the great skeptic, though I was surprised by what I read, somehow I was never able to marshal any real doubts. Everything seemed to fit in so well with what had been happening since I'd arrived. Just like the letters R, B and A would fit into the empty spaces around the E ECC lettered in gold on the burial urn to spell REBECCA.

Just after midnight, exhausted and close to defeated, I hit upon a desperate plan. It wasn't hard to find holes in it; I found even more than Maria did. We just couldn't come up with anything better.

———

I re-hid Zandie's papers, shoving them back between a couple of the video cassettes on the shelf.

Maria saw what I was doing and said, "Wouldn't it be better if you could fit them around a cassette inside the cardboard sleeve?"

"I don't think there's room. Let me see." I pulled out a cassette from its sleeve and put it down on top of the VCR, hoping to wrap the pages around it.

The cassette began to vibrate.

The video recorder was on.

I switched on the TV. And there I was in real time standing in front of the TV watching myself stand in front of the TV. Someone—most likely Humpert—had somehow disconnected the red operating light and the small mechanical counter on the VCR, but the machine was on and recording, nonetheless. The attached camera with its built-in microphone commanded a good portion of the room. It was centered on the chaise lounge—the only real place in the lab to sit—where we'd been poring over the very document they were searching for, discussing how we might use it against them.

So that was why Victoria had decided not to torture us—easier to just let me tell her everything she needed to know on tape. That also explained the radio: loud enough to cover the minimal sound of the video tape running, but soft enough not to interfere with recording our conversations.

I checked the tape in the machine. It was almost at the end. But the VCR was in the six-hour mode, and we'd been in the lab less than three. Humpert must have accidentally started recording somewhere in the middle of a cassette that had already had something on it.

I rewound the tape to the beginning and hit play.

It began with Victoria in bed with a distinguished-looking gentleman. This may have been the tape Cranick had tried to blackmail Victoria with. It certainly wasn't very incriminating; they didn't even make it all the way to sex—not actual intercourse anyway—though Victoria was gently denigrating everything the guy did. Anxious to get the part on us erased, we fast forwarded through this and through most of the next two men, both of whom had come over while I was at the house.

With the investment executive, Victoria was merely flirtatious, blowing hot and cold, and laughing at the way he caressed her. The second guy, the attorney she'd met at Club Gatsby, screamed once as Victoria "accidentally" ripped his erection with her fingernails, drawing blood. Then she giggled. If Victoria had taped me, fortunately it wasn't on this cassette. Maybe it was on the part that had just been recorded over.

I skipped ahead to where Maria and I appeared. Then, when the tape reached the part just before I pulled the pages out of their hiding place—at a point where neither one of us was visible on the recording—I stepped out of camera view. Leaning back in, yet staying out of the frame—I hoped—I hit the red button to record over what came next.

The new recording wasn't likely to win any major awards. Maria fell asleep on the chaise. I pretended to doze lying beside her. I didn't figure anyone would be coming for us until they thought the tape had recorded its full six hours. Still, I stayed alert: ready to yank out the tape, pop in another and stash the first one in a pile of Zandie's books. Maybe they'd think Humpert's tampering had somehow screwed something up and kept the machine from recording. Maybe they wouldn't.

Later, when the tape finally clicked to a stop, I let myself relax and slept fitfully. I dreamed of Ann.

It was late the next afternoon before Leo and Humpert came and got me.

CHAPTER 43

"Sit down, Steve—or Gavin, I guess it is." Victoria was still in her bathrobe. She stopped massaging her temples and patted the waterbed beside her. Humpert and Leo had left us alone. They were probably watching through the one-way mirror. "I know you're afraid of me, but I'm not going to hurt you. At least, not now."

I sat, but about as far away on the bed as possible, as if that would make a difference. I didn't bother to deny I was afraid of her.

"You've had a rough time recently, Gavin. I know it. But your rough time could be over now. You could join me. Humpert's sicker by the day. It doesn't matter what the doctors say. I've been through this before. And I can feel him dying—slipping from me—in every cell of my body. You could take his place. But my boys have to trust each other. And I have to trust you."

Victoria paused, clearly looking for a response. I kept my mouth shut.

She smiled at me radiantly, a Madonna from a stained-glass window. When she continued, her voice was soft cotton, soothing and comforting. "With me, you could find a home. With me, you'll be out among the real people of the planet, the movers and the shakers. The famous and those who control the famous. Forget Harrison Armstrong. We'll find a man who'll make him look like pocket change."

She stretched out her hand to me. I let her grasp my fingers but resisted her gentle tug and remained where I was.

"Maybe I'll never find 'the man of my dreams,'" she added with a sad, self-deprecating smile, "but I will be coddled and pampered. And adored. Believe me."

"And me...?"

"You'd be with me. Helping me. Close to me. Privy to my secrets. *All my secrets,*" she said suggestively, reminding me of the drawings downstairs. "And I'll take good care of you."

She slid over next to me. As our thighs rolled together on the waterbed, her hand went to the back of my neck. I sat there rigidly. Maybe she'd never find the man of her dreams, but I'd found the woman of my dreams. And she wasn't even a woman; she was a monster, an abomination, the vile creation of a man who was himself a creation of who knows what?

Her fingers kneaded my neck. I thought of Cranick, of Al. Was it now my turn? But before I could break out of her grasp, Victoria suddenly understood why I was pulling back. She laughed, shaking her head in amusement.

"Calm down. Relax. I should have made it clear to you by now there's no way on earth I'm gonna take you into my bed. Not seriously. You're perfectly safe on that score."

She tousled my hair and chuckled again, not viciously, but in the condescending way of an insensitive teacher, laughing at the homely little adolescent with a crush on her.

"It's not your fault you want me, Ste... Gavin. But I'm not the kind who can go to bed with just anyone. Sure, I've had my share of disappointments—suitors who sooner or later turned out to be pathetic specimens—but it wasn't like I ever knew that beforehand."

Oh. How are you supposed to feel when the Nazis announce they're executing every man in the village, but, needless to say, they aren't going to bother with you?

As her fingertips massaged my neck, her robe opened. Above the slight swell of her stomach an extended nipple quivered hypnotically. Slowly, gently, she eased my head down and slipped the nipple past my lips.

It stiffened even more. I must have sucked at it automatically: a pungent liquid spilled into my mouth. My eyes were closed, but in a silent explosion my head filled with a warm red glow.

"With me you'll have power you can never have on your own," Victoria crooned.

The glow intensified. Like the liquid, it was bitter, yet in an extraordinarily pleasing way. Victoria was speaking of the men she'd had, the men she would have. I wasn't specifically aware of exactly what she was saying, but I suddenly realized what fools they all were.

They all thought they were such a big deal. They all would have considered themselves better than I was. Maybe I couldn't have Victoria. Maybe I wasn't good enough, but—primped and poised, strutting or sauntering—didn't they always end up yielding everything to her, begging for her favor? I sucked harder. Tasting her strength—Victoria was so far above me she could bring everyone else down to my level. And below. After all, when it came right down to it, weren't we all worms? No, not worms; serpents, snakes in the grass, ready to do each other in for the slightest advantage. The thought gave me a deep satisfaction. And a strength of my own—to defy the bullshit myth of human beneficence, and jeer at those who claimed any motivation beyond feeding their own bellies and elevating themselves over their neighbors.

The breast went dry, but she had to pull my head roughly away before I stopped sucking. Her strength was clearly physical as well. I wiped my mouth. The residue on the back of my hand was a sickly yellow. Like an addict, already worried the effects might end, I bent down toward the other breast. But she shoved me away.

"Enough for now. If you're with me, there'll be plenty more later. But I need that grimoire. I need to understand exactly who I am; exactly what forces are at work here."

She took a bottle of eye drops off the night table, leaning back against the pillows as she released two drops in each eye.

"Like anybody else," she said, blinking against the artificial tears, "I just lived my life and never really thought much about it. Even though I knew there were things about me that were...different...things that developed over the years that even I found hard to believe. But now, with Humpert getting sick and the way I was feeling and everything... It isn't that I'm not all I once was, you understand. But with that grimoire I can make certain I remain all that I am and become everything that I can be."

Her words and the sudden uneasiness in her voice reminded me of what I'd read in the manuscript the night before:

> The human flesh that clothes such a demon, such a psychic parasite, is mutable—mortal to disease and injury. I can attest to that all too well myself. Though my understanding is that barring such fatal incidents, he (or she, as I suppose we should call such a being if it has taken mortal female form) could remain viable and even grow more desirable indefinitely...though only and precisely to the extent of his or her increasing confidence.

CHAPTER 44

Leo took me back down to the old lab in the basement. Humpert was watching the tape on the TV. I tried to act appropriately surprised by the recording but he wasn't paying any attention to me anyway. Maria was sitting silently on the chaise. The radio was finally silent. Victoria trailed in a moment later. I wondered if she'd stayed behind to wash off her breast.

"Well?" she said to Humpert.

He paused the tape. "Nothing about the grimoire so far. But I did see him hide some papers."

"Did you get them?"

He shook his head. "He must have moved them later. It was just a small sheaf of papers though—too slim to be the grimoire."

"Didn't they even discuss the grimoire?" Victoria asked.

"Not yet. But there's a lot more I haven't seen."

"Well, Steve," Victoria asked, "do we need to watch the rest?"

"If I give it to you, what happens to Maria?"

Victoria threw me a Mona Lisa smile. "What do you want to happen to her? If you're going to be with me, what do *you* think I should do with her? After all, you brought her over here."

Almost distractedly, Victoria crossed over to one of the mirrors. She examined her face for a moment, then pulled out a brush from the pocket of her robe and began brushing her hair. When she'd finished, she motioned me over beside her. I couldn't help thinking how much better I looked standing next to such a woman.

"Humpert joined me in 1938," she said. "He was thirty-one. Actually, he was thirty-four by the time the lactating started, though he enjoyed sucking on my breasts like a baby from the beginning. I got Leo in 1958, when he was thirty-three. As you can see, the years have been easy on them. We've got a good thing here. Do you want to let Maria screw it up? She's as much a threat to you as to me. I'll let it be your decision."

Maria was visible in the mirror, right over my left shoulder; I focused on one of the drawings on the wall instead, catching the sharp intake of her breath as I said, "I guess she has to die."

"Are you certain?" Victoria asked.

I nodded, the taste of her milk still bitter in my mouth.

"Say it."

"Yes. She has to die."

"Thank you, Steve," said Maria, very softly.

"Gavin," Victoria corrected. "Of course, she was going to disappear no matter what you said, Gavin. But I thought it would do you good to make the choice."

"Good move, stud," said Leo.

"Welcome to the club, Arnold," said Humpert.

Suddenly I felt like strangling him with the stupid lamb's wool sweater he had tied around his neck. It couldn't have been big enough to fit him anyway.

"Thanks, Humpert. By the way, I loved your artwork," I added sarcastically, apropos of nothing, waving at the collection of conquests on the walls. "It's so edifying."

"Those?" he answered. "Victoria did those. She can draw anything she sees."

"I'm also a whiz at potholders," snapped Victoria. "Who cares? I need that grimoire, Steve. Now!"

I walked over and pulled the manuscript out of a stack of books. At first, Victoria didn't want to believe that was all I had. Then she ordered Humpert to go get her glasses from her dresser because she didn't have her contacts in. As he trudged off, she turned the pages over in her hands several times without even unfolding the letter fold, never mind trying to read anything. She seemed shaken by its size and insignificant appearance.

"It's all in there," I said. "Everything about you."

"You've read it all?"

I nodded. "The material about you is toward the beginning, starting around page three. Farther back, he's got complete details on all the ceremonies, including yours, and four or five other spells that at least occasionally worked."

"Did he say where they came from?"

"The one..." It seemed ridiculous to say *the one he used to create you.* "Your spell was in notes left by somebody named Rebecca."

"Yes! That would be exactly right."

"The rest?" I shrugged.

She gave a dismissive wave, "Doesn't matter." She quickly unfolded the manuscript and flipped past the first page.

"Careful," I said, "The paper is old and crumbly."

She shot me an annoyed look, but became more gentle. Turning to page three, she peered blindly at the page. Then she walked over and sat on the chaise, switching on the reading lamp. When that didn't seem to help, she put the document down and pulled out her Virginia Slims and a lighter from the pocket of her robe. While she took the first few puffs, waiting for her glasses, she studied my face as if trying to guess what I already knew, but she didn't ask.

A few moments later, Humpert returned. Victoria took her glasses, found the right section and began reading. We all just watched her. Her lips moved silently. Leaning forward toward her, Humpert's entire clumsy body looked expectant. Leo was watching me as well—and Maria.

"I *am* supernatural...miraculous," Victoria beamed, "Of course, I always knew that."

"Had to be," said Humpert devoutly.

Victoria kept reading and her face darkened. Then, "The next section is titled, 'Educating the *Demon*'. *He* should talk about demons. And that son of a bitch calls what he did to me, 'education.' My earliest memory is of him taunting me about the scabs on my legs and chest. He never even gave me a real name. 'Victoria' was an insult, the name of the wretched old queen. Calling me Venus mantrap was his idea of a joke—he used to tell me that with my looks, I'd be lucky to catch flies. And that scar he gouged into my face... No one's ever been able to remove that."

"'The enduring symbol left by a ceremony designed to tie her to me in subservience forever,'" I said, quoting loosely from the document. "'Conducted in expectation that her aspect would soon improve—before it became clear how uncomely she would always remain.'"

Victoria glared at me. I tried to appear sympathetic. "If it's any consolation, Zandie was fairly sure that particular ceremony didn't work."

"Actually, he didn't care whether it had worked or not. Not once he saw how I was turning out." Her index finger started tapping spasmodically against the pages she was holding. "I can remember when I first left here, buying beautiful clothes and being afraid to wear them because I thought people would make fun of such an ugly girl, trying so hard to look attractive. And sexually..." She shook her head as if to clear it of those memories.

She skimmed through the rest of that page and flipped to the next one. I sat down on the couch, slipping her lighter into my pocket. It had just occurred to me how it might come in handy.

Suddenly, Victoria grew very still. Her jaw relaxed, then a tiny smile appeared.

Seconds later, she beamed with relief. "What this is saying is that I'm just as desirable as I think I am for as long as I think I am. Isn't that right, Steve?"

"You're asking me?"

"You read it, didn't you?" The hand holding the pages dropped to her side in mock exasperation. I was afraid she might lose her place and miss the key point. She added, "Zandie once told me that, but I didn't really believe him."

"Uh huh. It does say something like that. At first."

"At first?" She read on silently, standing up and taking a step or two. Concern spread across her face, and then sudden horror. Her eyes darted from me to Leo to Humpert, as if she were cornered. Then she began to re-read it out loud.

"'But the creature is so unstable and so uncomfortable in this world that she may reach a point where—even were conquests available to her—she would need them to be ever greater, until even that cannot reassure her, and significant deterioration sets in. Her concentration may wane. Small physical problems may plague her. Her joints may ache—her mouth may grow chronically dry. This I know only too well, being such a creature and having reached such a state myself.'"

"Zandie!?!" exclaimed Victoria, interrupting herself. She continued reading. "'Once begun, this decline, which may proceed to full and complete deterioration, is often rapid and...'"

Constricted, her voice quivered to a halt. The document slipped out of her hand.

I picked it up, finding her place easily. "'...this decline, which may proceed to full and complete deterioration is often rapid and is...irreversible.'"

"'Irreversible,'" I repeated. It was the last word of the last line on the page, which I quickly turned. "That's all he says about it. The next page gives a formula for producing mind shadows of the dead on someone's flesh."

Groaning hard, Victoria doubled up as if she'd been kicked in the stomach. She collapsed to her knees. "Help me," she cried.

"Let's get her to the chaise," I suggested, tossing the pages aside.

Leo stared at me as if I were speaking gibberish. Humpert, who'd seized the manuscript the instant it hit the ground, stuck it under his arm, and we helped her to her feet.

Victoria winced when I touched her back—something was bulging under her robe.

"Let's get this off," I said.

"What are you doing?" demanded Leo, belligerently.

"We... I've got to see what's under there."

I tore off the robe, more roughly than was necessary. Underneath, Victoria's body seemed compressed, stunted. The pinkness of her skin had deepened. It might have been darkening even as we watched. The bulge on her lower back pulsed. A smaller swelling was beginning to fill the space between her left breast and shoulder. The smell of charred flesh and singed hair surrounded her.

Someone gasped. Leo moaned. Desperately, Victoria pushed me back so she could catch sight of herself in the mirror, but when she did, she recoiled from the image. Her face was contorted. Her darting eyes grew imploring, beseeching, but beseeching no one in particular. Her breathing came in spasms, and now in each breath was an ululating little cry of panic. She dropped back onto the chaise.

"Fight it, Victoria. Fight it!" Humpert was thumbing through the manuscript even as he spoke.

I switched off the light by the chaise as if to shelter Victoria from it.

"You know you can be beautiful," Humpert pleaded. "You're probably the most lusted-after woman who ever lived. Remember who you are. *Remember!* You are Victoria and you are gorgeous. Remember—for all our sakes."

Her eyes calmed somewhat. Their movements slowed. But within the bulge on her chest a half-serpent, half-human face rose to the surface, pressing itself in three-quarter profile against the membrane of skin—an ear, a nose, a single unseeing eye, a lipless grimacing mouth. Then it receded back into the tumor.

"What the..." Humpert cried.

I thought he was reacting to Victoria, but Humpert held the manuscript close to his face. He glared down at me suspiciously, then moved over underneath the bulb hanging from the ceiling. "I think this page has been altered."

"What?" cried Victoria with desperate hope.

"Really?" I asked, heading toward the light, collecting Maria with a hand on her back.

"Yes. It has, Victoria. *Yes, it has!* And not only that, but a page is missing here. We've got fifteen... and the next one is seventeen."

"Let me see," I said, coming up behind him. His face filled with comprehension as I yanked down on the pull chain of the light with all my might, tearing it loose and submerging the room in darkness.

I knocked Humpert away from us. He yelled for Leo. I reached toward where Maria had been standing. And found nothing. Then Humpert was upon me, hitting me off center, but knocking me to the concrete floor—the fingers of my left hand smashed by his knee. I tried to scramble away; his hands closed like a bear trap on my right leg.

A shaft of light! Not ten feet away. Maria had found the door. But she was just standing in the opening.

"Get out of here!" I screamed as Humpert's full bulk dropped on top of me, compressing my rib cage. My arms and legs were pinned. My body tingled with growing panic. The light in the hallway went out, and once more the darkness was almost complete.

"Shit!" Close by, Leo had stumbled on something. I hoped Maria was long gone.

A small dull shape swept through the air. I didn't realize it was Maria's cast until I heard it smack into flesh. Twice. Then Humpert was coughing, choking. I kicked myself free, lunging after Maria, finding the door, just as my coat was seized from behind. Pivoting quickly, I slammed the door on the arm that held me. Bones cracked. The cry could have been Leo's. Maria and I dashed away, shutting out lights as we went.

The sentence I'd altered in the manuscript had originally read, "full and complete deterioration is often rapid and is *reversible*," and the next page had continued, "only by a restoration of the creature's diminishing faith in itself." Adding the "ir" to "reversible" and putting a period after the word had been easy. The only problem was that none of Victoria's drawing pens quite matched the faded ink of the manuscript.

We darted up the cellar stairs, Maria leading the way and me as close behind as humanly possible, clutching at the stabbing pain in my chest, listening for pursuit.

The door at the top of the stairs was locked.

I shoved it and swore.

Shoving it again didn't help. Leo hadn't locked it behind us when he'd brought me back down there. Humpert must have done it, perhaps remembering O'Ryan stumbling in on Victoria and Leo when they were disposing of Cranick.

I put my shoulder into it like they do on TV. And bounced back, nearly falling off the top step and tumbling backwards, clenching my teeth against the shooting pain in my chest. I knew I'd thrown away Cranick's keys, but I checked my pockets anyway. With no windows and the bulkhead exit sealed, this basement itself made a hell of a tomb.

"There is one way," I said. Quickly, I told Maria about the built-in ice box in the P.A. room, explaining how we'd have to sneak past them to get to it.

It was her turn to swear.

CHAPTER 45

Cautiously, we worked our way through the darkened labyrinth, alert to the slightest stirring, ever ready to leap into the scant protection of the closest cubicle. Maria was breathing hard. My chest throbbed with every step.

The light was on again in the lab. The door was halfway open. We stopped about ten feet back. We could hear three separate voices inside. Victoria sounded more concerned with reassuring herself she'd be all right—and Leo and Humpert more concerned with helping her do that—than anybody was about the faint prospect of us getting away. They must have been convinced we couldn't get out.

"That missing page," said Humpert, his sharp voice carrying better than Victoria's or Leo's, "that's the important one. But at least we finally know the condition *is* reversible. And that the information on how to reverse it exists."

I squeezed Maria's hand, whispering and gesturing in the dim light to show the route to the P.A. room and the old ice box: past the door to the lab and the mess of lab equipment, through the curtain, a quick right, and it's right there on the left. I indicated I'd go first. It'd be crazy to try to sneak by the door together—no telling where they were standing in the room or what they could see. We shared what was meant to be an encouraging glance. Maria took a deep breath like a diver about to go under, then released it softly through her mouth. I was tight, ticking with nervousness like a homemade bomb.

Slowly, skittishly, I started forward. The patch of light that fell from the lab into the hallway reminded me of watching Victoria in the bathroom. A drop of sweat slid down my back like a hot chill.

I was two steps from the door when the beam of light doubled and filled with a huge shadow.

For an eternal millisecond my body wouldn't respond.

"Don't worry, Victoria," soothed Humpert. "That page'll be ours in no time. And then he'll be taken care of."

I ducked backwards and hustled quietly back down the hall. Maria was already gone.

"Just be careful you don't end up shooting yourself," Victoria rasped angrily. "Or one of us."

I slipped into the altar room. The statue of Asmodeus was still in pieces on the floor, the altar broken open, the air dusty. I flattened myself against the wall on the far side of the open door. And almost sneezed. I could hear Humpert plodding down the corridor.

He stopped once; the hallway light came on. He stopped again, right outside the altar room. He may have peeked in, but I doubted he was expecting us to be this close by. He made one more stop, probably at the next room down.

Was that where Maria was? I wondered anxiously. But he soon pushed on.

Putting my hands on my knees, I lowered my head like a spent runner, trying to settle myself and to clear the grit from my throat. A glass of water would have been nice. An open window would have been nicer.

I waited until I was sure Humpert was gone, then crept back out into the hallway. Maria was still nowhere in sight. I did a quick check of the four closest cubicles—no Maria. Then the next two. It was hard to believe she'd hidden much further back than that.

Was she ahead of me? Was she behind me?

I had no idea what to do. Victoria and Leo were probably watching the rest of the video, but they weren't going to stay in the lab forever. Humpert could come back anytime. The only thing that made sense was to head down to the P.A. room. And—if Maria wasn't there already—to wait for her as long as possible. Of course, there'd be no way of telling whether or not she'd already been there and gone.

Conscious of the smallest scuff of my soles on the concrete, I headed back down toward the lab. Getting past the door was going to be easy; Humpert had left it closed. The ten feet after that were much more heavily cluttered with equipment than this part of the hall, but I still had to step carefully.

Right on to La Perdita's tail—her furious snarl electrified the silence.

Startled, I cried out, leaping back, reflexively grabbing at the pain in my injured ribs, brushing against a crystal globe perched atop a small display case. Before it even hit the ground, I was searching for another place to hide as La Perdita dashed off through the lab equipment. The globe smashed against the concrete floor.

I was halfway back to the altar room when Maria appeared down the hall in front of me, peering cautiously around the corner, checking out the noise. Frantically, I waved her back out of sight.

I made it into the altar room just as the lab door slammed open. Voices spilled out.

"That way!" Victoria ordered.

Leo muttered something.

"They went *that* way," she screamed. "Are you deaf? Get going! They couldn't have gotten far."

Hiding behind the door wasn't going to cut it this time.

The hole I'd knocked in the top of the hollow altar when I was searching for Zandie's body was big enough to slide in through—just big enough; my coat snagged for a moment on the way in. It was also big enough to reveal me cowering there if Leo came too close. Of course, I could always leap out of this trap like some insane jack-in-the-box. Then all I'd have to deal with would be an oversize football player and his gun.

Through a hairline crack in the marble, I watched Leo's legs turn into the room. He pushed the open door against the wall. Nobody behind it. The altar was the only other hiding place: either crouching on the other side of it or—as would soon be obvious—in it. Once again, I began searching through my brain for something I could say, something I could claim that would get me out of this.

I caught just a glimpse of Maria hurrying past the doorway, headed toward the P.A. room.

Go, Maria, go! Once she got around all the junk in the hall, the way would be clear to the ice box and the outside. *After that, how long would it take to get the sheriffs out here?*

Was there a chance she might not even call them, knowing I was wanted for murder?

Leo was mumbling to himself. He was inches from the altar. I could practically read the lettering on his college ring when a deep scraping sound came from down the hall, like something heavy and wooden being dragged across concrete.

He froze.

A roaring cascade of breaking glass—Leo was moving even before the sound died down. Maria had given herself away. It didn't even surprise me. Moving whatever she'd moved to create that long scraping noise wasn't something she would have had to do to get past, and she couldn't have done it by accident. I only hoped she could make it through the ice box before Leo caught up with her. It would take him forever to force his bulk through that tiny compartment, if it was even possible. It had been a tight enough squeeze for me.

I freed myself from the altar amongst a confusion of noises. Leo reaching the jumble of equipment in the hall—plowing his way through it, pushing things aside, cursing. More glass breaking. More scraping. It took a while. Seconds? A full minute? Then I heard his footsteps on the concrete, running free on the other side. Victoria following ponderously.

A rash of excited cries and then silence.

I imagined I heard someone running outside the building, though I realized that was impossible through the stone walls. I strained for the slightest sound, only to be jarred by an earsplitting electronic squeal, which tapered into a crackling. Then the basement filled with the full weight of the National Anthem.

CHAPTER 46

I had a moment of confusion, in which it actually occurred to me that we might be saved, as if the forces of goodness and light would arrive to the blaring of martial music like the cavalry in a western or the gunships in *Apocalypse Now*. Then I realized it was just the damn P.A. system, fired off at full power. And then I felt vulnerable, exposed. A division of Russian tanks could be rumbling toward me under cover of that musical barrage.

The anthem receded and became an eerie backdrop for Victoria's voice.

"Steve, I've got Maria. I'd forgotten about the old ice box. Pretty clever. Only she didn't quite reach it."

I didn't believe her. I didn't want to believe her. It was almost as if I couldn't believe her. *Hadn't I heard running outside?*

No, I hadn't.

Carefully, I peered out into the hall, but I couldn't see past the curtain at the end. Maria was on her way to get help. If she'd gotten to her home phone or her car, it could come anytime. Worst case, it might take an hour or two, maybe even three, but it was a big basement, and I could hide. No way Leo could have caught her with the head start she had. It took him too long to get through that mess outside the lab. Victoria was bluffing. It was all over for her, and she was hoping against hope that I'd fall for her bluff and give up the missing page in time for them to take care of me and get out of there before the sheriffs arrived.

I took a step out into the hall. She had to be bluffing. Because if she wasn't, I was dead and I couldn't possibly accept that I would die there like that—still young—for no good reason except that I'd hung around an attractive woman for a few days hoping to get laid when I should have been moving on.

Except for the slimmest of chances—being picked up by Maria hitchhiking, leaving her uncle's that first night exactly when I did—I never even would have met Victoria. I hadn't believed in any cosmic plan since childhood, and I knew that the slimmest of chances—turning left instead of right, leaving now instead of later—melodramatically deciding to carry a gun on a drug deal—these things killed people every day. But even after Dell and Stephen, I still couldn't bring myself to believe that after all these years and all I'd been through, my own death could be so casual, so trivial. Maria must have escaped.

"Hello?" Maria's voice came through the P.A. My first instinct was that it was a trick, a recording. "I told you Victoria, Steve didn't wait around for me. He left before I did."

The words trailed off into a cry of pain. "And then I suppose he threw the latch on the ice box door from inside the ice box," said Victoria. Which of course couldn't be done. But I appreciated Maria trying to save me.

"She's not going to make it, Steve," Victoria continued, her words swollen with bitterness and tainted with desperation. "You can listen to her die, courtesy of modern electronics. It won't be quick, and it won't be easy. And before she dies—just before she dies—we'll cut the fetus out of her. It'll be pretty small, so we'll have to slice out a big enough hunk to make sure we've got it. You know, searching through all that mystical mumbo jumbo in Zandie's books, we found a ritual that was supposed to attract someone's perfect match to them from anywhere in the world. It called for the flesh of two people who died in agony. I remember that because Humpert said that it seemed like a tough way to get a date. Now Maria certainly counts as a person—in spite of the way you've been treating her. Whether the fetus counts as a person, I guess depends on your politics. But that probably doesn't matter, since there's virtually no chance that ritual actually works. Still, it should be fun to try. And all you'll be able to do is listen. Not being man enough to do anything about it."

"Or," called Leo in the background, "you could come down here and try to stop us, couldn't you, stud?"

"We don't expect that, Steve. But why don't you come to us, and we'll let Maria die peacefully and the fetus stay where it is. If you're quick, and if you lead us to that page, and crawl and grovel as well as we all know you can, I might even let you live. I might even still allow you to join us. I don't have to kill you. You aren't going to cause us any trouble. I might let you join us—of course I might not—but what choice do you have?"

What choice did I have? And even if by some miracle I got out, when it came right down to it, everything I'd ever pinned any hopes to was gone. What did I really have left? Nothing.

"This is your chance, Steve," Victoria said, a moment later. "I'm here all alone now. It's the perfect time for a rescue. Or a little semi-private groveling, in front of just me..." Maria screamed out in sudden anguish, "...and what's left of Maria."

At the end of the hall, the curtain moved. I ducked back just in time. I cut myself painfully scrambling back into the dusty altar, but Leo hustled right on by.

Now both Leo and Humpert were behind me. Victoria *was* alone.

I struggled with the weight of my fear. My instincts were to stay hidden, to avoid confrontation for as long as possible. It wasn't rational; they'd find me sooner or later, and in the meantime Maria would be tortured to death, her unborn fetus ripped from her womb. Still, it was hard to leave the closest thing I had to safety, no matter how temporary it might be. A non-swimmer doesn't jump easily from a sinking ship to a life raft, even if the raft is drifting farther and farther away every second. The longer I delayed, the slimmer my already slim chances grew. But remaining didn't call for thought or action. And it wasn't agonizing.

I dragged myself out of the altar just as Victoria returned to the P.A., all pretenses gone—furious, frightened, a slight treble of hysteria in her voice. "Don't cross me, you bastard. I need that page. I know you've got it, and you're going to give it to me."

Maria's shriek was elongated, dying out and then revitalized by some new torment. I shook my head hard. I didn't want to imagine what was happening. Three more screams came as I advanced down the corridor, through the broken glass and the jumbled mess, the evidence of what Maria had done to save me. I could smell my own fear. My throat was dry and gritty, though the taste of bile was in my mouth.

Stepping through the curtain, I could see an empty corner of the P.A. room. My heart was thudding, echoing through my body, worse than when I watched Cranick assaulting Victoria, worse even than during the most ludicrous of my sexual encounters with her. At that moment, I would rather have died than have had to confront her. Much rather. I was sure I was going to die anyway. One way or another. But before that death, that emptiness...? I couldn't have been more terrified if my blood had turned to liquid fear.

Why? Why was I so fucking terrified? Was it the milk that I'd nursed from Victoria—from the demon?

The fault, dear Brutus. I could hear Stephen—the real Stephen Witowski—saying the words. His favorite quote. Repeated from the time we were in ninth grade, studying the abridged version of *Julius Caesar*. Repeated so frequently, it was soon abbreviated to just the first four words: *The fault, dear Brutus.* Then later, *TFDB.*

The fault, dear Brutus, is not in our stars, but in ourselves, that we are underlings.

Not in our stars, but in ourselves, quoted Stephen Witowski. Stephen Witowski who'd put a rifle in his mouth and pulled the trigger.

Humpert was right; Victoria was a touchstone, powerful, overwhelming, even in her present condition—perhaps especially in her present condition. Dealing with her had already confirmed every self-doubt I'd ever had—my worst suspicions and nightmares had become self-evident truth. I didn't want to know what vile new revelations about myself and the race that spawned me lay beyond even that. I didn't want to know what she could make of me—or, more accurately, have me make of myself—before she allowed me to die.

I edged down the hall toward the P.A. room, each step a conscious effort. Creeping up beside the doorway. Not yet looking inside. A groan came through a speaker on the wall behind me, startling me. Then came a small sob, as if Maria was absorbing the suffering rather than filling the air with it as Victoria wanted.

"I hope you're aware of what your cowardice is making me do to this poor creature, Steve. Up till now I've kept it to her body. There are a lot of different tools and utensils in here. Don't make me use the more horrible ones. I'm not that kind of person, but this is self-defense, and you're forcing me to punish this innocent girl instead of you. What do you want with that page anyway? It won't do you any good. It won't get you out of here. But it could make all the difference in the world to me. How can you be such a selfish bastard?"

Yet another cry from Maria.

"Now her face has been sliced. Do you know what that means to a woman?" Victoria was as furious with me as if she actually believed I'd done it. "And it's going to get worse."

Tentatively, I hazarded a glance into the room. Four or five feet away, Maria sat in a straight-back chair. A fine stream of blood ran down one side of her face, and she was clutching her stomach as if she'd been punched. Victoria stood in front of her, back to me, her pink robe wrapped around her once again.

As Victoria stepped back and started to turn, I ducked out of sight, sure I'd been seen. Or almost sure. I might have run if I hadn't been so afraid of definitely giving myself away. One of Victoria's hands came into view, dark and rough, the knuckles huge, the fingers strong, yet misshapen, setting the knife down on the table by the door, picking up a pack of Virginia Slims Menthol Lights.

When she spoke into the microphone again, she spoke softly, as if she knew I was just outside:

"I'm going to light a cigarette now. It's not good for my health, but I've been under a great deal of tension lately." Her chuckle had jagged edges. "When I'm finished you can put it out for me like a good little gentleman. Either that or it's going out in one of Maria's lovely brown eyes. And then we're going to have that baby. Right here. Right now."

A pause. Drawers opened and closed. Then the sound of a match being struck and Victoria inhaling and exhaling the first drag. "You can't do this to her, Steve. You can't be that much of a coward. That page is nothing to you, but it means everything to Maria and I."

She sucked in another puff and let it out, then continued, "Leo, Humpert, get back here right away. I'll need you to hold her down, Humpert. And Leo, you'll have to do the really grisly cutting. You two hear me? Hurry."

"On my way," called Leo, sounding close by. Humpert's indistinct reply arrived a second later. He wasn't much farther away.

Did Victoria know I was out there, exposed—the way she'd known from the bathtub and dancing on the altar? Was she playing with me?

I had to do something before Leo and Humpert arrived. But what? I snuck another peek. I could hear Leo's heavy approach. The knife was still on the table, the blood drying on its tip. Though I had something else I could use as a last resort, the weapon was a godsend. Victoria had her back to me again, holding the microphone in front of Maria. Leo was coming down the next corridor. Victoria wound her hand into Maria's thick curly hair. I slipped into the doorway. Maria's eyes met mine. Someplace behind me, Leo cursed as he banged into something heavy and stumbled. I could be on Victoria before she could react. I reached for the knife. A blade at her throat would get us out of there. We could lock Leo and Humpert in the lab. No problem. And Victoria?

Victoria.

Maria screamed as Victoria twisted the handful of hair. The scream became louder—more anguished. I'd pulled my hand back without the knife. The ghastliest shriek yet covered my desperate escape as I fled from the doorway, from the pink-robed back. And from the horrible understanding in Maria's eyes.

CHAPTER 47

I stumbled round the corner and into the crypt. To the top wall vault, the one that was still covered. The one that came up underneath the back porch. Leo must have heard me dashing off. He might even have seen me. Any second he'd be coming to take me back to Victoria.

"A few more puffs should do it, Steve," came over the speaker outside in the hall.

I tore at the capstone. It was no longer sealed, of course. I'd merely shoved it back in place. But it wasn't going to come off. Several of the fingers on my left hand were swelling thanks to Humpert's knee, and it was difficult to grip. Somehow, I forced it open. And put it down carefully, quietly. Panting. Hearing tiny echoing moans I barely realized were my own. I heaved myself up and halfway in.

I wasn't alone.

"I think we should do the right eye," said the P.A. "Where's Humpert?"

In my panic, I hadn't even noticed the smell, but now with the dead flesh pressed against my own, my eyes watered and my nostrils were full of it.

"Humpert?" called Victoria.

Where was he?

I jerked myself forward over the corpse. My forearms and shoulders scraped against the concrete. The stench was warm, sticky. Like cotton candy against my face. All those plans and dreams about the evolution of the human spirit I'd shared with Stephen and Dell and Ann and all the others, all those songs I'd written about mankind as the soul of the cosmos. It wasn't that many years ago. Once left on my own, how quickly I'd come to this. Desperately, I clawed my way onward, expecting my ankles to be seized at any second.

"Hold her," ordered Victoria.

The dead man and I came face to face. Our heads wedged against each other. Something slick and wet touched my lips, and I tasted his blood. A crack of gray light glowed above us. Jamming my knees under me, I drove my back up against the stone that covered the vault.

It yielded. A quiet scrape as it slid to the side and onto the soft ground. The fresh air rushed in.

The night was clear and balmy, moonlight filtering in even under the porch. My body was halfway out of the tomb, my face pressed against the cool earth. Like a worm. Or a snake. I was safe. I was free. I could easily get out of there before Leo or Humpert could get to me, and I heard no pursuit.

"Hold her head back, Humpert," Victoria's words were thin and distant.

"He's not going to show," said Leo. "He doesn't have the balls."

I was safe. I would live.

Maria would die.

"Hold her eye open," said Victoria. "Wait... get the knife, Leo. We'll cut the lid off first."

But Maria would die anyway. No matter what I did. No matter what I went through.

"One last puff..."

I almost lost a shoe, but my legs finally came clear. Even if she told Victoria about the missing page, Maria would die. And I couldn't kid myself that I could get help up here in time to do any good. I would live, but already barely tasting that life, I could see what I would live as.

Over the P.A. came a long deep exaggerated toke on a cigarette. What I had done to myself was worse than anything Victoria could have done.

"Fuck it. Cut her, Leo. Listen to *this* scream, Steve."

"STOP! STOP IT, VICTORIA! I'm here! In the crypt."

"Get him!" Victoria ordered.

I looked down into the grave I'd just escaped from. At Peter, the Englishman, naked and now as emaciated as Cranick. His ear had hardly bled at all. He hadn't been castrated but his throat had been sliced about as far as it's possible to slice a throat.

Rather than try to squeeze past him again, I grabbed him under the shoulders and pulled him back out of the way. He weighed almost nothing and came almost all the way out. I was well past being squeamish.

I climbed back into the grave, resigned. Then I turned over on my stomach and slid down toward the opening. I was going to die, pissing on a forest fire. It didn't matter if anyone or no one would have cheered. And it wasn't for a better world. Ultimately, it was for me. I was going back because I didn't want to be the kind of person who wouldn't go back.

The fault, dear Brutus. TFDB.

CHAPTER 48

Leo and Humpert grabbed me as I slid out of the grave. Humpert's left arm hung at his side.

"Get your hands off me," I ordered, having nothing to lose. "If you want that missing page."

Strangely enough they obeyed.

Leo peered into the tomb. "It's open to the outside? Where's the body?"

"What's left of him is lying under the back porch."

"Like I told you," Humpert said, "Victoria is more powerful than ever. That happened the first time they were together."

"Looks to me like she sliced his throat," I said, starting back to the P.A. room as if the trip was my idea.

"I did that," said Leo. "He was already dead. Not easy either, draining blood from a corpse."

"Blood for that ceremony that night." Humpert sounded apologetic.

"And the ear?" I asked him, getting a small shamefaced shrug of the eyebrows in return. "Killing Cranick might have been part accident, but she did Peter deliberately."

"She wanted to see if she could," said Leo. "To see if maybe that was what she needed."

"She likes it, doesn't she? It's more fun than just turning them into derelicts."

"She's a dominant natural force," said Humpert.

"She's a witch," I answered.

He snorted. "Don't be childish. There's no such thing."

"That's reassuring."

We entered the P.A. room. The smell of death was as strong as it had been in the tomb. Victoria turned.

"Jesus!" I muttered.

Her body was twisted. The skin on her face was as brown and brittle as if it had been baked. A flap of it hung down from her forehead, partially covering one yellow eye. Her dingy hair looked seared around the edges. Her lips and fingertips were a dark purple.

"I never thought you'd show up," was all she said.

I brushed past her to Maria who was limp in her chair, blood still seeping down her cheek. I grabbed her cast with both hands as if I was comforting her.

"Giving yourself up was stupid," she said. Her smile said differently.

"Is she really worth dying for, Steve?" Victoria asked scornfully.

"She is. I am. You aren't," I said without turning around. I noticed that the cigarettes and a pack of matches were now on the counter beside Maria's chair.

"Where's that page?" Victoria said it like a general giving orders to a lieutenant—but a lieutenant who was holding a gun and pissed off.

"I need a cigarette."

"A Virginia Slim? Isn't that sweet."

"It's an old cop trick, Victoria," I said, smiling at Maria. My lips didn't even quiver. I knew I was going to die and that was okay. It was actually better than the alternative I'd been facing minutes before. "To cover the stench of decomposition. And to get the taste of it out of my mouth."

"Take one. You don't have to worry about picking up the habit long term."

Still facing Maria, with my back to the three of them, I stuck a Virginia Slims Menthol Light in my mouth. I didn't need the butane lighter in my pocket; I used Victoria's matches. Just before I would have scorched my fingers, I swung around and lit the cigarette with the flame from a single rolled up page of paper. As realization slowly emerged on their faces, I dropped the last ashes to the floor and crushed them out under my shoe. Then I did the same with the cigarette.

"It was wedged under my cast, Victoria," Maria said with satisfaction. "You *should* have bargained with me—but you were so certain Steve had it. That's one of the problems of being such a sexist, I guess. You simply assumed that with something that important it would be the man who'd be controlling it. Still, another twenty seconds and I probably would have told you about it anyway."

"And then you'd have been dead," I said to Maria. She nodded.

Victoria's misshapen face slackened. Her mouth hung open, though no sound escaped as she crumbled to a sitting position on the floor.

Leo charged over and slugged me in face, knocking me to the floor, too. "You bastard!" he yelled.

"Watch it, motherfucker. I'm the only one who ever read that page."

Victoria's head jerked up. Her mouth was a stiffened gash, her nose scarcely more than a bump of cartilage. Her skin was taking on a purplish cast, and it was as if her features were vanishing. Still, at my words a flicker of hope ignited in her eyes.

"Stand up," I ordered her, doing so myself. "And take off your robe."

She did as she was told. Slowly. Painfully. Her body had shriveled. The half-serpent, half-human face bulging out over one breast was clearly visible, a death mask, charred even darker than the rest of her, yet more human now than her own face. The thick dark liquid leaking from her nipples was eating through the skin below, opening holes in her abdomen, revealing rotting flesh and, in one spot, three skeletal fingers.

"Turn around," I ordered.

Three inflamed boils the size of saucers infected her back. Two had burst open, revealing small clumps of hair and several teeth among the pus.

"That page, asshole," Leo demand. "What did it say? Believe me, we can have you begging to tell us."

"I wouldn't be in such a hurry if I were you," I snapped.

I led Victoria to the mirror over the sink. A jagged crack scarred its surface.

"Take a look," I said. She held up her hand in front of her face, as if to protect herself from a blow. The fingers were shriveled and webbed, the hand twisted so badly it was barely a hand. "Do you really believe *that* can be made beautiful again. Do you really?"

Victoria—or rather the wreckage of rotting flesh that had once been Victoria—began to cry. A single tear the color of thin blood slid down one cheek.

"You're dead, Kennan," Leo cried, raising his gun, living up to my expectations.

"No," sobbed Victoria. "No!"

Shivering, she grasped my shoulder. "It's you," she whispered. "You know what I can be. You can save me, Steve."

"My name is Gavin."

"You know how much you wanted me." Her arm slithered behind my back, still strong, pulling me to her. It wasn't sexual; it felt like she was just trying to hang on to someone who had wanted her so much. Maybe the last man who would ever want her. Her stench was sickening. Her scaly cheek scraped against mine.

"The problem, Victoria, is that I'm an asshole." I was on safe ground there. No one in the room was likely to contradict me. "I'm incredibly shallow. I didn't actually want you. I had no idea who you were. I didn't even know *what* you were. I wanted your tits, your ass, your blonde hair, your blue eyes, your body. Your fragrant, delicious pussy. And I'll bet it was fragrant and delicious. Even your asshole was probably perfect. Maybe it was even a more perfect asshole than I am. Put that all together and that's what we've all decided is desirable nowadays. You were the fucking White Rock woman of 1982. You were first prize. Or as close to it as I was ever likely to get. You were success!"

"And she can be again," Humpert was pleading.

"No. No. She can't be. Look at yourself, Victoria. Take a good look. You're getting worse by the second. And look at me. Can you honestly believe that there's any way, any time, anywhere that a shallow motherfucker like me could ever be made to want..." I flicked my hand at her reflection in the mirror as if I was flicking away a bug, "...*that?* That any of the men you've ever known or are ever likely to know could ever be made to want you?"

And then I said, "Kiss me, Victoria."

"Kiss you?" she wheezed, confused.

"Kiss me, seduce me, make me want you, make my dick stir even the tiniest bit."

I took her in my arms and pulled her to me. She held back. Her breath was like a draft from a charnel house. Her skin was slick, greasy. "You're too far gone. The page made that clear. But if you honestly believe you can make me find you anything other than sickening, then do it, kiss me. Now."

With a sudden desperate leap, her mouth was on mine, her decimated hands holding my head in place, her dry, desperate tongue working to get inside my mouth.

I let it happen. Our tongues met. Then something seized my body, my whole being—a repulsion so deep and so profound she must have felt it through every part of her body that touched mine. I would have vomited but I'd eaten nothing in so long there was nothing to vomit. Still, my diaphragm spasmed and the bile came up, filling my mouth, covering both our tongues. We gagged simultaneously and—unable to bear more—I shoved her off me. Once again, she collapsed to the concrete, coughing, writhing into a tangled fetal position.

Humpert looked like he might be sick, but Leo—though visibly shaken—still had his gun on me.

"You'd better get out of here," I warned them, as if I could do something about it if they didn't. "It's over. Get out."

They shared a confused glance. The gun came down slightly. Then Leo drew a bead on my stomach once again.

"I said, get out!"

Suddenly, Victoria began to convulse on the floor. Something green and viscous was draining from the cavities in her abdomen. And Leo fired the gun once, twice, three times. He kept firing until the thing on the floor had been stilled forever, and the gun was clicking empty. Then, realizing what he'd done, he snarled with fear and defiance like a rebellious child, wheeled, and vanished through the door. Humpert nodded, raised a sad little smile, and followed him. I didn't know what would happen to them without Victoria. I didn't care.

SATURDAY, APRIL 3 TO WEDNESDAY, APRIL 14, 1982
ZANDIE'S GRAVE

"To have her here in bed with me, breathing on me, her hair in my mouth—I count that something of a miracle."
– Henry Miller

CHAPTER 49

On the way out of the old church, I'd found Victoria's purse on the kitchen table and settled our account for the $193 inside. Maria and I were exhausted, but neither of us wanted to sleep at her place. Instead, we drove to the Traveler's Inn in San Cristobal, where, without thinking, I rented a room in my real name. It was off the beaten path and close to the hospital.

We both took long showers and fell into the double bed. When I woke up nine hours later, we were wrapped in each other's arms. A few minutes after that, Maria woke up. I gave her a kiss and we simply held each other. Gingerly.

Most of my left cheek was a vivid maroon, like the scar of an old burn. I might have injured it dropping down into the altar or forcing my way through the tomb, but that was also the spot where Victoria's face had rubbed up against mine. My chest and the fingers on my left hand were badly bruised and my arms and legs were scraped up but not seriously. As for Maria, aside from the cut on her face and a very sore scalp, she'd lost the nail on her right thumb. Earlier, she'd minimized what Victoria had done to her as, "Mostly she pulled my hair and told me I'd better scream like hell." I found out later that whenever she didn't scream loudly enough, Victoria slowly forced her knife under Maria's thumbnail.

We lay in bed luxuriating for several hours, talking about our lives and about what we might do next, not avoiding what had just happened but not talking much about it either. Strangely enough, there really didn't seem to be much to say about it. Every once in a while, we'd just look at each other and shake our heads or reach out and hold each other.

At one point, Maria turned, looked at me uncertainly and said, "What are we going to do about...?"

At first, I thought she was talking about the fact that I was still on the run, still wanted for murder. Then I realized that wasn't it at all. "Penelope's husband?" I asked.

She nodded.

"I have no idea. But we can't just let it go."

Eventually we went out to CVS and bought Band-Aids, Bactine and some surgical tape just in case I needed to strap up my chest. As tender as it was though, I was reasonably sure I hadn't broken a rib.

On the way back, I said, "We should eat something."

She nodded. "It could be a long night."

We stopped at Martin McMulligan's. I couldn't bring myself to order anything made with flesh, so I got something called a "veg-wich delight" and left most of it untouched. Maria picked at a small salad.

Back at the hotel, we made some plans for the immediate future.

And then we made love.

Neither of us thought this was the start—or the rebirth—of a romance. It was clear to us both that while we wanted and needed to be together just then, that it was just a convalescence. I'd failed Maria too profoundly for her to ever settle for me. As for me, making love to Maria was suddenly a delight and a revelation. Because *making love* was the best description—not *making love* as an empty or nearly empty euphemism for sex, maybe even good sex, maybe even great sex, maybe even the best sex I ever imagined possible with Victoria—but actually *making love*, expressing how I felt for this astonishing woman through a shared sensuality.

Shockingly, dishearteningly, I recognized that for me this was happening for the first time since Ann. Maybe, I'm ashamed to say, for the first time ever.

I'm not big on sweeping general statements, but here's one: When it turns out that the woman of your dreams wasn't even a woman—wasn't even human—it's time to reevaluate your dreams.

About 2:30 a.m., we slipped into Cristobal Bay Hospital through the emergency room as if we were patients. I'd wanted to spare Maria this, but she'd insisted on coming. We took the service stairs up to the third floor where her uncle lay.

Except for the first sentence—the continuation of the one I'd altered—the page I'd taken out of Zandie's manuscript had nothing on it that might have helped Victoria, though it did explain a bit more of her history.

Having found Rebecca's ritual, Zandie had created Victoria when he'd first begun to decline. Though he wanted to create a male—and was bitterly disappointed to get a female—he soon realized Victoria's sex might not be all bad. Obviously, he felt inferior to the middle class he ridiculed and pretended to scorn. What's more, all *his* conquests were females, and that counted for little in his day. Victoria, on the other hand—if she developed into a female Zandie—could get the men. And since she was "a mere woman" and he was her creator, he was confident that, no matter what, he'd always be able to dominate his Venus mantrap completely. In effect, her conquests would become his, not only ending his deterioration but making him stronger and surer than ever.

The problem was that he didn't realize it was going to take a number of years for her to evolve into a beauty—particularly in the face of his constantly growing disappointment in her. The term Venus mantrap quickly became a mocking insult.

Ultimately of course, Victoria's powers reached fiery extremes beyond anything Zandie imagined possible. Unfortunately for him, by then she was long gone. And even if she was somehow psychically tied to him—and even if that spell binding her to him had produced some lasting effect—she believed he was dead. She hadn't come back until she herself was failing and anxious for renewal, though Maria had wondered if Victoria wasn't trying to prove herself to the Zandie she carried around in her head right up until the end.

That didn't help Zandie, though.

The third floor of the hospital was quiet. O'Ryan's room was in the opposite direction from the nurse's station, and, in any case, no one seemed to be at the desk. I don't know if I would have killed him—I'd gone there hoping to convince myself that it wasn't necessary. But if I wasn't at least considering shutting off the machines or perhaps making one of them accidentally malfunction, I wouldn't have snuck up there in the dead of night.

But O'Ryan was gone.

O'Ryan, who'd told me he'd been saved by Maria's great aunt, the original proprietor of the store, whose name was still above the door, Penelope Delgado. I probably should have begun to suspect him, even before I'd read Zandie's reference to "Penelope, my new helpmate." But I hadn't.

And now Zandie was gone.

The startled charge nurse—whose personality was as stiffly starched as her uniform—first threatened to call security on us for being up there. When she realized who Maria was, she grew embarrassed.

"We tried to phone you," she explained. "Repeatedly. Your uncle regained consciousness yesterday morning. Even that was a miracle. He looked so much better, but unfortunately, he was out of touch with reality. All that damage to his skull... Thought he was a young man again, primping and preening like a peacock, flirting with all the nurses. And he did look so good. Not like he thought he looked of course, but...well, as you know, your uncle was...*is* still a very handsome man. Like I say, he was flirting with all the nurses. In fact, at first, he got extremely upset when they tried to leave him alone. But after a while, he just grew quiet. Then he ordered everybody out. Sometime this afternoon he disappeared. The police are on the lookout. He couldn't have made it far in his condition. Besides, how difficult can it be to find an old man in a hospital gown?"

When we got back to O'Ryan's, he'd been there and gone. Little was missing. A few clothes. The urn with Rebecca's ashes. And another one of the serpent knives. For some reason, a plaster bust of Andrew Jackson was sitting upright on his bed. We talked about how ironic it was for Victoria to have almost killed the person she was seeking and wondered when Zandie first suspected who *she* was. My guess was that it was probably when he got Cranick's letter. Maria thought it wasn't until he discovered we were tearing up the church, looking for his bones. In his senile condition though, it was hard to say what he may or may not have realized—or how clear any realization he did have could have been.

Then Maria said what we'd both been thinking.

"It doesn't matter if he's crazy, does it? If he thinks he's desirable then...?"

I shrugged. There was nothing more to be said. It looked like Zandie was back in business.

It was late the next day before I thought to return to the old church—after I re-read the final page of Zandie's manuscript:

> "For the sake of my good wife, Penelope, the woman who had saved my body, if not my soul, I'm trying to be a Christian—I've lost at everything else anyway. But Christianity always ends up making my blood ache, and I simply can't face spending eternity buried in an undistinguished hole in Corpus Christi Cemetery. So, when my time comes, let me be entombed as Zandie, not O'Ryan—though he may be the better man—and if possible, let me be interred in my old house, on my old throne..."

On it, not *in* it, though I wasn't sure how that would work. Did he want to be mummified?

We found him there, seated on his throne, dressed in a 1920s tuxedo. He looked forty-five years old and quite handsome. His time didn't appear to have come. Not at all. If he hadn't been so pale he would have looked as if his life as Zandie was about ready to begin again. The urn with what was left of Rebecca's ashes was placed at his feet, next to that human skull that he'd had gold plated all those years before. His arms were hanging down over the sides of the throne—the serpent knife on the floor underneath his left hand, soaked with some of the blood that had poured out his sliced-opened wrists. *This is MY body. This is MY blood.*

Why did he do it? Most likely it was the brain damage, or the confusion caused by the sudden transformation or some combination of the two. Most likely. And I'm certainly no fan of believing something because you want to believe it. Yet, in the absence of any evidence one way or the other, I very much want to believe that after becoming Zandie again and acknowledging who he was—with Rebecca's ashes and the gold-plated skull and the serpent knife—my friend Jonathan O'Ryan simply decided he didn't want to return to being the creature he used to be.

I can certainly understand that.

EPILOGUE

"The end of a melody is not its goal: but nonetheless, had
the melody not reached its end it would not have reached
its goal either. A parable."
– *Friedrich Nietzsche*

I stayed with Maria in her apartment behind O'Ryan's. Vantana Chemical kept phoning, trying to locate Al—Maria had nothing she could tell them.

According to the *San Cristobal Times*, the autopsy on the body of Lyle Cranick confirmed that he died in a fire. Oddly, his internal organs were more badly burned than his skin. The article didn't say whether there was any problem with the time of death. As for his medallion—I've come to think of these faces on my forearms as medallions—it reappears occasionally to this day.

Perhaps these medallions do have something to do with my feelings of guilt. Logically I can tell myself there's no rational reason for me to feel guilty about Cranick: whom I didn't kill and who was in fact trying to kill me. Yet the face comes, and I feel guilt. Or is it that the guilt comes, and I get the face? Dell's face is with me permanently. And so is Victoria's. And she—it—wasn't even human. Unfortunately, over the years other faces have joined them, but that's another story. Several other stories actually. Some days the medallions are more vivid, some days fainter. Years ago, on an island off the coast of Vladivostok, I stumbled on a spell that might have countered the effect and made them disappear permanently. After thinking it over, I decided not to try it. The faces are a good reminder.

⸻

My final job at the old church was to deal with Victoria's remains. I did it alone, sneaking over there early while Maria was still sleeping. It wasn't pleasant, and I won't go into the details. I'll simply say that only one burial vault in the crypt could still be covered by a functioning face plate, so Peter won't be spending eternity alone. After I finished, I threw away the clothes I was wearing but I couldn't get the smell out of my nose for days.

Legally at least, Maria was O'Ryan's next of kin and would inherit his property, but she had absolutely no desire to keep living there. After a week or so, I helped her move into a small two-bedroom apartment in one of San Cristobal's tree-lined neighborhoods, directly across from a park and six blocks from the beach. The next day we went to an animal shelter, and she picked out a weird looking retriever-husky-poodle-etcetera-etcetera mutt. It might not have been the ugliest creature ever to walk the planet, but it had to be in the top ten. Maria named it Steve.

"Since my name is Gavin," I said, "I'm not going to take that personally."

"In that case," she smiled, "I'll call him Gavin."

The day after that, April 14, 1982, I had her drop me off by the Shell station at the stop lights on the highway. Since I was still wanted for murder, I was headed for Mexico. Maria had offered to drive me, but I wasn't quite selfish enough to allow her to leave herself open to an aiding and abetting charge. I'd given her the contact info of both my brother and sister, and gotten addresses and phone numbers for her closest relative—a cousin—and three of her best friends. I'd lost too many of the important people in my life to take a chance on losing track of Maria.

Zandie's manuscript was in my gym bag, and I'd stuck another copy safely in a money belt around my waist.

Also, in my money belt I discovered later—five thousand in cash that Maria had slipped inside. The bust of Andrew Jackson that O'Ryan had left on his bed turned out to be hollow, with $77,777.77 stuffed inside it. I was convinced the number must have had some great significance to him, especially since Jackson was the seventh president. Then Maria noticed the note tucked in with the cash, listing each time he'd added money along with the running total, which ended at $73,356.89. So apparently the significance of the number 77,777.77 was that O'Ryan couldn't add.

I once had a particularly annoying host of a network morning show keep pressing me about what my investigations have taught me about the meaning of life. Finally, I just said, "All I want to say about that, Herb, is "Seven...seven...seven...seven...seven...seven..." Then I paused, looked him straight in the hairpiece and in my most portentous voice intoned, "*Seven!*"

Herb had no idea what I was talking about. Neither did I, of course. But the internet did. By the time I realized what was happening and tweeted out that it was all a joke, there were probably 77,777 different explanations online detailing the cosmic significance behind my dumb-ass comment.

I try not to do that kind of thing anymore.

As for the five grand Maria slipped into my money belt, since this was the eighties, I treated the money as the purchase price of shares in the financial life of one Gavin Kennan—me. Those shares have paid dividends and today Maria doesn't have to worry about where the money for her next meal is coming from. Or the financing for her next documentary. Or the one after that. Or... Let's just say she's in excellent shape financially, professionally and personally. She's been with her partner over thirty years now, and they have a son—Jonathan Albert Delgado—who occasionally works with me. Her daughter, who I insisted on naming Maria, was born on Christmas Day, 1982, with a full head of bright red hair. That's why we did the genetic testing and discovered that she was mine. She hates it when I get too effusive about her, so let me simply say that she's by far the most important thing in my life, and a far better human being than I will ever be.

That five thousand was extraordinarily generous and desperately needed, but it was nowhere near the best gift Maria ever gave me.

In any case, on April 14, 1982, I didn't know I had the money. So, while getting into Mexico wouldn't be a problem; getting there might be. And rather than actually hitchhiking and taking a chance on being rousted by the police—which happened from time to time—I needed to find likely candidates to cautiously ask for rides, the way I'd done when I'd first met Maria.

The first car to pull into the Shell Station was yet another damn Mercedes, this one driven by a yuppie in his mid-thirties in a suit and tie and the shiniest pair of shoes I'd ever seen on a human being who wasn't in a dance recital. He pumped his gas listening to some self-help tape—maybe from RAM?—that was blaring from the car at an annoyingly loud volume. His red, white and blue bumper sticker quoted Ronald Reagan, "Government is not the solution. Government is the problem."

No point in even asking.

I walked over and plopped down under the giant fig tree where Ann and I had once camped with a small contingent of the people with whom we believed we were going to change the world. Now, I sat there alone. Waiting for someone to pull into the Shell station who was enough like one of those people that they'd give me a ride.

The gigantic branches spread out above me in all directions. Some of the fullest and the most beautiful were still braced by those guy wires. That was comforting, especially sitting underneath them, but this time I wasn't tripping and it no longer felt like any kind of a metaphor for anything.

Sometimes, I thought, *a cigar is simply a cigar.*

I did notice that a couple of the branches had been removed—apparently recently—and one cable hung down limply, no longer supporting anything.

Fortunately, before any additional arbor-born cosmic insights arrived, a woman in an older Chevy Citation with Arizona plates pulled off the highway and into the gas station. She climbed out and stretched as if she'd been behind the wheel for hours. She had a well-scrubbed, open look and rich coffee-colored skin. Her black hair was tied back. Her body was sturdy and self-aware. She reminded me of Ann. An older, stronger Ann. Of course, in those days a lot of people reminded me of Ann. That still happens from time to time too.

I picked up my bag and went to ask for her help. And that's how I met Abigail Lincoln—yes, *the* Abigail Lincoln. But just then even she had no idea she would someday be *the* anything. Nowadays I'm even more frequently reminded of Abby than I am of Ann.

My life from that point on of course has been described in far too many books and articles, and distorted beyond all recognition in one movie, even though it was years before I would become—in the hyperbole of two different TIME Magazine *Person of the Year* covers—"the Man Who Rediscovered Magic." That term 'magic' always makes me wince. But I suppose people are going to persist in describing those few bits of knowledge my team and I have uncovered over the years as magic—right up until the day when better minds than mine can explain how or why any of it works.

A certain amount of nonsense goes with the territory. The TIME covers weren't even the worst of it. Some idiot—yes, I know he was the Vice President of the United States, but you haven't met him—once even tried to nominate me for the Nobel Prize in Metaphysics. The only two problems with that are:

1. I don't deserve it. And
2. The prize doesn't exist.

Still, though the hype about magic does sometimes get out of control, it's not like it's completely baseless. As I've mentioned several times,

Maria dropped me off at the stop lights and I met Abby on April 14, 1982.

On April 14, 1865, Abraham Lincoln was shot.

On April 14, 1912, the Titanic hit an iceberg.

TIME Magazine, my non-existent Nobel Prize and similar bullshit notwithstanding, I've got a lifetime of empirical evidence that the universe doesn't care one way or the other about me. Yet for whatever reason or for no reason at all, it was on April 14, 1982—the anniversary of the day Abraham Lincoln was shot and the day the Titanic was struck—that I climbed into Abigail Lincoln's car and halfway to Los Angeles we smashed into a truck full of dry ice, and my life quickly got weird enough to make me think of my time with Victoria as normal.

ABOUT THE AUTHOR

Barry Maher may be the only horror novelist who has ever appeared in the pages of *Funeral Service Insider*. In his misspent youth, his articles were featured in perhaps a hundred different publications and, in order to eat, he held nearly that many different jobs. Sometimes he lived on the beach. Not in a house on the beach. On the beach. With the sand and the seagulls.

After a sentence with a Fortune 100 company, he started speaking professionally. He told stories to audiences across the country and around the world: His client list a Who's Who of multi-national corporations and large associations. You may have seen Barry on The Today Show, NBC Nightly News, CNN, CBS or CNBC, or read his *Slightly Off-Kilter* syndicated newspaper column.

On the downside, he's actually been incarcerated twice. Once for not making a left-hand turn out of a left-hand turn lane, and once for aiding and abetting a loiterer. He's deeply repentant.

A while back, Barry lost the ability to tell time, courtesy of a baseball-size, cancerous, brain tumor. He awoke from having his skull cut open without the tumor but with the story of *The Great Dick: And the Dysfunctional Demon*. Find him at barrymaher.com.

THE END?

Not if you want to dive into more of Crystal Lake Publishing's Tales from the Darkest Depths!

Check out our amazing website and online store or download our latest catalog here.
https://geni.us/CLPCatalog

We always have great new projects and content on the website to dive into, as well as a newsletter, behind the scenes options, social media platforms, our own dark fiction shared-world series and our very own webstore. Our webstore even has categories specifically for KU books, non-fiction, anthologies, and of course more novels and novellas.

Readers...

Thank you for reading *The Great Dick*. We hope you enjoyed this novel. If you have a moment, please review *The Great Dick* at the store where you bought it.

Help other readers by telling them why you enjoyed this book. No need to write an in-depth discussion. Even a single sentence will be greatly appreciated. Reviews go a long way to helping a book sell, and is great for an author's career. It'll also help us to continue publishing quality books.

Thank you again for taking the time to journey with Crystal Lake Publishing.

You will find links to all our social media platforms on our Linktree page. https://linktr.ee/CrystalLakePublishing

Follow us on Amazon:

MISSION STATEMENT

Since its founding in August 2012, Crystal Lake has quickly become one of the world's leading publishers of Dark Fiction and Horror books. In 2023, Crystal Lake officially transitioned into an entertainment company, joining several other divisions, genres, and imprints, including Torrid Waters, Crystal Lake Comics, Crystal Lake Games, Crystal Lake Kids, and many more.

While we strive to present only the highest quality fiction and entertainment, we also endeavour to support authors along their writing journey. We offer our time and experience in non-fiction projects, as well as author mentoring and services, at competitive prices.

With several Bram Stoker Award wins and many other wins and nominations (including the HWA's Specialty Press Award), Crystal Lake Publishing puts integrity, honor, and respect at the forefront of our publishing operations.

We strive for each book and outreach program we spearhead to not only entertain and touch or comment on issues that affect our readers, but also to strengthen and support the Dark Fiction field and its authors.

Not only do we find and publish authors we believe are destined for greatness, but we strive to work with men and women who endeavour to be decent human beings who care more for others than themselves, while still being hard working, driven, and passionate artists and storytellers.

Crystal Lake Publishing is and will always be a beacon of what passion and dedication, combined with overwhelming teamwork and respect, can accomplish. We endeavour to know each and every one of our readers, while building personal relationships with our authors, reviewers, bloggers, podcasters, bookstores, and libraries.

We will be as trustworthy, forthright, and transparent as any business can be, while also keeping most of the headaches away from our authors, since it's our job to solve the problems so they can stay in a creative mind. Which of course also means paying our authors.

We do not just publish books, we present to you worlds within your world, doors within your mind, from talented authors who sacrifice so much for a moment of your time.

There are some amazing small presses out there, and through collaboration and open forums we will continue to support other presses in the goal of helping authors and showing the world what quality small presses are capable of accomplishing. No one wins when a small press goes down, so we will always be there to support hardworking, legitimate presses and their authors. We don't see Crystal Lake as the best press out there, but we will always strive to be the best, strive to be the most interactive and grateful, and even blessed press around. No matter what happens over time, we will also take our mission very seriously while appreciating where we are and enjoying the journey.

What do we offer our authors that they can't do for themselves through self-publishing?

We are big supporters of self-publishing (especially hybrid publishing), if done with care, patience, and planning. However, not every author has the time or inclination to do market research, advertise, and set up book launch strategies. Although a lot of authors are successful in doing it all, strong small presses will always be there for the authors who just want to do what they do best: write.

What we offer is experience, industry knowledge, contacts and trust built up over years. And due to our strong brand and trusting fanbase, every Crystal Lake Publishing book comes with weight of respect. In time our fans begin to trust our judgment and will try a new author purely based on our support of said author.

With each launch we strive to fine-tune our approach, learn from our mistakes, and increase our reach. We continue to assure our authors that we're here for them and that we'll carry the weight of the launch and dealing with third parties while they focus on their strengths—be it writing, interviews, blogs, signings, etc.

We also offer several mentoring packages to authors that include knowledge and skills they can use in both traditional and self-publishing endeavours.

We look forward to launching many new careers.

This is what we believe in. What we stand for. This will be our legacy.

Welcome to Crystal Lake Publishing—Where Stories Come Alive!